ILLERA'S DARKLIETE

A FANTASY

GAIL GERNAT

DARKLIETE BOOK 2

ANDREA James
PUBLISHING

Gernat's second book... yet another fantasy that keeps us turning the pages, wanting more. Gernat's fiction is filled with life... believable fantasy... a good rainy day read.

Maggie Lacroix
    Wynterblue Publishing

LERA'S SORROW - (Darkliete Book 1)

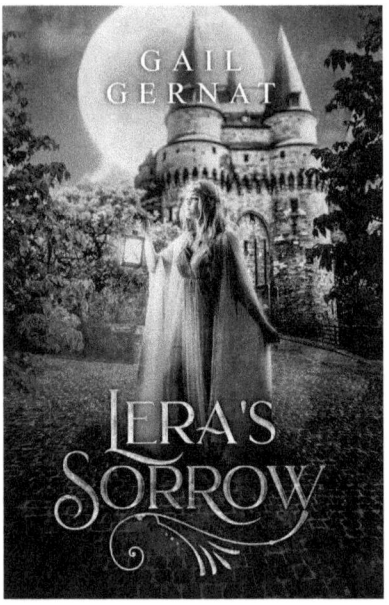

Lera and her cousin have completed their long childhood and their training as healers. Sent to their grandparents back in Madean, they must negotiate the strange new world, attain their werwinstans. Fate intervenes in the shape of handsome young Ian, very human and very poisonous to the elven. Trying out her independence for the first time in her life, what will Lera decide? Where will she discover her loyalty to lay, with love or with duty?

DEDICATION

First, in memory of Corbeau, joy given wings. I miss the brightness of your feathers and the pleasure you spread like sunshine. Rest in peace happy spirit.

For Maggie who began the adventure with me. The candle flickers a lot, but it still burns.

For Tabitha who helped me finish it. It will come around.

Many thanks to Andrea James Publishing for taking a chance on me.

Especially--

For all the dear readers who start the journey with me.

Human Towns, Swamp, Rivers, Mountains, Rolling Hills, Shul.

PROLOGUE

The high, thin keening of the wind could not compete with the wailing of the male infants. King Korul clutched the two screaming babies awkwardly as the big dappled gray horse shifted restlessly under him. The waves slapped against the cliff, shooting plumes of spray that reached up to his position overlooking the path to the rocky beach below. He watched as the pikemen prodded the reluctant priestesses as they clanked down the steep and narrow incline. They often turned to look up to his position high above, one bare blonde head and one midnight-dark one twisting around, yearning for a last glimpse of their children.

The blonde fell to her knees, grasping with all her strength on a sharp upthrust boulder on the edge of the path. The king could hear her screams, floating on the mourning wind. One of the pikemen prodded her from the hold, and she slid, tumbling down ten feet before she could regain her footing. Using the distraction, her dark-haired sibling made a break, scrambling back up the path to her child. The leg irons slowed her enough that the guards caught her with ease, brutally whipping her around and back down the path.

Just offshore, a vessel lay at anchor, tall prow rising into the clear, cold sky. A small skiff awaited the priestesses on the beach, holding four burly rowers with oars shipped. The party reached the strand of pebbles. The head guard unlocked the leg irons, and the women made one more attempt to return to their children, but they were easily stopped by the pikemen across the only trail to the top. Defeated both women got into the boat, and it was pushed into the foaming waves.

Halfway to the ship, the priestesses stood facing him. Korul snarled a smile back at them.

"You wanted to go home, so go," he bellowed down at them, stirring the infants to another storm of wailing.

The women spoke in unison, their hands waving arcane patterns in front of their faces as they glared up at him.

"Know this Korul, King of Frain, that cursed you be and cursed you are from this moment to the next world. We are the priestess dark; we are the priestess light. You befoul our very memory. We place your actions before all the gods of this world and the next. Hear our cry to the dimensions beyond ours. All your work will be in vain, and you will cause your kingdom to fail; to enter the darkest region of the netherworld where you will be imprisoned as you have imprisoned us. And a woman will lead the way to your destruction. Your throne will be maggots, and you will be king of only your hate-filled self. We pronounce the cursed of the damned upon you forevermore."

Korul bellowed a laugh. "You witches can't scare me. I own your land. Your people are my servants, and you are nothing but my whores."

His laughter was rough and crude, smothered in rolling thunder from the clear skies. The thunder grew louder as black clouds boiled from the horizon, covering the sun. The King kneed his horse back from the cliff as the skies opened. Hail pounded down, drowning the cries of the infants in his arms.

Lighting struck right behind him whipping his steed into a swift canter.

A mile or more from the cliff, Korul saw the shack of the horse girl. He swerved his mount aside there and took shelter under the ragged roof. Timidly the girl crept from one dirty corner.

"Come here, girl," the King demanded. "Take these howling brats."

The girl reached up and took the babies, scuttling back to her corner with them. She soothed their cries to whimpers. The king dismounted and stood in the doorway watching the hail and rain pound down; flinching from the closer lightning strikes.

The babies gradually quieted in the horse girl's arms. As suddenly as it came, the storm abated. The king mounted and turned his stallion to the door.

"My Lord, wait, the children," cried the girl from the corner, struggling to her feet with the two boys.

Korul looked down at her from his royal height. He gazed slowly around the hut, taking in the poverty and squalor of the surroundings. A slow smile spread across his cruel features.

"You keep them. They are now yours to raise," and lifting his hand he spurred his mount out of the door.

The castle of Frain was dismal, damp in the aftermath of the storm and the chimneys didn't draw well anymore. Dallia, the queen, was seated next to the best fireplace, squinting at the needlework in her hands. The firelight glowed on her copper tresses bound in green velvet. She dropped the needlework as he entered and rose to meet him.

"My Lord," she murmured in a voice sweet and low.

"Dallia," he laughed, "it's done. The witches have been sent back to their own land where they can practice sorcery to their heart's desire."

He picked her up and swung her around.

"And the infants?" the Queen inquired as he placed her back on her feet.

Korul bellowed a laugh. "I disposed of them. Gone. Vanished. Missing."

The Queen paled. "My Lord, you didn't harm the children? The gods look ill on those who harm the innocent."

"Look," he retorted loudly, "you nagged me and nagged me until I got rid of those women. 'I won't share your bed or bear your heir with them living under the same roof.' Well, I got rid of them. I got rid of their little bastards too so there will be no claims to the throne except for your children. You are supposed to be happy."

"But my Lord, they were just babies; they were innocent."

"By the Thunderer and his Bolts, there is no pleasing you woman. You will fulfill your part in this bargain and provide me with an heir. Now!"

Korul grabbed her by the arm and dragged her up the stairs. Servants scurried to clear the room. She fought him, but her strength was useless against his battle-hardened muscles as he manhandled her up the stairs in spite of her struggle.

"Korul!" she yelled as she managed to free an arm. "You cannot treat me like one of your concubine women! I am your queen, and you will treat me with the respect I deserve."

Korul turned to her, his face red and throbbing, "You are a woman, and you will bear my seed. I have waited long enough for your favors. Come now!"

"I'm not some cheap tramp you can pick up at the town market. My father..."

With a cry of incoherent rage, Korul raised his fist and struck Dallia on the side of her face. A piercing cry escaped her lips as she lost her balance and tumbled down the long steep stairway. Korul stood frozen at the top for long moments; galloping down to where she lay in a boneless heap at the bottom.

"Jurgen, Jurgen you old quack," he roared, "there's been an accident, the Queen has fallen, somebody get Jurgen, quick. By the Thunderer and by my Sword if someone doesn't come here immediately I'll have you all drawn and quartered. Jurgen!"

CHAPTER 1

*I*llera bent over the grunting sow. The strong reek of the pigsty made her wrinkle her delicate nose as she ran her hands over the straining pig.

"Please, my lady, can you help 'er? We uns is really going to need those piglets if the raidin' keeps up. Is there anythin' you can do?" The pig girl, Shani, wrung her hands and wiped them on her tattered, dirty skirt.

Illera went down on her knees in the soiled straw, oblivious of the damage to her long, saffron gown. With one hand on the pig's head and another on the distended belly, she began to murmur to the straining animal.

"Easy, girl, easy. You can do this, just a few more pushes and your babies will be here. Easy, easy, shhhhhhhhhh."

Her dainty hand on the pig's abdomen stroked back and forth, back and forth. The sow relaxed, the taut muscles becoming flaccid and her eyes closed.

"Okay, now!" spoke Illera in a commanding voice.

The pig strained, and a small tail appeared. With a cry the pig girl fell to her knees at the pig's rear, assisting the tiny piglet from its mother's body. Illera took the tiny body from the pig girl's hands. She wiped it with some of the clean straw and lay it beside its mother's belly. Slender fingers massaged the small animal's chest, and with a snort, it began to squeal. The sow raised her head and nuzzled it. With a grunt, she lay back down and another piglet, this one head first, appeared.

For the next few triumphant hours, Illera and the pig girl watched as the sow presented them with twelve new babies, seven of them female. As Illera rose to go, the girl grasped her slender hands in her own thick and grubby ones.

"My lady, 'ow can I thank you. Without 'elp Aquiwin would'a died with all her children. I can niver repay you!"

"It's okay, Shani. I'm very happy I could help you with her."

The pig girl glanced down at Illera's gown. "Oh, my lady, I've ruined your dress."

The distraught girl fell to her knees, her face tight with sorrow and grief.

Illera laughed. "It's all right. I have many dresses and what value is a dress compared to thirteen lives, twelve of them just starting. Don't be upset."

"My lady," Shani muttered, turning back to the sow.

Illera smiled and slipped from the pigsty. Dawn was streaking the sky with golden fingers, painting the seven tall, white towers of the castle with bright rose and yellow strokes. Her father's dark blue and white pennant fluttered from the tallest turret of the donjon. The white griffin rampart, gilded with the sunrise, appeared to be flying as a lazy wind caressed down its length. Illera smiled at the illusion.

The magpie sailed out of the sun, gargling a welcome to her. Illera raised her arm and the bird settled on her wrist. Immediately her feathered friend began croaking and bubbling in the most serious manner.

"What is it, Maggie? What do you want me to know?" Illera asked the bird; her head cocked to one side in imitation.

The rising sun struck the gold and copper threads of her hair surrounding her head with halo, but it didn't impress the noisy bird who tried more and more urgently to convey the message. She launched from Illera's wrist and flew towards the castle, scolding as she flapped. Illera squinted her eyes against the light as the magpie circled the castle twice, dipping earthward at the barbican. She arrowed back, aligning on Illera's outstretched arm. A long series of magpie conversation burbled from her throat.

"Is someone here?" asked Illera.

The bird gave one loud squawk and lifted her wings overhead.

"Is it a good visitor? Someone I want to meet?" she inquired.

The magpie thrust its beak between its legs and made a strangling sound.

"Hide?" the princess suggested.

The bird leapt from her hand and flew warbling into the sky. Illera turned away from the castle and started towards the Royal River. It passed her home swiftly, but narrowly, stitched together by seven bridges giving the farmers and herders access to the warm, rich and fertile other side. The second bridge was not far, arching high out over the roiling waters. This was the path the herds took on their way to lush grazing pasture.

Illera didn't step foot on the wide planks of the bridge, but ducked under, slithering down the bank and then climbing up into the wooden supports. Wriggling her way to the middle, she prised open a square wooden panel. She flipped into the narrow tunnel thus revealed and sealed the panel back into its place.

Long years ago, when her mother ruled here beside her father, the Queen had insisted that the secret passageways and tunnels be built into the castle. Illera often wondered if her mother knew that she would someday be in dire need of these escapes. People often told her of her mother's uncanny wisdom; how she knew so many things and Illera again felt the pang of growing up without the woman of whom everyone spoke glowingly.

She pattered down the dusty tunnel, burning with curiosity. The magpie had been her companion for so long, but was still so incomprehensible. Her father often chided her for listening to the bird, but when she understood what Maggie wanted, it was always the correct thing. So she hurried, anxious to discover why she needed to hide.

The tunnel rose sharply and ended at a rough stone wall inside the rampart. Illera stood on tiptoe to peer out of the glass eye set into the stone. It gave her a good view of the outside. Dozens of men were practicing swordplay on the grounds of the outer bailey. They appeared fully occupied, so Illera slipped the catch and slid from her hiding place. She hurried across the short grass to the inner gate and trotted inside without notice. The stable was close so she escaped in there. The stabled horses greeted her with friendly whuffs. She stroked the soft, inquisitive noses as she hurried by.

At the rear of the barn, she shoved aside some shovels and vanished behind the panel, snapping it shut just as a groom came to investigate the noise. The tunnels were dusty, and Illera sneezed, freezing in her tracks to hear if anyone noticed. The walls were very thin in this part of the maze, and she could hear the old groom moving around, whistling to the horses. He seemed undisturbed, so she rushed to her rooms, high in the middle tower.

Closing the secret passage tightly, she crossed the floor and locked the door to her rooms. She paused; then stopped in front of the fancy glass mirror that had been her mother's. She laughed as she regarded herself. Her dress was filthy, caked with pig dirt from the knees down, and smudged with horse dung at the hem from her passage through the stable. Dust and cobwebs covered her from the top of her golden chestnut hair to the grime ground into the bottom of her soiled gown. But the widely spaced violet eyes sparkled with mischief, and the dimples showed deep in the cheeks of her delicate, pointed-chinned face. She laughed out loud once more, then slapped a hand over her mouth afraid that someone might hear.

She stripped the filthy clothes from her body, leaving them in an untidy heap on the floor. A few steps brought her to the bathing room. The water jar was full, if cold. She sponged herself off with the chilly water and dried on the warm fluffy towels from the shelves. Turning to the dressing room, she chose a dark, sturdy dress, unlikely to be ruined by dusty passageways or well-used stables. She took her copper hair down and combed the dust from it, braiding it and piling it again on top of her head.

Loud fanfares from trumpets heralded the arrival of the visitor and made her hurry. She ducked back into the secret passage and went down the winding stairs to the musician's gallery. It was empty, so she tiptoed out, looking down at the great room through a loosely woven tapestry. Her father's seat was beneath her, but the rest of the room stretched out sturdy stone walls and massive roofing beams ahead and below. Huge wall-hangings decorated the perimeter walls depicting scenes of farmers, their lands, and livestock. Over the enormous, roaring fireplace the larger than life portrait of her parents hung. Tables lined the walls on either side, flanked by tall, ladderback chairs. The rushes on the stone floor were thick and deep, muffling foot sounds.

The heralds on either side of her father's seat blew their trumpets again, and a small entourage of travel-stained men entered the door and walked up the aisle to stand before the king.

A thin man led the group of four. Pale dirty hair protruded beneath his helm, and the device on his red and green shield was a black dragon. He held his head high, looking down a large and reddish nose; his sword hand continually twitched towards his weapon.

"Announcing, Sir Kyle of Frain, emissary of King Korul, come to see King Ian of Madean on matters of great importance to both great countries," the herald announced in a ringing voice.

Illera heard her father speak directly below her. "Welcome, Sir Kyle if you come in peace. I would not care to test the temper of your liege in war, but if for war you have come then you are indeed ill come."

Sir Kyle went down on one knee and lowered his head in a fraction of a bow. The others in his train followed his example. "Good King Ian, I indeed come in peace. Just now King Korul has enough enemies and would sue for peace with your land. Indeed, we have heard that you yourselves have fallen upon the hard times of war. These pirates of Carnuvon attack both of our ships, choking our trade. The Shul raid, destroying towns, farms and villages. They loot and burn and savage the land so that the peasants go hungry and cry for relief. King Korul would forge an alliance with you, to fight against these invaders from sea and mountain."

"Then you are welcome Sir Kyle. Go, refresh yourselves, we will speak more of this when you are rested."

The Franians rose and were escorted to guest quarters by the servants. Illera returned to her rooms pondering what this all meant. Maggie was unlikely to be wrong, yet peace with Frain sounded like something good. She decided for the time being to remain in hiding.

The musicians were in the gallery when the evening meal was served, so Illera chose a spot behind the hangings on the main floor of the great hall, just to the left of her father's seat. The hall was crowded tonight. Her place, opposite her father at the head table remained empty, but his three war leaders and the four visitors from Frain filled the sides of the table. The lower tables were jammed with the rest of the knights, squires, yeomen and ordinary men come to swell the ranks of the soldiers at the castle. Servants scurried back and forth, trying to cater to all the men gathered to eat at the King's table.

Sir Kyle asked the King, "I thought you had a daughter?"

Illera stiffened behind the heavy curtain. "Yes, I do indeed have a daughter. But quite often she is involved with the local people. She has quite a talent for helping with livestock, she does."

"And I was told she is of marriageable age?"

King Ian sighed. "I fear that, perhaps like her mother, my daughter will never marry. She has a...a somewhat willful spirit?"

"Ah," retorted Sir Kyle.

"Nonetheless, she is a lovely girl and as I have said very talented."

Sir Kyle scratched the side of his nose. "My King also has a son of marriageable age. Torul has turned nineteen this year past, and Korul thinks to find him a suitable wife."

Ian laughed. "I fear my daughter would not feel she was a suitable wife for any man."

"But are not daughters subject to their fathers, particularly if their fathers are the king?"

Ian leaned forward. "Illera is special. You might barter another princess for the sake of the kingdom, but Illera...she is like the wind that blows over the land, or the mountains that make up its spine. I could no more give you my daughter than I could give you the soil that grows our bread. She is my heir, my only child, and she will inherit the Kingdom of Madean when I pass on. I hope she can find a brave knight to share the throne with and provide Madean with princes to rule after her, but Illera belongs here. I believe a mate will be her choice. Like it was with her mother; she is much like her mother."

King Ian looked up to the huge portrait hanging over the fireplace. As a younger man, he stood there, a proud smile on his shapely lips and a hand resting on the shoulder of a beautiful seated woman. The face was familiar to Illera, she saw it every day in the mirror, but the hair was like sunlight on snow, unbound and falling about her shoulders, accenting the delicate, pointed chin and wide spaced, violet eyes. The artist had captured a sense of otherworldliness, as if her mother didn't belong on this earth, and the only thing tethering her was the hand resting gently on her shoulder. Illera sighed, longing for the mother she had never known.

Sir Kyle puckered his lips and drew his eyebrows up. "But surely King Ian, if the very life of the kingdom were at stake...?"

Ian sighed, blowing down his snowy beard and drawing his eyebrows fiercely together. "Can you tell me just why you are so interested in Illera? Is the kingdom at stake?"

Smiling, Sir Kyle stroked fingers down his sheathed sword. "My liege, King Korul, is an eminent statesman. It is his.... uh... hope to unite Frain and Madean. Together we could make a much better stand against Shul and the Carnuvon pirates. Now, of course, the easy way is through an alliance, Torul, and Illera. And, if that cannot be arranged, then perhaps, and I say just perhaps, King Korul might think that it would be better to conquer Madean than to have an unsecured border."

Sir Kyle stared upwards at the many candles flickering on the gold and crystal chandelier. Illera saw her father's face grew red. He sat his throne stiffly. An arm shot out, shaking a finger at Sir Kyle.

"Sir," the King spat, "if you think to abuse my hospitality and threaten my kingdom and my daughter, then perhaps t'would be better that you should hurry to horse and home again before my patience is exhausted."

The knights on both sides of the table shifted restlessly, hands going to sword hilts and chairs surreptitiously pushed back.

"You mistake me, sire. I do not make policy, I merely guess at what my liege would think. I do not presume upon your hospitality. Indeed, my only task here is to assure you of peace with Frain and attempt to make an alliance with your sweet and warm country."

"So long as your mission is a peaceful one," retorted Ian, face stiff and voice hard.

"It is indeed, sire. I think only of what is good for Frain, and Madean as well. It is well known that your years are adding up, what have you now, ninety summers?"

"Not that it is your business, but I have eighty-four summers, and my health is excellent," Ian snapped back.

"Still, one must be realistic, at that great age things can occur suddenly and can a young girl of but twenty summers cope with the loss of a beloved father and the running of a kingdom at war?"

"Sir, this discussion is ended!" King Ian rose from his place and stalked from the table.

Illera felt the pain of stiffened, straining muscles and realized that her shoulders and back were clenched to the point of spasm and her jaw was aching with the pressure of her teeth grinding together. She relaxed her muscles, telling herself that her father would never agree to have her leave Madean. Maggie was right, this was trouble, and she needed to hide. She would remain hidden until these noxious visitors had left; as if she would leave this beautiful and bountiful country for the dark and cold northern lands. She tiptoed through the hidden passages to the kitchen where she gathered some food supplies and disappeared back into the walls.

High on the front right turret, overlooking the barbican, Illera made her nest. An irregular chink in the stones gave her a small window to watch the comings and goings below, and it allowed the magpie entrance. It was a small room, the floors, and walls lined with furs and linens; the place where she played as a child. A few of her old dolls were still scattered over the furthest sections from the window. Right below the watchman's tower perch, it gave an excellent view of the entire castle and the long straight approach leading to the outer walls.

Maggie flew in, gargling her usual welcome. Illera stroked the pinto feathers, making soothing sounds to the bird. She was ruffled, refusing to settle down, hopping to the window and shaking herself. Illera sighed, what now?

The sound of a rider thundering across the drawbridge drew her attention. The horse was lathered, head hanging down, heaving for breath on the outer bailey as the rider explained to the guards with extravagant gestures, repeatedly pointing back down the road. One man dashed off to the keep, as the others rushed in all directions, gathering weapons and mounts. In a short time, her father appeared, mounted on his giant black war-horse. Most of the knights of the castle were with him, armed and mounted. The king leaned down and instructed Sir Garth, his most trusted knight, turned his horse's head and galloped out of the gate followed by most of the men from the castle. The rider rode a fresh horse at King Ian's side, pointing down the road to River Blend. Illera watched until they had vanished from sight, and she could no longer hear the thunder of the horse's hooves on the heavy clay of the roads.

She stayed immured in her little room, leaving only to gather more food and attend to nature. It was a long, weary time. She tried to recapture the simplicity of childhood, playing with her discarded dolls, but it was hollow, all the magic long since burned away by maturity. Maggie came and went at intervals that made sense only to the bird. On the evening of the third day, just as Illera felt she could stay inside no more, the trumpets hailed the return of the king.

Her heart clenched into a tight fist at the sight her father and his men presented as they dragged themselves up the approach. Half the men were missing, and many returning were bandaged and bloody. Even the mighty war-horses were disheveled and dragged their great hooves, stirring up dust to cloak the dispirited riders. Illera sped from her tower room, through the back passages to the musician's gallery above the great hall. It was deserted at this time of day. She watched her father hobble in, limping badly on one leg. Sir Kyle swept him a deep bow. Her father waved it away and settled in his chair.

"Your majesty, I hope the battle went well?"

"No Sir Kyle, it did not. The pirates were gone by the time I reached the River Blend and along with them, our grain crop, all of last year's produce and the new spring grain. Now the farmers will have no food until the grain ripens in the fall. Indeed, I'll have none myself. I cannot eat if the farmers don't and I cannot eat what doesn't exist."

"But if there was no battle...?"

The King wearily flopped his head into his hands. He made a muffled reply.

"I'm sorry sire; I couldn't hear you."

With a deep sigh, he lifted his head. "The pirates returned. They bombarded us with some sort of missiles. When they landed, they killed everyone they could reach. Half my knights, half my knights...." His reply trailed off into muttering once more. "You must excuse me. I must go and attend to the wounded."

The king rose and hobbled from the great hall, head hanging. Sir Kyle smiled and slapped his hands together, striding after the broken man.

Illera ducked back into the walls. She trotted, counting the doorways by their latches. At the panel before the stables she halted, breathing deeply of the dusty air, catching her breath. She tiptoed to the glass eye and squinted out. The men lay in their barracks. Few moved, most lay as if dead; bone weary and injured. Illera could see the stooped back of the physician moving slowly from bed to bed, ministering to the wounded. The dame followed closely behind him carrying the sizeable woven basket of supplies. Her gray-clad corpulent body barely fit between the narrow rows of wooden platforms jammed into the barracks to accommodate the men impressed into the King's service. Illera watched her father limp slowly through the wide open door. The physician tottered over to him and gave a low voiced report with much hand-wringing and head shaking. She had never seen her father look so despondent. The physician moved back to the men, changing bandages and anointing wounds with wine and oil. King Ian moved slowly from bed to bed, encouraging the men and speaking consoling words to them.

As he approached her position, slightly behind the wash-stand, she slipped the catch and slid from the narrow opening. His snowy head whipped towards her.

"Illera, where have you been?" he hissed.

"Father, I'm so sorry. Is there anything I can do to help?"

"Illera, answer me. I'm too tired to play games with you, where have you been?"

"Maggie warned me, father, and I have been hiding. I won't be sold to Frain!"

Ian sighed and dropped his head to his chest. Raising it again, he placed both hands on her slender shoulders and looked deep into her eyes.

"Illera, my darling, darling girl, the last thing in the world I would want for you is to leave Madean and me. But you must realize, when one is born to royalty one has obligations, duties to the land and to the people. I know you are aware of that and that you do your best to take care of the people around you. You do a wonderful job, and I am proud of you. We have suffered a bitter defeat. All our food stocks are gone, taken by the pirates. Many of our men are dead, slaughtered like sheep. These are the men that we need to grow more food, to take care of the land and the women and children that are left behind. I will not consent to this marriage to Torul of Frain unless there is no other way to save Madean and her people, but my darling; it may come to that. You may have to sacrifice yourself for the land you love."

Illera backed a step away from her father, watching his hands fall wearily to his sides. "No father. I cannot leave you, and I cannot leave Madean. What if my mother returns?"

Ian grimaced. "No child, I've told you often your mother will not return. She said herself, that as one of the ageless ones she should not have been with me. I was most blessed to have her company for the time she was here and even more blessed that she allowed you to be conceived and brought to birth. You were her final gift to me, but it was final, and I wish, oh how I wish you wouldn't keep dreaming of your mother's return. She's gone to her people and her land."

Tears formed in Illera's eyes and dripped unheeded down her cheeks to splash on the dusty stone of the floor. "She left you, father, she didn't leave me, and I have to believe that one day, one day when I need her most, she will return for me."

"Oh Illera," began Ian.

The tramp of spurred boots rang on the cobblestones outside the door. With a quick glance over her shoulder, Illera vanished back into the walls. As the catch snicked tight, she heard the loud voice of Sir Kyle and a shudder left a cold trail up her spine.

She hurried back to her room, gathering her cloak, basket, and candles and made her way through the passages to the longest of them. It was a long trip to the edge of the forest, more so when it was underground through long disused tunnels. She walked for hours with only the flickering candle for company. At last the stone stairs rose under her feet, and she dragged up them, slowly and wearily until she reached the heavy stone doorway. Grunting she shoved the massive block aside on its rails and exited into the fresh air of the forest.

First moon was just rising, hovering on the battlements of the distant castle. It was full and golden tonight, shedding a steady even light over the dark boles of the trees. Illera blew out the candle and traveled swiftly through the dark trees to the silver forest, where the ghostly birch dominated the land, regal and pale against the strengthening light of first moon. Second moon was following close behind tonight, a slender blue sicle half the size of first moon. The double shadows made finding the herbs and mosses she was collecting difficult, and she had to exercise great care not to pick the wrong plants.

Her eyes were aching and her basket nearly full when she heard the low, rumbling growl. She straightened from the base of a huge silver birch and stared straight into glowing green eyes. She immediately tore her gaze from the predator's, looking down its long, tawny length stretched on the branch above her. The rumble intensified. Illera began to talk to the lion in a soft voice. Her voice rose in a gentle wordless song. The growl stopped, and the tautness left the muscles of the creature. As Illera continued, the lion sprang down from the branch and sat in front of her. Illera went down on her knees in front of the beast, just inches away from the six-inch ripping fangs. With gentle hands, she reached out and stroked the long whiskers on either side of its face. The big cat purred with pleasure. Illera rose and took her basket, walking slowly back to the entrance of the tunnel. The lion padded beside her. At the tunnel, Illera spent a few moments petting the animal, lit her candle and disappeared into the dark hole, closing the rock behind her.

The trip back to the castle was even more difficult, for she was weary. Her heart seized with anxiety every time she thought of leaving Madean, and she knew she couldn't go away whether the kingdom depended on it or not. So, she tried to hurry with her burden and finally made it home. Careless, she dropped her things on the floor of her room and crawled into her bed for a few hours' sleep.

The maidservant, Sar, woke her, opening the curtains and caroling a good morning. Illera came groggily awake. A steaming tub was waiting for her in the bathing room, and she sank into its depths gratefully. After breakfast she went through the castle to her father's rooms, every nerve straining to the sound of the Franians, ever ready to duck into the secret passages within the walls. Undetected by outsiders she made it to the King's quarters. She knocked loudly. Her father's servant opened the door.

Propped up with pillows, her father was dwarfed by the massive four-poster bed. The heavy red velvet draperies accented the pallor of his face as he flinched away from the bright morning sun. Illera felt a pang of alarm run through her at the sight of him.

Forcing a smile to her lips, she said, "Good morning father. How are you today?"

His normally clear blue eyes were cloudy, with sagging pouches of flesh below them. "I've had a hard night, child. And you? You look tired."

"Well, I was a little busy last night," she replied.

Her father groaned. "What have you been doing now? How often must I tell you not to go out alone at night? What about wild animals?"

Illera laughed. "I have more to fear inside these walls than from the animals of the forest. Besides, I needed some things. How else can I make you better?"

The King covered his eyes with both hands. "Illera!"

Illera plumped down on the bed beside him, placing one delicate hand over his blue-veined one. "Father, our fighting force is cut in half. You know the physician is an idiot and half of those left are going to die. I can't let that happen. So just let me start with you, and then I'll go and treat the injured men in the barracks."

"Illera, it is not fitting for you to be in the men's barracks."

Illera didn't reply, but turned back the covers exposing the King's leg. A deep slash started just above the knee spiraling down across the calf to the ankle. It was a dark, throbbing red with lines spreading into the pale flesh beside the wound. Illera drew a deep breath.

"Father, why didn't you tell me it was this bad," she scolded.

Ian shook his head and looked away. She sorted through her basket, removing a woody, pale blue mushroom. She gave it to the manservant.

"Make my father some tea with this. Hurry and bring it to him immediately it has steeped."

The manservant hurried off to do her bidding. Next, she placed a number of tiny dark green leaves in an ewer of water, stirring slowly until the water turned a deep amber color. Then she washed the wound, being as gentle as possible, but still, the King winced with every stroke. When the slash was as clean as she could make it, she wrapped it with moss of the palest green and covered it with fresh bandages. Then she sat with him, silently stroking his hand as he drank the blue tea, making faces at its strong, pungent flavor. As he drifted off to sleep, she gathered her things and went to treat the men in the barracks.

Illera was again hidden behind the tapestry in the great hall. She held herself very still although her muscles ached and her bones groaned with weariness. She wiped the sleep from her eyes, anxious for a hint of what her Father had agreed to with the Franians. King Ian looked tired and beaten, although his wound was the memory of the scar, well healed from a week ago. The tables were filled with the recovered warriors, and only her absence at the head table was obvious.

The Franians were jubilant, drinking deeply and talking loudly. Sir Kyle gazed around the great hall with a possessiveness that made Illera sorely uneasy. His laugh was like sanding paper on her nerves.

"Well, King Ian, a toast to the success of our venture," Sir Kyle loudly proclaimed, raising his goblet high.

The king lifted his cup in a weary hand in reply, followed by his men at the table.

"To the union of Frain and Madean!" yelled Sir Kyle followed by the Frainians and with less verve by the men of Madean.

Sir Kyle continued, "So, you can expect my contingent to arrive sometime next month. As soon as I return, the bride price will be sent, along with men of arms, food supplies, weapons and horses. You drive a hard bargain you old fox."

King Ian grunted in reply.

"But I have yet to see the maiden. Should she not have returned after this great time?"

"Never fear, she is about. I have spoken to her on many occasions since your arrival."

Sir Kyle's voice took on a sly note, "Yes, I heard of her healing in the barracks. It appears that she has more than talents with just livestock. In fact, some of my men thought the healing of the wounds of your army almost uncanny."

"They were young and healthy, well fed. So their healing was nothing unnatural. We have an outstanding physician."

"But the men themselves told me it was your daughter who did the healing."

"The people hereabouts think a great deal of Illera," retorted Ian, growing angry.

"But I could not bring home to my prince a woman who was...shall we say...tainted."

Ian rose to his feet, followed by his men, "Are you calling my daughter tainted?"

"No...no my lord," soothed Sir Kyle, "it's merely that I, for one, have never seen the maiden. Even you, sire must admit that to be at Seven Spires for two weeks and never see the princess, who should be acting as hostess, is somewhat unusual."

Ian slumped back to his seat. A wave of his hand and his men followed suit. "My daughter has no wish to see you or to meet with you. As I told you on the first night, she does not desire to marry and move from Madean. She belongs to this land. So, as you are the cause of her going, she has no wish to see or be seen by you."

"But Sire," Sir Kyle interposed, "there can be but one reason not to show me the girl."

"Pray tell, sir, what that might be?"

"Either the maiden is tainted, or is of such repulsive features that you fear to show her to me."

Ian towered over the Franians, furious in his wrath. His soldiers drew swords across the table from the strangers. "By the Thunderer and his Bolt, you men try my patience. You force me to sell the one most dear to me in order to save my country from starvation and then have the gall to call my daughter unfit for the cur offspring of your lord. You need nothing more than a womb to bear the plagued offspring of your lord's whelp. I'll guarantee my daughter to be of sound health and virtue. If not, you may claim my throne as your own. By all that's holy, I have had enough of you arrogant pig droppings. Take your horses and leave!"

"But sire, it is the middle of the night," replied Sir Kyle flabbergasted.

"I don't care if it is the second moon of Kyrian, you will be gone from my demesnes immediately! See to it," he instructed Garth, and he strode from the room.

Illera hurried after her father, catching him in the corridor outside his quarters.

"Father, tell me you didn't sell me to the King of Frain."

"Illera," Ian began but dissolved into sobs, clutching her to him as weeping racked his body.

CHAPTER 2

Illera threw her arms over the lowest branch of the ancient spreading oak. She swung her leg over and pulled herself upright on the limb. Moving close to the trunk, she inched upward. The magpie fluttered around her face, trying to force her down from the tree.

"Come on Maggie; I just want to see it. You know I won't hurt anything," Illera used her most soothing voice.

The magpie squawked louder and tried harder to hinder Illera's climb. She persisted, gently pushing the bird aside with one free hand as she inched up the bark with the other. Very slowly she made her way upward, clinging more tightly as the branches grew narrower. With an almost human yelp, Maggie left her, winging away into the clear summer sky. Illera scrambled higher, securing a position looking down into an untidy pile of sticks. Three featherless, gray blobs opened their eyes and began to gape at her. Illera smiled down at them and reaching into the pocket of her dress with one hand, tossed slivers of meat to the babies. Maggie sailed in with an indignant sound and covered her young ones, hiding them from Illera's view with outspread wings.

"Oh, Maggie, I just wanted to see your children. You know I would never hurt them."

Maggie turned her head away; pretending Illera wasn't there.

"Okay, I get the hint, I'm leaving."

She placed the remaining slivers of meat on the branch where the magpie could easily reach them. Then she slithered down the branch to one below. An imperative squawk from the bird made her halt.

"What is it, Maggie? I'm leaving, okay?"

Maggie gargled back a reply, looking down the road to the approach. Illera stopped and listened. Under the muffled begging of the baby magpies, she could hear the faint thunder of hooves.

"Thanks, Maggie," called Illera slipping down to a concealing branch where she could see the road.

The approaching party was magnificent. Two banner carriers on snow-white mules rode first, their pennants snapping in the wind. Illera's heart sank at the sight of the black dragon on a field of blood red. The other standard sported a galloping white horse on sky blue. Behind the mules trod two of the largest war-horses she had ever seen. The furthest stallion was coal black, caparisoned in sky blue and ridden by a dark-haired man in shining silver armor. The nearest was golden with a white mane and tail, also caparisoned in sky blue, ridden by a man with hair the color of his horse's coat. He was also clad in mirror bright armor. A chestnut palfrey with a white blaze and four white stockings was led at rein behind them. She counted twelve pairs of knights behind them, each riding a well-decked out war-horse and carrying many weapons. Behind the knights came ten pairs of bowmen, trotting and carrying their longbows in their hands. After them shuffled twenty pairs of donkeys, each laden to the point that the animals looked like walking bundles with long ears in front. A mixed herd of scrawny cattle followed, Illera guessed there were about twenty head.

She sighed; this must be the party from Frain come to steal

her from her land. Usually, Maggie gave her warning of bad things, but she was occupied with her new family, so Illera understood why the bird had failed to caution her. The unrest in the kingdom bothered her, and the pinch of hunger was not something she was used to. Her father said this train would bring food, enough for the farmers to survive until the crops were ready. But still, how could they expect her to leave here. It was part of her soul.

When the last bovine passed, switched repeatedly by a dusty boy, Illera slid down from the oak and followed the entourage at a distance. There was total confusion on the outer bailey as the Frainians worked with the guards to organize a march to the inner castle and a reception by the king. She slipped past the milling throng and ducked into one of the passages, passing under the confusion and into the castle. In her rooms, she could hear her father bellowing orders below and at the mention of her name, disappeared again, exiting into the stable this time.

The loft afforded her a good view of the proceeding. Her father greeted the guests royally, accepting the loaded donkeys and giving them to the care of the yeoman in charge of supplies. Sir Garth took charge of the soldiers, sending them to the barracks beside the stable. The grooms took the war-horses and bedded them down beneath Illera's hiding place. The confusion moved indoors, and all was quiet below.

Illera descended the ladder from the loft, and walked among the new arrivals. She knew every animal around the castle, but her favorites were the giant horses that the knights rode. She moved to the two huge animals from the front of the procession. The golden stallion whickered at her, and she stretched out her hand and firmly stroked his broad cheek. Stabled next to him was the black. When Illera approached him he snorted and stamped, shaking the stall walls.

"What's the matter?" Illera asked him.

His eyes rolled redly in his head, and the massive hooves beat a tattoo on the walls. Illera laughed, watching his ears swivel towards her.

"Shhhhhhh big boy. You know you don't have to be afraid of me," she whispered to him.

Gradually the great head bent closer, arching down above her. Her hand crept forward, and she scratched behind the curious muzzle. He lowered his head, and she placed her forehead on his, closing her eyes and communing with the powerful creature.

"I never thought Abbadon would let any creature so close to him except me," a warm voice said directly behind her.

Illera jumped and whirled around at the same time the horse threw up his head and snorted fiercely.

"Whoa, big fellow. It's me," the man said, reaching up to catch the halter and pull the big head back down.

The horse bared his teeth and shuffled backward in his stall.

"Now what did you do to my horse?" asked the man as he turned to her.

Illera stared up at him, speechless. He fitted his animal well, being the tallest man she had ever seen, with broad shoulders blotting out the light from the doorway. He had a strong face with wide cheekbones and deep dimples now smiling down at her. His hair was as black as Abbadon's hide, but it was his eyes that held her mesmerized, large and dark, just the color of the sky at twilight, fringed with long black lashes and they bore straight into hers. Her heart thumped wildly in her chest.

"I...I don't know what to say," Illera stammered. "I was just... ah... getting acquainted with the new horses."

The stranger laughed, a rich, hearty sound that made Illera smile in return. "It's okay. I'm just surprised. Abbadon has one master, me. Anyone else approaching him usually gets stomped flat, and here I find you head to head with him."

"I'm sorry," Illera replied. "I was just talking to him, and he is so beautiful. I don't think I've ever seen a more splendid animal."

The stranger's smile grew wider. "Thank you. I think the same thing. Lark, that's my brother, and I fought over him as a colt. But I won; so Abbadon's mine, and Lark got Appolon there. He's not a bad animal either."

"No," Illera agreed, "He looks fabulous. Until now my father's horse was the best one in the stable." She pointed to King Ian's war-horse across the width of the building.

"I thought that was the King's horse," said the stranger with a frown on his face. "Don't tell me you are the princess?"

His eyes wandered down her body, and Illera looked too, noting the smudges of dirt and straw sticking to her front. Her hem was in its usual soiled state. Dust and cobwebs were smeared down her arms and across her face and hair. A long run, where the fabric had caught on a branch exposed the cotton petticoat below. Illera blushed, embarrassed.

The stranger straightened and held out a hand. "My lady, I am Raven, squire of King Korul, sent to escort you to your betrothed, Torul, prince of Frain."

Caught, Illera could do little but extend a dainty, if soiled, hand to him. He raised it to his forehead and bowed over it, releasing her immediately. Raising his head, he stared. Illera fidgeted; uncomfortable under his gaze.

"Sir, you embarrass me," she snapped staring right back at him.

"Your pardon my lady," he replied looking away. "Rumor has it that the princess of Madean is an ugly hag that Torul will have to be blindfolded to beget an heir on, and yet I see before me the most beautiful woman I have ever seen in my life."

Illera looked at the floor, not knowing how to reply. Twisting her fingers together she said, "I'm sorry Sir Raven, but I resist this union and I refused to meet with the other messengers from your country. By that, they inferred my appearance."

Raven smiled broadly. "I'm not Sir Raven yet. When we return successfully from this mission, King Korul has promised us our spurs."

"Us?" inquired Illera.

"Lark and I. My brother."

"Surely, the mission is not that important. You could lose me, and it wouldn't matter," she ventured hopefully.

Raven smiled sadly. "I must not fail. We were not royal born, but our mother was the horse girl, and shamefully treated for having us without wedlock. Not until we were ten was there a man brave enough to dare the villager's scorn and take her for his own. So if Lark and I earn our spurs, then we honor her, as she deserves."

Illera turned away. "I don't want to go. I belong here. This is my land."

Raven turned her back, looking down at her, "I'm sorry, but we don't always get to do what we want. If it were up to me, I would leave you here and move Torul in with you. This is a much more pleasant land than Frain. I too, have no choice. I must take you back to my liege."

Illera looked away. She pulled free from his hands and strode out the door and straight to the keep and her rooms there. She hurled herself on the bed and began to weep, soaking the pillow into soggy clumps. When she was drenched from crying, she summoned her servants and had them prepare a bath. She chose her best gown for dinner, a royal purple that accented the color of her eyes. The maids took an hour to fix her hair with amethyst and golden chains. She hung a golden torque set with amethyst around her neck and went to the meal looking her best.

Her father's smile of gratitude at her appearance almost made the lump in her throat burst into tears again, but she was determined not to embarrass herself in front of the Franians again. She nodded graciously to Raven as he took his place beside her and held out a hand to Lark, seated at her other side. He was like and unlike his brother, an inch shorter, but still gigantic compared to the men of Madean. His hair was golden and his eyes the same dark blue as Raven's. The dimples and wide cheekbones were similar, but Lark had a full-lipped mouth, curved now in a pleasant smile. He greeted her as courteously as his brother as they took their seats.

Illera could see her father heave a sigh of relief as she behaved herself and she felt a pang of sorrow at the discomfort her disobedience caused him. However, he was unfair to sell her for the good of the kingdom. She ate very little at the banquet and spoke not at all, even though both Raven and Lark attempted to engage her in conversation during the meal. Before the last course, she pleaded weariness and escaped to her rooms and another storm of weeping.

As soon as she opened her eyes the next morning, the serving maids were there, supervised by Sar. They had cedar chests brought in and began to pack her clothes. Illera sat on her bed, just watching as her dressing room emptied of its contents and the offensive boxes were filled one by one.

"This can't be happening. This is not real," she ventured to Sar when the other maids left to fetch more dried lavender to pack in the folds of her garments.

"For shore 'tis 'appenin' my Lady. But a few days 'ence and you'll be gone from all ar lives. 'tis a shame too by all I'm 'earing."

"What do you mean Sar?"

"I canna' tell, my Lady. T'wouldn't be fair."

"Sar, by all that's holy, if you know anything about the situation I'll be facing please tell me. Have I not been a kind and considerate mistress to you?"

"Aye, you 'ave, but still, they'd cut out ma tongue were they t'find I'tol you anythin'."

Illera stretched out her hand in entreaty. "I am being sold to Frain so that you and the rest of the kingdom might have food in their bellies and you refuse to tell me what you know that might help me there. Sar, that is unfair. Remember how I braved my father's wrath when your little dog went missing? Do you remember how we searched together, in the pouring rain for hours until I found him in the poacher's snare? Do you remember how I defied my father and your King to stay with you until we knew he would survive and the wound of his that I healed? Sar, if you have any fondness for me at all, please tell me what you know."

Sar tiptoed to the door, checked both ways and then locked it. She came to the bed and sat beside her mistress. Illera held her hand in her own icy ones.

"Well, my lady, I made th'quaintance of one of the gen'lmen sent 'ere to 'elp with t' pirates and t'Shul. An' I know you is a fair raised lady, but when a man and woman a been t'gether, sometime t'man, well 'e's like to talk after. Well, this 'ere gen'lmen, 'e is tellin' me 'bout Frain and Korul and Torul. Seems a dreadful place t'me. They says as 'ow Korul, the King 'ad a beautiful bride an 'e beat 'er so 'er's a 'alfwit now. An' still 'e made 'er bear 'is 'eir, an' that almost killed 'er. An' 'e said Torul was worse than th'father, 'a cruel, selfish, spoiled brat' was th'words 'e used. I remember 'um."

Illera swallowed the bile that rose in her throat at the thought of such a marriage.

"Oh Sar, how am I going to endure it?"

"Well my Lady, th'gen'lmen said as how your escorts is fine soldiers, good men, 'onest an' true. Maybe they can 'elp you?"

Illera sighed. "No, I already asked Raven. He said that they would win their spurs for bringing me to Torul. It seems to be very important to him, and his brother."

"Well, my Lady, I wouldna' give up. Try the brother. I be thinkin' 'e took a shine t'you. I seen 'im lookin' when you weren't."

Illera ventured a feeble smile. "I think I'll try my father one last time. He's got to understand reason and if I tell him what you told me, maybe he will change his mind."

Sar lept from the bed, "My Lady, you must'nt tell 'im 'ow you know. If th'gen'lmen learns I been talkin' who knows what'll 'appen t'me."

"Trust me, Sar; I won't let on how I know. You're safe."

Illera rose and dressed quickly, choosing from the few gowns left unpacked. Then she hurried off, to find her father. She wandered around the castle, asking the servants and finally tracked him down in the library. Lark and Raven were with him. She hesitated and then entered.

"Father, I need to talk to you."

Ian lifted his head, and a gusty sigh ruffled the fringes of his beard. "If this is about not going to Frain, I don't want to discuss it anymore. That's final."

"But father," she continued as Lark and Raven stood at her approach. "I have information that will change your mind. I know it will. If you love me, you will listen."

Ian shook his head. "Illera nothing can change this. Nothing."

Illera stood before him, just the width of his desk separating them, "Please listen, if only you knew what kind of people you are selling me to, you can't know and still send me there. I've heard that Torul is a selfish, spoiled brat and Korul is so cruel he beat his wife until she became an idiot."

King Ian looked at the messengers from Frain. Lark and Raven refused to meet his eyes.

"Is this true?" he asked them.

"Your majesty, as lowly squires it ill befits us to criticize our betters," replied Lark.

"But is what my daughter said true?" he insisted.

Raven looked at him and then Illera. "It is true that many of the serfs speak ill of the King and his son. For myself, I have not had a lot of contact with either of them, only the knights of the castle during training."

"What about Korul's wife?" persisted the king.

Lark shuffled his feet. "It is true she has lost her mental faculties, but I heard it was due to a fall."

"Father!" Illera insisted.

The king rose. "What would you have me do?" He paced back and forth before the tall windows behind the desk. "Most of the grain and other food supplies have already been distributed. Would you ask me to force starving people to watch their children die while I retrieve the food from their mouths to save you from a spoiled child of a husband?"

Illera drew back, shocked to the core of her being at his answer. "But you love me?"

Ian stopped, spread his hands on the desk and looked at her. "Yes, child I love you. If I could take your place, I would. But I love Madean too, and I love its people. I could not sacrifice them for your happiness if I wanted too. Besides what of the warriors from Frain bedded inside our very walls? They would make sure that you go to Torul as agreed."

Illera shook her head. "I never agreed."

"I agreed for you!" roared the king like a wounded mountain lion.

Illera took a quick step back and stumbled into Raven. He put a warm hand on her shoulder to steady her. The clang of running footsteps interrupted the conversation. A page burst into the room.

"Sire, sire," he gasped, "the signal fires have been lighted."

"Where," demanded king Ian, obviously relieved to have a problem he knew how to handle.

"Southward, from Southern Reach," the boy replied.

"Tell Sir Garth to ready the men at arms and the grooms to prepare the horses," Ian commanded.

The boy dashed from the room.

"Excuse me, gentlemen, I must don my armor."

Raven interjected, "Sire, I request that Lark and I be allowed to join with you in repelling these invaders."

Ian gave him a long look and nodded. The three men strode rapidly from the room.

Illera watched from the south tower of the barbican. Her father, Raven, Lark and most of the men galloped over Third Bridge and through the waving fields of young grain. She watched until her eyes strained to discover the dust rising in the distance. She felt hollow inside, almost as if she had died and part of her was missing. Her father loved her, but not as much as he loved Madean. The whole universe had been shaken and rearranged into a different pattern, and she just didn't know how it functioned anymore. All her certainties had vanished.

The next day she wandered like a ghost from place to place, visiting the special people, animals and places that she had loved to go: Shani and her tribe of pigs, Jorul the shepherd boy with the flocks and droves, Meigid, the ancient withered man in charge of the cattle, and the old groom Stave and the few horses that remained. She walked through the little villages clustered close to the castle; spoke a farewell to the tearful people there.

On the second day, she walked to the forest and drifted through the soothing verdure that had once been a place she valued above her life. The birds and small animals came to her and climbed about her head and shoulders. The deer brought her fawn to eat from her hand, and the lion lay purring at her feet for hours while she scratched him.

On the third day, Illera visited all the bridges over the Royal River, gazing for hours into the foaming depths and listening to the hidden messages in the song of the water. Distorting it all was the gray fog that settled over her life when her father refused to protect her. Her spark was gone and her energy low as she dragged herself from place to place awaiting the inevitable.

Illera was dawdling her way back to the castle when the war party returned. She didn't even lift her head to see them trot by. Her father in the lead, sat proud and strong, followed by Lark and Raven, their huge mounts dwarfing his. The rest of the men trailed behind, but seemed cheerful and uninjured. Illera shuffled along in their dust when they passed.

Her father met her at the steps to the keep. "Illera, I want you to dress well tonight and attend the banquet. We are honoring the brave men who defended Southern Reach tonight in addition to having your farewell supper. I need you to be there."

Illera nodded dully and brushed past him taking note of the order of importance in his words. She was oblivious to his stare of perplexity that followed her into the castle. In her rooms, she prepared herself with difficulty. Most of her things were packed, ready for the journey tomorrow. She couldn't make herself care, for nothing mattered anymore. Sar helped, doing more to prepare her for the banquet than she did herself. One of the maids brought a new gown, a shimmering periwinkle blue, and they dressed her, piling only the front of her hair up, leaving the back long and rippling down her back. Illera barely glanced in the mirror and absently thanked them for their help. With dragging steps, she descended the wide stone staircase to the meal.

All the knights rose in deference to her entrance, but she didn't even nod to them or smile as she usually did. Even the clatter they made when they sat could not pierce the gloom that enveloped her.

"My Lady, you look especially beautiful tonight," Lark complimented her.

"But sad?" questioned Raven.

Illera looked vaguely at them.

"You are not becoming ill, I hope?" Lark ventured again.

Raven laughed. "Torul would think ill of an ailing bride."

Her father raised his goblet in a toast. "My dear, to you, and your journey. I have no more fears of your safety."

The rest of the people in the hall followed the king's lead and toasted her.

The king continued, "Why my child, you should have seen these men fight. Why if I had five of them I would have no fear for my kingdom at all. We repelled the Shul without a single casualty. That warhorse, how magnificent. He fights like seven men. Did you know Illera, that Raven has promised me one of his get?"

Illera shook her head in answer to her father's question.

He continued, "And I have a special surprise for you. In Southern Reach, I found a warrior maiden, a fine fighter, and a splendid woman. She is descended from some warriors of Sorwelk, trapped here when their boat was burned. She has agreed to be your companion on your trip to Frain, and perhaps, if you get along well, she will stay with you there."

The king beamed his pleasure at her. Rising to his feet, he gestured to the lower tables. An enormous woman rose to her feet. Illera would not have believed it was a woman except for the small, flat breasts accented by the curve of her armor. Her blonde braids were worn in a circle at the crest of her head. A tall fore-head led down to small, round eyes and a puckish upturned nose. Full red lips were the most feminine thing about her. Her clothing was similar to what the fighting men wore, leather and metal. A short skirt left muscular thighs and calves corded with muscle exposed.

King Ian waved a hand, "Ashera come up here and meet my daughter."

The gigantic woman made her way through the throng and curtseyed clumsily before Illera. She watched, knowing if she was herself she would be astonished, but not feeling much of anything. She nodded at her.

Ashera said, "I am most pleased to meet you Princess Illera."

Again Illera nodded. The giantess curtseyed again and returned to her seat.

"So my dear, what do you think?"

Illera regarded him wearily and shrugged. Ian glared at her a moment and turned his conversation back to Raven and his war-horse. Illera pushed around the food on her plate and let the rest of the meal swirl around her, taking less meaning from the babel of the words than she had from the noise of the rushing river. She noticed that all the foods were her favorites, perfectly prepared and served, yet each course tasted like straw to her tonight and she only picked at the offerings. The banquet seemed interminable, and she longed for the quiet of her own bare rooms.

"Illera!" snapped her father.

Illera looked up, vaguely registering the anger on his face.

"If you cannot be civil enough to answer a polite question, perhaps you should leave the table."

Lark stammered, "It's alright...I..."

"No!" the king cut him off. "I raised my daughter to be a lady, not some common milkmaid who knows no better. Illera..."

Illera jumped to her feet, the gray around her sundering and falling away in brittle pieces. A fury and pain flowed over her, stealing her breath and trembling her muscles.

"Shut up, you hateful old man," she screamed.

Ian's face sagged, and his jaw hung open.

"You raised me to be a whore, to be sold to the highest bidder who can take care of your country when you can't. How dare you lecture me on courtesy? You haven't even the courtesy to listen to the voice of your own daughter. How I despise you," Turning to the room she looked at all the shocked faces. "I despise all of you, using me to save yourselves."

She threw down the napkin and tore from the room, closely pursued by tears that threatened to scald her. She ran aimlessly until her breath was short and she was gasping. Coming to herself, she realized she was at the top of the tower. She paused and the enormity of what she had said hit her in the stomach like a powerful kick from one of the war-horses. She staggered to the edge, peering out through the crenellations. A chilly bracing wind caressed her face, drying the sweat and tears. As if the wind was a signal, the gray enveloped her again, leaving her devoid of feeling, wrapped in thick bands of uncaring. Her life was remote, distant from her hollow self. It was better than that pain, the one that made her mouth open and spew hurtful things; far better not to care. Perhaps a permanent uncaring would be the best.

She placed her elbows on the battlement and drew herself up; standing looking down, down the moon touched face of the outer wall. The moat glimmered far below, its muddy water painted silver now, hiding its green scum and unwholesome appearance. If she jumped outward as she fell she should hit the rocky soil around the moat and not the dirty water itself. She spread her arms, a giddy feeling of exhilaration beginning to well up inside her. She would know how Maggie felt to fly.

"Illera," a voice behind her almost made her lose her balance.

"Go away," she replied her voice soft and distant as the gentle wind.

Lark spoke again, "Illera, you can't do this. It will plunge Madean into war with Frain."

"I don't care. They don't care about me, not even my father."

"Can't you see this was the hardest thing he has ever had to do. Harder even than losing your mother."

"No, I only see that I am being sold for peasants. Go away! I want my last moment to be peaceful."

Lark was moving slowly closer. "Illera you can't do this."

She turned her head to regard him. "Yes, I can. It is my life, and if I don't wish to sacrifice it to a spoiled, selfish brat, I shouldn't have to. So, yes I can."

With a furious squawk, Maggie flew out of the dark into Illera's face. Lark used the distraction to cover the two remaining steps to her. Maggie fluttered and scolded while Illera batted at her with her hands.

"Let me fly with you Maggie," she cried as she bent her knees and shifted her weight forward.

Lark seized her by the waist and lifted her from the edge holding her close to his massive chest. She battered him with her fists and kicked at him with her legs.

"Release me, you have no right," she screamed through clenched teeth.

He placed her on her feet and grabbed both her hands in one fist and held them tight.

Bending his head, he spoke close to her ear, "Illera, I know you don't want this, and I don't blame you. I wouldn't want it either. But I promise you, by the mother, I was born to that if you are unhappy, or if Torul mistreats you in any way, I will rescue you from him and bring you back to your father and Madean, even if I have to kill him."

An earth shudder rippled through the stones of the tower. Illera clutched tight to Lark. She thought about his words. Pushing away from him she stared into his eyes.

"You swear?" she asked.

"Yes Illera, I swear."

CHAPTER 3

*I*llera awoke in the pearl gray light of a day just beginning. The sky outside her window was painted in delicate pastel shades of yellow and peach and the morning chorus of birds was tuning up to burst into vibrant song at the sun's first peek over the horizon. She lay in her bed, eyes wandering around the barren room, noting the absence of anything that would make it personal to her, except for her mother's large, glass mirror.

If only her mother were here, she wouldn't be making her go to a life of misery. Illera was as certain of her fate as she was her knowledge that the sky was blue, but her father wouldn't listen. Her mother would understand. Hadn't she left her own land and lived with her father for long years, always grieving for the place of her birth? Hadn't she finally forsaken the man she loved in order to return to the place she belonged? Yes, her mother would know how she felt. At least she had loved her father, not been forced to marry a cruel, selfish, spoiled brat. She needed her mother.

Slowly a plan coalesced in Illera's mind, firming as the details began to stand out sharp and clear. She bounced from her bed and began rummaging through the empty drawers and chests remaining in her room. She found a good-sized hemp bag in which the maids had carried the lavender. She dumped the remaining flakes of the flowers onto the floor, wiping the inside of the bag clean. She took the flint and tinder from the fireplace and located her hoof knife and pick in a chest of things to be given to the poor. They were together in the sheath, so she placed them in the bag as well. The remainder of a spool of sturdy cord followed them.

Then Illera dressed in the clothing she had selected yesterday. She blessed whatever whim or depression made her choose the olive and brown tweed divided skirt and jacket. The orange blouse was too bright so she exchanged it for a dull brown one from the discard chest, leaving her own intense one in its place. She plaited her hair in a single long braid down her back, took her long black leather riding cloak and descended the stairs with her bag in hand.

Only a few servants were stirring this early. She slipped out of the back door and made her way to the chicken yard where the goose girl was feeding her charges. Illera smiled and waved to her in answer to her greeting. She went to the granary and filled the bag she carried from the oat bin. With a grin, she twisted the mouth of the bag closed and fastened it with a bit of twine. She secured it to her belt and returned to the castle.

"Where is the girl, Thunderer take it? If she has vanished, I'll have somebody's head," Illera heard as she entered the kitchen.

"Is something the matter father?" she asked sweetly.

Her father turned at the sound of her voice. A mighty frown on his face smoothed away at the sight of her.

"I thought you were hiding." He cleared his throat.

Illera pondered a moment and said, "Father, I'll leave with the messengers, but won't you please reconsider. I feel marrying Torul will be a disaster. I feel it in the marrow of my bones."

Ian smiled sourly at her. "I suppose it will. What else could it be with two spoiled brats joining together."

"Father!" exclaimed Illera shock ringing through her voice.

"Yes," he continued, "I thought I raised my daughter to be a good and caring person, but you have proved me wrong. Such a pity I didn't realize it earlier when I could have done something about it, but I guess it will be Torul's problem from now on."

Illera felt as if a knife were disemboweling her. Her breath was short, and her stomach knotted painfully.

"Father." She shook her head, and a single tear dribbled down her cheek as he turned from her and marched from the kitchen.

Following him to the great room, she noticed Ashera, Lark, and Raven already at breakfast at the head table. Despite her pain, Illera forced herself to join them. As the food was set before her, she chewed and swallowed everything on her plate and asked the serving girls for more. She ate until she could barely breathe and another mouthful would make her void the contents of her stomach. Lark and Raven were watching her with lowered brows. Ashera was eating twice as much and never noticed Illera gorging on ham, eggs, bread dripping with butter and honey; all washed down with quaffs of fresh milk.

"Princess Illera, are you all right?" Lark blinked, and his eyes wandered from her face.

She looked up at him and smiled. "Yes, I am fine. The last few days I didn't feel much like eating, but now my appetite has returned."

"Do you always eat like this?" He waved a hand in his brother's direction to silence his guffaws.

Feeling puckish, Illera gave him her widest smile. "Of course not, almost Sir Lark, quite often I eat much more."

Raven no longer able to contain himself burst into loud peals of infectious laughter, joined by Ashera. The astonishment on Lark's face made Illera join in as well.

Lark ventured another question, "Then how do you stay so slim if you are so fine a trencherman?"

King Ian cut in crossly, "Can't you see this is just another scheme to make you leave her here. She hopes to put you off, so you return to Frain without her and counsel Torul to avoid her."

"Come, sire," retorted Raven as his eyes twinkled at her, "I hardly think her capable of such perversity."

"Nor would I have thought so until recently." The king's face sported a mighty frown.

Illera smiled politely and excused herself, feeling as if the considerable meal was going to come back up then and there. She made it to her room and flopped on the bed. The nausea and whirling sensation in her head finally left, and she rose and went downstairs, collecting her bag and her cloak from where she left them. Her father waited at the main door of the keep. Down the stairs, over his shoulder, she could see the servants loading her baggage onto the donkeys. The two banner carriers were waiting beside their white mules. Abbadon and Appolon were saddled, waiting for their riders and a scruffy white war-horse dozed beside them.

Illera walked toward her father as he gazed over the activity on the inner bailey.

"Goodbye, father," Illera noted the cold in her tone, freezing her features to match as she moved past him.

He caught the sleeve of her jacket as she went past. "Illera, I'm sorry at the harsh words that have been spoken between us. You will leave, and I won't see you again for a long time, if ever. I want you to know that I do love you, more than you can ever realize. I'm sorry that you are unhappy about this match, but I had no choice."

Illera could see the sincerity in his eyes and hear it in his voice. His eyes were rheumy as if he might cry at any moment. He looked like a beaten, defeated old man. She felt the barriers crumbling inside her and took a step towards him.

"Father, you were the only man I loved, and I love you still. But I know you are making a mistake, I know it. I am going, and I wish it were as before, before Sir Kyle ever stepped foot into Madean. The thing that hurts the most is feeling that you don't love me anymore. That's the only reason I am leaving."

"Oh child, if only you could know just how much I do love you. You can't believe how hard this is for me as well."

"But it's still not enough to believe in my feelings."

"I have to do what my head tells me is right, not my heart."

Illera ducked her head. "I know." She raised her head to look into his eyes. They were glistening with unshed tears. She felt her own grow shiny. "Father, remember that I love you and I always will. I can't continue angry with you, and please, when you hear the reports of me, don't grieve too much. Don't blame yourself; I do know this is the only thing you can do under the circumstances. If only we'd had more time…"

Her voice thickened, and she could speak no longer. Her father drew her into his arms and held her, his tears dampening the top of her hair while hers fell to his shirt and darkened the fine material. Raven and Lark slipped past the embracing pair and went to the horses. Ashera stopped beside them

"My lady, we have a long way to travel today, and it would be best to get started." Ashera's voice grated like metal on Illera's ears.

With a final hug, she turned from her father and descended the steps to the courtyard. Raven strode from the stable leading the tall chestnut palfrey with a strange contraption on its back. Lark came up beside her.

"What's in the bag?" he asked nodding to the sack tied at her waist.

"Oh, I brought that to get acquainted with the horses," replied Illera remembering her plan.

She opened the bag and went to each of the four donkeys, taking a palmful of oats and holding it out to each. Then she fed a handful to each mule and Ashera's white steed. Appolon reached eagerly for his share and whickered at her. Abbadon greedily shouldered him aside and gobbled down a handful of oats. Illera approached the mare and held out a hand. The chestnut lowered her head and delicately nibbled the offering. Abbadon tried shoving the mare aside and taking her share, but she laid her ears back and bared her teeth. Abbadon back away. Illera laughed, Raven and Lark, joining her.

"Enough," called Ashera from her mount, "We must be off before the sun's overhead."

"This mare is a gift from Torul to you my Lady, her name is Copper," said Raven as Illera inspected the horse.

"From Torul?" asked Illera, "Did he select her personally?"

Raven darkened, blushing to the roots of his hair. "No, my Lady. I chose her, but Torul said to bring you a mount."

At Lark's snort, Illera inquired, "Did Torul really send me a mount?"

Raven blushed even darker. "Well, he said to see you had a reliable animal to enable you to reach Frain."

Lark laughed aloud. "You might as well tell her the truth Brother. Torul wanted you to have a donkey, but Raven thought a donkey wasn't good enough for a princess, even an ugly princess, so he picked the best palfrey from our mother's herd for you. Torul has no idea."

Illera looked up at Raven watching him grind his teeth while giving murderous looks to his brother. Lark swung up on his horse, and the banner carriers mounted their mules. They gathered the reins for the donkeys.

"How am I supposed to ride this horse? It needs a saddle," asked Illera puzzled by the contraption on the mare's back.

"It's a side saddle, my Lady," replied Raven.

Illera looked at him puzzled. His hands encircled her waist, and he lifted her to the tall chestnut's back. Blushing furiously again, he arranged her legs into the proper configuration and placed her feet in the stirrups.

"Thank you, Raven," she murmured, taking pity on his embarrassment. "But this seems a very unstable way to ride."

The party moved out, passing through the inner gates and onto the outer bailey. Illera refused to think that this might be the last time she passed these beloved walls.

"Why do Franians enforce the indignity of sitting a horse in such a manner on their princesses?" she asked in an attempt not to think of the more important event taking place.

"A,...uh...maiden must be protected...from....uh...uh... damage," Raven looked pointedly ahead.

"Damage?" inquired Illera innocently.

"Er, yes...damage."

"What sort of damage?" she persisted as they crossed the outer bailey and exited the barbican. The hollow ring of the hooves over the drawbridge made her bones ache.

Overhearing their conversation, Lark was laughing so hard he was having a hard time to sit on his horse.

"Uh...well... it is said that...uh...damage can occur if a maiden rides astride a horse...so, therefore...we...uh...use a sidesaddle for maidens of virtue." Raven occupied his hands twisting his horse's mane.

Illera forced a strained laugh. The approach vanished beneath the swift-moving animals, and she mentally said goodbye to the spreading oak with Maggie and her babies. A sob caught on the sound of the laugh. Raven gave her a strange look.

"Is something wrong?"

"Oh, I must be damaged a lot then, for I have ridden astride since I could first walk." She hiccuped to keep the sobs down.

Raven gave her a warm smile. "My mother says it is all foolishness, but the men of Frain love the superstition, so you must have a sidesaddle. I wouldn't worry."

Unable to contain the pain that threatened to burst her asunder, Illera kicked the long-legged mare into a gallop. She rushed ahead of Lark, Ashera, and the banner carriers. Raven followed, overtaking and swinging Abbadon in front of her to slow her headlong flight.

"I'm sorry Illera, but you must stay with the party."

She looked at him as slow tears leaked from her eyes. "Can the party move a little quicker then, for if I don't get away from the castle, I'm going to burst."

The understanding dawning in his eyes made her sob harder. He turned and gestured for the rest who joined them at a swift trot, the best pace the donkeys could maintain.

"Get away from the girl," Ashera growled chasing Raven back to Lark while she paced her horse with Copper. "Ladies of her sort don't like to be bothered with riffraff like the two of you."

Ashera babbled on for hours about her family and her heritage and how she grew up as an outsider in Southern Reach. Illera tuned her out, concentrating on the rhythm of the horse beneath her as the miles added up, removing her from her home. The vast green plains, dotted with small farms gradually gave way to low hills with flocks of grazing sheep. The road wound on, and the forest dipped over from the west to meet them, and soon they were traveling through the brushy woodland of widely spaced mixed trees.

"I need to stop." She pulled Copper to a shifting halt.

"We need to make some miles your highness," the warrior woman replied.

"Then I'll stop myself." Illera slid from the palfrey.

Ashera yelled at the banner carriers. The ground felt unstable after so many hours on horseback and Illera stretched her back and legs and walked around in an exaggerated fashion to limber up her muscles.

Lark dismounted and walked up beside her. "Is something the matter my Lady?"

She knew now was the time. "Yes, Lark, my rear is sore, I am perishing for a cup of tea, and I have to ease nature."

A grin quirked his mouth. "I guess it is past noon, so we can take a break. The horses need to rest a bit anyway. Ashera, escort the princess to a suitable shrubbery."

Illera had not counted on this twist. Still, she went meekly with the warrior woman to a stand of dense bushes, taller than she was. Ashera stood right beside her. She scraped a hole and then turned to the woman.

"Ashera, please, would you stand the other side of the bush. You can hear me, I'm right here and…and it embarrasses me to have someone watching."

"Certainly my lady," she replied moving to the front of the shrub.

Illera rustled around making small noises, concentrating all her power on calling some birds. Two tiny brown thrushes came in answer to her summons. She scattered a handful of grain around in the duff of the forest floor and stole away; putting more and more of the low bushes between her and the rest of the party. The thrushes scratched and rustled through the fallen leaves making a lot of noise, precisely as if she were still in the same place.

The forest grew thicker and denser as she stealthily moved west and south. She called other creatures to come and obscure her trail. The possum and raccoon were the first to answer, and she scattered them a handful of grain. A pair of stags arrived and followed behind her, covering her marks with their sharp hoof prints. When she reached a rocky outcropping, she left them a pile of grain as a reward. She entered the forest again, removing her boots and wading down a small stream. It retook her east, but it would hide her tracks better. When her feet grew numb, she left the stream, dried herself and put her boots back on. A helpful beaver covered her exit point with mud and the imprint of his own body.

She could move faster now, feeling that they would find it impossible to follow her trail. She trotted through the forest, keeping to the fringes where the trees were farther apart. She ran until her lungs were about to burst, then she walked until she was able to run again. She repeated that pattern, always keeping to the edges of the forest, ready to duck in among the bigger trees if she should see a person. As the sun was celebrating the day's end with red and gold banners in the sky, she reached the part of the woodlands she knew well. Looking away from the sun she saw the castle, its seven tall towers rosy in the declining day. A sharp pang knifed through her, but she firmed her mind and continued. The first bridge over the Royal River was almost in the forest. She watched for long moments, but the structure seemed deserted. She dashed from the cover of the trees and flew over the bridge as fast as she could run. She was no sooner over the span when she dived back into the concealing trees. She knew this land so well she could travel in the dark and did so until she found herself in a part of the forest not as familiar. She made a nest of leaves and pulled her cloak over her, falling asleep instantly.

Fingers of golden light pried at her eyelids. Illera snuggled deeper into the warm hollow her body had made. A number of small stirrings around and over her pricked at her consciousness. The decaying scent of leaves and needles filled her nostrils. This didn't feel like her bed. She opened her eyes. A dozen or more small, furry, long-eared bodies cuddled around her. She yawned and stretched, dislodging the bunnies.

"Good morning. Are you hungry?"

She scattered a handful of oats over the ground and smiled as the little ones hopped around picking up the grains. She took a handful herself and chewed the tough material slowly, grimacing a little at the musty taste. Rising, she shook herself off, looked around briefly and continued following the forest to the south.

On her right, the mountains were growing taller, thrusting sharp knife-edged peaks into the sky and the land itself rolled more deeply, with many gullies; rushing streams in their bellies. Illera climbed and descended, climbed and descended.

The sun was directly overhead when her attention was drawn by a low moaning. She turned mountainward and scrambled up a sharp incline. On a flat place, enclosed by tall granite boulders, she saw a creature that was new to her. It looked like a man, yet not a man. The back, arms, and legs were covered with plates of tough brown scales. The creature was bald, with a series of ridges beginning as a crest on its head and growing larger down the spine until they vanished from sight beneath a thick skirt of pounded, woven bark. The hands and feet sported sharp black claws instead of nails, and the face bore a vestigial muzzle with long canine fangs protruding from the upper jaw. A festering wound twisted from the creature's armpit around to the middle of the back near the waistband of the skirt.

Illera approached cautiously, murmuring in the low singsong voice that was so successful with other animals. The wounded beast turned its head and regarded her with bleary orange eyes with horizontal pupils like a goat's.

"Hello, I see you are hurt. Is there anything I can do?" she asked in case the creature had speech.

"You can go and let me die in peace," the beast snarled at her.

Illera knelt down in front of it. She noticed the red streaking from the edges of the slice. "I know a bit about healing, would you let me help you?"

The creature yelped. "As if a human would help an ogre to do anything except die!"

It lay its head back on the rocky earth. Illera reached out a hand, holding it over the wound. The ogre snarled and grabbed her wrist with one hand. Looking straight into its pain-racked eyes, she sent it the thought she would and could help. The grip on her arm weakened and fell away. The beast shrugged.

"Help if you can. There's little enough you can do."

"I'll be right back." She surveyed the surrounding landscape.

She slithered down the rock and back into the forest. Searching, she finally found a clump of birch trees. There was not as much of the healing moss as she liked, but she picked it and placed it in her bag. She scouted around some more and found the blue mushrooms. A cluster of fleshy trilobate plants caught her attention, and she picked a double handful of them. She raced back. The creature had not moved.

Illera had no pot to make tea, so she gave a mushroom to the creature, who stared at her brows furrowed and finally put it in its mouth and began to chew. She took the fleshy leaves and slit them with her hoof knife, letting the sap drip into the open wound. The creature hissed and spat, jumping from his place on the rock only to sag down again a few feet further on.

"I'm sorry," Illera told him, "Usually I can process the juice, so it doesn't sting, but I can't here. I hope you can put up with the pain."

The ogre growled something incomprehensible. Illera continued, squeezing the sap into the wound, angling around the creature's body until she got to its armpit. Then she took the moss and packed it over the gash. She gave the beast another mushroom to chew on and sat beside it to wait. Every few minutes she ran her hand a few inches over the moss bandage.

The day declined and the night stole upon them. Illera continued to run her hand over the treated wound. The creature panted beside her. Twice more she gave him mushrooms and gradually his breath quieted, and he fell asleep. Nearing dawn, Illera herself dozed off. The creature's stirring woke her.

"What manner of thing be this?" It towered over her.

Illera rose to her feet. When it was wounded on the ground, the beast had not seemed so tall nor so massive. The moss hung in tattered strips from the thin red line of the wound. The skin around it was pink and healthy. The beast stood, bunching its prominent muscles.

"It looks good today."

"What are you?" it asked her again.

"I'm just woman. My name is Illera."

The creature ducked its head. "I am Frak, Windsinger of the tribe belonging to Targ of the Shul. Why would you, a woman, heal me, an ogre?"

"Pleased to meet you Frak. And why would I not heal you? It was in my power to do so, and you were in need, how could I withhold that from you?"

The beast shook his head. "Your manner of thought is strange to me. I will think on it as I travel home. Know this, Illera, human woman; Frak Windsinger owes you a life debt."

The ogre bent his head to her once more, then left, climbing the steep hillside as easily as a mountain goat. Illera took a handful of grain and chewed it thoughtfully as she descended.

This part of the country was not familiar to her as were the castle environs. To reach her goal she needed to head east, to find Faerie Bay. Taking her position by the sun, she walked towards it, gradually descending from the hills to lower ones then rolling grassland. The forest was left behind. At first, she felt nervous and exposed, but she realized that they could not track her and Madean was a big place to search for a single missing maiden. So, she tripped along delighting in the warm sun and the sounds of life surrounding her from the singing of the meadowlarks and finches to the comforting hum of insects. There were farmhouses and people scattered through the countryside, but she could see them well enough in advance to avoid going near.

The sun traveled overhead and moved to warm her back as she headed towards the invisible sea. The land smoothed out, becoming flatter and the farms were closer together and harder to avoid. The sky darkened as the clouds piled overhead. Illera had barely enough time to get her cloak fastened before the Thunderer let loose with his bolts and rain.

Feeling the exhaustion of the miles and the healing, she staggered and fell, so she found an overhang on the lee side of a slight hill and folded herself into it, with only her cloak exposed on the outer side. It was a little dryer than the fields, but chilly. Her stomach was beginning to complain, but she told it to be quiet and tucking her hands in her armpits, curled into a ball and slept, lulled by the drumming of the storm overhead.

"Ow!" She unfurled, hurling herself out of her meager shelter.

A small boy stood before her holding a sharply pointed stick.

"See, I tole you it war somebody." He said to the taller boy beside him. Both boys were dressed only in frayed, ragged pants. The pouring rain sluiced over their heads and cascaded down their skinny naked chests. Their feet were bare and callused. A small drove of sheep bleated around them, eager to be gone to the shelter of a fold.

"Who are you?" demanded Illera.

"I be Kest, and he be Ades," the taller of the boys told her. "We's just watchin' th'sheep."

"Yes, Lady, come w'th'us. You c'n shelter within th'sheep an us," the smaller one put in.

"Thank you," Illera told them.

They set off with their small band of animals and Illera trailed behind them until they came at last to a cozy stone pen, roofed tight with heavy timbers and thatch. The boys bedded the sheep down, and soon the warmth of the animals crept through the structure. The children offered her a share of their supper of well-cured bacon, cheese, and bread. Illera gratefully accepted, offering them, in turn, some of her grain. It was a silent and solemn exchange. The boys shook out some dusty hemp bags and made her a bed. Illera sagged down on it and was instantly asleep.

The bleating of the sheep leaving for the pasture in the morning woke her, and she continued on her journey. This day was gray and dull, the sun choosing to hide its face behind a thick swaddling of clouds. Illera persisted, trudging east, trotting when she could, but walking at as fast a pace as she could maintain most of the time.

The land was inclining downward, the grass growing sparser and changing from a fine bladed variety to one with coarse, sharp edges. The tang of the sea was in her nostrils. She hurried. The southern curve of Faerie Bay spread beneath her. The low sandstone cliff guarded the bay and Illera searched for a downward path to the glittering white sand. The rock was sheer and unbroken, gliding smoothly to the sea. Illera flopped on her belly and inched backward over the cliff, hanging on with hands as her feet scrambled against the rock for toeholds. Her muscles gave out, and her fingers slipped from the edge. Down she tumbled to the beach, the hard curve of the rock guiding her path. She landed stomach down and winded; gasping for breath.

Feeling dizzy when she sat up and more than a little disoriented, she gazed around at the strange area. The sand had an unnatural shimmer and the blue-green waves rolling onto the beach had a glamour about them she had never seen. The cliff rose up, sparkling walls against the roiling sky; particles of mica shining without the sun. Farther down the beach six long brown shapes lay in careless abandon on the sand.

Illera went towards them, straining her eyes and making out that they were seals. Half of them humped over to the water and dove into it before she got close. Two others moved to the edge of the water, waiting to see what she would do. When she continued, they too took to the depths. Only one lay in the shining sand watching her approach. She began her song. Its head came up, and it watched her with white-ringed eyes. She admired it from a distance for a few minutes, pleased at the sleek mottled coat and large shining eyes. She shook her head, for the seal seem to change, elongate and grow legs and arms. It stood upright and walked towards her. The song died in her throat.

He had the same grizzled hair as the seal; a thick, sleek beard covered his face and continued down his chest. His loins were covered with a sealskin garment, but hairy legs protruded from that. His eyes were large, dark and seal-like and his teeth small and pointy when he smiled. He stopped a few feet from her and regarded her with his head cocked to one side.

"Lera?" he asked.

"My name is Illera, if that is what you are asking."

His nose went up into the air, and he sniffed. "You are human," he stated.

"Yes."

"And yet not."

"Who are you?" Illera took a step back, frightened as she had never been of animals.

His smile was daunting. "I am the guardian selkie. Why are you in Faerie Bay? This is no place for humans."

"I've come to find my mother," declared Illera.

The selkie nodded his head. "The daughter whom Lera bore to the human who stole her heart."

She looked at the selkie, unsure what to answer.

"It was my understanding of the bargain that you were to remain human, not become part of the Sidhe."

"I...I don't know anything about a bargain. I've only come to find my mother."

"Why?" the creature demanded in a voice of iron.

"Well, you see, my father...uh...made a marriage alliance for me, without my agreement, to this...uh ...person who has a nasty reputation. And ...I...uh..."

"And you have this feeling of doom about it," the selkie finished for her.

"Yes, exactly," replied Illera wondering how the creature understood so perfectly.

"That is the elf in you, that sure certainty of the outcome of your course in life."

"Oh, then..."

"You are right, of course. The marriage alliance will be a

disaster. But, for all that, you must go through with it. You are half human, and as a human, there is no place for you among the Sidhe."

"No," cried Illera stamping her foot, "I'd rather be dead than have Torul as a husband."

The selkie gave her a sly smile. "I can do naught for you with regards to your mother. Only Sidhe can travel to our land, and you are half human."

"Has there never been a case where a human, or part human traveled to your land? I've heard the legends."

The selkie nodded his head. "It has happened, but as you know from your legends time moves differently in our dimension. Any who leave the here and now can only return decades or centuries in the future. All they know is dead and gone. It drives humans mad. That is why we do not permit such travel anymore."

"But I don't want to come back. I just want to go and stay there forever, to be with my mother and get to know her."

The selkie's eyes began to glitter. "You wish never to return to Madean?'

"Yes, I wish to leave here and never come back."

"I understood you resisted the marriage because you had no wish to leave Madean and yet now you flee from it?"

Confused, Illera shook her head. "Yes, I felt at first I couldn't leave Madean, but since Madean throwing me out, then I feel I have no choice but to leave."

"Even if it plunges Madean and Frain into centuries of war?"

Illera hesitated. "I can't marry Torul."

The selkie nodded his head as if he had made a decision. "Very well, remove your dress, the weight will pull you down too much."

Illera stripped off her cloak, jacket, skirt, and blouse and stood there in her camisole and bloomers, shivering a little with the wind blowing about them from the sea. The selkie nodded again, taking her arm began to pull her towards the ocean.

"But, but Mr. Selkie, I can't swim," she protested.

The selkie snorted. "I can't imagine a creature that cannot swim. But you don't need to in this instance, for I shall take you."

The hands hardened to claws, piercing her skin and it smiled at her with a hungry rapacity that terrified her. She pulled back, digging her heels into the sand and struggling against the painful grip.

"Now little halfling, remember you wanted this, you wanted to disappear." It snarled at her.

"I wanted to go to my mother," Illera screamed pulling back towards the shore as it dragged her ever deeper into the water. She could feel its hunger, a burning desire to feed on her flesh. Horror swept over her.

"Can't always have what you want," it snapped back, becoming more bestial by the moment.

Illera screamed; a terrified shriek howling from her throat.

"Hang on!" She thought she heard the words drifting to her on the wind.

The selkie looked over her shoulder and snarled again. It tried to drag her faster, but she fought harder, flailing at it with her free hand and kicking it where she could. She leaned back towards the shore, dipping her shoulder into the chilly waters. A thrashing sounded behind her. The selkie let her go, and she tumbled under the waves, fighting to get her feet beneath her again. A great commotion was stirring up the sand and churning the waves into foam. As her lungs were about to burst, a large hand pulled her upright, and she found her footing.

Waist deep in the water Lark and Raven fought with the selkie. They were fully clothed in their armor, and Illera felt a thrill of fear that one or the other might slip under the waves and be pulled down by the weight. The selkie fought ferociously, brandishing a silver sword, but the men battled even more fiercely. Ashera caught Illera by the arms and pulled her back to the sand where she stood shivering and riveted to the action in the water. It seemed like hours that the men exchanged blows with the selkie. Finally, Lark turned a thrust and Raven plunged his sword into the beast, running it through to the other side. The seal man collapsed, and the warriors dragged him through the surf to the shore to deposit him at Illera's feet.

She knelt down, feeling the life running out of him. She rushed for her pile of clothes and snatched up the bag. Tearing it open, the grain spilled to the sand. She sifted through it until she found the fleshy leaves and slitting one open she dripped it into his deep piercing. She placed her hands over the wound and concentrated. The blood stopped, forming a gelatinous mass under her hands. She applied the remains of the healing moss and held it there with her hands, willing life and strength into the creature.

"What are you doing?" demanded Lark.

"I'm healing it."

"Are you demented, that thing tried to kill you?"

"It was only doing what it thought was right. It's a living creature, and it doesn't deserve to lose its life because of me."

The selkie opened its eyes. "I was taking you below the waters to kill and eat you," it told her candidly.

Illera looked square into its eyes, "I know."

"So why should you heal me?"

"As I already told another creature, why not? If I can do good, should I not?"

The selkie nodded. "I understand, but do you?" He lay back on the sparkling sand.

As she concentrated on the selkie's words, Illera saw with depressing clarity that despite the pain it might bring to her, that she must go to Frain, and if it must be that she marry Torul, then the lives of generations would be saved by her sacrifice.

She poured her strength and healing into the selkie, finally collapsing beside it in the sand. Ashera wrapped Illera's cloak around her and sat close sharing body heat. Lark and Raven had a fire of driftwood pieces going. Raven came over and put a cup of hot soup into her hands. The pieces of meat were still hard and the broth watery, but Illera thought she had never tasted anything quite so good. She drank it to the last drop.

As the day was declining, the selkie rose. The wound was only a memory on his hairy chest.

"Lady Illera, my name is Shwawnigon. As you know in the Sidhe, our names have power. You have my name and my loyalty."

It bowed low over her hand then strode to the sea. It waded out until the water reached its waist and turned back to her. A strange glow surrounded it.

"You will travel north and thereby save the kingdom, and by saving the kingdom, you will save yourself, and the Darkliete sent from beyond to illuminate this world. We will meet again, Illera, daughter of the Sidhe. I will tell Lera her child fares well."

The selkie dove into the water and vanished from their sight. A cold wind was rising, making Illera aware of the tears that tracked down her face and the damp underwear she was wearing, covered only by the soiled cloak.

"Why are you crying my Lady," Lark inquired softly. "He was your enemy and tried to kill you."

"But he made me know myself," was her whispered reply.

CHAPTER 4

$\mathcal{L}$ ark was a speck trudging back to them from the west and Raven a similar spot moving towards them from the east. Illera warmed her hands over the tiny flames as she watched them grow larger in tiny increments. Crouching beside the princess, Ashera placed the last stick of driftwood on the flames.

"I hope they found a way up and off this accursed beach." Ashera rubbed her hands briskly.

Illera looked past Raven to the sea where the setting sun blinded his eyes and dyed the waves crimson, violet, orange, and magenta. She noted the line of his shoulders and the way he held his head.

"I don't think Raven found any access to the grasslands."

The warrior woman grunted. "Maybe the other one was more successful."

Illera turned to watch Lark, her eyes straining to pick out his silhouette against the darkening cliff. She noted his normal jaunty stride was shorter and he appeared to lift his feet against the sand with more effort.

"I don't think Lark found anything either." She sighed.

"By the Thunderer, do we have to live here the rest of our miserable lives. Surely others have come to Faerie Bay and left again?"

Illera smiled up at the taller woman. "I'm sure they have. But I came not intending to leave, and I think you probably came down about as precipitously as I did."

Ashera chuckled. "Yes, that we did. We come over that headland with the sound of your screams in our ears; the horses nearly foundered. The two squires were down off their horses and over that cliff before I even clapped eyes on you being dragged into the water. T'was a rare sight indeed to see them tearing over the sand like that, and what could I do but follow without a thought as to how we were going to make it back up that cliff. And a good thing too, I was there to drag you out before you drown."

Illera put her hand on the other woman's arm. "Yes, Ashera, I never did thank you for pulling me out. I do appreciate your help, and I'm sure that the kingdom will someday owe its freedom to your assistance today. Thank you."

The giantess looked startled. "You are very welcome my Lady, but it is unnecessary to thank me. No one ever thanked me before for doing my job."

Illera smiled at her and turned back to the fire. The men were coming closer as the sky grew ever darker; the heavy cloud cover blanketing the light over the land. Raven broke into a slow jog, arriving with a slight puff.

"Cliffs, just those smooth concave cliffs all the way to the headland and the open sea where they get taller and sharper. There is no way we could climb out of here eastward."

Illera sighed. "I thought as much. This bay is like a bowl, a safe enclosed harbor for those from the other dimensions. It's almost like a trap some plants use to catch insects."

Raven looked at her with one eyebrow raised. "Well, I for one refuse to be the insect in the trap. We are going to get out of here."

He was still gazing at the surrounding rocks when his brother reached the fire.

Lark said, "There is nothing that way for miles on miles. I feel sure I could walk all the way around the bay, and the walls would be the same height and the same slickness the whole circumference. Anyone have any ideas?"

The group was silent, staring morosely at the dancing flames.

Rubbing his chin, Raven rose and pointed to the cliff. "I have an idea, but I don't know if it will work. We need to make a human ladder. I think the cliff is about four man heights, and we are fair sized men, so I think if we climb on each other's shoulders, one of us should be able to reach the top."

"That won't work." Lark thrust his hands in front of him as if pushing away a foe. "The cliff curves in and away from the beach. If we stood on each other's shoulders, we would still be twenty feet from the lip of the grasslands."

"No look," Raven explained, "If I lie down and brace my feet on some rocks and you stand on my shoulders, but you are against the curve of the rock, then Ashera does the same, Illera should be able to crawl up our bodies and reach the top of the cliff."

"Let's try it. Right now." Ashera leapt to her feet. "I don't want to spend the night on this spooky beach."

In the failing twilight, Raven carried out his plan, bracing his feet on a small boulder. Lark climbed over his back and braced his feet on his brother's broad shoulders. With his hands braced against the slick rock by his face, he called for Ashera. Raven groaned as her weight was added to his brother's. She shifted and moved until she felt secure against the portion of the rock she faced. Illera watched as Raven gritted his teeth and firmed his muscles to hold his position. At Ashera's call, she grasped Raven's sword belt and pulled herself over his body. She balanced a moment on his shoulders, grasped Lark's sword belt and pulled herself upward. Ashera had her feet placed, so there was no room for Illera's on Lark's wide shoulders. She stretched herself, caught her toes on the top of his head and pulled herself up with Ashera's sword belt. The woman's body was easier to clamber over, and in moments she was standing on Ashera's shoulders. Her fingers were still six inches from the lip of the cliff.

"I can't reach it," she called.

"Get higher," commanded Raven with a grunt of pain.

Feeling sorry for him, Illera wobbled up to Ashera's head. Her hands were over the edge now, but she could not summon enough strength to pull her body upwards. She bent her knees and gave a little hop, throwing her elbows over. Her maneuver unbalanced the ladder and the three below tumbled to the beach. Grunting with effort Illera wriggled her way onto the grass, the sharp blades slashing at her hands and face. Panting, she flopped on her back staring at the darkening sky. A pale shape blotted out the clouds, and a warm nose blew grassy breath into her face.

"Appolon," she laughed catching hold of the great head with both hands.

The stallion jerked upright and pulled her to her feet. She hugged the giant animal. A nudge at her back made her turn. Abbadon was dark against dark. She gave him a muscle-straining hug.

Moving around to the saddles, she searched through the saddlebags, feeling vaguely uneasy as she stirred around the clothes and personal belongings stored inside. There was no rope. She contemplated tying the reins together, but there would not be enough length to be of any use to her companions still trapped on the beach.

Illera spied a white blur in the distance. She moved towards it, realizing it was Ashera's horse. The animal was feeling stubborn tonight, moving off when Illera approached. They played tag for long minutes until, she resorted to her song and the gelding stood while she came up to him. The first thing she saw was the length of stout rope secured to the front of his saddle. She loosened it quickly and hurried back to the edge of the cliff. She tied one end to the cantle of Appolon's saddle and tossed the other over the edge.

"Catch the rope."

Soon a yell drifted to the top. She led Appolon forward, and within seconds Ashera was gasping at the top. She released the rope and Illera coaxed the stallion back to the edge. Another yell and Lark joined them. They repeated the performance and Raven was back with them, to whickers of joy from Abbadon.

Ashera gathered underbrush and grass twists and soon had a fire roaring on the cliff top. Picketing the horses in a hollow some distance away, they used the saddles for pillows; resting from their ordeal.

"How did you find me?" Illera watched the dancing pictures in the coals as her fingers twisted plaits of grass. "I thought I covered my trail pretty well."

Raven laughed. "We almost didn't. Your father had us searching through all these dusty passageways hidden in the castle walls for a day. He seemed certain that you would have hidden there."

"It was me, your Ladyship," cut in Ashera. "I didn't think you'd go back to a place you'd been tossed out of. So I went around and asked all the village people if they'd seen you. Found a crofter who was resting from cutting down a tree when he saw you dash over First bridge. I knew then you were heading south. So, I got the squires, and we followed you. Picked up your track where you left the forest, and then I met up with Kest and Ades. Good kids, knew 'em when I was in Southern Reach. Got real nice parents them two, and they confirmed it was you we were chasing."

Illera sighed. "I thought I was very clever."

Lark laughed. "And so you were. You had that forest back to Seven Spires so confused with tracks I don't think anyone could have followed you there. We just went straight back to the castle because we thought that's where you would head."

In the hollow Appolon and Abbadon snorted, one of them stamping his huge feet, making echoes through the turf.

"I think you were just naïve. You should have given the boys a false name, that would have confused us for awhile." Raven glanced at her from lowered eyes.

Abbadon neighed, a loud ringing sound.

"See, even my horse agrees with me," Raven told her laughing.

Appolon answered the other stallion's call with one of his own adding a lot of snorting. Illera bolted upright.

"The horses are restless; I'll go see what's wrong."

She retreated into the dark, looking back at the trio talking in low tones around the fire. Reaching Abbadon first, she stroked his heated side and spoke to quiet him. He nodded his head up and down then pushed his nose at her, snorting. Raven materialized out of the dark to join her and the horse.

"What's the matter, big boy?" He rubbed the dark nose.

Illera ducked under the horse's neck and next to Appolon. His eyes were wild, and he half reared, narrowly missing her feet when he returned to the turf. He turned his head and nudged her as Abbadon had done.

"Something has these horses very upset." Illera stroked the golden neck with a firm hand.

A loud ululating cry burst split the night. Before Illera could gather her senses, Raven was at her side and tossed her to Appolon's bare back, throwing her the reins. He swung up on his horse, and they raced for the campfire. Ashera and Lark were swinging their swords against a band of thirty or more swarthy men. The firelight danced on their barbaric garb flashing on gold rings in ears and noses and long gold chains dangling from their necks. Dark, baggy clothing obscured their outlines making it difficult to judge just where to strike. Yelling and laughing, they attacked. Raven swung his war-horse into the fray without hesitation. Illera watched him lean over and snatch his sword from its scabbard on the ground. Whooping he straightened up, urging Abbadon on. The horse fought as fiercely as the rider, kicking back with both back feet and disabling his opponents. His front feet smashed with deadly results, crashing into the pirates and cleaving them into pieces. When his legs were impeded, he shoved them down and trampled them under churning hooves.

Raven fought like a demon, swinging his sword overhead so fast it was a blur. Lark and Ashera fought back to back; a growing pile of bodies circling them as testimony to their prowess with the sword. Illera knew Appolon was as trained as Abbadon, so she let him move into the conflict. More and more raiders came out of the darkness to swell the ranks of the attackers. Appolon moved forward, Illera guiding him to the area with the fewest pirates. He struck and one of the men vanished beneath his mighty hooves. She urged him forward with her knees, and he entered the fighting with flailing feet. She simply hung on and let him respond to his training.

"Illera, get out, get away," screamed Raven his face a mask of fury.

Her concentration slipped just as the huge stallion lashed out with both hind feet. Illera slid from his back to her backside on the bloody ground. She jumped up and tried to regain his back, but he moved away from her; fighting his way to Lark's side. A man grabbed her from behind. She twisted in his hands, staring up into a dirty grinning face.

"How nice of you to invite us to your little party." A spray of spittle bathed her face. "That bonfire was a lovely touch to call us in."

Abbadon appeared out of the night. He drove his teeth into the man's shoulder and lifted him high into the air. His mighty head tossed and the pirate sailed through the air. A sharp swang sound and the man's head left his body; Raven's sword flashed red in the firelight. He kneed the horse closer to her, reached down and swung her up behind him. She fastened her arms around his waist in a frantic grip, and her legs clamped to the horse.

Raven battled his way to Lark and Ashera. Appolon was almost there, fighting as well as three men. A fresh wave of pirates rushed upon them, cutting off Raven. Illera could hear him cursing under his breath. She closed her eyes, shutting out the sights and sounds of the slaughter.

She heard a voice, below the threshold of normal hearing, a voice like gravel rolling down an incline, but singing. It reminded her of the wind in the trees rising until it resembled a howling blizzard in the winter. Then it faded away.

She opened her eyes and looked around trying to locate the singer, but only the sounds of battle roared in her ears. The fighting reached a fever pitch. Raven was pushed further and further from his brother and Ashera. Appolon went down, pulled and pushed by more bodies than he could resist. A pirate leapt to Abbadon's back, slashing down Raven's right arm with a knife. Without thinking, Illera whipped Raven's belt knife from the scabbard and stabbed the man. He slid from the black's back with a whimpering cry. Abbadon thrust backward and the pirate vanished into the night. Raven's blood poured over them and the horse as he switched the sword to his other hand. Illera tried to hold on to the wound, but he was moving too much, spraying his life's fluid all over the muddy battlefield.

The wind was picking up, driving before it a wall of fog. Thin and wispy at first the fog thickened to the point that Illera could no longer see Abbadon's ears just an arm's length away.

"Lark?" called Raven, hearing only the sounds of confusion and the clang of sword on sword.

With a fierce squawk, a magpie dove upon them. Raven raised his left hand to bat it away. Illera dug her fingers into him.

""Don't," she cried in his ear, "that's Maggie. She'll show us the way out of here."

"Not without my brother." Raven ground his teeth.

"Maggie." The bird alighted on Raven's head her head cocked towards Illera. "Find Lark and Ashera. Take us to Lark and Ashera."

With a squawk, she fluttered ahead, flapping madly to allow the horse to keep up. As they moved through the fog, Lark materialized off Abbadon's right shoulder.

Raven leaned down. "Lark, are you all right?"

Lark laughed at him. "Of course, why wouldn't I be with just a little scuffle like this?"

They heard Maggie's gurgle as she reappeared out of the mist, tugging Appolon by his forelock. Lark saluted her and leapt to his mount's back. A few steps further they found Ashera, driving a sword through a pirate who lay spread-eagled on the ground. She seized Lark's hand and swung up behind him. Maggie next took them to the untidy scatter of their belongings. They grabbed their saddles, saddlebags and most of their armor. Maggie chattered at a frantic pace, and they followed her to Ashera's white stallion still tied securely in the dip. The warrior woman slid from Appolon, saddled the white and mounted. They followed the magpie once more.

Illera clamped both hands over the deep slice in Raven's arm, concentrating on getting the bleeding to stop. It lessened by degrees and ceased as they traveled through a gray world with no sense of where they were. An hour passed before the veil thinned, and thinned again becoming wispy tendrils. Silvery trees surrounded them, a gentle, open forest of beech, ash, and birch. Maggie lit on Raven's head again. She gurgled an incomprehensible message to Illera and looked longingly to the north and Seven Spires.

"Go Maggie. Go back to your family and my thanks for this night's work."

With a final burble, the magpie launched herself and arrowed home. Lark led them to a towering rock, thrusting to the stars from the sandy loam of the forest floor. Wearily they dismounted, keeping the horses close and making a semi-circle with their gear on the landward side of the rock.

"Can someone make a small, very small fire? I just need enough to boil a kettle of water for tea," asked Illera.

Lark groaned. "Surely you can't insist on a cup of tea now. We are too tired to gather wood and make you a cup of tea."

Illera pointed to Raven, slumped on the ground. "It's not for me. It's to make medicine for Raven."

Lark looked at his brother and moved to his side. Looking up he said, "My apologies Lady. I am tired from this day's work and have wronged you in my thoughts and speech."

Illera smiled at him. "Forget it, Lark. There is no need. We are all tired, but Raven needs attention. I'm going to gather some supplies."

Ashera trailed Illera as she picked the needed medicine from the forest. They returned, Illera, her skirt full to overflowing with moss, leaves and mushrooms and Ashera, her arms loaded with wood. Lark shaved the wood into kindling and started a small fire while Ashera took the kettle and went to search for water. Illera examined Raven's arm in the flickering light.

The cut started in the middle of the bicep and traveled in a straight line to the wrist becoming shallower. It was deepest at the elbow, and Illera was alarmed to notice the tendon had been sliced and was just hanging together. She blew out her breath and shook Raven's opposite shoulder.

"Raven?" She shook him again. "Raven, I have a problem."

Blearily he opened his eyes. "What can I do for you, my Lady?"

"When the pirate cut your arm he almost severed the tendon. I can try to fix it, maybe, but it is going to hurt, a lot. But, if I don't try, you could lose the use of your arm altogether. What do you want me to do? I warn you, I've only worked on animals, never humans."

Raven sat up in alarm.

"Don't move," Illera told him. "The more you move around, the greater the likelihood of the tendon parting and if it does that there is nothing I can do to fix it."

"My Lady, please, if you can do anything, do it. I don't care how much it hurts, if I lose the use of my arm, I stand no chance of ever becoming a knight, and I must become a knight."

Illera could hear the panic starting in his voice. "It's going to be okay, just don't move until I can repair it."

Raven froze into immobility as Illera rose and approached Lark.

"Raven's arm is bad, and if I'm going to fix it, I need a sewing needle and fiber. Do either you or Raven have such an item?"

Lark shook his head. "Neither of us carry woman's tools."

Ashera loomed out of the dark with the pot of water. "Neither do I, but I do carry an awl to mend harness and such."

Taking the water Illera divided it into two portions, adding leaves to one and mushrooms to the other, and setting them beside the fire to boil.

"Watch the medicine Lark. Let the leaves boil until the water turns dark. Take the mushrooms off as soon as the water boils and bring it to Raven to drink."

She went with Ashera to her saddlebags and received the awl. It was very sharp, but too large for her purpose. She returned to the fire and thought. Seeing the slivers from the kindling, she picked one up. Borrowing Ashera's knife, she made it smaller, with a tiny hole in one end. Then she put it in the tea of leaves boiling on the fire. She went to Abbadon and plucked a hair from his mane and tossed that in the pot as well.

Ready, she approached Raven. "Can you and Ashera come here and hold Raven down? It's crucial that he not move at all."

The others complied, Lark holding him tight across his chest and other arm as Ashera steadied the injured arm and wrist. Illera threaded the sliver with the horsehair and bent to her work. She firmly fastened the two ends of the tendon together, heaving a sigh of relief when the last knot was tied. She wiped the sweat from her forehead and smiled at the others.

"It's okay; I got it." A grin split her weary face.

They released Raven, and he sat up looking ill.

"I'm sorry I had to hurt you," she placed a shaking hand on his shoulder, "But I mended the tendon and once your arm heals it will be fine."

Raven smiled at her. "It didn't hurt my Lady. You have a fine touch."

Illera laughed. "I know it hurt; I felt you flinching."

Raven grinned, "Not as much as losing my arm would have."

Illera poured the cooled leaf tea into the wound and packed it with moss. She gave Raven a drink of the mushroom tea, and he was soon asleep. Moving to Ashera, she treated her small cuts and slices. Lark had only a small gash on the back of his hand, but Illera packed it in moss. They joined Raven in slumber.

Abbadon was cut around the legs, and she needed a long time to wash and pack his wounds, but Appolon was roughly hacked on his legs, flank, and belly. It took her several hours to clean and bandage his wounds. The sky was beginning to pale by the time Illera finished.

Stirring up the fire, she put some fresh wood on the coals. Following Ashera's path from the night before, kettle in hand, she found a rill of water where she washed the kettle and refilled it, returning to the campsite. She put the water on to boil and checked her patients. Raven woke as she moved the moss to check the wound. He looked at the thin pink line that remained and flexed his hand.

"My Lady," he began, "Illera," She looked at him, noting the dancing blue motes deep within his eyes. "Princess, I don't know how to thank you."

"Forget it, Raven; you were hurt defending me."

"No, that was my job, and knights get hurt all the time doing their job. But, nobody I have ever heard of has been given a second chance as I have. I don't have the words to tell you, my Lady."

Illera put a finger to his lips to stop him. She shook her head.

He moved her finger aside and held her hand, "Lady, I pledge you my sword. Next to my liege, the king, you have my service and my loyalty. And I swear, by the mother that bore me that I will protect your life and happiness should it cost my own in return."

As thunder rumbled from the sea, vibrating the land with its power Illera pulled her hand from his and stood. She smiled down at him, embarrassed.

"Thank you, Raven. I seem to be collecting loyalty these days." She moved to the fire. "The tea should be hot, come and have breakfast with me."

"Gladly my Lady," he replied, springing to his feet.

The others joined them, chewing on tough jerked meat washed down with the delicate mint tea Illera had made. They stomped out the fire, packed their gear and mounted the horses.

"The Lady rides with me." Ashera thrust out her chest.

Illera looked at Abbadon and Appolon but approached the ill-tempered white gelding. Ashera reached down a hand, but Lark lifted her to ride pillion behind the warrior woman. They headed away from the rising sun, determined to put miles between themselves and the pirate-filled sea. Lulled by the rhythm of the horse, Illera soon nodded off, her head against Ashera's broad back.

She woke with a thump and a whoosh as the air escaped from her lungs. She lay gasping, staring at the bright blue of the sky overhead. Two heads obscured her vision.

"My Lady, are you all right?" they chorused.

Unable to reply, Illera twisted on the hard ground as she

struggled for breath. A welcoming draught blessed her lungs, and she panted in soft grass. Lark lifted her to her feet, his face anxious. Ashera joined the group still mounted on her horse.

"He spooked at a rabbit and jumped. I felt you slide but couldn't do anything 'cause he tried to bolt." Ashera smacked the prancing beast roughly on the neck.

"Why do you ride such a creature?" Raven's voice dripped sarcasm. "The Lady could have broken her neck, then where would we all be? Probably have to be outlaws for the rest of our days with King Korul and King Ian both after our heads."

"Sorry my Lady, not all of us can afford fancy war-horses. Some of us take what we can get," snapped Ashera.

Illera waved a hand at her in dismissal. "My fault for falling asleep."

"But you wouldn't have fallen asleep if you hadn't been up all night tending our wounds." Raven glared at Ashera with a half snarl.

"Peace, peace," cried Lark. "We have enough enemies to fight without going at each other. However, I do think Illera would fare better on a well-trained animal. She can ride with me on Appolon. He's not likely to spook."

"Abbadon is smitten by her. I think she should ride with me." Raven thrust out his chin.

"A Lady should ride with a woman, not a man," Ashera insisted.

Lark opened his mouth to reply, but Illera cut him off. "I know Appolon is wounded, and so is Raven, so it would be better if I stayed with Ashera for now, until we are sure that both are completely recovered."

Ashera smiled in triumph as Lark and Raven glared at each other. Lark lifted her to the white's back, and they set off again. Many slow miles passed beneath the hooves before Illera fell asleep again.

Hands lifted her from the horse's back and her second awakening was better than the first. When she regained her feet, she looked around the town of Southern Reach. It was a dilapidated, sleepy town; the main street of packed sand lofted clouds of dust into the warm wind as the horses plodded behind a servant to the large stable. A double row of wooden houses lined the way, and through the gaps between the buildings, she could see more houses of the same sort. The short, local people, in brown or cream colored clothing, ambled about their business, often turning to stare at the strangers. They looked like the typical people of Madean, but their normally sturdy bodies were thin and their faces pinched and hollow.

The travelers stood in front of the only stone building, a two-story structure, towering over its single-level neighbors. A series of three shallow stone stairs led to the double, wooden plank doors decorated with heavy wrought iron latches and hinges. Leading the way to the doors, Ashera banged on the surface. A hollow echo reverberated. She knocked again.

Illera jumped when the doors swung open, and Raven caught her before she could tumble down the steps. A white-haired couple dressed in creamy, pale robes bowed low over their hands. When he raised his head, Illera noticed the old man had piercing green eyes that bore through her, giving her the feeling he was reading her innermost thoughts.

"Welcome Lady Illera, our princess. We are so happy that you have been found. How may the humble town of Southern Reach serve you?"

Baffled, Illera turned to Lark. He replied, "We need only lodging, food and a good bath would be most welcome Headmaster Dela."

"Certainly, squire. Please enter. I will send and make sure your horses are properly cared for. The chestnut mare is most well. There are some who will be sorry to see her leave."

The old couple warmly welcomed Ashera, inquiring about every detail of her adventures as they followed Dela into the town hall. He led them to a back room where the community kitchen was busy, and Illera detected the savory odors of roast and bread. The others sniffed the appetizing scents.

The headwoman told them to be seated at a long trestle table, and soon a trencher was set before each one of them. Filled with sliced meat, potatoes, vegetables and three large slices of bread, the long tray was dripping with gravy.

"We are so grateful to your father for the provisions he sent," the woman told Illera. "Without them, we would be unable to feed ourselves, let alone you. And your squires, why they saved our barley harvest from the Shul."

"Please, tell me about it?" requested Illera.

The woman sat down across from her as she continued eating. "For the last few years, since I was a girl, the Shul have been coming into our land and raiding our ripe fields and granaries. They steal the best of our herds and flocks. And it has been getting worse. For years they left us enough to live on, if just to assure themselves a steady supply, but lately, with their new leader, they have been taking everything and burning the fields, barns, and farms whenever they can. It has been a long hungry time. But now your father has sent us supplies, and we are so grateful."

Illera swallowed around a large lump in her throat.

The woman continued, "This year, when the barley harvest came in, the Shul came as usual. But your father, bless his wisdom, had prepared signal fires for when the enemy came, and we lighted them. He was here so quickly, and he brought these fine squires with him. Of course, we had our own Ashera then, but it is hard for a single fighter to repel a horde of Shul. They drove the ogres away. Targ's clan actually fled rather than try to fight against the band your father led."

"I have been impressed with them too," Illera said softly, "Why just last night..."

A strong hand drove fingers into her thigh and stopped her. She glared up at Ashera.

"Tis bad luck to speak so, my Lady. I would respectfully ask you to refrain."

Illera nodded, and Ashera removed her claws. Illera rubbed her leg and nodded ruefully at the Headmistress.

"I'd best be busy anyhow." The woman rose and bustled off into the kitchen.

"Why did you do that?" Illera asked. "I was only going to tell her how well you fought."

Ashera shook her head bottom lip outthrust. "You have your ways and we fighters, ours. I do not insist you do your things our way, allow us to have our own traditions."

"Of course," Illera agreed, "But I don't see..."

"No, Princess, you do not see."

Illera closed her mouth not speaking a word, while they finished eating. A small girl came and timidly showed them to the bathing room. Illera was impressed that the small dusty town would boast such an amenity. There was a wide sunken pool where heated water lifted languorous fingers of steam into the air. The area around the bath, cobbled with large flat stones, had a series of benches circling the walls. The girl left them towels, washing cloths, and lavender scented soap. Ashera stripped and jumped into the pool while Illera was gazing around.

"Come on," she called.

"Do you mean together?" Illera's jaw was slack.

"Of course."

Illera turned her back and removed her clothes, holding her dress in front of her until she could slip into the water. Ashera laughed at her and splashed. The little girl came back and took their soiled clothing, leaving soft cotton robes for them to put on. Illera washed quickly and got out, dressing with her back to Ashera. When they finished, they moved to a cozy room with a large bed. Illera crawled under the covers and was soon asleep.

After a hearty breakfast the next morning, they packed their things and saddled the horses. Illera was pleased to meet Copper again, although Abbadon refused to let either of them alone, lipping Illera's clothing and nipping at the mare. Lark took the lead as they left Southern Reach, leading them parallel to the mountains. Illera remembered her flight through here and vaguely wished she could be alone to travel the length and width of Madean. When the day waned, they found a sheltered copse of trees with a stream nearby and bedded down for the night.

It was a bone-chilling scream, a shriek that went up and up in pitch and volume until Illera could feel it vibrating in the marrow of her bones that woke her shortly before midnight. The horses snorted and plunged trying to break free and fight the noise. Lark and Raven scrambled into armor as Ashera dragged Illera to the horses before she was even awake.

She threw her on Copper's bare back and yelled, "Run, get to your father. He'll see that you make it to Frain."

Heading Copper in the right direction and slapping her smartly on the rump, Ashera turned back to Lark and Raven. Illera could hear more screams, and then the clash of weapons before Copper's swift strides took her too far from the fray to hear. Copper was born and bred to run, and Illera wrapped her legs around the mare's barrel and urged her on, anxiety for her companions chewing at her nerves like wolves with a carcass. It became too much; she slowed the chestnut to a trot, then a walk. The mare stood still, blowing and huffing while Illera strained her ears for the sound of other hoof beats. She circled the mare, trying to pick up the sounds of battle. She heard a scuff, a small animal moving through the grass.

Copper reared up, and Illera grabbed at her mane to stay on her back, but horny, callused hands grabbed her and ripped her from the mare's back. Bundled into a stinking sack, she was slung over the back of her captor. It moved off, jiggling and bouncing

Illera on its broad back. She squirmed around until her head was upright, hearing the clomp of Copper's hooves behind her.

The horse scrambled several times as though she was slipping on rock and Illera was unmercifully jounced around before the creature that was carrying her dumped the bag on the ground. She fell out on her side.

"Lark! Raven!" She stretched her hands towards them as she spied them sitting bound and gagged against a wall of rock.

The brothers hung their heads. She could see the rise and fall of Lark's chest as he sighed and Raven shook his head. Ashera was nowhere to be seen. One of the Shul guarding the men walked over and kicked the two of them several times. Raven wriggled upright again while Lark lay where he had fallen. Illera tried to go to him, but her captor seized her wrists and lifted her into the air. The other Shul chortled with laughter. Angry, Illera attempted to kick the beast while swinging and engendered even more merriment. It tired of its sport and dropped her on the ground. When it turned its back, she crept over to the men, shoving Lark into a sitting position again.

She started to speak, but a quick shake of Raven's head told her to be silent, so she tucked her back against the rock and hunched between them, feeling very small and vulnerable.

The Shul brought their spears and prodded the captives to their feet. The path wound steeply upwards, sheer rock on one side and a murderous drop on the other. Without room for resistance should they have an opportunity to fight, they had no avenue of escape.

Climbing through the night, dawn's rays illuminated the tallest peaks as they came to a high pass. There was snow on the ground, and the terrain was icy. A sharp wind prowled the pass, freezing exposed skin with its breath. Illera slipped several times, twice going to her knees. The ogres laughed and prodded her with spears. She struggled to keep up. In front, she could see Lark's hands getting white and knew Raven's would be the same.

The next time she slipped, she tore the legs off her bloomers. Struggling ahead through the progressively deepening snow, she wrapped Lark's hands in the thick material. Dropping back, she did the same for Raven. He smiled at her with his eyes, which was reward enough. The guard roared at her and struck her with the butt of his spear, sending her tumbling through the snow perilously close to the edge. With loud cursing, another trudged through the snow and pulled her back to the trail. A grunt and a buffet smote her as he set her between the two men. Illera forced her legs back into the rhythm of the march.

The trail peaked and tended downward; the snow shallower and the wind, although strong, lacking the fangs it had at the higher level. They marched on until dark and then kept moving through the blackness of the night. Second moon was three-quarters and first moon only a memory, so the stars were out, sharp, clear and indifferent.

As they traveled through the night, Illera was prodded more and more often. Even Lark and Raven were stumbling. The ogres finally called a halt at a deep cave. The humans were pushed to the back, and a roaring blaze was soon going at the front of the cave. Curious as to what they used for fuel, Illera crept to the front. The creatures were roasting game over the flames, and her mouth began to water. One of them noticed her and gestured for her to go to the back. Illera stood up her full height.

"I'm hungry, and so are my friends. We can't walk anymore unless you feed us." Her posture was tall and her face composed although she shivered with cold and fear.

The ogres began to laugh. They seemed to find everything she did hilarious, so she stomped closer and pointed to the rabbit in the middle of the flames. They laughed harder, but one removed the carcass and tossed it to her. She bowed and thanked them, moving to the rear of the cave to the sounds of laughter.

She removed the gags from the men, but when she tried to untie their hands, the guards moved in and stopped her. Tearing the rabbit in pieces, she held a piece in each hand in front of Lark and Raven and let them tear the meat off with their teeth.

"How did you get this food?" whispered Raven between bites.

"They seem to think I'm amusing. They laugh at everything I do, so I just asked."

Lark snorted, "Well I'm glad you're funny, although from what I've heard that's very unusual."

Illera shrugged. "Where's Ashera?"

"They took her somewhere first, when we were held there in those rocks waiting," Lark tried to wipe his greasy lips on his shoulder.

"Is she all right?"

Raven shrugged. "I don't know. Are we?"

Illera pondered for a long moment. "Yes."

"What?" hissed Lark. "What do you mean we are all right? We are captives of the Shul, in the mountains, freezing, starving, and half dead from walking and you say we are all right."

Illera looked at him, a deep wash of serenity flowing through her, "We will be. We will be fine."

"How do you know?" asked Raven.

Illera shrugged, staring at the cave floor. "I don't know, I feel."

He smiled, streaks of rabbit grease shining in the firelight. "Yes," he said slowly, "I think I feel it too. Search for it Lark, feel around in that heartless old chest of yours and see what you come up with."

"Nothing," he whispered back.

When the men had eaten their portions, Illera tore into hers. The grease ran down her fingers and stained the sleeves of her garment. When only the bones remained, she took them to the fire and threw them in. She could see the flames, but the fire was burning on nothing at all, a magic flame.

She returned to her corner and was soon fast asleep, her head pillowed on Raven's lap and her feet on Lark's. It seemed she had no more than laid her head down when the ogres were prodding them up again. She lurched to her feet with groans for her sore and aching muscles. For a few seconds, her ankles wobbled, and her feet would not hold her, but exerting her will and she made them take her weight.

Leaving the cave, they traveled upwards again and back into the snow. By noon, they were descending again, and that was the pattern repeated over and over until she lost track of the way they had come. When for a longer time they had been spiraling down, the path widened enough for two to walk safely abreast, but they stayed in their single file, while the Shul went in pairs. The land flattened, and Illera gazed at the blue and purple mountains enclosing a wide plateau. Shrubby gray-green vegetation became common, and she noticed unripe berries on most of the bushes. The soil was thin and stony, caught in hollows, folds, and dips. Many dwarf pines struggled to grow in some of the deeper crevasses. In the middle of the plateau was a village of low, round dwellings, composed of two-foot-high rock walls with animal hide rising from it to form a circular tent. They sported intense colors in with feathers and strips of bright cloth. A roaring bonfire in the center of the town burned on nothing at all, like the one in the cave and many Shul milled about the flames. To one side Illera could see a corral, with Abbadon, Appolon, Copper, Ashera's white gelding and three short, spotted ponies.

The prisoners marched to the village. The biggest hut sported wide banners of red and yellow and was decorated with red and yellow circles and bars painted around the circumference. Yellow feathers lined the doorway. The trio was pushed through the leather flap that served as a door and into the warmth of the building. A stone vessel filled with grease shed light, heat and stink into the space. On a throne, opposite to the door sat a gigantic Shul, wearing solid metal armor with plumes of yellow feathers at each massive shoulder. The ridges of his crest were tremendous, large and a vibrant orange instead of the common brown. Ashera stood to one side, well within reach of the ripping talons on his fingers, as a dozen other Shul shifted about the edges of the space. Illera and the two men were shoved before the throne.

"Is this the one you were telling me about?" The creature growled.

"Indeed, mighty Targ, this is she." Ashera bowed as she approached the throne.

"It doesn't look worth much. How much gold?"

"A lot of gold your mightiness, probably more gold than you have ever seen."

"But if I send a messenger, he will be killed before he ever reaches the lowlands."

"Send me, your highness. I will deliver the message and return here with the gold for you."

The creature laughed. "You want me to trust you to do my business? You will run away."

"No, your mightiness. On my honor, I will return."

The creature laughed louder, stopping suddenly. "Here is what we will do. I will send my messenger, and he will go with you. Should anyone attack him, you will die, and I will kill these immediately he returns to me. So guard my servant well."

The ogre gave commands to his people. The prisoners were taken to another building, this one with solid stonewalls, roofed with skins. They saw Ashera mounting her horse. At her back were two ogres riding the small ponies with spears at the small of her back.

They were pushed into the jail building, and the skin flap was tied down on the outside. This one was a quarter the size of Targ's home and the rock walls held the chill. The grease lamp was small, and the three huddled around it, trying to get warm. Illera picked at the knots holding the men's hands behind their back, managing to pick them apart just as the flap opened and a tiny ogre carrying a metal bucket stepped in.

It wore a long woven bark garment and a fur cloak that rose

over a huge hump on its back. The bucket contained scraps of meat, berries, and bark. It set the bucket in the middle of them and gestured for them to eat. Lark and Raven dug into the mess with numbed hands, but Illera stared at the female.

Squalling sounds issued from the hump. Keeping her eyes on the prisoners, she reached around and pulled a baby forward. It was round, pink and human looking but for the eyes. Illera stepped forward with her hands outstretched. The female jumped back, alarm on her face. Illera talked to her in her sing-song voice, and the creature cocked her head. Illera moved forward, and the ogress showed her the baby.

"He sick," the ogress told her.

"What's the matter?" Illera made cooing sounds over the child.

"A lung cough," the mother stuttered.

Illera told her, "Let me help."

"How you help Targ child?"

Illera smiled at her and took the baby from her arms. "On my horse, the...the...mare, reddish colored," at the mother's nod she continued. "There is a bag full of plants. Bring it here to me with some boiling water, and I can help your son."

The female nodded, looking at Illera and her son. Then she went to the flap and scratched at it. It opened, and she left, leaving her baby in Illera's arms. She sat next to the flames to keep the child warm. The ogress soon returned with Illera's herbs and a pot of boiling water.

Illera gave the child to its mother and placed the blue mushrooms in the pot of water. When it cooled, she took the infant from his mother and dripped the decoction into his mouth, rocking and singing to him. Lark and Raven fell asleep on one side of the room, and the mother sat on her heels; her eyes never leaving Illera's face.

Hours later, the child coughed, then coughed again. He gave a deep sigh and fell into a restful sleep. Illera placed him in his mother's arms.

"He will be fine now. All better."

The ogress peered at her with lowered brows. "All better? No sick?"

Illera nodded. "No sick."

With a fearsome display of fangs, the mother smiled. She packed the baby onto her back and scratched until the guard opened the tent flap. With one last look, she vanished into the night. Illera stretched and curled herself around the lamp. Sleep was waiting.

Babble outside the flap in the morning woke the prisoners. The ogress was back, bringing boiled grain and eggs; fare much improved over the night before. Before they finished eating, males and females were pushing into the little building asking for Illera's help. She mended broken limbs, infections, and wounds from weapons until her supplies ran out. As the last patients shuffled out of the door, a voice like gravel made her turn.

"I thought it could only be you. I know no other who heals the enemy."

Illera smiled up at the ugly visage of Frak Windsinger.

"And how are you?" she inquired.

"My health is excellent and has been since you healed my death blow. My mind, however, is sick with musing and speculation."

Lark slid between them. "Who is this Illera?"

She moved him gently aside. "Just a friend."

The ogre laughed. "I move from patient to friend. You are remarkable for a human."

Illera smiled at him. "I have a wide circle of friends, most of them not human."

"Ah, then, I suppose I fit," Frak replied. "I must go, I just needed to be sure it was you. Targ is going to ransom you for a pile of gold. Just be patient, you will not be killed, just the two men. Once the messenger returns with the ransom, you will be escorted to your father."

"No, Frak, you cannot kill my companions?"

"Why not? They are the enemy."

"They are my friends. As I told you, I don't have many human friends, probably just these. Isn't there some way you could talk to Targ, so they are set free?"

Frak laughed, then stopped seeing her anxious face.

"Ah, I perceive you were not joking. I will try to do what I can, but I am only a Windsinger, not a leader. I doubt he will listen to me."

Illera placed both her hands on the massive forearm. "But you will try, won't you?"

Frak nodded and left the tent.

Raven and Lark looked at her as if she had taken leave of her senses.

"You're asking a favor of a Shul." Raven shook his head disgust written large across his features.

"We kill Shul; we don't bargain with them." Lark straightened and made stabbing motions with his arm.

Illera looked at them, wondering why they hated their captors so much. "They are people too, Lark, Raven. They just want to survive and raise their children and be happy. Why do you think they are so evil?"

"Well, because, well....they are, that's all," stammered Lark.

"They kill us all the time." Raven nodded his head.

"But I wonder who started the killing?" Illera asked them. "Those answers are so far back in history we will never have them. When all the races came here first, we all got along, but now, war with everyone all the time. Someone has to stop."

The men looked at her astonished. She held their eyes. Long moments passed until Raven smiled and placed a hand on her shoulder.

He said, "I'll think about it."

Illera laughed. "That's just about what Frak said when I spoke to him."

Raven and Lark looked at each other and retreated to their side of the lamp.

That night's supper was of far better quality, though served in the same container. The ogress left as soon as they finished eating and pausing at the entrance, one eyelid closed in a solemn wink and she was gone.

Illera looked at Lark and Raven and cocked her head to one side. Before sleep overtook them, Illera heard singing. Rising she went to the door flap. It was a voice of gravel, grating and rough, yet with the wild wind and weather in it, somehow familiar.

"See, humans sing and Shul sing. There's not that much difference."

Raven smiled, looking down, refusing to continue the argument. Lark looked ready to start over again when the door whisked aside and a small male entered.

"Come," he commanded.

Raven scrambled to his feet, following Illera and Lark out of the hut.

A thick fog surrounded them, making visibility nil. Illera held onto the boy in front and Lark held onto her and Raven to him. They stumbled across the village realizing when they passed the fire only by the warmth of the fog.

They moved to the coral, where Abbadon and Appolon greeted them with snorts of pleasure. Copper made for Illera and pushed Abbadon out of the way. The mounts were saddled, and their belongings were strapped behind the saddles.

"Has my ransom been paid already?" asked Illera surprised.

The boy lifted one coarse finger to his lips and gestured for them to mount and follow. They stayed tight together, fearful of losing each other in the mist. Traveling slowly, even the sounds of horse's feet were muffled by the dense moisture surrounding them; they ascended into the hills. Gradually, the land rose curving to meet surrounding mountains. The boy halted. The fog was lighter up here, but still thick enough to obscure all but ten feet in any direction.

The boy pointed ahead. "Go this trail, stay this trail. Long, long, keep go. Come Swift River; you know way." Bobbing his head, he vanished back into the fog.

"Thank you Frak Windsinger," called Illera gently into the mist. She thought she heard a low chuckle.

"You think that old ogre did this?" whispered Lark to her as she started down the trail.

"Yes."

"I can't believe that he could call the fog," argued Lark.

"Why not? Ogres didn't believe that I could heal them, but they do now."

Nonplussed, Lark had nothing to say. Abbadon surged into the lead, eager to be away from the ogres. Illera hurried after him, afraid of separation in this weather. The trail was sufficiently wide for a single horse and rider, but there was no passing room. It wound downwards in a series of sharp switchbacks and Illera watched to make sure she missed no turning to sail off into the fog-filled void. The horses inched downward with stiffened forelegs. The path leveled out, and the incline was reduced as the mist grew lighter, feathering away into the darkness of a moonless night. They picked up the pace a little, moving at a normal walk.

It seemed an endless journey, moving in blackness and hearing small, dislodged rocks tumbled down to unseen depths with a fading rattle. On and on they traveled. Illera's eyes grew weary of trying to focus on the midnight dark horse against the blackened sky and landscape. Only the occasional flash of starlight on Raven's chainmail and the hollow clomp of Abbadon's hoofs reassured her that he was still ahead.

Despite the chill of the air, Copper was sweating. When they reached a wider spot on the trail, a cove surrounded on three sides by sheer gray rock, Illera stopped the mare.

"I think we need to rest the horses," she called to Raven, keeping her voice low.

Abbadon backed up to the wide spot. Raven nodded and dismounted. Lark rode up next to them.

"We should keep moving. What if the Shul are following us?" Lark leaned over from his tall saddle.

Raven dismounted. "Then we stand a better chance of escaping them if the horses are rested. Those switchbacks were steep, and it took a lot out of them. I think an hour's rest will do us all good."

Illera slid down from her horse, found the brush in the saddlebags and scraped the mare off. She pulled her as close to the rock at the back as she could get and huddled between the mare's legs wrapping her cloak tightly against herself. The wind seemed alive, prying into every nook and fold, working its way inside to chill the flesh. In too short a time, Raven told her to mount again. Illera stood, but was unable to reach the sidesaddle stirrup on the tall mare. Lark lifted her to the animal's back, and she followed Raven back to the trail.

The horses were fresher now, walking eagerly. The trail was beginning to rise again, and soon they had climbed into the snow. As the sky lightened ahead of them, they crested the pass. Shuffling through belly-deep snow, they watched the sun peek through the jagged peaks ahead. The trail angled steeply downward again, plunging them back into night. They kept moving, chewing the tough jerked meat for their breakfast.

The trail inclined downward still and they trotted, able to make better time in the daylight. The sharp drop made Illera nervous, and when Copper's feet slipped, she threw herself to the cliffside of the animal. The mare caught her footing again, and they continued more slowly.

As they were rounding a sharp bend and the incline

narrowed to the point where a rider could just barely stay on the horse with one foot squeezed against the mountainside and the other hanging over open air, Illera heard cursing ahead of them. She turned to look at Lark who shrugged. Rounding the curve Abbadon stopped. Illera raised herself as tall as she could to peer around him.

Ashera's bad-tempered gelding blocked the way, his feet braced wide. Ashera, dismounted, was trying to tug him over a cleft in the trail, the matter of a single foot's width, but the war-horse would not budge. The ogre sat his small pinto patiently ahead of her. Ashera cursed again, bringing a snort of amusement from behind Illera. She slapped him on the shoulder, but he leaned back further and managed to take a step backward.

Raven kneed Abbadon forward. The white laid back his ears. Abbadon moved closer, crowding up against the gelding's tail. He tried to turn his head, but Ashera had a firm grip and was pulling him forward. He lashed out with one rear foot, unbalancing himself and Ashera hauled him ahead. One foreleg slipped into the crevasse and the other planted on the other side. He whinnied. Ashera yanked on the reins, and he pulled the foot from the rock and hobbled forward, the back legs joining the front one on the other side. Illera could see the blood running down the leg from the knee to the pastern.

Abbadon stepped delicately across the gap, followed by Copper and Appolon. They moved smartly until they reached a wider section of the trail. Raven dismounted and went to Ashera. Illera followed, joined by Lark.

"...betray us for money?" Raven was saying as Illera approached.

"I was trying to save your lives!" Ashera sneered, drawing herself to her full height.

The ogres watched them curiously. Illera kept one eye on them and one on the cliff edge while listening to Raven and Ashera argue.

"No, you found some way to get to Targ and thereby save your own skin."

"I thought she would be gone to her father. That's where I sent her," yelled Ashera pointing at Illera.

"You didn't even know she was captured when you went to make your bargain with the Shul?" Raven yelled back.

"No, but I was claiming to be her servant. I knew she would ransom me."

Raven turned his back and threw his hands into the air. "I've never seen a worse bodyguard. You should have gone with her, then, you could have fought off the Shul when they attacked her."

Ashera's face grew red. "Yes, I should have, but instead I stayed behind to save your miserable hides. Grateful aren't you?"

"Grateful? Grateful for what? That you led us into a trap?" Raven had his fist clenched now.

"If I hadn't asked for an audience with Targ, they would have killed you on sight never mind drag your sorry ass all the way to his den. Yeah, I saved your lives!"

"Raven," Lark grabbed his brother by the shoulder.

"You didn't protect Illera!"

"Who are you to be calling a princess by her first name? You forget who you are squire." Ashera's voice dripped with sarcasm. "You should be herding pigs or whatever it is your mother does. You don't deserve the rank of even a squire."

Raven lunged for Ashera, and she backed against the rock face drawing her sword. Lark grabbed Raven by both arms and Illera hurled herself between the two of them. Ashera and Raven were both panting with rage.

"Stop!" Illera commanded. "Ashera, did you do the best you knew how to do under the circumstances?"

"Yes!" Ashera snarled, staring at Raven past her blade.

"Then fine, but you owe Raven an apology for the slur on his mother." Turning to Raven, she said, "And you owe Ashera an apology for questioning her motives."

The combatants stared at each other. Raven shook his brother off and approached Ashera.

"I am sorry Ashera, I should not have questioned your motives, but should have ascertained the facts before I spoke. My sorrow that your honor was impugned." Raven's face was white and calm.

Ashera snarled and rammed her sword into its sheath and mounted her reluctant horse. She kicked him hard in the belly and trotted off down the trail, the ogres behind her.

Illera sighed and felt a hand on her shoulder.

"Ashera was right about one thing, my Lady," Raven told her, "I should not call you by your familiar name. My apologies, Lady."

Illera laughed. "Raven, and you too Lark, I give you both permission to use my given name. In fact, I request that you use it. My lady and princess and all those titles are suffocating."

She held up her arms so Raven could lift her to Copper's back as Lark trotted Appolon after Ashera.

When settled, Illera bent down from Copper's back and told Raven "Did you see the ogres when you were fighting? They watched with fascination and something I couldn't quite put my finger on, surprise maybe. Do you think ogres quarrel between themselves?"

She straightened and sent Copper after the pale tail of Appolon, hearing Raven right behind her. They caught up with Ashera and the ogres around a couple of the bends. Moving steadily along until the light began to fail, the ogres showed them to a round cave with enough room for horses and people. Over a small round hole in the floor, one beast struck his flint. It immediately burst into bright yellow flames. He shared what grain he had in his saddlebags between the animals and Raven made a stew of the jerked meat, boiling it until it was only the toughness of shoe leather. After eating, Illera rolled in her cloak and was asleep almost before her head touched the stone.

Lark shook her awake. "My Lady, I mean Illera, the ogres have run off. They knew we were the prisoners for ransom and knew we had escaped somehow. I think they will run back to their people and tell them and we can expect pursuit. We must hurry back to human territories."

Illera moved stiffly to Copper's side and followed Raven from the cave to the trail. They moved downwards, trotting the horses on all except the steepest slopes.

The noise of the Swift River was audible long before they came to the bridge. It foamed down the side of the mountains in a series of rapids and small cascades, roaring, and spraying. The bridge, composed of knotted rope, barely wide enough for a horse to pass, over the wild river made Illera's stomach clench. A series of rough driftwood boards comprised the floor, uneven and tippy.

Raven dismounted and examined the rickety structure. "You have to lead your horse across. It is too difficult for him to balance, especially with a rider on his back."

He led Abbadon out onto the span, moving with confidence. The black clopped along behind him as if he were walking to his stall. Illera, gulped, releasing a breath she did not know she was holding when he safely reached the other side. Then she moved onto the span. It was wet, slippery from the spray leaping from the river. That same spray dampened the bottom of her riding skirt, making it swirl heavily around her legs. Copper picked up her nervousness and skittered uncertainly behind her, tugging on the reins at the wrong time, making her footing more insecure.

One of the boards was missing from the middle of the bridge. Illera looked down to the waters below, mesmerized by the power of the river. Raven yelled at her, so she moved, jumping over the opening, just as Copper threw up her head. The reins slipped from her fingers, and she felt a sharp impact on the side of her head. The largest fish she had ever seen breached and hit her. Instinctively, grabbing the slippery creature, she tottered on the edge of the board, flailing for the rope sides with one hand, but the fish fought and forced her over the side into the foaming waters. As she fell, she saw Raven halfway across the span, coming to help her and many more of the rainbow fish jumping over the bridge then the water took her.

It was cold, fearsomely cold. She was buffeted and twirled, tossed from one rock to the next. She would be forced down, down to where the water was still colder then hurled up into the air to gasp what breath she could before it sucked her down again. A rock impacted her shoulder. She tried to grab on to it, but it was slick with green slime, and her numb fingers slid off. Upright she sailed over a small cascade, throwing her arms high in the air, in case someone could see her. At the bottom, the current inhaled her, dragging her along the smooth rocks of the bottom. Illera held her breath until she was ready to burst. In a spray of foam, the water tossed her up again, lifting her body half out of the water. She panted, drawing in spray and water with the air. Down she went again, striking her knee against a curving rock and tearing a wide gash in her skirt. A series of cascades alternately forced her up and sucked her down, the last time, purling along the bottom, she couldn't hold her breath any longer, and felt the blackness creeping in. Finished with her, the river tossed her aside as it curved around in a wide oxbow.

Rough hands pounded on her back. Pain ripped her in two; she could not breathe. She coughed, coughed and gagged. The pounding continued, and someone was holding her and shaking her. She continued to cough, deep racking explosions, tearing her apart. Her stomach turned, and she vomited all over the legs in front of her face.

"Oh shit!"

She heard vaguely. She could not concentrate, hacking up her essence until at last her lungs cleared enough for a few deep draughts of air. Between coughing and vomiting, she started to shiver, her teeth chattering and body shaking wildly. She was dragged across the damp surface of the rocks and up into a cluster of shrubby bushes. The pounding stopped, and she was laid down on the mossy ground, shaking and coughing. She heard dry snapping sounds and a few snorts. A stained and disheveled Raven came into view; his arms were loaded with sticks. He piled them in front of her and started a tiny fire. Illera tried stretching out her hands to the heat, but the shaking of her body made it impossible.

"Take off your wet clothes," Raven told her.

Illera shook her head, feeling the movement was lost in the trembling of her body she whispered, "No," in a voice that cracked and made her cough again.

He brushed the hair back from her face. "Illera, you have to get out of those wet things. Otherwise, the chill will kill you. I can see your lips and hands are already blue."

"Can't," she croaked back, retaken in a fit of coughing.

Raven sighed. "Forgive me, Lady."

He stripped her soaking outer garments and boots from her body, tossing them in a muddy pile beside the reluctant fire. When she protested, he left her soaked undergarments on her. With Abbadon's saddle blanket, he rubbed her down until her skin was tingling and she smelled of horse. He took his spare shirt from the saddlebags and put it on her. It hung to her knees, but the warmth of the dry cloth was the most incredible luxury she had ever felt. Then he wrapped her in his cloak and placed her next to the fire.

"I have to get more wood. Stay right here," Raven commanded.

Illera nodded, not trusting her voice to say anything. Abbadon nudged her from behind, but she could not summon enough energy to stroke him. Then she felt a sudden warmth as the great war-horse lay down at her back. She snuggled into his cozy heat with her head pillowed on his belly. The shivering slowed and gradually stopped. Raven returned and built the fire higher. He spread her soaked and tattered garments on sticks beside the heat to dry.

Illera heard a loud "Hallo" from across the river. Lark and Ashera stood there, Copper trailing behind Ashera's war-horse. She could see them gesticulating and arguing. Finally, Lark turned Appolon plunged him into the water. The current swept them downstream. Ashera gave her a long look and continued riding down the river. Illera closed her eyes for a moment and opened them to see the dark blue gaze of Lark right in front of her nose. She started, eliciting a loud snort from Abbadon.

"My lady, are you all right?" Lark asked, his voice anxious.

She nodded. "I told you to call me Illera. That's what friends do."

Lark laughed. "Of course, Illera. Is anything broken?"

She shook her head. "Don't think so, just lots of bruises."

His hand was warm and comforting on her forehead. "Then sleep. When you wake, we'll take the time to see how you are. Everything's going to be all right now."

Illera closed her eyes, listening to the soft sound of the brother's voices.

"Yeah, there must have been two hundred of them, all hidden in the bushes and behind trees, just waiting."

"You think she was leading us into a trap?" Lark inquired.

Raven chuckled. "I was leading brother. I don't know what to think. They know their mountains better than we do, so possibly, that ogre sent with Ashera fetched them for the ambush. I just don't know."

"Well, I know that we have to get her out of here as soon as possible. Once a Shul gets an idea in its mind, it doesn't quit until it's got what it wants or it's dead."

"Yeah," Raven returned, "And they want gold for Illera. By all the gods Lark, when I saw her in the mud, I was sure she was dead."

Lark laughed. "Never seen so tough a princess."

Raven agreed. "She's not what you'd expect."

Double hoofbeats drummed as Ashera and Copper joined the party.

"See, I told you there had to be another bridge," the warrior woman said in triumph.

"Yes, Ashera, you were right. But Appolon got me here anyway."

The warrior woman snorted. "Stupid squires, haven't got the brains of a squirrel between you. Raven, you could have been killed racing your horse through the rough brush and rock like that."

"Could have been, wasn't Ashera."

"But..."

"Ashera, I don't want to fight with you," snapped Raven in a louder voice. "And there is still the matter of an apology you owe me."

"Shhhhh," commanded Lark, "The princess needs to rest."

The conversation died, and all she could hear were the cries of the night birds and the snapping of the campfire.

CHAPTER 5

*A*bbadon shifted, moving away from her. Illera flung one arm from under the covering and tried to hold him in place, but the giant war-horse eased away from her and scrambled to his feet. Her eyes felt too heavy to open, so she lay her head on the ground, still warm from the horse's body, and drifted between sleep and waking. Sounds rustled around her: voices too low to hear without concentrating, the crackle of the fire, water being poured from one container to another, the clink of equipment being packed, leather straps being tightened, the snort and stamp of the horses, the tramp of feet, birds chorusing in the background.

A warm hand brushed the hair back from her face, and a soft voice called, "Illera, Illera."

She tried to open her eyes. The bottom one obliged, but the top eyelid merely pained without moving or giving her sight. Tiny rocks and bits of leaf were all she could see without moving, so she twitched her head to one side. Lark bent over her. He slipped an arm behind her shoulders and helped her to sit up. She heard a loud groan but could not place its origin.

"Yes," he crooned, "I know it hurts, but it's not safe here. The

Shul could find us at any moment. We have to be moving, now."

Trying to move her stiff and unyielding limbs was beyond her ability.

"Can't move," she whispered in a voice she did not recognize.

Raven hunkered down in front of her; his face shadowed in the misty light of early dawn.

"Hey, princess, I need my shirt." His grin was infectious, and she tried to respond.

Illera looked down; noticing the only thing she had on beneath the cloaks that covered her was a man's shirt and her underwear. She could feel her cheeks growing warm. Leaning away from Lark's support, she struggled to bear her own weight. Shaking she rose, wincing at the pain in her muscles and bones. Her hip was the worst, aching with horrible intensity. Lark and Raven hovered beside her, ready to catch her. Tottering the few steps to the fire, she took her ripped and frayed skirt from the stick holding it over the heat. She slipped it over her feet and pulled it up to fasten, but when she touched her hip, she collapsed in a heap on the ground. She looked at the injury. A large chunk of flesh had been scraped from the hipbone down her leg. The injury was a hot red with purple and blue blotches surrounding it. Lark bent closer to look.

"My lady, that doesn't look good. Can't you put some of your healing plants on it?"

Illera tried to smile, but it hurt too much. "Yes, Lark I could, if I had any. I used all my supplies on the Shul."

"Could we pick some for you?" Raven sounded anxious.

Illera gazed around at the scrubby forest and shook her head.

"I need a birch forest. That's where the moss grows, but sometimes I can find other things in a pine or spruce woods. There's nothing here though that I can use."

"Here now, you two shouldn't be bothering the princess when she needs to get dressed," called Ashera. "Go away and afford the Lady some dignity."

Raven snorted. "We were concerned that she might fall. The river gave her a sound beating yesterday."

"If care needs to be given, I'm the one to do it," Ashera made shooing motions with her hands.

The brothers moved away to attend to the horses and Ashera seized Illera's blouse from the stick, tearing another long run in the fabric. Sighing Illera shrugged out of Raven's shirt, the chill of the mountains and early morning seeping into her aching bones. She hurried as fast as her reluctant body allowed, buttoning up her blouse and jacket and throwing the cloak around her shoulders. Ashera smiled a triumphant grin at her.

"See, my Lady, it's not so bad once you get moving."

Illera nodded her head and hobbled to Copper. The mare dropped her head and rubbed her face on Illera, knocking her down. Lark was there in an instant, lifting her to her feet.

"My Lady, can you ride?"

"I have to, don't I Lark? And aren't you supposed to use my name?"

Lark grinned, lifting her to Copper's back. The bruised hip made her hiss with pain. Doubled over, she caught the reins and urged the chestnut forward. Illera bit her lip to keep from crying out at every step the mare took. Raven seized the horse by the bridle.

"No, Illera, you ride with me on Abbadon."

Illera smiled, an anemic thing. "I hardly think Abbadon's stride is any better than Copper's."

Raven lifted her down, tossing the reins to Ashera.

"Maybe not, but my arms can cushion you a little, and you won't have to hang on."

Raven mounted the black and Lark passed Illera up like a parcel. Raven cradled her in front of him and moved off, Abbadon moving slowly, with great care. Lark and Ashera followed. Illera soon relaxed against the motion of the horse, her sore hip outside away from any pressure. She watched the scenery glide by, alert for any trees that might shelter useful medicine. As Raven's arms grew weary, Illera rode with Lark and then Raven again.

They traveled down the southern bank of the Swift River at a gentle walk until they came to the main road to the north. A mean village perched on the bank of the river, a matter of a few straw huts on either side of the dusty road. A scattering of scabrous children watched from the doors of the buildings until fearful parents hustled them inside.

The bridge was wide and secure, resting on stone pillars embedded on either bank and in the middle of the river. The horses crossed, and Illera had a flashback to the last time she tried to cross the Swift River. She squirmed in Raven's arms.

On the other side, they decided to switch again. Lark lifted Illera down, and Raven dismounted to stretch. Illera peered into the distance, noticing a pale grove some miles from the road.

She pointed to the trees. "I need to go there."

Lark and Raven turned to look.

"It's too far from the road, My Lady," Ashera told her. "We need to get you to King Korul as quickly as possible before anything else goes wrong."

Illera smiled at her sweetly. "But if I am better and can ride then we will make much better time."

"And I say we keep on going. The gods know what could be hiding in that vale. It could be a horde of ogres or pirates. No, we have to keep to the main road. If we'd stuck with that, we wouldn't have had any of this trouble." Ashera stuck out her bottom lip.

Raven gave Ashera a smile that was half snarl. "If the Lady needs medicine then we have to go to that grove of trees. Being in pain is no joke and speed is not as important as getting there."

Before Ashera could reply, he mounted and turned Abbadon's head towards the trees. Lark and Illera mounted and quickly followed him. Ashera stubbornly reined her gelding to a standstill, fighting with Copper who tried to follow Illera. Arms crossed over her breast; she watched them gallop towards the woods.

Between the pale trunks of the trees, Lark lowered Illera to the ground. Moving stiffly, she examined the undergrowth, picking various leaves and placing them in her skirt. She shuffled back to the squires who had started a tiny fire and had a kettle of water boiling. Illera smiled as she made her various teas. Retreating behind a dense bush, she treated herself, packing the wound on her hip with moss and washing the various bruises and swellings. She packed her eye with the moss as well and dressing once more; she returned to the brothers. The fire was out, and Lark mounted, ready to continue. Illera handed some thick, furry leaves to him and Raven, keeping a handful for herself.

"Chew on these. They are a bit bitter, but they will invigorate you and give you energy," she instructed.

Riding back to the road, Illera began to feel better. In the same position when they returned, Ashera glared at them with anger in every line of her face. Illera mounted Copper and Ashera spurred her mount down the road. The others galloped to catch up. As the miles passed beneath them, Ashera gradually slowed the pace and rode abreast of Illera with the squires behind them. Wide golden plains on their right and rolling hills leading to sharp bluish mountains on their left hemmed them in and only the gently rolling dusty road led endlessly on, heading for the cold north. The days blurred together into a seamless haze as they moved over the land.

They stopped for the night at a traveler's hut, a small wooden building on the side of the road. King Ian had built many like it, a simple affair of boards and flat roof with four bunks, a table and half a dozen chairs in front of a small fireplace. The local people kept it stocked with firewood in a crib out back, in exchange for a reduction of their taxes. Raven rode to a village they could see nestled in the hills in the distance. Lark insisted Illera lay down on the hard, narrow bunk while he and Ashera made the fire and fetched water. She listened to the warrior woman's grumbling on the way to the well and the return.

"Ashera, stop it. Come right out and tell me, just what is your problem?" Lark stomped about the small cabin.

Ashera faced him, drawing herself up to her full height, just an inch or so below his. Her face was hard and unyielding.

"King Ian put me in charge of his daughter. I was to be her guardian and companion on her trip to Frain and here you two louts have taken over, boss me around like a serving wench and have turned the princess against me." Ashera slammed the pail onto the table sloshing half its contents onto the floor.

"What? Are you mad woman?" howled Lark, dropping his armload of wood on the floor.

Illera sat up, holding out a hand as if to prevent the escalation of the argument.

"My brother and I were sent to Seven Spires by the king of Frain to escort Illera back to his castle and his son. That is our job. We were sent specifically to be in charge of the princess until she could be delivered to King Korul. She's our responsibility."

"No," Ashera yelled back, "she's mine. Her father gave her into my charge!"

"And King Korul gave her into ours." Lark's voice rose in a bellow.

Illera tried to interrupt. "And I am in charge of myself. The three of you are my escorts."

Lark whirled on her. "With all respect my Lady, I think it is important to settle this issue of jurisdiction. Who is in charge?"

"Yes," Ashera agreed, "Who is in charge of your safety, the men sent from Frain, or the woman picked by your own father?"

Illera rose from the hard bed, crossing the floor to stand in front of the two.

Softly she said, "I am in charge. Not Lark nor Raven, and not

Ashera. Myself, I am in charge."

Ashera sneered. "Yeah, I know. You are in charge and go running away so as not to go to Frain and make all this trouble for us, your lowly servants."

Illera felt her hand move of its own accord as she slapped the woman across the face. Ashera flushed red with more than the force of the blow, her hands coiling into fists, stiffened at her sides.

"I am lenient with the people who work for me, but I think you forget yourself. I am the princess, and I will be Queen of both Madean and Frain. If you feel unable to display the proper respect my position deserves feel free to leave my service and return home." The frost in Illera's voice would chill a summer's day.

"My Lady?" Ashera turned pale.

"You are dismissed," Illera told her in a ringing voice.

Ashera stumbled out of the door, heading for the attached stable. Illera turned to Lark who was staring at her with his jaw hanging.

She snapped, "If you feel it necessary to question my authority you may leave and return to your King. You are also dismissed."

"My Lady," Lark went down on one knee and bowed his head, "I beg you not to dismiss me to my lord. That dishonor would kill my mother, a fine and kind woman, who desires nothing more in this life but to see her two sons succeed at court. I could never return knowing the shame my failure would bring upon her. I request mercy."

Illera's face softened, and she placed a hand on the top of his golden head.

"I'm sorry Lark. This constant bickering is fraying my nerves like an old donkey rope. Of course, you don't have to leave, unless you want to."

Lark leapt to his feet. "Never, my Lady. I have sworn three

ways to protect you. Now you should be resting, for one more good day should see us at Dragon's Lair in Frain where the pages and your luggage should be." He led her back to the bunk.

Illera nodded and lay down, listening to the distant thunder of Ashera's mount as they cantered away, wondering what she had just done.

Turning on her side to watch Lark build a fire, she said, "Please, call me Illera."

He turned and grinned. "I am sorry my Lady, when you behave as one of us, one forgets you are indeed a princess as you just proved. It is good to be reminded of one's station and to keep one's proper place."

Illera groaned. "If you go all formal on me, like Ashera always was, I will go all royal on you and dismiss you and Raven."

Lark laughed, going to the door when he heard the sound of horses galloping to them. Raven strode in, a burlap sack in one hand and the other dragging Ashera.

"Can someone tell me why one of our companions was traveling the wrong way?" he demanded.

Ashera wrenched her arm from his grasp. "Don't ever touch me again pig. I told you, the princess dismissed me."

Raven turned to Illera for confirmation. Illera nodded.

"I am tired of the fighting between the three of you, so I told Ashera I was in charge and she questioned my competence. I dismissed her."

Raven moved to the bunk and sat down. "Illera, I don't question your competence, but I do your knowledge. While you know your kingdom better than anyone I've ever known, you know nothing of Frain. I've always found that it is a good idea to surround oneself with competent people when entering the unknown. Lark and I know the country very well, but I've seen Ashera fight, and you can use all the protection you can get. You don't know what you are riding into at Korul's castle."

Slowly, Illera nodded. "You are right Raven. Ashera will you rejoin us?"

The warrior woman smiled a feral grin and Illera did not like the triumph in her eyes, but she bowed her head to Illera.

"As you wish my Lady." Ashera strode to the other bunk and stretched out.

"And I," Raven clapped his hands, "Have brought a haunch of mutton and bread for our supper."

They settled down to eat as the warmth of the fire crept through the cabin.

The road wound, twisting over the hills and diving into the vales. Small villages dotted the land and flocks of sheep scattered as the horses cantered through them. Illera felt her heart lift as the meadowlarks caroled in the clear blue sky. As the sun warmed the land, the scent of blossoms perfumed their journey. The road ahead split, one broad path curving to the right. A weather-beaten sign hung drunkenly from the shaft of a broken spear driven deep into the earth. The name Ocean Perch was carved sloppily on the shingle of weathered wood. Illera pulled Copper to a halt to look at it, staring for long moments while the horses snorted and blew. Appolon crowded in close.

"This is the road to the northernmost town in Madean." Lark touched her on the elbow.

"I know. I've never been out of Madean before. It doesn't feel right to know I'm leaving my...my place."

He turned his horse and continued at a swift walk. Raven followed.

"My Lady?" inquired Ashera.

"Yes, I'm coming," Illera said, as she headed Copper down the main road, tears threatening to spill from her eyes.

Once over the border, the character of the land began to change. The hills grew steeper and the meadows smaller. Shrubs and larger trees increased in number until they were traveling through a dark spruce and pine forest, where the boles towered above them, and the sun presented only in warm dapples of light sprinkled on the open duff of the forest floor.

"Is all of Frain so grim?" she asked the brothers riding ahead.

Raven reigned back to ride beside her, forcing Ashera to the rear. His grin was wide and warm.

"I thought maybe you wished to ride with your thoughts, but I'm glad you are curious about my land."

Illera sighed. "I think I must be if I am to be Queen of it. Don't you think I should know something about it?"

Raven laughed. "I wish most of the rulers felt as you do Lady."

"Illera," she corrected.

He smiled at her again, brushing a thick overhanging branch away. "We call this section the Black Forest and this whole area the Bloody Hills. There is a lot of warfare here between Frain and the Shul. These hills are rich with iron for weapons and farming implements. This forest supplies most of the wood for what building that goes on in Frain. Mostly foresters and a few miners live here with their families. King Korul has a number of hunting lodges scattered through the forest."

"What does he hunt?" Illera asked curious about the animal life.

"Well, the dire wolves of course. They are his favorite. Then there are elk, deer, lion, griffin, and dragons."

"King Korul hunts dragons?"

"Only when he has to. Like most people, he leaves them alone if they leave us alone, but I remember about five years ago, I was a child, newly come to the castle. We had this little dragon preying on one of the mining communities. It had killed more than half the population, so Korul led an expedition against it. Lark and I went along to care for the horses. It cost five good knights as well as the maiden used for bait, but now its head hangs in the great hall of Korul's castle."

Illera shuddered. "You used a maiden for bait?"

"How else would you get a dragon to a spot where you could ambush it?"

"I don't know. I've never had anything to do with dragons. They don't live in Madean."

"Don't worry. Lark and I are familiar with them, and we will protect you. Besides, it's very unusual for a dragon to attack humans without provocation. That small one that I was telling you about, I think, although they never said so, that the miners were working too close to its lair."

Illera nodded. "Yes, that makes sense. Animals always do things for a reason. It's just people who are so hard to figure out."

Raven laughed as Illera continued, "Where are we going?"

"We are going to a town called Dragon's Lair. It's the largest town in the forest, and the Earl of this province lives there, Lord Darnovam. He's...well he's not my favorite character. Anyway, there are a lot of foresters who live at Dragon's Lair. And the pages were instructed to wait there with the donkeys and your luggage. It will be safe, and we can all relax for a little while anyway. I'm looking forward to it."

Illera smiled ruefully looking down at her tattered and frayed garments. "I guess I need my luggage badly. It will be good to have something decent in which to make an impression on Korul. I could imagine his reaction if I showed up in these rags."

They laughed together as they continued through the dense woodland, Raven pointing out different plants and animals to her as they traveled. His pleasant conversation was an anodyne to the growing anxiety that plucked at her mind. The sun set, making the trail seem darker and ill-intentioned. Once they heard the howl of wolves in the distance.

At first moonrise, they approached a clearing. In the middle, Illera could just make out wooden palisade walls stretching like the wings of a predator to the stygian edges of the forest. Tall, wide wooden doors were closed. Lark stood well away, where they were clearly visible and yelled to the doors. Two metal helmeted heads appeared over the sharp points of the logs comprising the walls.

"Who goes?" came the challenge.

"Lark and Raven of the horse herd, squires of King Korul on a mission of escort to princess Illera of Madean, betrothed of Torul, and her companion."

The group heard the sound of weapons rattling, and a horse galloped away behind the walls. The travelers sat on their horses watching first moonrise through the trees, gilding everything with its golden light. They could see the light glinting off the helmet and weapons of the guard watching them from the palisade. A horse galloped to the gates.

"Halloo," the guard called down to them. "We'll open the man gate. Dismount and enter one at a time with your hands away from your bodies."

They slid from their horses and approached the small door opening in one of the larger gates. Lark went first, stooping to enter. Appolon ducked and scraped his saddle against the wood on either side. Raven followed and Illera after him. Ashera brought up the rear, and the small door slammed and was bolted behind them. Illera felt a sinking sensation in her stomach at the sound of the bolt rasping home.

Men at arms lined both sides of the entry, swords ready and hands on pikes. Lark and Raven stood still, holding their arms from their sides. A chieftain approached with a lantern and thrust it first into Lark's face and then into Raven's and Ashera's.

"This is the princess?" he asked with a sneer on his lips.

"No," Lark turned his head and indicating with his chin, Illera hidden in the shadows of the horses.

The chieftain swung the lantern in her direction, shining the light in her eyes. She could see his eyes gleaming in the light, travel down her body and back to her face.

"What manner of trickery is this," he snarled.

"There is no trickery," replied Lark.

"No? It is well known that King Ian's daughter is of such surpassing ugliness that Torul has taken ill in protest to wedding such a hag. This little beauty be no hag."

"Nevertheless, this is King Ian's daughter, princess of Madean," returned Lark evenly.

Illera could see Raven's hands clenching into fists. She smiled at the captain.

"Tis indeed a wonder that Torul knows my appearance when he had never seen me, nor did his envoy Sir Kyle. Or perhaps in Frain, the standards of beauty and ugliness are different from in Madean." Illera used her haughtiest tone.

"My pardon, princess," the chieftain replied. "I will conduct you to the Earl immediately."

He offered her a leg up, and Illera struggled into the awkward sidesaddle and followed him down the broad street. Her companions mounted and followed behind. The houses in the town were strange to her, being made of logs, low to the ground with tiny windows showing flickers of lamplight. Some buildings had carved wooden signs hanging in front, and from the sounds, Illera assumed they were establishments for drinking or less savory occupations. Dragon's Lair was surprisingly large, the palisades fading into the darkness and houses hugging the ground in every direction. Tall pines loomed over the houses making the town part of the forest that enclosed it.

In the center of the streets, Lord Darnovam's castle reared its hideous head. Obviously built by a madman, it lurched three to five stories into the moonlit sky, with an odd tower jutting here and a square, windowless block stuck on there. It seemed an amalgam of building styles; partly stone and partly wood, round cupolas supported by square beams protruding in an unfinished manner. The entire building swarmed with soldiers dressed in patchwork uniforms of leather, cloth, and bits of metal, but their weapons were sharpened and shiny, the hafts polished with use.

Ushered into the entryway, they trod down corridors lined with stuffed hunting trophies, dead animal eyes staring at them. Shields and weapons decorated the wooden walls. The great hall was similar. Antlers were used to hold swords and pikes, and the flat dead eyes of slaughtered animals were everywhere. A fire was roaring in the large open fireplace, the only stone structure Illera could see. On a carved chair, resembling a throne, sat a narrow man, splendidly dressed in plush red fabric inset with cloth of gold in the slashes. He was dark, sporting a small pointed beard on his triangular chin. Yellow-brown eyes and an extremely long nose reminded Illera of the foxes of her forest. The shrewdness behind the look cautioned her to tread carefully with this lord of Frain. She held her slender hand out to the man and waited for him to arise and come to her, noting the flicker of surprise on his face. His lips tightened into an imitation smile as he rose and grasped her hand, bowing over it and lifting it to his forehead.

"Welcome to Dragon's Lair princess," he told her in a voice both deep and sarcastic.

"My pleasure, Lord Darnovam and my apologies for my appearance. I'm afraid we have been sorely set upon by the Shul," she replied in her most haughty tones.

Lord Darnovam gestured, and a chair was brought for her and placed beside his at the fire.

"Your servants may go to the kitchen." He dismissed them.

"Your pardon," Illera interposed, "I have been through such an ordeal it would be a great favor if you would allow them to remain close by. I fear I may be overwrought and have an attack of the vapors should they be separated from me."

Darnovam gave her a small sour smile and instructed the serving girls to bring food and drink for the party.

"If it is your wish, my Lady, they may dine at the fireplace." He inclined his head a fraction.

"Thank you, kind sir. I shall be sure to mention your graciousness to King Korul when we meet."

Darnovam's eyes slid sideways, watching Lark, Raven, and Ashera sit on the hearthstones.

"Most unnecessary, I assure you," he murmured.

The serving girls brought a meager supper of bread and stew. However, the wine jugs were full, and they plied the brothers and Ashera with plenty of drink. Illera refused to touch the beverage, asking for tea instead. The food stuck in her throat as she tried to eat in a dainty manner befitting a princess under the gimlet eyes of Lord Darnovam.

"I trust the food was sufficient to your station Princess?" The earl looked pleased.

Illera smiled, aware of the verbal trap he was setting for her. "Of course, my Lord Darnovam, one can't expect one's accustomed victuals at an outpost so far from civilization, but adequate for the moment, yes quite adequate for the moment considering the circumstances."

From the corner of her eye, she could see Lark suppressing a grin, and Raven placed a hand over his mouth to stifle his laughter. The earl shot a black look at her.

"Now, my Lady, may we offer you some wine? Of course no doubt it will not be up to your exacting standards, but please, try our vintage."

Illera wrinkled her nose. "No thank you, I don't have much of a taste for wine."

"Then perhaps you will try some of our brewing. Dragon's Lair is renown for its way with the hops."

"Again, thank you Lord Darnovam, but beer upsets my stomach and makes me feel ill, so thank you, but no. However, a bed would be most welcomed right now. The trail has been long and tiring. Or a bath, that would be the most delightful thing you could offer me at the moment, followed by a warm bed and some sleep."

Darnovam smiled into his beard. "Then my Lady, please allow your attendants to remain and enjoy our hospitality."

Ashera piped up, "Yes, my Lady, please allow me to remain. One of the serving girls wants to speak with me about Southern Reach. It would be a great favor."

Illera could feel the warnings dancing along her nerves, strengthening the anxiety already building in her but she smiled to the lord, "I have been through a harrowing few days, and I would feel much better if my servants would stay near me."

"But my Lady," pleaded Ashera, stopping when the earl held up a hand.

He spoke, his voice hard and demanding. "But surely if your attendants have given good service they deserve a little reward for their hard work. Or do you subscribe to the view that servants are lower than the dogs that feed on the droppings of our tables."

Illera looked at the brothers and Ashera seated at the fire-place, trying to convey her warning with her eyes alone, and rose from her chair.

"Really Lord Darnovam, these verbal sparrings are fatiguing when one has traveled all day. If any of my entourage chose to remain and sample your cellars, they may, but I will rest better knowing someone watches over me."

She caught the flicker of understanding in the eyes of the squires, but Ashera leapt to her feet, and sketching a cursory bow followed one of the serving girls.

"My Lord," Raven bowed low, "we are also tired from the last few days and would be best served by retiring with the princess."

The Earl's mouth drew down in a sour smile. "Very well, Mista will show you to your rooms. A bath will be prepared my Lady, at once and you may all retire. However, I insist on sending some of my finest vintages for your attendants to taste. I simply must have input from people outside my own jurisdiction. How else can I trust that I am improving my stock?"

Illera nodded and followed a small, bone thin woman through the twisting corridors and up three flights of wooden stairs. The servant led her to a suite of drafty rooms. The outer room was an odd shape, having seven walls, furnished with a table and six chairs, with two straw pallets in one corner. One wall sported a series of shelves containing a number of bottles, jars, carvings, and parchments that were strange to Illera. The next chamber was the bedroom, large and wide with a single giant wooden bed in the middle of the floor. A small fireplace on the outside wall beside the tall, thin window contained a newly lit flame, dancing feebly on damp logs. It did little to dispel the chill from the musty room. On the far side of the bed, one of her chests sat, already opened. A wash of anger coursed through her at the sight.

Mista opened the only other door in the chamber and showed Illera a small bathing chamber with a round tin tub steaming in the middle of the floor. A stand holding a washbasin and jug graced the back wall with shelves containing linens over it. The rooms were barren and repulsive, and Illera knew if she were to behave like a princess she would protest.

"Mista, that is your name, Mista?"

"Yes, my Lady," the woman bowed her head, backing away from Illera's presence.

"Are these rooms the best this...this pitiable excuse for a castle has to offer?"

"Ah... ah...of course my Lady? There are no better 'ceptin' m'Lord's own."

"It is disgusting. You may tell your Lord that and not fit for my attendants let alone myself. I will speak to King Korul about this, this failure of hospitality."

The woman's eyes widened as she backed from the room and scurried back the way she had come. By the time Illera walked into the first chamber, a lovely young woman with a large bosom, most of it on display, was serving Lark and Raven.

"See to it that I am not disturbed," she told them in lieu of what she really wanted to discuss.

She returned to the bathing room and stripped off her soiled and frayed clothing. The water smelled unpleasant to Illera, sulfur and bitter. She sorted through her opened chest, finding the bag of her medicines. She chose the astringent leaves and scattered a handful of them over the surface of the water. It turned a blood red, gradually clearing to an appearance of normal water, but Illera was warned. She washed from the water in the jug on the stand and tossed her dirty clothing into the tainted bath. Taking her herbs with her, she climbed into the huge bed. The sheets were chill and damp. She huddled into a ball and tried to sleep.

A banging, rattling noise intruded on her rest. Illera tried to turn over and ignore it, but it continued, and the new spot on the bed was cold. She sat up. The fire had faded to ash, and the wind whistled in around the window. She went to it as a dark shape battered against the pane. Illera jumped back, stifling a scream at the suddenness. The shape hovered, pecking at the glass. She slipped the catch and opened the window and the bird tumbled in. It gurgled at her and perched on her shoulder, rubbing the side of its head against her face.

"Maggie?' whispered Illera unable to believe it was her old friend. "What about your babies?"

The magpie made soft shushing noises at her. Maggie grabbed a lock of Illera's hair and pulled her towards the outer door, chattering softly in the back of her throat. Illera tiptoed to the door, opening it a crack. Lark lay propped against the wall, a line of spittle running from the corner of his mouth, down his chin and across his chest. His arms were not placed naturally at his sides but lay at awkward angles. Illera opened the door slightly more and caught sight of Raven in a boneless heap against the other wall. His head was on the floor and his backside canted up the wall. One arm was twisted behind his back, and the other was straight down in front of him bearing the full weight of his body. She could hear men whispering around the curve of the oddly shaped room. Maggie tugged her back into the room.

Illera dressed quickly in warm clothes, all in black. She braided her hair back from her face and donned a fresh cloak. The bag of herbs went at her belt, fastened tightly. She took a dagger and sheath from her chest, and attached that to her belt beside the bag. The magpie watched her with fascination and a small burble now and then.

Illera checked the drop from the window, noting she must be in one of the overhanging parts of the castle for there no other structures close, even beneath the window. Closing it tightly, she turned to Maggie. The bird fluttered towards the door, walking solemnly out of the crack Illera opened. Illera bent to check the brothers, noting their breathing was shallow and labored. Lark had a number of fluid-filled pustules on his visible skin. Quickly Illera reached for her herbs, selecting two and crushing them, forcing the bits between his open lips. He twisted under her hands at the bitter taste and pungent aroma. She stroked his throat to make him swallow. She crossed to Raven, giving him the same mixture.

Maggie lingered just out of sight of the rest of the room. Illera stood behind her, listening and trying to plan her next move. She could hear the voices of three men in the other room as well as the clatter of the bones rolling in a dice game.

"Shit, Mogr you al'us wins!"

"Nuthin' like a li'le extra. Gonna get me a war-horse. Jest like them 'uns those squires rode in on."

"Shit Mogr, why'n ya jest take one a them?"

The third voice spoke, "You dummy. We gotta kill them animals. What if old Korul comes snoopin' aroun' and finds 'em. Probably be th'meat in yer stew fer the next few months."

The men laughed.

"When's we gonna take 'em?"

"Gotta wait. Th'Lord said ta wait 'til second moon rising 'cause th'princess wouldn't drink th'wine. Had ta stick it in her bath water an that takes longer ta work."

"Shit, wanna get it over an get back ta th'castle."

"Screw this up, an th'earl will gi'ya ta th'witch an she'll have yer balls fer breakfast. Cost th'earl plenty ta get th'old hag to gi'him that powder."

"Witches gi' me th'screamin' jeebies."

"Do that ta us all."

"How much longer?"

"Roll th' bones, ya meathead. I'll let ya know when's time."

"Mogr, ya know how far ta Sea Reach."

"Yeah, if'n we go now, an fast, should be thar about noon, day after ta marra."

"Them pirates gonna be waitin'."

"Suppose ta be. Can't never trust them'uns. Soon as double cross ya as spit."

"Shit, Mogr yer not suppose ta win agin."

"Quiet Droove or ya'll wake her highness."

"Roll th' bones."

Illera peeped around the corner, noting the three guards gathered in one corner. They were throwing the dice and quaffing beer as they played. Her attention wandered to the shelves and one particular pot decorated with arcane symbols. She signed to Maggie. The bird lit on her wrist that she held high over her head. Spreading her wings, the bird glided to the shelf. She indicated articles with her beak and Illera shook her head no until she came to the pot.

Nodding vigorously, Illera watched Maggie remove the lid, scoop up a beak full of powder and glide over the steins of beer and deposit the contents of her beak in one glass. She walked back to Illera, and they repeated the procedure until each guard had a large dose of the contents.

The powder worked fast. The first guard slumped into the corner, ruining the dice toss. The second tried to strike him for that and ended collapsed over his body. The third guard stood, lurched drunkenly to one side and tumbled to the floor as he tried to move towards Illera.

She turned her attention to the brothers. A few soft slaps brought Raven semi-awake, but Lark was more difficult. She fed him some more of the leaves, and he opened his eyes wearily. Raven had righted himself and was trying to stretch out the stiffness.

"I overheard them talking, and they are planning to sell us to the pirates. We are supposed to leave at second moon rising, so we don't have much time. I have to find Ashera, and we must hurry. Do you know where the horses are?"

Raven nodded, "Yes, I'm the only one who can take care of Abbadon. The grooms couldn't touch him."

Illera helped him to his feet and returned to Lark. She shook him hard then slapped his face again. Pushing her hand away, he staggered to his feet.

"Yeah, I heard," he muttered, "but right now I have the worse hangover in the world."

Illera jumbled through her bag producing a sliver of pink and silver fungus. Silently she handed it to Lark. Another smaller slice went to Raven.

"I'm going to try to find Ashera. You get the horses and meet me at the side of the castle nearest the road," she told them.

Illera replaced the cover on the pot, wrapping it tightly with one of the scarves from her chest as she left the room. With Maggie gliding ahead and leading the way, Illera followed the magpie through the twisting corridors and down a set of narrow wooden steps. Another long hallway and second set of stairs confused Illera as to her location, but Maggie seemed sure, so she followed her. The bird stopped with a soft squawk, perching on the doorframe with her head hanging down, peering into the room. Illera tiptoed forward.

Ashera lay with six other girls and women in an untidy heap in front of the enormous fireplace. The wood had burned down to glowing coals, and the room was in deep shadow. Illera moved stealthily to Ashera's side, the bag of herbs in her hand. She gently shook the giantess's shoulder, but Ashera was oblivious. Illera crushed the herbs and forced them between the woman's closed lips, stroking her throat to make her swallow. One of the other girls began to stir. Illera hunkered down on the floor and froze in position. The girl rose and went to the fire, stirring it and adding fresh wood. The flames blazed up, and the girl returned to her spot on the floor. Illera tried to rouse Ashera, slapping her gently and shaking her shoulder. The woman sleeping against Ashera began to grumble and gave the warrior a shove. Illera eased away carefully, tiptoeing backward to the door.

She shook her head at Maggie and whispered, "Lark and Raven, outside."

The bird flew back the way they had come, leading Illera down another set of stairs, these ones made of stone. A small heavy door was latched and bolted. Illera drew the bolt, wincing as it shrieked like a mountain lion with an arrow in his flank. She waited long moments before opening the door a crack and sliding out. First moon was far overhead, and she could see the faint glow preceding second moon behind the branches of the trees. The crunching of boots on gravel betrayed the presence of a guard. Following the magpie around the building, Illera stopped to let other patrols go by as she hid in the dark crevasses of the walls. In one inky pool ahead, she could make out the lighter shape of a horse and the blaze and stockings of another. Crouching, she ran to the squires. They boosted her onto a normal saddle, and she flashed them a smile.

Raven looked grim and whispered, "I think I killed a guard outside the stable."

"I'm sorry, Raven, but what else could you do. We have to get away from here."

"It feels wrong to kill my own people." Illera could see the corners of his mouth pulled down and dark creases of a frown on his forehead. "It's just wrong. We're supposed to be on the same side."

Illera leaned towards him, placing a hand on his arm."Having arrangements to sell us into slavery isn't being on the same side."

Leaving Ashera's mount tied to a post, Raven nodded and headed the horses down the eastern road that would lead to Korul's Castle, but Maggie flew in his face, chattering in muted tones until they turned north and trotted swiftly away from the castle. Behind they could hear the commotion moving down the road to the east.

The single guard at the outer palisade walls was asleep. The gate here was small and little used. Lark dismounted and crept up behind the man. He clapped one hand over his mouth and Illera tied the man's hands together behind his back. Lark gagged him with a strip of heavy cloth torn from the man's tunic.

Raven slipped the bar and opened the door, Illera and Lark crept through, pulling their horses behind them. Shutting the door carefully from the outside, he joined them. They urged their mounts to a gallop. The road twisted and snaked through the pines with quick choices to make between many side roads. Raven led the way uncertainly, pausing before a large road swinging west. Illera startled at the sound of manic laughter as Maggie flew in Raven's face, turning him from that path to the northern one. Second moon was well above the trees now, and the double shadows made treacherous movements out of bushes and tall pines. With Maggie leading the way, they raced down the narrow forest road.

It folded through the dark woods, twisting back on itself. They set their horses at top speed; Illera holding Copper back for the slower war-horses. A dark shape eclipsed the moon. Maggie shrieked and flew back to them, fluttering in their faces. A second time the moon vanished behind the bulk of something large. Raven pulled his horse to a stop. Abbadon shivered and snorted. Appolon tried to leave the trail and hide in the trees. Copper reared and threw herself about, causing Illera to bless the normal saddle she rode.

"Dragon," called Raven as the shape crossed the moon again.

"Small one about ten or fifteen feet," agreed Lark.

"What do we do?"

"Hide in the trees," Raven told her.

They turned off the trail and tried to ride under the branches, but the brush was too thick. Dismounting, they slapped their horses sending each one away in a different direction as they waded through the undergrowth, looking for a suitable hiding place. In the distance, Illera heard the howl of a wolf. Stopping under a fragrant spruce, she called and sent forth her calls to all the other animals that might assist them against the dragon. She poured all her strength into the call and became dizzy, sitting down suddenly in the scattered needles under the tree. Lark and Raven dove down beside her as a blast of fire scorched the tree where they had been standing.

Scrambling on hands and knees, they crawled to another sheltering spruce with branches that reached almost to the forest floor. Sitting silently against the trunk of the tree, they listened. The flapping of leathery wings was close; then the tree exploded into fire. Leaping to their feet, they ran, dodging between the close growing boles, whipped in the face by branches. Illera turned her head once to see their pursuer.

It was as Lark said, about ten feet from snout to tip, the color of blood or the hot coals when the fire dies down. The wide wings were double its length. It dangled four legs of equal length, all armed with razor-sharp ripping talons. The face surprised her, being pug-nosed with long tendrils around the mouth and over the eyes. The large dark eyes bore into her own, filled with terror and uncertainty. Around the sinuous scaly neck was a sharp, barbed metal collar. Illera stopped.

Lark and Raven each pulled one arm and dragged her behind them.

"Let me talk to it. It is in pain," she instructed them.

"No way Lady, if you stop you will be in cinders." Lark yanked her forward.

Illera tried to concentrate on the dragon, singing to it. It paused, alighting on the ground. A shrill wailing came from the beast and Illera pulled free from the squires and faced it. It took a step towards her. She stood still and sang to it. Desire warbled from its mouth, and it came closer. Lark and Raven drew their swords, prepared to try to kill the creature but Illera held up her hands. The dragon placed its snout in her hands, the feelers reaching out and caressing her face.

A high shriek, more mental than physical, shook the forest. The dragon whipped its head back. It shouted its defiance, but the shrill voice dominated. The reptile slashed its head from side to side, warbling and pleading in its cries. The voice was implacable. It turned its head away from Illera and spat, causing the tree where the spit landed to burst into flame. Illera backed away from the creature. Lark and Raven were watching her closely, following her every move.

The dragon howled again, a cry of purest agony, then it charged, spitting at them as it came. Lark pulled Illera to one side as Raven jumped the other way. A low growl behind him made him leap forward over the flame. Six large dire wolves crept from the shadows, fangs bared. The dragon leapt for the sky, fighting its unseen controller. Illera skirted the fire, moving to the wolves. The brothers shouted behind her. She sang to wolves, and they approached and rolled over at her feet. From a tree behind them, a lion leapt and rubbed his face against her leg. Lark and Raven watched, swords at ready and horror on their faces.

With a blood-curdling scream, the dragon stooped, spitting fire at the group on the ground. One of the wolves leapt high into the air, catching the reptile by the edge of one wing. The wolf fell flaming to the ground, its cries of agony joining with the dragon's.

Horrified, Illera rushed to it. It licked her hands as it died.

Tears streaming down her face she shooed the rest of her animal protectors into the screening trees and ran, dodging the gouts of flame the dragon hurled at her, screaming a warning before each one. Lark and Raven ran at her side.

Second moon was eclipsed by another larger shape.

"Now what," gasped Raven, springing to one side as burning spit flew by. "All we need is a second dragon."

Lark craned his head around, "Not another dragon, griffin maybe."

Illera stopped, panting for breath as the dragon rose to meet the other animal. She could see it clearly in the moonlight, silver and shining. The wide white wings carried a body much like that of the lion, with the long tail tufted in feathers. The sharp eagle's beak was night black and gleaming in the pale moon rays, and its crown of thick feathers made it seem more massive than it actually was. The four feet were taloned with tools every bit as sharp as those of the dragon.

They met in mid-air, the white griffin and the fiery dragon. The griffin flipped over, presenting a barrier of claws to the oncoming dragon. It was moving too fast to turn and raked one wing and one side of itself on the griffin's claws. The dragon flapped madly, trying for height, but with lazy sweeps of its pinions, the griffin ascended above it. It stooped on the dragon, which dodged, plummeting towards the trees. The evil voice shrieked in the background. The dragon snaked its head around and spat at the griffin. The bird merely shrugged aside in the air, and the fire flew harmlessly past it. The dragon zoomed up from the tree line, screaming, spitting fireball after fireball at the griffin. With one high piercing cry, the griffin turned on a wingtip and positioned itself over the dragon. It drove all four sets of talons into the dragon's spine. The dragon snapped its head backward, but before it could spit, the griffin drove its beak into the reptile's throat. The dragon spasmed in its death throes in the claws of the griffin.

Leisurely, the bird descended, depositing the dragon at Illera's feet. Lark and Raven faced the creature with swords but she walked to it and reaching up she caressed the pristine feathers and sang to it. The bird lowered its head and stretched its wings one after the other. Illera gave it a final caress, and it launched itself into the air and vanished into the moonlight. She turned to the dragon.

It looked smaller in death, battered and hopeless. Illera removed the tight metal collar with the barbs that cut into its neck and hurled it into the darkness of the night.

"I'm sorry I can't help you," she told it as she caressed the feelers into place, "But at least now you are free."

She began to sob. Lark and Raven sheathed their swords and approached her warily.

"It's okay," Lark ventured, "It's all over now."

Illera shook her head. "You don't understand."

"I don't understand why you are crying for a dragon?" Raven told her. "It was trying to kill us."

"No," she contradicted, "it wasn't. It was the person controlling the dragon who was trying to kill us. It only wanted to be free, to live in peace. Didn't you see how it fought against that control?"

Lark shook his head while Raven nodded, "Yes, it screamed before it shot fire at us. It was warning us, wasn't it?"

Illera nodded, the tears streaming down her cheeks. Raven took her in his arms and held her.

"What are you?" he whispered.

"I don't know," she replied, as her sobs become hiccups.

"Could you call our horses?" he asked. "That is if the dire wolves and lions haven't eaten them."

She nodded, but rested against his chest, trying to make the sorrow drain away so she could continue.

CHAPTER 6

$\mathcal{A}$ night bird sang somewhere; lost in the gold and silver dappled darkness; a mournful, haunting rise and fall of liquid notes. A soft night wind blew cool through the pines and spruces whispering an accompaniment. In the far, far distance, a pack of wolves sang to the sky. Illera trudged unheeding of the special beauty of the night, following Raven and Lark, concerned only with putting one foot ahead of another.

Raven halted so suddenly she bumped into him. Putting a hand on her shoulder to steady her, he held a finger to his lips for silence. She listened hard. The crackle of flames teased her ears, and she caught a faint wisp of smoke on the breeze. Peering around Raven, she could see a tiny flicker to the right, down a steep slope. A hint of movement in the shadows drew her eyes to Lark slipping from shadow to shifting shadow until she could no longer track his movements.

Raven eased her back until they were sheltered under the wide drooping branches of a giant white spruce. Illera placed her back against the trunk and slid to the ground.

"Are you tired, my Lady?" Raven whispered.

"Bone weary, Raven, bone weary. I miss Madean. It's like a toothache that won't give me any rest or peace."

The branches rustled as he sat down beside her.

"When I first went to Korul's castle I felt like that. Except it wasn't the country, I missed as much as my mother and all the horses. If Lark hadn't been with me, I don't think I could have stayed."

"You love your mother very much don't you?"

She could hear the smile in his voice as he answered. "More than I can tell you. Maybe you'll get to meet her once you become Queen."

"I think I'd like that. Tell me about her?"

He laughed soft and low. "I don't know what to tell you. What does a son tell about his mother? She is the King's horsewoman, and she takes care of the breeding herd. I've seen her ease a colt from its mother's body when everyone else had given up on both of them. I can't count the number of foals she's raised herself when something happened to the mare. I think one of my earliest memories is sharing my bed, well it was just a pallet of straw on the floor, with a long-legged bay filly. A lion had killed her dam, but mum rescued the little one and brought it home. She's just an incredible woman."

"It sounds that way. What about your father?"

His voice hardened. "My real father? I don't know who he is. If I ever find out, I think I'll kill him for what he did to my mother."

"Why?"

"He left her. She has two sons, and he leaves. And he took her without wedding vows. She never told us about our father, just that we were special by birth. That's all she ever said, Lark and I were special because of him. She must have loved him dreadfully to flout all the customs of the land for him and still, when he abandoned her, never say a bad word about him. But that's the kind of woman my mother is, the warmest heart in all of Frain."

"Does it hurt not to know your father?"

Raven rose, and paced the single step to the downward sweep of branches and peered out. Turning, impaled in a shaft of silver light, he stared at her. Illera saw the turmoil on his brow and the hard glint in his eye. He shook his head.

"It makes me angry, what he did to my mother. I don't think I want to know him."

Illera sighed. "I want to know my mother. She left on my first birthday."

Raven sat beside her again. "Your mother left you?"

"Yes, when I was one year old. I don't remember her, only the picture that hangs in the great hall of Seven Spires. You asked me who or what I am. I really don't know. I know I look like her, but what else of her there is in me, I can't tell you. I never knew her, and it hurts. I think that's why I can't stand to see anything else hurt, because my abandonment is always with me."

Raven put an arm around her shoulders. "Well my Lady, we are both half-orphans, and they say the gods care for orphan children."

"Does that mean that the gods care halfway for us?" She smiled, a small quirk of the lips.

Raven started to laugh. The branches whipped aside, and Raven surged to his feet sword drawn.

"Sit down, you great fool," snapped Lark. "You are making enough noise to attract an army from Sorwelk."

"Sorry, Illera and I were talking..."

Lark cut him off. "Enough. There are about five hundred Shul down in the hollow, all armed to destroy. I think they are hunting us. Ashera's promise of gold has well and truly come back to haunt us, and now those beasts will be on the Lady's trail until they are satisfied and Targ's coffers are filled."

"We better move out. Which way?"

"They look to be heading northeast. That's the logical place to look for Illera as Korul's castle is that way, so if we head straight north and swing back to the castle in an arc, we should avoid them."

They slipped from the shelter of the tree and moving as silently as possible kept the declining moon on their left. Illera could not imagine how many miles passed beneath their feet as the night wore away. When the right-hand sky was brightening, Raven called a halt, and they crawled into a nest cupped in the exposed roots of a towering pine. A chuckling stream bubbled through the forest a few steps from their hiding place. Lark carefully swept all their tracks into anonymity with a fallen branch. Sleepily, Illera called a blue jay. It perched overhead and kept watch for them. Tumbled together in a heap, they slept the day away.

She opened her eyes to a fuchsia and gold sunset streaking the sky. The bluejay was prancing up and down her body, uttering harsh little strangling noises. It fluttered to her hand, and she sang it her thanks before it winged away into the brilliant heavens. Raven had her enclosed in his heavy arms, and one of Lark's arms was around her hip and stomach. She squirmed out of Raven's embrace and carefully lifted Lark's torpor weighted limb. Scrambling to her feet, she made her way to the brook, hearing her stomach rumble as she drank her fill. She leapt the sparkling span and wandered through the woods in a short circle, picking cones, leaves, and fungus. When her skirts were full, she returned to the hollow under the pine. Raven and Lark were gone. Gathering twigs and bark, she started an insignificant fire and sat down to wait.

The twilight settled in gentle layers on the forest. Illera divided her gatherings into three portions and ate her own, hunger making short shrift of politeness. The brothers were still missing. She spent her time as the night darkened the world around her calling the horses. She was deep in concentration, trying to reach out to the animals when Lark burst into her consciousness. He seized her shoulder and shook her, snapping her head back and forth.

"Where were you?"

Stunned, Illera just looked at him. His mouth was drawn down at the corners, and fury smoked from his eyes.

"Where did you go?" he demanded again, giving her a little shake.

Illera pulled herself away from him and stiffened herself to her full height. "I was attending nature and gathering food. If you are hungry, there is your portion."

She pointed at a small heap of pine nuts, watercress, dandelion leaves and fungi beside the fire. His breath whooshed out of him, and he plumped down on the ground beside the miniscule fire.

"I'm sorry, Illera. You had us scared to death. Raven is still out there looking for you. I don't think I've been that worried since the rattler nailed my brother."

"A rattler nailed your brother?" Illera sat on her side of the fire. "That sounds interesting. Tell me about it, please."

"Yes, well, he was a hair-brained fool of a kid, always scaring our mother half to death. Well, one day he went out to try to find this mare that was missing, and he found her all right. On the side of a cliff, just past a nest of rattlers. Wasn't smart enough to leave the horse and get help, no he had to jump the snakes and try to ride the mare out over them. Of course, he didn't make it, one of them bit him on the ankle, right above the boot. But, being Raven, he managed to get to the horse, jump her over the nest and down the cliff to our mother. I'd never seen my mother so worried. Sat up with him for three days, dose after dose of snakeweed she poured down him. He survived though. You have to give him that, he's tough."

"Thanks for telling my embarrassing stories," floated a sarcastic voice out of the dark.

Raven followed, striding into the faint circle of light the fire provided. Illera and Lark laughed. The brothers ate their handfuls of food.

"I called the horses," Illera told them.

"What do you mean?" Lark arched his brows upward.

"I called them, asked them to find us. If we wait here, they should come."

Lark waved his hand through the air, brushing her remark aside. "That's superstition. We have to get moving; the Shul are in the forest."

Raven agreed, nodding his head. "We can't move that much faster with the horses. The trees are too thick, so we should keep moving."

Illera sighed. "I really did call them, and they have all the gear. It would be nice to cook something to eat."

After dousing the fire, they rose and walked northward. Lark laughed.

"Why don't you call a rabbit and we can kill that and eat it?"

"I don't call animals to me for their destruction. It's not like that." She halted and glared at him.

"You mean you can't." The squire laughed.

Raven contradicted, "I wouldn't say that about the Lady, Lark. We've seen some powerful strange things."

"Then I challenge you. Call something and tell us before you do so we can be sure that it is really you doing it."

"What do you want me to call?"

"Oh, let's make it a good test. Call an elk. A bull elk, with a large rack."

"I can't control the size of the animal that answers," Illera warned him.

She stopped walking and called, a silent mental effort. They resumed the march, Lark smiling, triumphant. A short distance ahead, they heard a rustling in the bushes. The squires drew their swords, but Illera stepped forward and began to sing. With great majesty, the largest elk they had ever seen stepped forth from the darkness. Its antlers stretched to the sky and the feeble rays of first moon reflected from the dark pools of its eyes. The brothers stood mesmerized as the huge animal lowered its head and sniffed Illera's outstretched palms. It raised its head and bellowed. Two more bull elk strode from the shadows, lesser animals, but still magnificent. Illera sang to the three of them. She thanked them audibly for coming and waved the squires forward to continue on their journey, the three great beasts crashing through the brush ahead and on either side of them.

In an awed whisper, Lark told her, "I've never seen anything like this. Where did you learn to call animals? Can you call people?"

"I never learned to call them, I've always known how to do it, and I've never tried to call people. I don't know if they can hear."

"I knew you could do it," Raven whispered. "You did it with the dire wolves and the griffin. You've called the magpie before too. I told you, Lark; the Lady is special."

The lead elk stopped, snorting. The travelers halted. Voices drifted to them from the dark. One of the elk at their side harried them to a thick-growing grove of berry bushes. They crouched as low to the ground as they could get. The deer stationed themselves on either side. The giant lead deer bounded off at an angle as six armed humans raced into the clearing.

"Just an elk," called one of the men.

"Keep lookin'. Th'Lord'll have our hides if'n we don' find 'em."

The soldiers scurried off into the night.

Illera and her two escorts waited for long dark minutes. First moon crept high in the sky shedding golden light softly on the forest and its inhabitants. One of the bulls snorted and began to move north again. The trio arose and followed in silence, sobered by the thought of two groups hunting them.

They trudged along as first moon descended and disappeared behind the trees, second moon following closely in its wake. An explosive snort from the elk on the left halted them. Illera heard swords whispering from their sheaths. Another snort broke the stillness of the night. They heard hooves pounding the earth in a cadence, one-two, one-two. Raven, crouched close to the ground, snuck forward, slipping from tree to tree. Lark drifted after him, and Illera followed. The taller trees gave way to a moonlit clearing carpeted with short, wiry grass and wildflowers, their colors dimmed by darkness. The elk hid in the shadows of the forest, but a moving shadow danced in one spot in the middle of the clearing. Illera spotted Raven from the corner of her eye sliding across the little meadow, sword at the ready. Closer and closer to the blackness he came, sword high, ready to cleave flesh and bone. She turned her eyes back to the darkness dancing a piaffe, a suddenly familiar shadow.

With a cry, she lunged around Lark, screaming at Raven to put his sword away. Lark seized her by the waist and swung her back into the sheltering trees just as the shadow gave a ringing neigh and Raven's sword began its descent. Illera screamed with anger and fought against Lark, pounding and kicking backward. She dropped through his arms and scrambled through his legs back onto the meadow. The darkness rushed at her, swerving to a stop at her feet. She hugged the big black animal, murmuring soothing words and stroking his trembling muscles. Looking up she saw Raven standing in the middle of the meadow, sword point down, buried in the sandy loam. It looked as if it was the only thing holding him up right now.

"Abbadon?" questioned Lark, running a hand over the big animal's shoulder. He snatched his fingers away as the horse snapped at them.

Raven tottered over. "By the gods Illera, if you hadn't yelled I would have killed my own horse. What was he doing?"

Illera paused in soothing the war-horse. "I think he was trying to get our attention. Perhaps the elk made him nervous, and he didn't think he could approach us? Is that possible?"

Raven shrugged. "I don't know? Abbadon usually just thunders through everything. Why not elk?"

"He's had a hard time, poor baby. Look at the sweat caked all over him." Illera rubbed a hand over his dirty shoulder.

Raven sheathed his sword and gathered twists of grass to groom the stallion. When Abbadon was rubbed down, he rifled through his saddlebags and found some jerky. The elk refused to leave the covering forest, so Illera thanked them with a song and watched as they faded into the night. Chewing the leathery meat, they continued north, Abbadon trailing behind them.

The character of the forest began to change. Towering stands of pine and spruce shrank into scrubby second growth, interspersed with large aspen. The open spaces between the trees snarled with shrubs, and tall bushes caught their feet and legs. It required such effort to push the face level branches aside and to avoid being slapped by the person in front's passage that their arms soon became as weary as their legs. Second moon sank behind the trees. The hills seemed steeper and the gullies deeper than the gently contoured deep forest. Illera stumbled more and more often, going to her knees only to be hauled back to her feet by one of the brothers. When they came to a fast, narrow river twinkling with rapids in the starlight, Illera plumped herself on a rock and refused to move. The shoreline of pebbles interspersed with large and small boulders offered patches of sharp poverty grass for Abbadon. Several feet back from the rocky shore were clusters of willows and other shrubs.

Unable to budge her, Lark and Raven made a small fire and stewed some of the meat. The warm broth slipped down her throat and warmed her from the inside. She sipped and listened to the busy rush of the river.

"I wonder how Ashera is?" she murmured aloud to no one in particular.

Raven sat beside her drinking his broth. "I wish I knew. I have a bad feeling about her."

"Ashera's tough." Lark joined them. "Some of the stories she told me; well let's just say the woman is a survivor."

"Like what?" enquired Illera sleepily, stretching back to lie against Abbadon's saddle.

"Let's see," mused Lark, "well, your father found her wandering alone on the southern coast of Madean. There was a burned Sorwelk ship not far away. He said he found a few bodies, they looked like Sorwelk traders, but no trade goods nor any other living soul. He said she was about five then, so he took her on his horse to Southern Reach. As he approached this Valkyrie woman comes screaming out at him, yelling in a language he doesn't understand. It was Ashera's mother, who had gone to the village to trade. When she went back to the boat to get the trade goods, here was the crew dead and the ship burnt. She said she searched for two days but couldn't find a trace of her daughter, so she returned to the village in mourning. Then King Ian rides up with the child, and she had thought he had done the killing and burning and was calling him out to a duel. When they got that straightened up, the King placed her under his special protection and gave them money for a house and to start up a smithy and an armory business.

I think the king and his troops were the mother's best customers and they prospered in Southern Reach. Poor Ashera, it seemed as nothing would go right for the girl and three years after that they settled there her mother died of the spotted fever. Now she was an orphan, and the town took care of her, but she was never happy. She wanted to be a warrior like her father or a smith like her mother. Since there was no one to teach her how to smith, she became a fighter. By the time she was thirteen, she had said she had killed twenty-one Shul during their raids on Southern Reach. She said they always tried to divert her before they came into the town to loot and she was catching on to their tricks. At least that's the story she told me."

"It's so sad, being without a mother," whispered Illera. "I wish I had known before; I might have tried to be nicer to her."

"Yeah," Lark agreed, "I think she is so, so pushy because she is afraid if she isn't people will just ignore her."

Raven grinned. "She's about as easy to ignore as a barleycorn in your shorts." Flushing red, he glanced at Illera. "Your pardon my Lady. I just never got on well with Ashera."

Illera waved his apology away. "We all have trouble with certain people. I think I was so focused on myself; I didn't see her. I hope I can make it up to her when we get to Korul's castle. How much farther do we have to go?"

Raven peered at Lark who looked around at the speeding water and the thick trees.

"I think, mind you this is only a guess, that we are about two days ride from the Bay of Hostages. That should be the Fear River. Of course, it could be a tributary. We should stay on this side of the river and head east soon. If we go too far north, we'll run into the swamp of ghosts and have to travel south again, so this is probably a good time to swing east. Then I think about six or seven days to Korul's castle, if no one or thing gets in the way."

Abbadon raised his head from the stubby grass he was grazing. His whicker rang through the forest. Raven jumped to his feet.

Raising up on one elbow Illera said, "Don't worry, it's just Copper."

Raven looked down at her, one eyebrow quirked. "How do you do that?"

Illera pointed. Four white stockings and a blaze low to the ground came limping towards them.

"Copper's markings are rather visible in the dark." She gave a low chuckle.

The mare limped over. A twisted piece of wire was embedded around her off front pastern. Illera rose and went to the injured animal.

"Lark, make tea," she commanded.

Raven bent over the injury. "A snare? Is she going to lose the foot?"

Illera examined the wound as best she could in the feeble firelight.

"I don't think so. I brought my herbs." She detached the bag from her belt.

Raven worked the wire loose and flung it into the night. Illera listened to him cursing under his breath as she washed and packed the ravaged foot with moss. The mare lay down beside Illera and Lark carried an armful of grass for the mare. Illera flung an arm around the mare's barrel and closed her eyes, instantly asleep.

Sharp pains in her bladder woke her, and she stuck her head out of the cloak covering her from head to foot. The cold air stung her nostrils. Shivering she rose wrapping the warmed leather around her. The fire had burnt out and the night was quiet, and still, the only sounds were Abbadon's slow movements and the sound of his teeth as he cropped the rough grass. The sky faded to gray on the eastern horizon, presaging the coming sunrise.

As Illera moved from the camp to the bushes, Raven materialized from the dark. She jumped. He grinned at her and returned to his post as she hurried behind a screening of thick bushes. Just as she finished her business and refastened all her clothes a gentle bump on her shoulder made her start and whirl around ready to yell at Raven for spying on her. Appolon's long face thrust into hers. She grabbed his bridle and scratched him behind his ears as her heart slowed.

She was about to step from behind the brush when a blood-curdling scream split the predawn air. Illera hunkered down, spreading the vegetation apart with her hand. A party of seven Shul descended upon the camp. Three of them were upon Lark, who was sleeping next to the fire. The other four were battling with Raven at the border of the trees. Appolon snorted and surged forward. Illera held tight to the reins and pulled him back.

"Down," she commanded him pulling earthward on the bridle.

Appolon shook his head. She pulled over and over until the giant war-horse went to his knees. She slipped her foot into the stirrup and swung up on his back. Appolon scrambled to his feet. He understood now and eased silently through the darkness heading for Raven. Raven was fighting for his life with a sword in one hand and dagger in the other, his back against a huge aspen tree. Illera saw his eyes widen as she and Appolon lunged out of the darkness. The horse clamped his teeth on one burly ogre's shoulder and lifted the howling creature high into the air, flinging it to the dirt. The powerful hooves trampled it. Illera winced at the crack of breaking bones and splat of rending flesh. Another tried to come at them from behind but Appolon lashed out with both hind feet, and the Shul went flying, landing back broken against a boulder. Appolon spun around, and Illera saw Raven run the point of his sword through one of the attackers and impale the other in the heart with his dagger. The one with the dagger ran off, heading back into the dark woods. The other collapsed and lay still as Raven pulled his sword out.

Turning, they saw Lark, trussed like a calf for slaughter over a Shul's back, being carried into the night.

"Stay here!" Raven, yelling a war cry chased the creatures.

Illera reigned Appolon to a standstill watching as Raven charged the fleeing ogres. The biggest turned, scooped up a massive boulder and hurled it at him. It caught him in the center of the chest and Raven was borne to the hard ground. The Shul escaped into the darkness. Illera kneed the horse forward until she reached Raven, pinned beneath the rock.

She slid down from the tall animal and tried pushing against the rock, Raven groaned with the pain, but she could not shift it. She ran back to the camp and snatched the reins from Abbadon's bridle, knotting them together as she ran. Raven's face was ashen in the strengthening light. She looped the lines around the rock and the pommel of Appolon's saddle. Seizing his reins, she urged him forward. He started then halted when the weight came on the saddle. Illera coaxed him, and he bent his head, dug in his toes and pulled. Leather creaking ominously, the boulder shifted, and Raven was free. Dropping the reins, Illera dashed to him.

"Thank you," he whispered.

"Lie still." She ran her hands gently over his body.

She removed the chain mail armor and the leather shirt underneath it. His chest was red and purple; the developing bruises beginning to rise. Her questing fingers told her that two of his ribs were broken.

"Your ribs are broken, but everything else looks good."

"Is that all." he tried to sit up.

"I think so, but then I don't know much about people. I've just healed animals remember. Can you make it to the camp?"

"I can try."

Illera did her best to hoist him to his feet and prop him up as he hobbled to camp. Appolon walked along beside them with Raven hanging to the saddle with his good arm. Illera deposited him on Lark's bedroll and hastily restarted the fire. She made tea and antiseptic, washing his wounds and packing them with moss and large, fuzzy, picky leaves.

"That's quite uncomfortable," Raven informed her.

"It's called knitbone and uncomfortable or not; it will heal you much faster than if you don't put up with it."

With a sigh, he lay his head down and allowed her to fix his injuries. She placed her hands on the broken ribs and concentrated. When she was sure they were going to be alright, she took her dagger and cut a large band of bark from the largest aspen. She trimmed it to the correct size and placed it on Raven's chest, lacing it together in the back with leather thongs from his saddlebags. She fed him the restorative tea.

"Rest," she told him. "In two or three days you will be as good as new, but right now, if you move around one of the bone fragments could puncture your lung. I couldn't help you then, so you must lie still for a little while."

"Lark?" he asked.

"It's okay. I'll find Lark."

"No, my Lady. You are the one they want the most. They must have thought that Lark was you, lying by the fire and that's why they took him. You must stay here."

Illera smiled. "I've left you firewood and water within easy reach, and there is food in the saddlebag at your right hand. Make sure you take it easy and drink the rest of this tea. It will help you heal."

She commanded Appolon to kneel and scrambled to his back.

She smiled and waved as Raven called, "No, my Lady. It's not safe. Illera, please stay here."

Illera followed the trail of blood leading back into the scrubby forest. Following the trampled bushes, Appolon seemed to know where to go and moved at a brisk trot. Not more than a couple of miles from the river, Illera found the Shul with Raven's dagger embedded in its chest. It hissed and spat at her when she dismounted.

"Let me help you. I can heal that wound."

"Get away. If you come close to me, I'll kill you," the creature snarled.

"I know you are in a lot of pain, but from the looks of things you will die unless you let me treat your injury."

The ogre laughed. "As if a human would save a Shul."

"I've already saved many Shul. After all, you are people too, why shouldn't I help you."

The beast returned her stare, its face a mask of perplexity.

"Then try, but I warn you, if you attempt to finish me off, it will mean your life."

Illera pulled out her bag of herbs and approached the creature. Its fear was a fetid stench in the clean morning. She pulled
the dagger with one swift motion, placing her hands over the
wound. Concentrating, she felt the blood flow slow and stop. She
packed the wound with moss and gave the creature the blue
mushrooms.

"You'll be fine. Just rest for a few hours. I would stay with you
until you are completely well, but I must find my other
companion."

The creature grinned, an awesome display of fangs. "I thank
you Lady, but your companion will be used to trap you."

"I figured as much, but I can't just leave him there. I wish I
knew what Shul feared."

The ogre looked at the brightening sky and back to Illera. He
coughed.

"I will pay the debt incurred for the return of my life. There is
no way you could use the information, so I will tell you. The Shul
fear nothing on land or water, everything is for our gratification,
but one creature alone brings terror upon us. The flying mouse
that wings its way through the darkness. That is why we hunt
mainly where there are none of them around or hide by night, if
at all possible. My life debt is paid." The Shul turned his face
from her.

"Thank you."

Mounting Appolon, she urged him down the trail, quickening
his pace. They cantered through the woods for several miles.
Topping a hill, Illera looked down into a small clearing. At the far
end, Lark, bound, gagged and tied to a thick tree was watching
her. Thick brush lined the open space, obscuring vision. Her ears
picked up a slight rustle behind the shrubs and the breathing of a
score of creatures.

Glancing at the sun, now clear of the horizon but not yet over
the trees, she wondered if her plan had any hope of success. She
closed her eyes and called with all her might. For long minutes,

the tableau held unbroken in the strengthening light. She called until she was dizzy. And they came. A twisting spiral, like smoke, fluttered out of the trees to the south and west and north, converging on her. She raised her arm and circled the edges of the clearing and the bats dove upon the Shul hiding there.

Illera could not repress a smile at the screams of horror issuing from the bushes. A stampede of ogres crashed through the forest, all heading west. The bats pursued. Illera rode at a leisurely pace to Lark and untied him. Barely had the gag been removed, when he burst out laughing. Apart from a few bruises, he was fine.

"My Lady, that was superb. I've never witnessed anything so funny in all my days. They planned this trap for you so carefully, and bats? Who would have ever thought ogres were afraid of bats?"

"No one, I'm sure. I healed the one Raven stabbed and he told me to pay his life debt." Illera untied his hands and feet.

They mounted Appolon and cantered back to the river.

Raven was on his feet, struggling to lift Abbadon's heavy saddle to his back. The black stallion sent a ringing greeting to them as they approached. Raven turned, clutching his ribs and grimacing with pain.

Illera slid over Appolon's rump as he slowed and trotted to Raven.

"I told you to remain still. Why aren't you lying down," she scolded as she helped him back to the fire.

"I had to go and help you. I was sure you would be killed." He grunted with pain and effort.

Lark dismounted and unsaddled Appolon, turning him loose with Abbadon and Copper.

"You need to learn to trust me," Illera told him, smiling as she settled him back on the bedroll. "As you can see, Lark is back, unharmed and the Shul have gone back to their own land."

"How many did you have to kill?" Raven squinted up at her.

She laughed. "I healed one, and that's all it took."

She tossed his dagger to him, the blade dark with dried blood.

Raven rose on one elbow. "That creature almost killed me, and you healed it? I can't believe you!"

She sat beside him and pushed him back gently.

"Healing that 'creature' gave me the key I needed to free Lark. Isn't it worth it to have your brother back?"

Lark strode up. "Yeah brother, what's the matter with you? I think I'm not worth the life of one of the Shul?"

He squatted down on his heels and brushed the hair back from Raven's forehead. Turning to Illera, he asked, "How bad is he and how soon will he be able to ride?"

"A couple of broken ribs. They would heal quicker if he would stay in one spot, but there's not much I can do if he won't remain still. If he stays quiet today, he could ride tomorrow morning and should be healed in, ah, about two more days."

Lark frowned at his brother. "Hear that. Stay still."

Illera scrambled to her feet and wandered through the edges of the forest and downstream beside the river collecting roots and leaves. When she returned she washed them and put them in the kettle with some of the jerky and left it to stew in the coals. Lark gathered firewood and water, ambling off to give the horses a good grooming. Illera checked Copper's foot and repacked it in moss. She sat beside Raven, her hand over the bark encasing his ribs and concentrated. He soon fell asleep.

When the sun had declined behind the trees, she woke him and gave him his portion of stew.

"Ummm, I didn't know you could make this kind of meal from bark and leaves. Hey, my ribs hardly hurt anymore."

He jumped to his feet. Illera grabbed his pants and tugged him down again.

"You need to stay still until tomorrow morning. You could re-injure yourself if you're not careful."

Lark backed her up, pointing to the blankets again. Raven reluctantly complied. They finished supper and washed up, then spent the rest of the evening contemplating the fire with their thoughts burning in their heads.

The sun rode the shorter trees surrounding them when they broke camp and headed east. The scrubby forest continued until midday becoming smaller and shrubbier, making their way hard going through brambles. Illera remarked how much more pleasant it was to ride rather than push through the clingy vegetation on her own two legs. Around them, the song sparrows sang, and the insects buzzed, assuring them that their enemies were somewhere else. So, they plodded without pushing the horses as the woods diminished and gradually gave way to short grassland. The birdsong changed as new species took over, but the hum of the insects was constant, making the horses kick and snap.

They moved more easily now that the hindering brush was gone, alternating between a gentle canter and a swift walk. The forest was a smudge on the horizon when they made camp for the night.

When they had eaten and settled for the night, Illera removed the bark and checked Raven's ribs.

"They seem to be healing very well."

"It doesn't hurt unless I move the wrong way." He hissed between his teeth as he did just that.

"Good. Two more days in the bark and you should be perfect,"

"Oh, so you think my brother's perfect," interjected Lark.

"Lark!" Raven protested, "If the Lady thinks I am perfect, that's good."

Illera smiled as they laughed. "I said he should be perfect, not that he is."

With good cheer, they retired for the night. The next days were repeats, the prairie flowing beneath their mount's hooves.

Only the wild things inhabited the wide prairie: birds, deer, lions, wolves, and bugs. The wind was their constant companion. Illera felt the greatest sense of freedom she had known since her father told her she must come to Frain, although her ache for Madean never left her. They skirted the edges of the Swamp of Ghosts, keeping miles distant from its deadly edges. From there they swung north again.

The character of the land began to change. The grasslands continued, the blades becoming ever shorter and wirier. The land shelved upward here, with long flat stretches of prairie then hills and another stretch of prairie. The further north they traveled, the rockier the land became.

As the horses surged over a shale-covered slope, Lark gave a whoop and spurred Appolon forward. Illera paused on the crest beside Raven. The land ahead stretched wide and green, dotted over most of its surface with horses. In the distance, a ragged skin tent waved in the persistent breeze; a blue pennant with a white galloping horse fluttering a welcome over it. Appolon was galloping flat out for a tiny figure in front of the structure. Illera looked at Raven. A wide smile plastered on his face, she could tell he wanted to be after Lark.

"My mother," he explained. "That's my mother's herd and her tent."

Illera smiled. "Go, greet your mother. She'll wonder where you are."

He looked at her grinning. Abbadon moved forward a few paces; then he reined him aside.

"My place is with you. We are supposed to be your squires, and we shouldn't both take off."

Illera kicked Copper to a gallop, and they raced after Lark, scattering mares and foals from their headlong charge. Abbadon pulled up snorting in front of a brown raisin of a woman, thrusting his soft dark nose into her cupped hands. The woman laughed, stroking his massive forehead. Raven leapt from the animal's back and grabbed his mother swinging her around and around while hugging her.

"Enough, you unmannerly lout, put me down," she demanded while laughing hard.

"But mother, I never get to see you," Raven cried.

"You can see me all the better on my feet. And you haven't introduced me to your princess yet. I taught you better courtesy than that," she scolded.

Raven placed his mother carefully on her feet and stepped back grinning. He lifted Illera down from Copper's back. His mother was of a height with Illera, having warm, kind eyes the color of clear tea. She had a broad nose with an interesting bobble on the end and a tiny rosebud of a mouth. Her body, though no longer young, was tough, lean and hard.

"My Lady, Illera, princess of Madean, betrothed of Torul and soon to be Queen of Frain, may I present Elisa, horsewoman for King Korul of Frain, and my mother."

Illera curtseyed as she would to another royal woman. Elisa blushed and waved away the greeting.

"You are most welcome to my humble abode your majesty. I have little to offer, but what I possess is at your service."

"Thank you kindly, Elisa. Your sons have told me much about you."

"Ah now, you great louts, what sort of stories have you been tellin' the lady to embarrass me," Elisa scolded.

Lark emerged from the tent munching on biscuits. Both hands were full of more of the flaky bread.

"You great hog," cried Raven lunging into the opening, "I hope you left some for me."

Elisa looked at Illera with a sigh of long-suffering. "I suppose I will be baking on the morrow. Boys! But come, my Lady, refresh yourself. If you wish to bathe and wash clothes, you are welcome. The castle is an easy day's ride from here."

"That would be most pleasant." Illera inclined her head.

Inside, the tent was large and comfortable. It had a screened off section at the back. Elisa gave Illera the only chair, a short, folding, backless affair and seated her at the rickety table, serving more of the flaky biscuit, fresh butter, a berry jam, and milk. Illera gratefully partook, understanding the brothers' greed at the tasty food.

After the repast, Elisa led Illera outside to a rocky outcrop. On the far side, a small stream issued from the rock, falling six feet and forming a shallow pool at the base of the rock before trickling off into the stubby grass. Elisa brought towels and soap, and Illera stripped with less embarrassment than she had ever had. Elisa scrubbed her grubby clothes as she scrubbed her grubby self.

"Have my boys acquitted themselves well?" Elisa focused on the clothing beating it against the rocks.

"Most well. I would have been killed several times if not for them. They are brave and noble squires, and I know they will be outstanding knights when Korul rewards them for this journey."

Elisa sighed with pleasure, a gentle smile on her face. "One tries so hard, but never knows how things will turn out. I always feared..."

She cut her words off.

Illera wrapped herself in the thick towel and sat beside the older woman, enjoying the warmth in the rocks.

"Elisa, tell me what you feared," she requested in her kindest voice.

Elisa ducked her head, pounding the cloth with zeal. "I always feared they would become like their father."

Illera nodded. "I can understand that. They must look like their father, so you would naturally think..."

Elisa shook her head and looked into Illera's eyes. "No, they resembled their father, not at all."

Taken aback, Illera paused, not knowing what to say.

Elisa laughed. "I don't know why I am telling you, of all

people this. I've not told a single soul a word about the boys' father."

Illera just looked at the older woman, wanting to know more but afraid to push.

"Do you...do you care about my sons?"

"Yes, very much," Illera returned softly, placing her hand over the other woman's where it rested on the rock.

Elisa looked up, looked deep into Illera's eyes, searching. "The boys aren't even mine," she said choking on the word. "They are royal bastards, orphans, abandoned by their father and mothers. You...you could not find a better bloodline to merge yours with in all of the world."

Her head hung down now, and she stared at the rock, speaking to the hard surface. Illera could barely hear her words. "They are cousins and half-brothers, although they don't know that. They had different mothers, sisters, but the same father. I have tried to the best of my ability to make sure that they grew up nothing like their father. He is evil incarnate."

"Who is their father," asked Illera quietly.

"Korul, King of Frain," Elisa choked out.

"Why are you telling me this Elisa?"

"You must marry a prince of Frain and unite the two king-doms. I wanted you to know there is more than one prince of Frain. When you are faced with Torul, you need to remember that."

Elisa whirled; stuffing the wet clothes into a hamper and ran back to the tent. Illera, clothed only in the towel followed her; her feet bruised by the wind-rounded rocks and slashed by the sharp grass. As she hobbled into the tent, Elisa grabbed her arm and drew her aside.

"I'm sorry, my Lady. I should not have deposited my burden on your shoulders, but you must, you absolutely must promise not to breathe a word of what I have told you. Please my Lady?"

Illera smiled. "I promise, unless the situation is life or death, they shall know nothing of their father from my lips."

She watched the relief course through Elisa. "Thank you, my Lady. Now if it is not too demeaning to your position, I offer you some of my clothes for the night while yours dry. We are much of a size."

At Illera's nod, she gave her a skirt and leather jerkin with a soft cream shirt. The skirt was snug over the hips and baggy at the waist, and she could not fasten the buttons of the shirt over her breasts, but the jerkin was roomy and covered her decently. As she was dressing, she heard Elisa scolding her sons to the bathing pool so they could be clean for their appearance at court the next day.

After a wondrous supper and more flaky bread, Illera was shown to a string bed. If felt like heaven after many days of sleeping on the ground and she collapsed into it, grateful that no matter what lay ahead, at least the traveling was done with tomorrow. She drifted to sleep lulled by the happy voices on the other side of the partition, cheered by their laughter.

They rode out under a fiery dawn, the blood-colored rising of the sun making the horses skittish. As the day wore on, the gloom increased, darkening the prairie with heavy cloud cover, until the land could bear it no more. The downpour was sudden and heavy, drenching the travelers before they could pull their cloaks around them. They trotted on through the storm, bedraggled and mud-spattered.

Well after midday, the castle loomed out of the dark and driving rain. Crouched on a high hill, the pile of black stone resembled a stalking dragon, in Illera's mind. It was half again larger than Seven Spires, and its approach was steep and curving. The outer crenelated walls towered over a sheer drop of more than one hundred and fifty feet to a rock and mud-filled moat far below. Tops of the barbican towers disappeared into the downpour. Lark pounded on the tall, dark, sealed doors behind the portcullis. With a shriek like a dying dragon, one of the doors crept open. A tall, bearded man peered out at them through the bars of the barrier. Lark yelled at him, but his voice was whipped away by the wind.

The man turned and bellowed to other knights inside. With the loudest shriek, Illera had ever heard, the metal teeth began to rise. Lark and Raven ducked under when the gate was horse high, and she followed; dread soaking her as surely as the rain. The outer bailey was short, spotted with tents under which cowered starving people and listless children who stared with hollow eyes. The inner gateway was solidly locked, and Raven had to pound for long minutes to attract the attention of the gatekeeper. He was a wizened man, holding an uncured cowhide over his head and cursing at them as they passed.

They dismounted at the stables and slopped through the flooded inner bailey to the keep. The doors opened as they approached, flanked by red and black liveried attendants. Illera entered Korul's castle and stood dripping on the flagstones. No one appeared to escort them, so they moved down the dark corridor towards the great room. The torches were widely spaced, leaving pools of deep shadow. Weapons decorated both walls, interspersed with unusual devices and pennants. Illera could not decipher where most of them were from. The sound of a commotion rolled towards them, the squires clapped hands to the pommels of their swords, as they strode into a scene of confusion.

A massive fireplace dwarfed a fire that burned fitfully on the back wall. A large empty throne of gold sat near it, upholstered in plush red fabric. On the far side, a massive stone staircase ascended up and up into a gloom of darkness. The four walls of the gigantic room were plastered, hung with animal heads of every creature in the known world, their sightless glass eyes staring down at the fight occurring in the middle of the room, in front of the throne. The tables and chairs were shoved back against the outside walls and all but obscured by the bodies of men milling around the contest, yelling and shouting encouragement for their favorite. The smack and thud of fist striking flesh brought renewed cheers and jeers. Illera stood in front of the door as though invisible, Lark and Raven on either side.

One fighter flipped and pinned the other, bringing the noise to a crescendo. The onlookers exchanged gibes and money. One of the men raised his head and stared at them for long moments. He was one of the shortest men in the bunch, but thick with a bull-like build and heavily muscled shoulders and neck. What could be seen of his face under wiry salt and pepper beard and mustache, was flushed and dominating all was the red, jutting protuberance of his nose. He smiled, revealing small teeth and moved cautiously towards them, balanced on the balls of his feet.

"Lark, Raven, and I presume this is the princess?" he remarked in a deep baritone as he stopped in front of them.

Illera pushed the hood of her cloak to her shoulders and regarded the man, staring straight into his colorless eyes. Lark and Raven bowed, going down to one knee.

"My Lord," they chorused.

"And you, little wench from Madean, do you not bow before your king?" One lip curled into a sneer.

Trembling inwardly, Illera curtsied, replying, "I do if I am aware of who he is. Having not been introduced, I find it hard to guess which of these many men is king."

Korul laughed; an unhappy sound. "I should think it would be obvious who is king among this crowd of louts."

"Certainly your majesty," Illera answered lowering her eyes.

"So, you finally show up and with just these two attendants," Korul remarked, his eyes sliding over her in a way that made her flesh crawl.

"We have had numerous difficulties, Sire. Shul and others have waylaid us. I regret that my maid and bodyguard was left at Dragon's Lair with Lord Darnovam who was less than hospitable."

"Really? I'm, afraid I've had a different story from Lord Darnovam. What's yours?"

"Your majesty, we have had a long wet ride. Could we discuss this by the fire?" Illera inquired.

The smile on the king's face made her blood run cold.

"It suits me to discuss this here and now."

Drawing a deep breath, she answered, "My bodyguard, your squires and I were drugged. I overheard our guards talking that Lord Darnovam had arranged to sell us all to pirates. It was necessary for us to escape from there. Without your squires it would not have been possible, and I know, I could not be here to unite Frain and Madean. I would respectfully request, Sire, that you send a messenger and bring my maid and bodyguard back to me."

Korul snorted. "Rise squires and tell me the truth."

Raven and Lark rose and looked at each other. Lark began, "Your majesty, it is as the Princess states. Lord Darnovam had plans to keep us from reaching you. We think he might have even employed a witch to prevent our escape."

Raven took up the tale. "We tried to rescue Ashera, the Lady's maid, and bodyguard, but it was not possible, so we had to proceed to bring Princess Illera here by ourselves."

Korul's hand struck quicker than a snake, smashing Raven across the mouth and sending blood spattering against the walls.

"How dare you, a lowly squire, use the given name of royalty. You befoul it in your stinking mouth," he roared.

Raven backed away and bowed his head. "Apologies your Majesty, my Lady."

Korul stomped to the throne. Uncertainly Illera followed, trailed by Lark and Raven. Sir Kyle moved to the King's right hand.

"Ah, yes, Illera, at last, we meet," he remarked as he stared her up and down, making her flesh squirm on her bones.

At the king's lack of action, she spoke, "Your majesty, pardon my asking, but why do you punish Raven for speaking my name but not Sir Kyle?"

Seated, the king grinned at her. "Sir Kyle is a knight in good standing in my army and head over many things in this house. Raven is stable sweepings."

"But it was my understanding that Lark and Raven were to be knighted as reward for their escorting me to this castle?"

Korul roared with laughter, laughing so long he had to hold his sides as the tears streamed down his face. The men gathered around the throne joined him.

"Ah, my dear, dear naive Princess, one says what one must to get the job done. I knew if I sent any of the others you would not make it here unsoiled, but Lark and Raven..." He had to stop for his bellows of mirth.

"Excuse me, your majesty, you mean..." enquired Lark timidly.

Korul rose from his seat, towering over the squire from the tall throne. "I mean you and your brother are fools and will remain as squires until you have absorbed enough of life to no longer be fools. If you wanted knighthood, you should have demanded it before the mission was accomplished. You have nothing to bargain with now."

Illera could see the hard set of Lark's and Raven's mouths and felt their disappointment running through her like blood. She was about to ask another question when a door slammed open. She turned. This had to be Torul. He was a carbon copy of his father with the exception of orange-red hair on his head and face. She could see the spoiled child in his face, one of angry self-absorption; all its lines spelled cruelty. She backed a step away from him. Korul rose and gestured him forward.

The King spoke formally, "Son, may I present to you, Illera, Princess, and daughter of King Ian of Madean, your betrothed. And Princess, I present my son, Torul, Prince and future King of Frain."

Illera curtsied as Torul moved towards her and grasped her hand. His was soft, cold and damp.

"My Lord Torul," she murmured.

His small colorless eyes roved up and down her body. One hand reached out, grabbed a breast, and squeezed. Illera pulled away, backing into Lark.

"Well, it seems I am the winner in this game of crowns. I was prepared for a hag of a wife, but you; yes, you are quite presentable. Come at once to my chambers so we may become better acquainted."

Illera's voice was frosty. "My Lord, you presume too much. I shall not go with you to your chambers until the vows have been said and recorded. And, my maid and bodyguard are missing. I cannot proceed with our wedding until Ashera has been found and restored to me."

Torul laughed, and it was an ugly sound. "You will do what you are told. I do not know what sort of freedoms your father gave, but here my word, and my father's is law. You will obey."

Her heart was thumping like a wild thing struggling to be free, and fear had turned her blood to ice water.

"I'm sorry my Lord, but your father just gave me a precious lesson on getting what I need first before I give what you want."

Korul and the men surrounding them chuckled. Torul's face flushed even redder and he lunged, seizing Illera by one wrist.

"Insolent wench, if you wanted your way it should have been before you arrived here."

Illera screamed, pulling backward with all her force, but she had no strength against the brute power of the Prince. Suddenly a sword whipped between them, pointing directly at Torul's throat. The Prince blanched releasing Illera's arm.

"We did not escort the Princess here to have her dishonored in front of her own people and ours," Raven snarled, his face a mask of hatred.

Lark had his sword out, protecting his brother's back. Korul was standing, icy rage in his eyes.

"Bring her in," the King bellowed.

Two of the men left at a run. Illera could hear her heart beating in the silence, as the room stood poised, waiting. Thud, thud, thud, breath was hard to draw in, as if even the air was reluctant to move in this frozen room. The sounds of feet and dragging vibrated on the flagstones. The two men returned, a limp figure slumped between them. They threw her at Illera's feet. A woman, face battered to anonymity, long pale hair streaming down her back, but clumps on the scalp bloody where handfuls had been ripped away. She was clad only in a thin shift of translucent material, blood visible in dried streaks down her legs and backside. Bruises on her hard flat breasts stood out in vivid detail through the cloth. Illera recoiled from this stranger. The woman moved, a faint croak issuing from her mangled throat and cracked teeth. Illera could not understand and bent closer to hear. Recognition and horror flooded through her, and she jumped back.

"Ashera?" She spun to face the King. "How could you do this to my servant?"

The King smirked at her. "When you ran away, I gave her to Torul in your place. After all, I promised him, and if you don't obey him that is what will happen to you too, so I advise you, DON'T PISS MY SON OFF."

Illera bent again to Ashera, willing healing into her broken body, giving her own strength.

Bending close, she whispered in one ravaged, bitten ear, "Ashera, if you love life come with me, follow me."

Illera rose, helping Ashera to her feet. "I want to go to my rooms now!" She used her most imperious voice.

Korul laughed. "Ask Torul where your rooms are,"

"Lark, Raven, get me out of here." Illera appealed to her last resource.

"If you make one move to help this bitch I will have you both killed and thrown to the dire wolves as bait. Your mother will join you in your fate."

Raven and Lark looked at each other. They nodded. Illera moved towards the door, the squires guarding her back, Ashera a dead weight on her shoulders. The soldiers scrambled for weapons and advanced towards them. A group of seven lunged between Illera and the brothers, driving her inward. The brothers fought their way to the doors and turned, noticing Illera's separation from them. Raven sprang forward; Illera sent him a message the way she did to animals, escape and be waiting to help. Throwing all her force behind Ashera, Illera ran for the stairs, bounding up them, pulling Ashera who spent her last energy to follow her mistress. Thighs burning and knees cramping they climbed, ignoring the corridors leading off from the landings. The stairs ended, and they raced down narrow corridors, their feet thudding on the rough wooden planks. The men were advancing slowly behind them; confident they could not escape. Illera and Ashera dashed into the room at the end of the hall, slamming and barring the door. Ashera collapsed in a heap on the floor, panting and heaving with a disturbing wheeze in her lungs.

The room was small and barren. A heap of dirty linens in one corner was the room's only furnishing. Illera went quickly to the window and threw open the shutters. Her heart sank at the sight of heavy metal bars blocking the way out. She turned as a heavy pounding on the door shook the little room.

"Open this up right now, and we can settle things properly," demanded the voice of Torul.

Illera waited silent and frozen by the window, exhaustion making her muscles shake.

"Fine, stay there until you starve. I'll give you one week to think about things, and then I'll break the door down, and the day I do that I'll be sending troops to Madean to conquer it. So think about it. You have one week to come out and accept your fate, or your country will be destroyed."

Sick at heart, Illera slumped to the floor, crying out for her mother, begging for help to resolve this horrible situation. Tears came then, burning from her eyes until they made a pool on the floor. Illera stared at the reflection, wondering how she could fix this. Like a cool caress in her mind blew the answer, repair what you can, one step at a time.

Taking a deep breath, she moved to Ashera. Opening the bag at her belt, she set out to heal the woman she had left behind.

CHAPTER 7

*A*shera curled into a corner, covered with the filthy rags. Unable to settle down, Illera paced the small space; four steps across, then eight steps from window to door and repeat. In the last two days she had brought about a physical healing of the giantess, but her broken mind was beyond Illera's skills. She worked herself to the edges of exhaustion and still, Ashera gazed vacantly at the walls. She would respond to direct commands, but initiated nothing on her own, nor responded to queries. Illera longed for the tools to reach her, make her bold and arrogant again.

The soft scratching vibrated through the door again. Several times during their incarceration they heard the same sound. This time, Illera lay on her belly and peered through the wide crack underneath the thick, rough planking. A pair of small feet wearing poorly tanned leather moccasins shuffled beyond. Bony ankles protruded, rising to a ragged fringe of tattered brown material. Illera scrambled to her feet and cautiously opened the door a crack, ready to slam and bolt it should a man appear.

The old lady scratched again on the door's splintery surface. She had tangled red and gray hair in a mat about her face. Her head lolled to one side, and one shoulder was markedly higher than the other. Her brown dress was ripped, soiled and very frayed. A dirty gray shawl draped around her shoulders and was clutched to her scrawny bosom with one skeletal hand. Illera opened the door and the woman hobbled in. She closed and bolted it again.

"Hello," she told the strange old lady.

The crone breathed, "Ha a aa."

She tottered to Ashera and crouched down beside her. The bony fingers brushed the tangled locks from the younger woman's face.

"Paaaa a baaabeee." She looked at Illera.

"Yes, mother, Ashera has been badly treated. Can you help her?"

The old woman shook her head violently back and forth alarming Illera who wondered if the frail neck could support such vehemence.

Pointing to herself she said, "Daaaalllllaaaaa, maaaaa Torul."

Puzzled Illera frowned. "Do you mean you are Torul's mother?"

The old woman nodded and began to cry, great sobs shaking her narrow shoulders. Illera sat down beside her and put her arms around the old lady, who turned her head and sobbed on Illera's breast, wetting the fabric of her blouse. The storm of weeping passed, and she became a dead weight in the younger woman's arms. Illera lay her on the floor beside Ashera and covered her with her own leather cloak. Rising she went to look out the window for the thousandth time.

The rain still pounded down, never stopping. Illera thought it must be extremely depressing to live where it rained so hard for days on end. Far below, the inner bailey was covered with a sheet of water, making a gray, rain pitted lake around the keep. She wished it would wash the castle away and free her from this dilemma.

With a shriek, the old woman bolted upright. Ashera started at the noise.

"It's alright, Ashera, this is Torul's mother." Illera placed an arm around her shoulders.

Ashera pulled away from her as though she were a poisonous snake, huddling as deep as she could get into the corner and making whimpering noises in the back of her throat. The old woman looked at her, then lurched to her feet. Her mouth pulled back in a grimace, exposing missing teeth. Hands outstretched she hobbled towards the door, pulling the bolt and leaving the door open as she staggered into the corridor. Illera dashed across the room and slammed the door, bolting it shut behind the retreating figure.

"It's okay now Ashera, she's gone," Illera told her gently, moving back to the writhing figure.

Ashera buried her face in the corner and would not look at her. Moving back to the window, she struck the sill with her fist, but it brought no relief, and neither did shaking the bars with all her strength. They were as solid as the door barring Torul from reaching them. Illera curled into the corner opposite Ashera and tried to sleep, but the cold and damp seeped into her bones, and she was unable to drift off. The walls and floor stole away body heat faster than it could be generated, so all she could do was shiver. Rising, she paced the floor again, a trapped animal in a cage.

The scratching was back at the door. Sighing, Illera looked underneath again. She saw nothing but the old woman's feet. At least it was a diversion from the thoughts and accusations marching through her brain. Cautiously, she opened the door. The lady straightened her crooked spine as much as she was able, thrusting a parcel wrapped in thick white linen into Illera's hands. Turning, she shuffled off down the corridor. Illera closed and bolted the door.

The package was warm and fragrant. Illera unwrapped it. A

dozen bread rolls oozing butter nearly dropped to the floor. Hastily Illera set them down. Beneath the bread, there was a layer of beef, warm and succulent. Illera's mouth watered. Wrapped separately she found a dozen large red apples smelling of sunshine and happiness.

"Ashera, come, let's eat," She bit into a roll, and the butter dribbled down her chin.

Ashera huddled in her corner. Illera divided the food and took a generous portion to the other woman. When it was placed in her hands, she began to eat, tearing into the bread and meat like an eagle on a carcass. Illera had all she could do not to bolt her own. She placed ten of the apples in her herb bag and reattached it to her belt. The room felt warmer after the food, but still, the rain pelted the castle, swaddling it in thick bands of gloom.

Pacing back to the window Illera watched a spot of darkness sailing towards her. The shape resolved into a bird, a black and white familiar form. With bated breath, Illera saw the soaking avian blown backward in the strong winds. It struggled mightily, then the wind dropped it, and it fell from sight below the window.

Placing her face as close as she could get, Illera still could not see the little form. It popped up, landing on the sill and startling Illera, so she stepped back, tripped over Ashera's outstretched legs and tumbled to the floor.

"Maggie, am I glad to see you. Gods know what you can do about this horrible situation, but I'm glad you are here. I thought something awful must have happened to you after that fight with the dragon."

The little bird cocked her head to one side and scolded Illera. Illera laughed. Shaking the water droplets from her feathers, she began to preen and scold as if Illera were at fault for the rain. Illera watched her with pleasure, happy to have one friend to share this imprisonment. Now her life-long friend was here, Illera knew she had to make an effort to escape.

The darkness increased, creeping from the corners to the middle of the room, blanketing everything with the same stygian cover. Maggie squawked and hopped to the door. Taking a deep breath and hoping, Illera sent a call to Lark and Raven: 'We're coming, get ready.'

She woke Ashera by shaking her shoulder. "We have to go now. You must stay right with me. Don't go away. Do exactly what I do or tell you to do. Do you understand?"

The blonde's eyes focused momentarily on Illera's. She nodded but then her eyes unfocused and wandered to the corners of the room. They approached the door together. Illera drew the bolt, praying for silence. It grated only slightly. She peeped out of the door. The corridor was deserted as far as she could tell with all the shadows. Torches were so widely spaced fifty men could hide in the intervals between the light. They tiptoed into the hallway. No movements were visible; no sounds audible, only their hushed breathing. Maggie poked her in the ear. With Ashera on her heels, they padded to the stairs. Runnels of water trickled down the corridor and puddles were revealed only by the drip, drip, drip from the leaky roof.

Pausing, Illera strained her senses to detect the presence of people, but only the sounds of drumming rain, howling wind and the groan of stone rubbing stone broke the silence. Carefully they eased down the stairs. Many were slick with water and Illera had to watch her feet lest she step in a puddle and crash down the staircase.

They were at the third landing, pausing before the descent to the next level. A rough hand snapped out of an inky pool nearly breaking Illera's arm.

"Now, now my little bride, just where would you be sneaking off to in the middle of the night? I can think of a cozy nest for the two of us," Torul hissed in her ear.

Ashera, catching sight of his face shrieked loud enough to wake the dead and bolted down the stairs at a dead run. Illera twisted in his grasp, bringing her knee up and into his private parts as hard as she could. As the air whooshed out of his lungs, Illera bolted after her maid, leaping down the stairs two at a time.

"You won't get away," Torul screamed in a high voice.

He hobbled after them, clasping the handrail with one hand and still half bent over. Illera flew down the stairs, her feet barely touching the stone and sliding through the puddles. Maggie launched from her shoulder and flew into Torul's face beating her wings about him. He let go of the handrail to fend her away as his heel splashed into a puddle. His feet slipped out from under him, and he catapulted forward, hurtling past Illera and bowling Ashera down the last three steps. From her position above, Illera heard the crack as he landed.

Rushing downward, she picked Ashera from the heap in the great hall. The light was already dimming in Torul's colorless eyes as she checked him and she knew she could do nothing for him. Pulling the larger woman along by the hand, she raced for the door. Sounds of men stirring were coming from all around.

They dashed through the door racing for the nearest pool of darkness between the torches. Illera halted abruptly, holding her breath as guards trotted by heading for the great room. As they passed the doorway, the women ran for the next shadow and the next until they had reached the outer doors of the keep. The commotion was rising behind them, so heedless of guards posted outside; Illera whipped open one leaf of the doors and hurried out, closing it securely behind them. The post was empty. Wind whipped the rain about in blinding sheets.

Uncertain of her direction, Illera whispered to Maggie, "Stables."

The bird fluttered ahead, and Illera followed the patch of white on her back. As they descended the stairs, the water came up to meet them, swamping their boots and soaking their feet with icy draughts. Illera plunged on, towing Ashera behind her. She could see nothing but the small pale spot of Maggie straight ahead. Colliding with the stable door, she bruised one wrist. Fumbling along the wood, she located the string and pulled it to lift the inside bar. The door groaned open a couple of inches, and they slipped inside.

It was a physical shock to be out of the storm, and Illera leaned against the door for long minutes trying to get her breath and orientation. Ashera shivered beside her and Maggie gurgled an incomprehensible message. The warm smell of horse and hay enfolded them.

"My Lady, would you take Abbadon," a voice in front of her requested.

Illera jumped with a sharp intake of breath. A warm muzzle thrust into her hands and a washcloth of a tongue wiped the water from the front of her cloak. A rustling beside her made her turn.

"I brought decent clothes and a cloak for Ashera," the voice told her.

"Lark?" Illera asked, uncertain in the impenetrable dark.

She heard a low laugh. "Yes my Lady, who else but your humbled squire. I need you to bring Abbadon; he won't let me near him."

She nodded, then chuckled for Lark could see no more than she could.

"Yes."

She felt hands lifting her and swung her leg over the saddle.

"This is Copper and here are Abbadon's reins."

Sounds of movement around her and then the door sprang open. She kicked Copper forward. The mare balked, not wanting to dare the storm. Illera was firm, and she moved forward. Appolon surged into the lead followed by an unfamiliar dark horse with Ashera riding. Illera kicked Copper and pulled Abbadon who forced his way ahead.

Appolon's tail was the beacon this time, and Maggie took refuge under Illera's cloak. The water was fetlock deep on the big horses, and they made loud sloshing noises moving through it. Torches outlined the castle door now, their wan light not penetrating to the stables and the downpour doused the flame if the torchbearer left the shelter of the keep.

The guard at the inner gateway lay dead, impaled by his own sword. Lark lifted the bars while still mounted and pulled the doors wide. They came with a rush and horde of peasants behind them. The people surged in, as relentless as the tide, pushing the horses back towards the stable. Lark commanded them to part and allow passage, but the mob was stampeding forward. Appolon forged ahead, and they made their way to the outer bailey. Here the flood had reached deadly proportions. Most of the peasants were in waist deep water, water that rose to the breasts of the horses. Desperate to escape to higher ground, the mob was frantic and near to violence. Lark moved aside from the horde.

The horses pushed through stragglers and water coming at last to the barbican towers. Chest deep in water, Raven grasped Lark's outstretched hand and vaulted to Appolon's back.

"The guards are tied," he yelled, "but I have to go up the tower to raise the portcullis. I'll meet you outside on the approach."

He slipped back to the water and waded to the stairs, disappearing into the thicker gloom inside. Minutes later the gates screamed in protest and slowly began to rise. The dammed water rushed out the narrow opening in a mill race down the approach. Illera, lying flat on Copper's neck, squeezed through pulling Abbadon. Ashera followed closely and Lark as soon as the gate had risen high enough.

Bellows rang through the darkness behind them, sounds of men running, weapons and armor clashing.

"Go," yelled Lark.

"We can't," Illera snapped back, "Raven's still in there."

Lark slapped Copper on the rump with the flat of his sword and she bolted down the steep and winding approach. Illera's heart was in her mouth as the mare skidded around the curves and slipped into the river flowing down the road. At the bottom, the mare pulled up, legs shaking, her whole body quivering. Ashera's mount stopped beside them, joined by Lark.

"Wait and watch." He pointed to the top of the barbican tower.

Illera could just make out a speck of a figure standing beside the pennant. Another figure joined the first, carrying a swinging lantern. A high ululating cry pierced the night and rain and the first figure dove from the battlement, arching downward to splash into the moat, not twenty feet from where they waited.

Raven swam to the edge and hoisted himself out, shaking the slime and mud from himself like a dog. He trotted to Illera and grabbed Abbadon's reins. Swinging aboard, he turned the black stallion east, and they all galloped into the streaming night. Looking back once under her arm, Illera saw lights and horses starting down the curve of the approach. She faced forward and urged Copper to her best speed.

The weather improved not at all, becoming colder and windier as the night progressed. The rain continued to fall in torrents. Making good time on the flooded roads, the horses trotted, and there were no eyes abroad to see where they went. Raven stopped to let the horses breath and reined next to Illera.

"The next decision is yours, my Lady. I think we should attempt the Swamp of Ghosts and Lark figures we should head south to your father. Whichever way we go, Korul and Torul are going to pursue."

"Torul is dead. He won't be chasing us."

"You killed Torul?" Raven's voice in the dark was incredulous.

Illera shook her head. "No, he slipped on the stairs and broke his neck. I had nothing to do with it. Well, nothing other than trying to run away from him. Why do you think we should try the swamp?"

"If Korul is sure we are in the swamp, he will spend his time chasing us. If we head to your father, it means war for his kingdom. Immediately. If we can get away, some people can be sent with a message to King Ian and warn him of what is going to happen. In fact, we have already arranged for my stepfather to take such a message and he should have left a couple of days ago. Korul will attack Madean regardless, but he will be so furious that I think he will chase us first and give your father time to prepare. But it is your decision."

Unhesitatingly she replied, "The swamp."

Lark nodded, and they crept ahead with the rain driving them forward. The horses followed Appolon, treading in his tracks. The ground sucked and pulled at the animal's hooves. Copper often stumbled, once nearly pitching Illera to the water, but she pulled her back to her feet, and they continued at a claudicant pace.

Pale blue and yellow lights winked on then vanished in the depths of the swamp. Moss covered trees were interspersed with tall grass reaching higher than the backs of the horses, all waiting to dump their burden of moisture on the riders. Vines strung their lengths from one tree to the next tying them together into a maze. Several times Illera heard the slither and splash of large animals moving from their wending path.

They eased deeper into the swamp. Lark found a hummock rising from the water. The grass was shorter there, and while the trees surrounded it, it gave them a clearing in which to rest. The thick leaves blunted the force of the rain, reducing it to random drops. They dismounted to let the steaming, shaking horses rest.

CHAPTER 8

*S*eated cross-legged on the soggy ground, Illera stared out at the pouring rain. The drops that dribbled through the leafy canopy overhead, made runnels down her sodden cloak. Her mind was as dismal as the weather, caught up in visions of unending war between Frain and Madean, her beloved people torn from the land and the brutal Korul master of the wide golden plains. Because she could not subject herself to the cruel and loathsome Torul, her land was going to be destroyed. Silent, hot tears slid from her eyes and joined the rivulets coursing down her cloak. The sky was growing lighter, emphasizing the darkness that lay upon her soul. Maggie uttered sleepy comments from under her outer garment, stirring from time to time. As much as her mind shied away from the idea, she had to accept it; she had ruined Madean.

Lark hunkered down beside her. "What is the matter, my Lady? Did Torul hurt you?"

Raven joined them, looming over their low crouching shapes like one of the ghosts of the swamp.

"I have destroyed Madean." Illera choked. "Korul will invade.

My father will fight, and the people will join him. They will all be destroyed because they are farmers and herders, not warriors. Korul will take the land, and pollute it and ruin it. There will be generations of war as Madean tries to throw off Frain's yolk, and it is all my fault because I could not accept that, that loathsome worm of a prince."

Lark shook his head. "Surely it is not as grim as all that."

Raven knelt beside her and put an arm around her shoulders. Turning her face into his shoulder, Illera sobbed, her heart broken. Her pain of soul was a shard of glass piercing and slicing her emotions to bloody meat; grinding her spirit to grisly tatters.

"Illera, look," called Lark softly, rising slowly to his feet.

She looked up with bleary eyes. Rounded shapes moved through the heavy rain coming towards her. A doe and fawn stopped a few feet from them and lowered their heads to nibble the short grass. Half a dozen rabbits hopped around Illera's feet while the trees fill up with a rainbow of birds, all twittering and rustling. Two black ducks waddled from the water, shaking their pinions dry. Their anxious quacks brought a small smile to her face. A tufted-eared head peeked around the bole of a tree; the slit pupils widened to round circles. The bobcat crept forward, belly to the ground until it could lay its head in Illera's lap.

"They don't want you to be sad," Raven stepped away from her. "Your tears upset them."

Illera looked up at him and smiled. "I didn't call them. They came on their own."

"All the wild things love you," he replied with a strange, far away look on his face. "And that is a great blessing."

The rain stopped. One moment the downpour was hurtling from the sky, the next, only the burden of droplets from the trees was falling to earth and water. The wind, however, continued, moaning through the swamp like the voices of dying children. Illera sang to the wild creatures in the key of the wind. They listened, perched or crouched in positions to watch the liquid notes stream from her throat; then they drifted back into the dim recesses of their home as her song ended; all except the bobcat. The sky was lightening as the clouds parted and watery morning sunshine leaked down into the open spaces. Stroking the cat, Illera stood.

"Where do we go from here?"

Raven shrugged as Lark responded, "I'm not sure, my Lady. I know that Korul will be hunting for us."

"What lies west of here?"

Raven replied, "If we go straight west, most of the way is swamp. There is a high set of hills, almost mountains, then the Bay of Hostages, where Korul slaughtered the women and children he held hostage from Sorwelk when the tribute was late. It is deserted and said to be haunted, so it's avoided by all. If we travel straight north, we reach the Black Sea, probably somewhere by the North Bay. A few fishermen are living there, and they are all loyal to Korul. East lies the castle as you know and to the south, we can reach the prairie and the forest and your home."

Illera thought. "I think the safest place is probably the Bay of Hostages. What do you think?"

Lark snorted and walked away. Raven watched him, then turned to Illera.

"I think it needs to be your decision, my Lady. If we head west, it means probably a week or more struggling through this mess with the danger of quicksand, or mud pits and nowhere to rest or cook a hot meal. I would say there are dangerous animals in the swamp, but then you are with us. But, when we get out of the swamp we have those high hills to get over before reaching the Bay. It will be an arduous trip."

"Lark, what's your opinion?"

Lark swung around to face them. "I think we should head north. We could reach the ocean in a day or two at the most. I don't think Ashera is up to wading through this muck to get to the Bay of Hostages."

"What about the fishermen?"

"Yeah, Lark, you remember how terrified they were of King Korul the last time we went that way. They would sell their own children to please him, and I can see them being quick to turn us over to earn his gratitude." Raven kicked at the ground with his booted foot.

"That man has no gratitude!" Lark shook his fist in their direction.

"But the fishermen don't know that," Raven argued.

"It's the Lady's decision." Lark turned away.

Illera thought, turning to look at Ashera, slumped on the ground, her pale blue eyes vacant and staring. She walked over to her and pulled her to a sitting position. Running her hands a few inches from the big woman's body, Illera made her decision.

"We head west. Ashera is physically fine and strong. It's just her mind that's broken."

Lark snorted and moved to boost Ashera onto her sturdy bay mount. Raven gave Illera a leg up, and the brothers mounted. The bobcat yowled at them and moved a few steps into the swamp.

"What does he want?" snapped Lark, his lips tight.

"He is our guide," Illera urged Copper after the cat.

"This is crazy, wandering through the Swamp of Ghosts after a bobcat."

Raven buffeted his brother on the shoulder. "Quiet Lark, or I will think you've lost faith. Whatever happens, this is our grand adventure."

Raven laughed, and Lark joined him, sharing a joke of which only the brothers were aware. As the horses stepped gingerly onto the waterlogged path, they trailed after Illera and Ashera.

The bobcat led them on concealed animal traces where the water was only hoof deep. Frequently they came to tussocks and humps covered with grass where the horses could graze and the riders rest. Mud pits bubbled, and other places of smooth, unruffled sand, open and invited their presence. Always, either near or at a distance the wailing voice of the wind, crying and crying until their nerves were as taut as a drawn bowstring. When the light levels sank low for the evening, or because of the denseness of the vegetation, the witch lights flickered and danced in many colors, crimson, blue, clear yellow, uneasy purple and evil green. The bobcat avoided these spurts of illumination, even reversing direction if one should suddenly appear on their line of travel. So they wove their way through the swamp, from dry ground to dry ground heading generally west.

The days lurched by in an uneasy procession, punctuated by the strange moans and heart-stopping screams from the recesses of the vegetation. The bobcat advanced circumspectly, in jerks and starts and switched directions often. The travelers were lost, trusting in Illera's way with wildlife to see them to safety. Ashera remained distant, obeying direct orders but still lost in the shattered recesses of her own mind. More than any of the others, she seemed to belong to this mournful place of flickering ghost lights and unnerving noises. Illera herself felt the hand of severe depression on her soul, her mind running in circles and terrified that again she had chosen the wrong path. She sank into silent continuous reverie and always the ache for Madean plagued her, an unhealing abscess on her spirit. On the fifth day of wandering, the bobcat led them to a larger hump of grass than usual. When they settled, he vanished into the darkening damp to hunt. Lark and Raven made camp while Illera settled Ashera onto a rude pallet.

"My Lady," Lark began, shuffling his feet, "all day today, we headed north, judging by the direction of the sun. It seems to me that we are making little progress toward our goal and perhaps we would be better served by striking out on our own rather than follow your furry friend."

Illera looked up from her position next to Ashera, and rose.

She stared out at the dismal surroundings. Except for the narrow bridge of soil, this tussock was an island, surrounded by dark, evil-smelling water and enclosed by wet and towering trees that seemed to stoop towards them for some evil purpose. She sighed.

"Does it matter?"

"What, my Lady?"

"Does it matter if we are lost? If Korul is chasing us, and we don't know if he is or isn't, but if he is, then the longer we take to traverse this place the more likely it is that he and his men will meet with some accident. That is all the better for us is it not?"

"Of course it would be, if Korul were chasing us, but how do we know?"

Illera called Maggie to her outstretched hand. The bird alighted with a flurry of wings. She whispered commands to the magpie and tossed her into the air. The bird climbed into the darkening sky and faded from view. Illera turned to Lark.

"Maggie will circle the swamp and tell us if there are others in here with us."

Lark paused, staring deeply into her eyes. "But if we don't find our way out soon we will be in trouble. The grain for the horses is starting to run short, and we have only a few more days of food left for ourselves. And pardon my saying so, but my Lady, you look near the limit of your endurance."

She smiled. "My endurance may be more than you calculate Lark. It is not the physical hardship that is taking a toll, but my concern for Madean. The more of Korul's men who die in the swamp, the less there will be to attack my home. I could spend the rest of my life wandering here if it would save my country."

Raven wandered over, depositing the tack on the ground.

"But you still don't know if Korul has followed us," Lark argued.

"No," Illera replied, "and that is why I worry."

"I wouldn't worry, my Lady," Raven interjected, "Korul loved nothing else on this earth except himself and his son. I can't see him destroying Madean until he has you in his power so you can watch the destruction. Then he will kill you slowly."

Lark snorted. "If you were so good at knowing what Korul will do, why didn't you predict that he would cheat us out of our knighthoods?"

Raven smiled and punched his brother on the shoulder. "Okay, I know nothing. I was just trying to cheer Illera up."

Lark pushed him back, and they ended up wrestling on the damp grass like children. The good-natured gibes and tussling left her unmoved, when normally she would laugh at the sight of grown men behaving thus. Illera watched for a few moments, then wandered to the edge of their little island. The ground fell off suddenly and a pebble dislodged by her toe made a deep plunk. She edged back from the brink. She began a circuit of the space to stretch her legs, cramped for hours on the horse. Ducking under low hanging branches and looping vines, her eyes chanced upon a large swathe of pale green. She reached forward and picked a handful. It looked like the same as the healing moss she used. She tasted it. Stretching forward over the roots of a large tree she collected all she could reach. There was still a copious amount hanging from the higher branches.

Illera clambered up onto the root, balancing with her feet wide apart on the algae slicked surface. She stretched and harvested more medicine, packing it into her bag. She was reaching for a final handful when her outside foot slipped, and she toppled face first into the dark water. She flailed for the surface, breaking through and gasping for air. The island seemed a mile away, and she wondered how she got so far from shore. She yelled for the squires as she tried an inexperienced paddle to the tree, but hard as she struggled, the further the land became.

The screening foliage burst apart, revealing Lark and Raven. She beat the water harder and kicked with all her might, but only succeeded in staying in the same place. Her strength was beginning to fail, and inexorably she was dragged away. Raven disappeared while Lark stood with mouth open, yelling instructions that she could not hear with the water in her ears. A sharp bump on her backside catapulted her body half out of the water. A scaly back slid past her face. Illera kicked harder, but still, the island drew further away. Raven popped back through the brush, a rope in his hands. He threw with all his might. It landed ten feet away. Illera struggled to reach the line, making almost half the distance. The reptile bumped her again, the rough and scaly hide acting like sandpaper and removing the skin from the back of one hand. She tried to push away from it, but it surfaced and seizing her arm, pulled her under the water. It rolled around and around, banging her head against the bottom, disorienting her and shaking her senseless. Her lungs were aching for air, and she felt she must breathe, even if it was water she inhaled. It released her, and she bobbed back to the surface, drawing great draughts of air into her aching lungs.

Disoriented she looked around. She could not see Lark, or Raven, or the rope. She could not tell which hump had been the one she came from. The reptile bumped her again. She struggled in the water, trying to see it. She tried to sing, but her lungs were too painful, and her blood starved for oxygen, making her voice a croak. Her arm was bleeding, forty or more large puncture holes making darker trails in the already black water. She called and told the reptile to go away, leave her alone. It bumped her again raising her body halfway from the swamp.

The predator shoved her to an island with a semi-circular bay. Suddenly, many little reptiles, all croaking and singing with voices like bullfrogs surrounded her. An inch to three inches long, they were long-tailed, with glowing yellow eyes that protruded from their miniature heads. The long delicate snouts opened to jaws lined with fringes of fine needle teeth. They encircled her, nipping with their sharp fangs, bumping and pulling on her skin. The large one, she assumed to be the mother, guarded her way out. Illera paddled for the steeply wooded shore, but the babies were thick, impeding her progress. The adult roared, a stunning vibration through the water and the little ones attacked in earnest. Illera flipped positions, rotating to face the mother and the open water and roared herself using both voice and mind. The reptiles froze. The little ones slithered to the adult, a plethora of tiny vees in the water. The adult opened its mouth, and the babies hurried inside. With one baleful yellow glare, the beast dove from sight and glided away followed by an arrow of water.

Illera struggled to the hump of land and catching a trailing vine, hauled herself from the water. She collapsed, gasping in pain and relief over an algae slimed root. Gathering her courage and strength, she rose and staggered inward. In the middle of the grass cloaking the center of the tussock, a pure blue flame flickered. She crouched down beside a twisted tree and watched the light; bleeding from a myriad of small punctures as well as the wounds down one arm. A strange fey feeling came over her, as if the consequence did not matter anymore. Her head spun crazily, and a wild giggle bubbled up from her throat. All the pain and fatigue vanished. Her body was miles away, and she was as tall as the surrounding trees as she rose and strode to the light. It hovered a foot above the ground and rose to a peak high over her head, about the height of Abbadon's ears. She could hear the faintest of hissing noises. It was a mesmerizing sound, regular, soft and enticing. Stopping about two feet away, she watched as the light brightened and dimmed, beckoning, calling. It danced for her. Moving sideways in a circle around the light she inspected it from every angle.

Her hand moved of its own volition, passing through the middle. It was not hot, rather it was colder than the air, and it brightened to a clear yellow where her hand passed. Looking down at her left hand, she noticed it glowed blue with clear yellow edges, the same colors as the flame, brightening and darkening as it did. Fascinated she watched her hand and the fire, lost in the radiant color and the drone of sound. Without willing it, her feet moved, and she stepped into the fire. The breath exhaled from her lungs, and distantly she knew she must move or die, but it was a far away notion, languid and unimportant. Exerting the power of her mind, she moved out of the phenomenon and gasped for air. She turned, but the light had vanished leaving only the drone and darkness, the pitch darkness of the middle of the night. Looking down, she could see that she glowed with the colors. She moved back to the spot where the flame had started, amused to note that her feet did not touch the ground, but now she floated above the surface as the flame had hovered a foot from the ground. Joy welled up in her, bursting over her in a fashion she had never felt before, taking her to dizzying heights. Serenity spread through her, and she thought, "Perhaps I am dead."

Inspecting the small grassy area, she grew restless, remembering Lark, Raven, and Ashera. She tried to find a trail with her feet, stepping down to the water, but her feet stopped above the surface. Daring, she bobbed out from the island, floating on the surface of the swamp water. She laughed inside herself and willed her presence forward. She went to the spot where she had crawled ashore and walked out from there, searching for the island where her companions were. She glided over the dark water, exhilarated by this new form of progress. The current had pushed her away from the island, so she took a shred of moss and tossed it on the water. It moved swiftly behind her, so she floated against the current, tossing the moss to determine the right direction.

An hour's gliding on the swamp brought her to a larger hump of land. Peering closer with the glow from herself, she could see gouges in the algae on the roots of one large tree. She hovered up over the roots and onto the land, willing herself in the direction that they had set up the camp. She heard the sound of horses cropping grass, the odd stamping of a hoof vibrated through the soil and her cocoon of light. Moving inward and around many of the looming trees she caught sight of a small fire in the middle of the grassy area, around which were Lark, Raven, and Ashera. Her heart was singing with joy as she approached them.

Ashera was facing her, and her eyes widened, her face contorting into a mask of horror. A scream of utter terror ripped from her throat. Lark and Raven surged to their feet, drawing swords and whirling to face Illera. Illera smiled and held out a hand as Ashera scuttled backward, trying to hide beneath the saddles.

"Begone demon of our Princess," commanded Lark with a quaver in his voice.

Their swords were pointed right at her heart.

"No, you don't understand."

Lark lunged at her. She skipped aside feeling the breeze of the sword passing through where she had been. Raven stood frozen staring at her. His face was pale and the blue eyes wide with fear, the first she had ever seen in him.

"No," commanded Illera, "don't. There is nothing wrong with me. It's just some kind of coating I picked up. I'm not dead."

Raven's sword wavered.

"Raven," yelled Lark, "It's a trick. The demon is trying to trick you."

Illera held out a beseeching hand. The fire glowed and writhed down her fingers, dancing and flickering with a hypnotic rhythm. Raven sheathed his sword.

"Raven, don't!" yelled Lark.

Turning to his brother, Raven said, "I don't care Lark. What have I got except my service to the Princess now? I would rather be with her in death than by myself in Korul's kingdom."

He stepped forward and clasped her hand. Illera felt the light draining from her into him. She settled gently to the grass. The ground was hard under her feet again. Raven glowed with a pale,

pale blue, faded from the brighter hue she had worn. His feet floated six inches above the grass. He laughed.

"Hey Lark, it doesn't hurt."

Lark glared at Illera, suspicious, gradually lowering his sword. Raven approached him. "Try," He held out a hand.

Lark clasped the hand, and the color flowed to him, diminishing even more in intensity. Raven turned to Illera, grinning. She smiled, wanting to participate in this new game but the serenity and joy had flowed from her to the flame. Her knees shook, and her lungs wearied from drawing breath. Exhaustion felled her like a blow to the head and Illera collapsed into a trembling heap. The brothers carried her to the fire and wrapped her in her cloak. They exchanged the glow again, and the radiance faded to barely discernable.

Something was nudging her back; a rhythmic shove, shove, shove, forcing her from slumber and pulling her mind from the depths of darkness. She forced her sticky eyelids to open a crack, perceiving the pearly light of early morning. A deep thrumming sound vibrated from behind her. Her eyes were so heavy; it was as if rocks were weighing down her lashes. Somewhere below, in the deep recesses of her mind, an alarm was shrilling, but she was tired. She wanted only to sleep. She felt so heavy, heavier than the war-horses, heavier than a castle, heavier than the world.

Sharp prickles now accompanied the shoving, piercing through her clothing and the cloying somnolence. Illera rolled over onto her back, peering into the golden eyes of the bobcat. Each limb felt as if it weighed as much as Copper and it took all her strength to lift one heavy hand and look at it. It looked odd to her weary eyes. It was her hand but covered with an ashy gray substance that flaked away when she rubbed her fingers together. The bobcat yowled at her as she let her hand collapse to her side, too heavy to hold aloft. Maggie winged down from the sky and sat on her chest, poking her in the chin, urging her to rise.

"Can't Maggie. Too tired."

A sharp beak thrust coupled with a claws-extended swat from the feline brought her bolt upright with pain.

"Hey, leave me alone," she yelled, her patience as short as her energy.

The bobcat backed away a few paces, but Maggie insolently squawked at her, urging some action. Illera tried to concentrate, but her mind was full of cobwebs. She looked around the campsite. The fire was dead; Lark and Raven sound asleep to one side. On the other side, Ashera stared at her with vacant eyes, and a thin runnel of drool coursing from her gaping mouth down over her chin. The sun was high overhead. That did not seem right, seconds ago, it was early morning, and Lark and Raven were always up early setting the camp in order so they could leave. Everything was wrong.

Illera forced herself to hands and knees, unable to summon the ability to rise. She crawled to Raven and collapsed beside him gasping for breath. She closed her eyes for a second, but Maggie was insistent, chattering in her ear and poking with her beak in all the tender places. The cat circled and yowled at her, dashing in for a slap every few circuits. Illera forced her eyes open. The short shadows of noon startled her mind, making a bounding panic underlie the irresistible waves of exhaustion.

Requiring her body to obey her mind, she got to her knees and shook Raven as hard as she could. He too was covered with the fine ashy residue that puffed away as she touched him. An incoherent groan was all she could elicit from him. She drew her hand back and struck him as hard as she was able across the face, his dark stubble scratching her palm. The deep blue eyes opened momentarily, unfocused. As the lids drooped again, Illera screamed at him. Briefly, consciousness flickered, then dimmed as his eyes sagged shut. She turned to Ashera.

"Come here," she commanded, fighting against the tide of sleep that threatened to overwhelm her.

Ashera rose and stumbled over.

"Don't let me go to sleep. Hit me if you have too, but don't let me sleep. Do you understand?"

Ashera stared at her vaguely. Illera tried to force her mind to think clearly. The bobcat prowled around them tense and nervous, and Maggie was gurgling and chattering, trying to convey some message. Illera stared and tried to concentrate. What had she asked the bird to find out? The answer rose in her brain like fish to bait.

"Is Korul in the swamp?"

Maggie gurgled and hopped up and down.

"Is he close to us?"

Now the bird became frantic, launching herself into the air and swooping in circles around Illera's head.

Fear blossomed in her, temporarily drowning out the fatigue. She rose to her feet and staggered to the horses, saddling and bridling the four of them. Hastily, with no organization, she threw their supplies into saddlebags and tied them to the saddles. She tottered to Lark, pushing him and shoving him to try to wake him. He refused to budge. She was frantic; her panic was beginning to break through. She used it to fuel her motions, fed it, thinking of the tortures Korul would inflict on her and her companions. She took a kettle from the pack and staggered, half crawling to the closest edge of the water. There she filled it with swamp water. Returning, she dumped it over Lark and Raven. Lark spluttered and sat up suddenly. Raven rolled away from her and closed his eyes again. Illera shook Lark's shoulders.

"You have to wake up. Something has happened to us and sucked away all our energy. I think it might have been the blue flame because Ashera is fine, but we have to get moving. It's afternoon and Korul is in the swamp and Maggie says he is close."

Lark looked at her vaguely, and Illera was not sure her message got through to him.

"Help me wake up Raven."

Lark rose, shaky on his feet and stumbled to his brother. Illera went to fetch another kettle of water. Staring at her reflection in the swamp, she noticed she was covered with the gray flakes. Setting the kettle aside, she washed her face. Immediately she noticed a difference. The fatigue, while still present faded somewhat. With that, she scrubbed herself earnestly, making sure every crevasse and fold of her skin was clean. The ashy and oily residue floated away, making a thick scum on the surface of the water. By the time she was done, her mind was clear, and although her body still longed to rest, it would obey her orders. She filled the kettle and returned to the camp. Lark was sleeping again.

Getting a rag from the saddlebags she washed, first Raven then Lark, clearing their exposed skin of the residue. Raven woke as she finished and sat up holding his head in his hands.

As she was cleaning his brother, she spoke. "I think we have to hurry and leave. Something happened to us last night, and we have slept the day away. That flame left some kind of ash on us that is draining our energy, and Korul is in the swamp, and he is close. We have to get moving. Shit man, move it."

He staggered to his feet without replying and made it to the horses. Hanging onto Abbadon's saddle he vomited into the short grass, spewing bile about the horses' hooves. The animal skittered aside.

Lark opened his eyes and focused on Illera's face. Sitting up, he too was sick, hurling the contents of his stomach towards her. Illera jumped aside just in time. She led Ashera to her horse and got her mounted. Raven seemed unable to get a foot in the stirrup, so she guided him, boosting him from behind to the best of her strength. He clenched the pommel and reins with both hands and bent over, holding his stomach. Illera got Lark on his feet, and together they staggered to his horse. She made Appolon kneel and guided Lark to his back. Copper was stubborn and refused to let Illera grab the bridle. Maggie was growing more agitated, insisting that they hurry. Finally, Illera, not up to chasing the skittering mare, told the bobcat to go and she followed him, splashing through the cold water. The chill in her feet seemed to drain what little energy she had. Her body was sluggish, and she concentrated on placing one foot ahead of the other as she followed behind their guide. The riders trailed after her.

The bobcat suddenly bounded ahead, forcing Illera to run or lose him. She forced her legs to a heavy trot, slipping from edge to narrow edge of the sunken trail. The feline was quickly disappearing into the tall grass and trees ahead. She broke into an all-out run, the horses trotting behind her. They ducked behind some tall screening grass just as the sounds of many horses, with riders talking in loud voices and cursing assaulted their ears. They churned the dark water to a gray froth as they splashed along Illera's trail. The cat had vanished, and Illera dare not try the swamp without a reliable guide. She stood panting, trying to keep the sound of her breath quiet. Lark and Raven were asleep, stooped over in their saddles, riding by instinct. Ashera regarded her with wide, frightened eyes, her mouth open in a silent scream. Copper nudged her from behind, and Illera pulled herself into the saddle. Holding her body at the ready for a sudden dash into the depths, she waited, tension singing through every fiber of her being.

Korul and his men paused, the leader of the group leaning far over his horse's shoulder, peering into the water. He straightened and turned to the king.

"They are just ahead. The water is still muddy from large animals passing."

Korul grunted. "Then hurry. I'll have that bitch in irons before the sun sets and I can just feel the pleasure I'm going to get from drawing and quartering those bastards of mine."

Maggie vaulted from Illera's shoulder and zipped past the king's nose squawking her most insulting call. The dozen or more knights behind him pressed forward as the leader slapped his steed into a canter, splashing past the place where Illera and her companions were hiding. The tall plumes of grass rippled in the speed of their passage, but did not part to reveal them. She waited until their noise faded between the boles of the trees and the birds and insects began to sing again. She softly called the bobcat.

He reappeared out of the dense grass and sat down, washing his face. He turned with great aplomb and trod daintily in the opposite direction to the king's party. They circled through the morass as the day declined and utter darkness gripped the lowland. Illera pressed on, unwilling to rest or eat, her nerves frayed by this dismal place and longing for wide-open spaces and sunshine. As the first moon rose, they came at last to longer stretches of dryer ground, interspersed with serpentine fingers of water. The bobcat trotted now, and the hooves of the exhausted horses echoed on turf. The water gave way to mud bogs and soon they were traveling through a damp and mossy forest. At second moonrise, the bobcat stopped and sat in front of the horses. Illera dismounted and stroked his head and tufted ears as she sang him a low song of thanks. He rubbed his head on her arm and leapt away, bounding back into his home.

Maggie winged out of the dark and grumbled irritably to Illera as she squirmed under her cloak to sleep for the night. Lark and Raven were still sleeping on the backs of their horses, but Ashera regarded her with wide, owl eyes. Sighing, Illera made Copper bow and clambered to her back, setting off to the west, guiding herself by the gold and silver moons. The weary animals plodded with heavy feet, but still, she pushed them. The brush with Korul unnerved her and gave her a pressing sense of urgency, forcing her to keep moving no matter how tired the horses were, or she was. The must escape and keep him interested in chasing her, thus sparing Madean a few more days or weeks.

She noticed the forest becoming dryer as the land began to

rise. She urged the horses onward, the way becoming steeper and the foliage lessening until they were traveling through rocks instead of trees. The horses stumbled repeatedly, and Illera could see that soon, either Lark or Raven was going to be pitched to the uneven, stony ground. Second moon was directly overhead when she halted, telling Ashera to get down. She pulled Lark and Raven from their saddles and settled them beside the giantess. Covering her three companions with their cloaks, she unsaddled and fed the last of the grain to the horses. With a mind troubled by urgency and sorrow, she joined her companions.

A songbird caroled joyously, joining the sounds of crackling fire, boiling water and the scraping of pots. Someone was humming under their breath; an ancient hill melody. She opened her eyes to long morning shadows and a bustling camp. The horses grazed on a narrow patch of grass just down the hillside. Raven was cooking something, and even Ashera looked more in tune with her surroundings. Lark came whistling down the slope, sloshing a kettle of water at his side.

"All right," he called as he saw her sit up, "how did we get here? The last I remember, we were in the middle of the swamp and you were lost."

Raven turned from his pan to hear her reply. Illera looked at them nonplussed.

"What do you mean? Don't you remember? You were with me all day yesterday...when we left the swamp...when Korul almost caught us...when I said goodbye to the bobcat...don't you remember any of that?"

"No, nothing," Raven stirred the food in the pan. "I remember you had fallen into the swamp and the current was pulling you away from the island. I threw you a rope but it floated out of reach, and then you disappeared under the water. I dove in, but it was all black, and I couldn't see anything. You were gone."

Lark put the kettle over the fire. "Yeah, Raven splashed around out there for over an hour looking for you. I had him tie the rope around his waist, so I could pull him in, but we couldn't find you at all. I finally gave up and pulled him out."

"You should have let me keep looking. I told you she wasn't dead." Raven bristled.

"I came back the same night, in the blue fire. Don't you remember that at least? Ashera was terrified."

Raven looked at the sky, brow furrowed, "I remember going back to the fire and changing into dry clothes. I remember thinking you had to be dead, no one survives long on their own in the swamp, but I felt you were still out there somewhere. Then, I remember waking up here this morning."

Lark nodded. "That's about what I remember."

Illera sighed. "I got pulled away by some big reptilian creature. It took me to a bay where there were dozens of little baby reptiles, all biting me. Look at my arm." She pulled up her sleeve and showed them the large and small puncture wounds, crusted with scabs and dried blood. "I roared at the little ones, and they swam to their mother, and then I climbed out of the water. There was a blue flame in the middle of the island, and I went over to it, and for some reason, I don't remember now, I went into it. It covered me all over, and I floated. It was the strangest feeling, but I floated off that island and followed the current back to where you were. You don't remember any of this?"

Puzzled, the men shook their heads. Raven whipped his pan of food from the fire and divided it into four portions, handing them around.

"What did we do?" Lark asked between bites.

"You were around the fire, the three of you. Ashera was terrified and hid under the saddles, and you tried to run me through with your sword. But Raven took my hand, and all the fire went to him, but it dimmed considerably. Then Raven gave it to you, and the two of you passed it back and forth."

"We were in the blue fire?" Raven shook his head as if he could not believe what she was telling him.

"Yes, all of us, but Ashera. Then yesterday morning, I couldn't wake up. The bobcat and Maggie both kept trying and finally I sort of managed to force myself to do things, but I was so tired. I've never been that tired in all my life. It was better when I washed the ash from myself, so I washed you, and Lark too. We got to the horses and ran from Korul and his men. The bobcat brought us out of the swamp, and I brought us here."

Lark hunkered down in front of her. "We were covered in ash?"

"Yes. All of us who had worn the fire."

He shook his head. "For years we have found bodies of those who died in the swamp, covered in ash and perfectly preserved, as though they were just sleeping. Some of them disappeared years before. That ash is one of the most dangerous phenomena in the swamp. We call it being taken by the Darkliete."

Illera thought. "I don't know. I think...maybe...we came very close to dying. I was tired enough to be dying, and the two of you weren't any better. But we passed the flame back and forth between us. Do you think that could have weakened it enough that we survived?"

Lark shook his head. "I don't know. I do know we were very fortunate."

Raven nodded. "I think you might be right. What would have enough strength to kill one person couldn't overpower three. Good lesson."

Maggie gave an outraged yelp and fluttered her wings. The travelers turned. Far down the hillside, a group of riders paused in a wide clearing. Trees cupped the group in a tight embrace, but the sunlight struck flashes from the pikes and swords they carried. The riders spurred their horses forward and under the covering trees. Lark doused the fire with water as Raven scrambled for the horses. Illera threw their things into the saddlebags and heaved her saddle onto Copper's back. She jammed the bit between the horse's teeth and mounted as she buckled the bridle.

Lark forced Ashera onto her mount, and they set off up the steep hillside at a spanking trot.

Maggie scouted ahead, finding the easiest way over the rocks. Lark followed close behind her, then Ashera, Illera, and Raven. Small rocks dislodged by the horses tumbled down the hillside in a continuous cascade. The animals slipped and scrambled, heaving higher and higher. After an hour's hard riding, they made the flattened crest of the hill. They stopped to let the horses blow.

The wind was piercing here, blowing sodden from the bay and driving low scudding clouds before it. It worked its way under cloaks and sought out their damp places to chill the flesh beneath. Illera turned, searching the lower levels for any sign of Korul or his knights. Close behind her Raven turned and pointed. Squinting, she could see their shadows slipping from tree to tree at the verge of forest and rock. They must have been watching Illera's band, and as if Raven's finger was a signal, they burst from the covering foliage and charged the hill.

"They're coming. We have to move."

Lark spurred his shaking mount ahead, and the others followed. They galloped along the crest of the hill, searching for a way down, but the ocean side proved too steep for the horses. The weary animals maintained the best pace they could, but Illera could see Korul and his men overtaking them. She heard Raven talking behind her and twisted in her saddle to hear him, but the strong winds from the sea blew his words away. She followed his pointing arm with her eyes and beheld the rocky beach littered with seals. She shook her head; it was too much to imagine the selkie among them.

The power of the wind increased, stiffening the travelers and slowing the legs of their steeds. The clouds lowered and grew heavy and Illera tried a few times to reach out and touch them. The far side became steeper and more dangerous the further they cantered to the north. The horses were dripping foam now, and their breathing was like a blacksmith's bellow. Illera pulled Copper to a halt. The chestnut hung her head, coughing and panting. Raven dismounted and came up beside her.

"I'm not going to kill the horses," she told him. "I can climb down this side, then Korul will chase me, and maybe he'll lose a few men getting down to the beach."

"Then I'm coming with you." He flung himself from Abbadon's back.

Illera shook her head. "You need to stay with Lark and help Ashera. There is no need for both of us to die."

Raven laughed. "My Lady, I swore to protect you with my life, and I will do just that. You can't think that Korul will let Lark and I get away after we defied him in front of his knights, do you?"

"I suppose not. I've been so involved with my own problems, I guess never gave any thought to yours. Sorry." She gave him a sweet smile.

She stepped to the edge of the cliff and lowered herself over. Stones tumbled past her head telling her that Raven followed. Carefully searching for footholds, she lowered herself an inch at a time down the steep and perilous rocks. Above and to one side, Raven loosened an avalanche of fist-sized stone, one of which struck her on the side of the head, threatening to bowl her from her precarious perch. She clutched the hand and footholds as her head spun, the whirling sensations making her feel ill. Only the chill hand of the wind, forcing her against the hillside kept her from falling.

Unable to move either up or down, Illera regretted what she had done in leaving the horses to climb to the beach. Raven moved parallel to her. He stretched out one hand and touched the side of her head. Her stomach rebelled and hurled its contents down the clean rocky face. She could see blood on his fingers when her tears cleared.

"My Lady, I am sorry. I should have stayed further away." Raven stared, face stricken.

He descended from her view. The wind cut off, and Raven's body was around her. The sudden warmth made her gasp. He went lower, exposing half of her to the cold.

"Move this foot here," he commanded, gently guiding her foot to a secure resting place. "Now this one."

Slowly and painfully, they descended the cliff, Raven guiding her feet as she hung on with her fingers and toes and moved to his command. The last step was steep, a five-foot slide of sheer rock. Raven let go and slid down on his belly. Rising he dusted himself off.

"Let go and I'll catch you." Legs braced, he spread his arms wide.

Illera shook her head, too sick and dizzy to try his maneuver. He tugged sharply at her foot, pulling it from the safety of the last foothold and she tumbled downward. She closed her eyes, astonished that they made it down the treacherous cliff face. Finding her balance, she turned, determined to take charge of herself again.

The seals littering the beach regarded them with mournful eyes. On shaking legs, Illera approached them and scanned the group.

"Shwawnigon, are you among the seals," she called over the pile.

The animals shifted restlessly, a few heading for the sea and diving in. Illera sighed.

Turning to Raven, she began, "I guess it was too much to..."

A man approached them from further up the beach, wearing a sealskin loincloth and a short, thick beard. He smiled as he approached, revealing pointed canine teeth. Illera paused on shaking legs as relief washed over her. He placed his hand on the wound on her head, and she could feel the strength returning to her limbs, and the spinning in her head retreated. He smiled his feral smile again.

"Turnabout. This way." He turned back the way he had come.

They struggled over rocks and stones and sank in the soft black sand of the smooth areas, but the selkie breezed along, and they had to run to keep up with him. Rounding a curve of smooth rock, Illera saw a tall prowed ship under full sail approaching the rocky shore where the land jutted out in a natural dock. The sails were furled, and the ship glided into the land. Sailors jumped to the stones and made the ship fast, running out a gangplank.

Turning her head, she saw Lark and Ashera leading Copper and Abbadon mincing down the steep path from the top. The selkie sped his steps and Illera began to fall behind. The sealman scrambled up the ten-foot-high nose of land, reaching down a hand to help her up. Raven boosted her from behind and together they hoisted her to the rough pebbles of the strand connected to the ship. Raven pulled himself up and helped her to her feet. The horses clattered over the gangplank. Illera and Raven staggered after them.

The sailors jumped aboard and pulled in the access. Turning to the land, Illera looked at the hillside. Korul and his men were charging down the steep path to the ship, their mouths open and she could imagine the curses that the wind was blowing away.

The sails zipped up the masts, and the ship regained headway, turning and sweeping to the sea majestically as Korul pulled his foaming war-horse to a halt at the edge of the rock. She could see the purple choler in his face and was tempted to reply in kind to the shaking fist. She restrained herself. Korul's archers moved to the fore, losing shafts at them. Lark caught her shoulders and pulled her to the wooden planks of the deck, covering her with his own body.

The wind filled the sails, and soon they were past all dangers of the land, heading down the Bay of Hostages to the open sea. Sailors gathered around them.

"Welcome to the Waiting, strangers," a short man greeted them. "I'm Captain Rivard, and this here's my vessel."

The captain was a short man, brown and lean with his eyes

wreathed in smile lines and a permanent grin embedded in the furrows of his face. A fringe of graying brown frizz encircled his shining bald head. A uniform of midnight blue bagged on his spare frame, but was as neat and clean as the rest of the crew and ship itself.

"Here now, show this boy where to set the animals." He appointed one sailor to the task.

Raven went with the horses to a compartment in the middle of the ship.

"An' you, take the lady and her crew to The cabin amidships."

Another sailor escorted Lark, Ashera, and Illera down a set of stairs so narrow it was almost a ladder. They were in a corridor lined with doors. The sailor took them to one door, opened it and left them. Illera staggered inside collapsing onto one of the sturdy wooden chairs.

The room was paneled in wood, warm and golden. A pair of narrow bunks, neat and tidy with cream-colored bedding, filled the space behind the door. A chest carved with whorls and abstract shapes of great delicacy decorated its foot. A round table with a raised edge around its circumference was bolted to the middle of the floor, and surrounded by eight of the sturdy wooden chairs. A small round window with a thick glass cover admitted light. The brass frame glowed with warmth in the daylight. Suspended from the ceiling, a brass lantern swung with the motion of the ship, echoing the colors of the frame. A set of floor to ceiling bookshelves made the fourth wall. Slats of wood kept all the volumes in their places. Illera tried to read the titles graven in gold on leather bindings, but it was written in a language with which she was unfamiliar.

Lark escorted Ashera to the lower bunk, and then came and sat beside Illera.

"Do you know who these people are?"

"No, I'm afraid I don't."

"Then how could we just jump aboard this ship. We don't know what they want."

"The selkie brought me. Besides what choice did we have? Strange ship who wants to save us or Korul who wants to kill us?"

The door opened, and Raven was escorted into the room. The sailor left as Raven sat down beside his brother. Before either could speak again, the door opened, and two tall, slender women entered the room. Dressed in identical flowing robes of sparkling white they moved regally to stand before the three companions. The woman closest to the door had a serenely beautiful face with strong cheekbones and a high forehead surrounded by hair the color of the summer sun. Her eyes were dark, dark blue with sparkling lights of cerulean and azure. She had full wide red lips and a strong nose. Her companion was almost a mirror image, but with hair the color of midnight.

"I am the priestess dark," began the raven-haired beauty.

"And I am the priestess light," returned the other.

"The selkie called us to your rescue,"

"so, we left our pursuits and came to his call."

"Can you tell us who you are?"

Illera rose, her legs trembling with fatigue and not a little awe. "I am Illera, princess of Madean. These are Lark and Raven my squires and my bodyguard and maidservant Ashera, who was brutalized by Torul, son of Korul until her mind was broken as badly as her body."

The priestesses moved to the bunk. The blonde turned back to Illera.

"The maid servant's body is well healed."

"Who accomplished this service?" the dark one asked.

"I managed to heal her body, but could do nothing for her mind," Illera replied. "I should warn you that Korul, King of Frain, is hunting us. He thinks I killed his son, but I did not. The brute fell down the stairs and broke his neck."

The two priestesses gazed at each other, a deep communing.

The most incredulous smiles of pleasure spread across their faces. They bowed to Illera and rose again.

"We thank you,"

"Princess, for this cheering."

"news of the demise of Korul's"

"spawn. You make"

"the world a cleaner"

"place to live."

The priestess dark ran her hands an inch above the surface of Ashera's face. Turning to her twin, she nodded.

"We can"

"heal the mind."

"of your friend."

"Give us."

"a few hours to prepare."

The priestesses glided from the room. Illera sank back down on the chair and lay her head on the table. The stress of the last few days rose up in her, and she wept, sobbing away the exhaustion and the terror. At last, there were other people to help them. Raven and Lark sat on either side of her and patted her back.

Illera caught her tears and forced them aside. She must be strong for Ashera was going to be restored to them and she had to make amends with the giantess. The door swung open, and Illera turned. Two children stood there; a raven-haired girl and a golden boy, both about twelve years old.

"Please Princess, would you come with me," piped the girl, "and bring the other lady too?"

"And the priestess asked me to escort you," the boy said indicating Lark and Raven.

Illera tugged on Ashera's arm until the woman rose and followed her. Lark and Raven disappeared down another stairway, and she felt a pang of anxiety at their disappearance. Trouble had appeared from every corner, and she felt vulnerable and exposed without their protection. The child led her to a dark room at the bow of the ship. The girl closed the door behind them and lit seven thick blue candles. A sweet scent pervaded the room. The child whipped the cover from a pair of deep tubs filled with steaming water. Flower petals floated on the surface of the water.

"They asked that you bathe and be clean for the healing. It is easier to heal with a clean body. Then the mind wishes to be in harmony." The girl spoke as though reciting from a manual. "When both of you are clean, princess you are to drink this. It is for protection, but the other lady, the sick one, can't have any. Her mind needs to be open. And here are the garments for the ceremony. The sick lady is to wear the yellow."

The girl nodded to a murky corner of the triangular shaped room. There was a wooden table bolted to the floor and on it a copper pitcher. A tall, cut-crystal glass was anchored beside it with straps. Beside the pitcher were two long silk robes, one a clear blue and the other yellow. Thick white towels and washing cloths were folded over the robes. The girl turned and left them to their bath.

Illera stripped Ashera and coerced her into one of the tubs. Once there she seemed to know what to do. Gratefully, Illera left her to her scrubbing and attended to her own. Ashera needed help to dry and dress herself. Illera did that service for her, giggling a little at the thought of her father seeing her performing the service for Ashera that was the blonde's responsibility. When they were ready, Illera drank a glass of the water from the copper pitcher. It was cool and faintly sweet with a lingering hint of peaches. She wished for more, but was told a single glass, so she restrained herself and opened the door. The child was waiting, with a wide-appealing smile, and led them down the corridor to another room.

This chamber glowed with light from a hanging glass chandelier sporting a myriad of candles. The light fractured and danced in splinters around the large room. A ledge of gold, glowing in the wonderful light wainscoted the dark and light striped wooden walls. The patterned walls were something Illera had never seen before, and she thought the effect was striking. The ledge was the only furniture in the room. On the striped wooden floor was a round carpet, woven in shades of clear yellow and intense bright blue. She thought it might be the same form of writing she had observed on the backs of the books, in the other room. She could not read what it said, but admired the intricate pattern it made and how the colors wove in and out of each other. It was almost hypnotic. She shook herself and looked away. The two children she had seen earlier were present, and two others, another boy, and girl of about fifteen, joined them. The girl in this pairing was palest blonde and the boy night dark. The four children knelt in a square around the carpet, but not touching it. The priestesses arrived. The blonde was dressed in a robe of rich, clear yellow silk embroidered around the hem with more of the writing in blue. The dark-haired woman was dressed in the same bright blue color Illera wore, but with yellow embroidery around the hem. Raven and Lark followed them also dressed in silk robes of blue and yellow.

"We have a balance," began the dark-haired priestess.

"Except for you," continued her counterpart.

"In the Darkliete,"

"all must balance,"

"and yet we need a balance,"

"for Ashera."

Illera swallowed. Hesitant and unsure she asked, "I don't know what you mean?"

The blonde priestess turned around the circle, pointing, "Dark, light, dark, light, dark, light, light."

"But you are neither; you partake of both dark and light."

"We cannot polarize the circle," the priestess light continued.

"Do you want me to leave?" Illera wished that would be the answer.

The dark priestess smiled. "No, we want you to anchor the circle. To stand at the center."

"and allow the power to flow through you and around you. To be"

"the nexus."

Illera could see Raven and Lark getting ready to protest. She nodded. If she could help Ashera, she owed her that. If she had not abandoned her at Dragon's Lair, her mind would still be whole and sound. The priestess dark moved her to the exact center of the circle. The acolytes on the outer edge shifted as she moved Lark and Raven into a kneeling position with them. Ashera knelt at Illera's feet facing outward, fear beginning to build in her wide blue eyes.

The candles blew out with a suddenness that made Illera jump. The room was steeped in darkness. She could feel it stealing into her very bones. The priestess dark and the priestess light began to sing; a melody without words in two-part harmony, a familiar, yet strange song to Illera. The sound wound around them in the darkness. Illera could feel her heart beating in the rhythm of the song. A pure blue flame flared into life around her. Her feet rose from the floor. She recognized the feelings of euphoria and serenity it brought. She glowed with the blue fire of the swamp, it reflected back to her from the eyes of the kneeling children, Raven, and Lark on the outside of the circle. The priestesses circled around in front of her, their hands joining together making shapes that reminded Illera of the shape of the flame, flickering around her. The priestess light knelt before Ashera, placing her hands over the giantess' shoulders. She stared into the broken woman's eyes. The priestess dark stood behind her. Her hands reached out to Illera, drawing some of the blue fire to them. Illera extended her hands. The flame flowed from Illera to the priestess dark down her body to the priestess light, up her arms, and to Ashera, enclosing her head in a brilliant blue aura.

Time seemed to stand still at the same time it was speeding

by faster than thought. It was a strange and disorienting feeling, but it was buried deep, deep beneath the feeling of joy and peace the blue light brought. She knew time passed, but it was without meaning. Her mind strained against the fabric of her being. Memories rose, parading through her thoughts as she flashed back and forth through her life and the experiences she lived. Faces and animals long forgotten, all viewed with a sense of detachment as if she were not herself, but a voyeur rummaging through her life. The world spun and tottered, held together by the color of the fire.

Ashera slumped back against her legs, pushing her from the center of the carpet. Illera fought to hold her position. The sound of a gong shivered through the air, and the fire disappeared in an instant. Illera stumbled as her feet touched the floor, tumbling backward to land on her bottom, Ashera pinning her legs with her greater weight. The priestesses hurried from the room.

The acolytes clustered around, holding pails of warm water. They washed her from head to toe, stripping away the silk gown, insensitive of her modesty. Illera was appalled under the weariness that engulfed her. One of the girls wrapped a warm and furry sheet around her. The next thing she knew she was lifted into the air and carried to another room. She managed to crack her eyes open enough to peer into Lark's disturbed and troubled face. She was asleep before her head touched the pillow on the narrow bunk.

The buzz of conversation woke her. The effects of the fire seemed much less this time, and she felt refreshed and alive. She stretched long in the warm bed.

"Well, look who's finally back with us." Raven laughed.

"You've slept for two days Illera," complained Lark.

Ashera sprang up from her chair. "And I have so much to tell you."

Illera sat up, catching the covers as they slipped, almost

revealing her embarrassing state of undress. She squirmed, remembering the day or was it two days before.

Lark and Raven stood. Raven attempted to imitate a trumpet. Lark moved his hand in a grand flourish.

"May I present," he announced, "the princess Ashera, daughter of Uggarick of Carnuvon, long lost and much searched for, now found."

Illera shook her head unable to grasp what the squires were saying.

"What?" she said inelegantly.

Raven laughed aloud. "Let the poor woman have some breakfast, Lark, before you go rearranging the world on her."

He strode to the door and ordered food for the princess, and returned, sitting on the edge of her bed. He took her hand in his own.

"I'm sorry Illera, but nothing is as it once was. Everything has changed. Do you remember Ashera's story?"

"She was the daughter of a Sorwelk trader?"

Lark continued the explanation. "That's what her mother told her to protect her. She was actually the only daughter of Uggarick, the King of Carnuvon. That's why the pirates have been attacking Madean for so long, they thought you had kidnapped Ashera, and they have been looking for her for twenty-two years. Ashera is a royal princess."

Illera laughed. "I'm so happy for you, but what of...of the other ....you know, with Torul..."

Ashera smiled. "It wasn't your fault my Lady, I mean Illera. I was stubborn, and I knew that you wanted me to stay with you, so I rebelled. I'm sorry I didn't listen, but everything is distant now, like a very bad dream, not even one that happened to me, just something I heard. But I am sorry I was so foolish."

"And I'm so sorry I left you there. That was the worst thing I could have done. I didn't know Korul and Torul were like that, or

I would have found some way to get you out. I feel so, so horrible about the whole thing. I..."

"Don't punish yourself Illera. It wasn't your fault. But you should listen to the rest of the news."

"What news," she asked, looking around smiling.

The door opened, and the two priestesses walked in, the priestess light carrying a tray. She deposited it on Illera's lap. Lifting the cover, Illera could smell fresh scrambled eggs and warm toast dripping with butter. Her mouth watered and her stomach growled.

Lark laughed. "Go ahead. You're several days behind us. We'll talk, you eat."

He turned a glowing smile on the priestess and took her hand. They sat arm in arm at the table. Illera felt a pang, for if Lark were leaving her who would help fight Korul when he attacked Madean. The priestess dark sat down on her bed beside Raven nudging him over with her hip. He put his arm around her shoulders. Illera felt another shaft of fear impaling her heart, and the eggs lost their flavor.

"My name is Rejoicing, and I am the priestess dark," the woman began.

Illera forced her face to keep smiling, but inside her stomach clenched and she was getting knots in her back.

"My name is special, and I tell it only to family."

"I am not your family..." Illera's voice sounded high and nervous.

The priestess dark smiled. "You are half-elven, and your vanderjar has solidified your werwinstans, and that confuses you."

Illera shook her head. "I understood maybe half your words."

Rejoicing laughed. "My sister and I were captured twenty-six years ago by Korul and forced to be his concubines. It was the gravest insult to our nation and our calling. We chose the Darkliete when we were children and trained for it our whole lives. Then that pond scum, Korul, invaded our country, just as we achieved the peak of our powers and captured us. When our children were born, one month apart, Korul arranged a marriage with a princess from the far land, and she insisted that we be driven out. He said he was going to dash our children, our sons, to pieces on the rocks after he drove us to the boat he had called from Sorwelk. We believed him for he is the king of evil. But Raven and Lark are those sons."

Stunned, Illera stared with her mouth hanging open. Then she laughed, with a sound that bubbled up and burst from her mouth with astounding joy.

"Their mother told me she wasn't their mother and that Korul was their father, but she swore me to secrecy. But neither of you seem old enough to be the mothers of men their age."

Rejoicing laughed. "In the Darkliete, people age differently. I am a lot older than you might expect."

The priestess light moved forward. "I am Laughter and Lark's mother."

"And I am most honored to meet you." Illera was unable to keep the wide grin from her face. "Where do we go from here?"

Raven jumped from the bed and continued pacing. "My mother tells me that you are half-elven."

Illera nodded.

"Elves left here long ago, going to another home somewhere else. But your mother visited here in her vanderjar. That's when a young elf leaves home and travels around. That solidifies a sense that elves have and that humans don't; the werwinstans or we might call it the land sense. That's why elves always return to the places where they were born. It is just too painful to stay away, it irritates the werwinstans. That's why your mother had to leave. She loved you and your father, but she couldn't stay away from home forever. She had to return. I know how much you needed to know that."

Slow tears leaked from Illera's eyes. She still missed her

mother but she also missed Madean fiercely, and if this was what her mother felt, then she could understand why she had to leave her year old child and return home. It was a great gift this understanding. She opened her eyes and stared at the watery figures of Lark, Raven, Ashera, Laughter, and Rejoicing and said in a small voice, "Thank you."

CHAPTER 9

The ship bucked and heaved through the water. The waves marched in steady succession beneath the stern as it rose and lowered; water caressing down the length of the vessel. The stern and prow did not seem to catch the same rhythm and as soon as one rose the other sank and vice versa. Illera gritted her teeth and braced her feet wide apart as she struggled to groom Copper, who had no problem accommodating the motion of the boat.

"I guess I need four legs too." She stroked the brush over the hard muscled shoulders as the waves tossed her against the glossy chestnut coat for the hundredth time.

She threw her arms around the mare's neck and hung on to her quiet strength. It could be worse; she could be like Ashera, confined to her bunk, unable to eat or move about. It just seemed that she could not catch the pattern of the sea and so, was tossed from port to starboard, bow to stern. A plethora of bruises on her shins and buttocks bore testimony to her inability to maintain her footing.

She picked up a hoof and began to clean the frog. The ship heaved, and she landed on her aching backside again. Copper blew a warm breath down her neck. Lark came whistling into the enclosure, stopping and grinning as he saw her scrambling back to her feet.

"Still having trouble?" He gave her a jaunty grin.

She shook her head. "Just a little. Don't know how you guys do it."

Lark laughed aloud. "Just in the bloodline. By the way, Rejoicing wanted me to ask you if you have time to talk. I'll finish with the horses if you want."

"Thanks," Illera said, striking her clothes to remove as much straw and dust as possible. "Where is she?"

"Starboard side, at the bow."

Illera nodded and left the small shelter. The wind caught her cloak and loose hair twisting them around her body, binding and blinding her. She unsnarled herself with a sigh and headed towards the beautiful woman looking over the railing. She too placed her hands on the rail and stared out over the gray and whitecapped water. The wind was driving low dark clouds before it, and the entire world seemed to be composed of shades of gray.

"It is a depressing day." Illera watched the waves dance past.

The priestess dark smiled without turning her head. "The dark is as important as the light."

"Of course," replied Illera uncertainly.

Rejoicing smiled. "In the Darkliete all involves balance. Night needs day. Male needs female. Good needs evil. Happiness requires sorrow. Life requires death."

Illera thought for a moment. "I'm sorry Lady, but I can't agree. For me, to say that happiness requires sorrow doesn't feel right. I don't have to feel pain to know I prefer feeling well. I don't have to be miserable to know I prefer to be full of joy. I don't want to disparage your beliefs, but I cannot hold them myself."

Rejoicing gave a ghost of a laugh. "It has ever been thus with elves. I thought being half human; you would see it our way."

"What do you mean, with elves?"

"The elven are a different species. Just as a wild lion is a different creature from a cat kept in the barn to hunt mice. They live at a different rhythm and see through different eyes. I am surprised that your mother loved your father enough to bear him a child. That is most unusual."

"I don't know anything about my mother's people, but Elves don't look much different from humans."

Rejoicing turned to face her. "No, most of the differences are on the inside. Elves find it hard to interact with people, human people. That is why it seems that when humans move into an area, the elven move away, slowly and gradually, taking hundreds of years; no doubt because of the werwinstans; but they go. My own theory is that the physical congruencies exacerbate the mental disparities."

"Ah...yes?"

The priestess laughed, a high tinkling sound. "I merely mean that we look a lot alike but think so differently."

Illera pondered, wondering if she thought differently from others.

The priestess continued, "And now you are wondering how I think and how other humans think compared to you?"

Illera nodded, surprised that the other woman could read her mind.

"You think differently from a human, but you don't think like an elf. It was my great privilege, many years ago, to assist one of the elven who had fallen on hard times. He gave me access to his thoughts through the Darkliete. It was an experience I will always treasure."

"But, what about me?"

"You are something different, neither human nor elf. I will treasure the taste of your thoughts also, for many years yet. However, I cannot categorize them, you are unique and must discover yourself for yourself. I envy you that voyage."

"So my ability to heal and to talk to animals doesn't spring from my elven blood?"

"Yes and no. I have never heard of your connection to the wild things from any other source. It is unusual. But the healing; that could be elven. The elves are divided into clans, and each clan has its own special talents. One of the clans has the ability to heal, the racial memory of healing plants and potions. If you are descended from those, then your abilities are natural, from your mother."

"But not the ability to communicate with birds and animals?"

"No, not that."

Illera watched the sea, thrusting away the question that had nagged her since first knowing the Darkliete priestess was Raven's mother. The pause in conversation widened, silence punctuated by wave and wind.

She blurted out, "Rejoicing, what happened between you and Korul? How did he enslave you?"

The priestess's face hardened, the corners of her mouth pulling down. She stared out to the horizon, and for once Illera could believe she was old enough to be Raven's mother.

"I have put those memories far from my mind, but I suppose since...Bifbats moana shifticmat orbicans..."

"Priestess, are you all right? Forget my question if it disturbs you."

"No, I will tell. My sister and I were raised to belong to the Darkliete. We studied hard and were inaugurated at a young age, only twenty-three. We served our people, the Sorwelk, well and attained mastery of the flame and girdle. But the king of Frain attacked; greedy for power and wealth. Our country was peaceful, just simple peasants growing their gardens and tending their flocks. But we had gold in the mountains, mined and shaped by the hands of our craftsmen into shapes and devices to please the mind and decorate the body. Korul feigned interest in the Darkliete and was invited to observe a ceremony. He broke the circle, and his men took my sister and myself captive and dragged us to their ship. He attacked the city and took hostages from every royal house and merchant's shop.

"When the people of Sorwelk were slow to pay tribute, he killed the hostages. We watched, Laughter and I, we watched the slaughter until the sands ran red and bled into the sea. Korul laughed the whole time. If I live to be two thousand, I will never see such glee on the face of another human. My sister and I he raped; over and over, like an animal, for many months. Then she got pregnant. He left her alone after that and concentrated on me. He wanted to disgrace us. You see, the Darkliete do not usually bear children. There is no law against it, just the tradition that one devotes oneself totally to the care and healing of others. A month later, I, myself, was pregnant.

"Raven was but a few weeks old when Korul drove us away. His new bride would tolerate no rivals to her offspring to be. Korul said our children had to die. We went back to Sorwelk in mourning, and we have mourned for twenty-four years, until you brought our sons back to us."

"Why did you never seek to come back, to look for them?"

Rejoicing sighed. "Fear. Fear of what Korul would do to us if he found us. Fear that the boys were already dead. Fear he would ravage Sorwelk again. Fear the curse we placed upon him would fall upon us."

Illera placed a hand on the taller woman's arm. The priestess dark turned to her and hugged her tight.

"I'm so sorry that you had such a bad life," Illera murmured.

Rejoicing laughed and released her. "No, it was not all miserable. There has been much joy, the strongest when we discovered our sons returned to us. Now Torul is dead, one of them must be made king of Frain, when Korul has been executed. That is what I needed to tell you. You are betrothed to a son of Korul, to unite Madean and Frain. We must destroy Korul and all his evil, and you must choose one of the sons of the Darkliete. It will balance the world again."

"Have you spoken to them about this?"

"My sister made the way plain before them this morning."

Drawing herself to her full height, Illera shook her head. "Much as I respect your opinion Priestess, I will not, absolutely will not, be forced into another betrothal that is not my own free and clear choice. You need to inform your sister, Lark, and Raven of that fact. They are honorable men, and I do not impugn that, but when I decide to marry it will be my choice and no other's."

Rejoicing looked as if she had been struck in the face.

"Princess," she began, "the Darkliete says this must be so, to restore the balance."

"You told me yourself that I don't think like a human or an elf. You cannot expect me to follow your belief or your political will. I will do as I see fit. I was coerced once. I will not be party to it a second time."

"Very well. I am not Korul to force an unwilling maiden against her will. But the world loves balance, and it will be achieved one way or another, whether you cooperate or not."

Illera smiled, a hand indicating the tossing waves. "The world loves chaos. At least that has been my experience. I would appreciate you for an ally, even if we disagree in this regard."

Rejoicing gave her a strange look, her brows furrowed and eyes opened wide.

"You still wish to be allies, even if you won't join with Lark or Raven."

"Of course, it is to both our benefits. Why would I not wish for peace between all our peoples?"

Rejoicing laughed. "I told you, you do not think like a human, or an elf. Illera, you are truly different."

The older woman put an arm around her shoulders and led her from the windy deck. They descended the ladder-like stairs to below deck. The absence of the wind was like a slap and Illera realized how much effort she exerted to maintain her position in the face of its strength. Rejoicing fluttered a hand in her direction and vanished into the quarters she shared with her sister. Illera assumed she wanted to discuss the prospects of peace between their countries further and felt astonished that she would just leave that way.

Deciding to check on Ashera now she was below; she opened the door to their room. Ashera moaned on her bunk, while Lark stood at the porthole and stared out at the furious sea. Raven was poised between sitting on a chair and standing. He rose as she closed the door. Lark turned and stared at her with a feral light in his eyes. Raven moved hastily to his side. Illera realized the trap the priestess had set for her.

"She told you her plan?"

Raven cleared his throat. "What plan?"

Lark laughed aloud, slapping his brother on the shoulder.

"What's the matter brother, afraid that she'll choose the better man?"

Suddenly they were both talking at once, their words mixing together and confusing her so that she couldn't understand either of them.

"I am the oldest..." Lark began.

"I am far more capable..." Raven cut him off.

"So the kingship should..."

"and you and I share..."

"By birthright be mine..."

"This love of horses..."

"So it is proper..."

"And I can protect you..."

"For Madean..."

"And I will always..."

"And Frain..."

"Enough!" snapped Illera. "I think you need to hear what I told the Priestess dark."

Raven and Lark were silent. Raven staring at her with entreaty and Lark with a confident certitude. Even Ashera was quiet, rising green-faced to one elbow to watch the scene.

"I told Rejoicing plainly that I have no intention of becoming betrothed to either one of you to further anyone's political aim. When, and if I marry, it will be my choice for my own reasons."

"But Illera," began Lark, "we've been through so much, for the sole purpose of uniting Frain and Madean. We are Korul's only living sons. I don't dispute your right to choose, but you must choose one of us."

Raven smiled and looked at her with the corners of his mouth pulling down. "You said from the beginning it was wrong to force you to marry a prince of Frain. I understand why you don't want either of us and I don't blame you. It was a vain hope you would choose me anyway."

He walked past her and out of the room his arm trailing across her shoulder.

"Wait," Illera called as she stamped her foot. "I want to discuss this right now and get it out of the way."

Raven paused in the corridor, turning inch by slow inch to face her. His face was tight, but he nodded and returned to the room, seating himself at the table. Lark sat beside him. Collapsing with weariness of the mind and heart, Illera joined them.

"I'm sorry." She paused, at a loss for words. "I think you both need to know how much I value all you have done for me. As I told your mother, I think you are both noble, valiant men. Men any woman would be proud to call husband, but I am not any woman. When my father dies, gods forbid, I will be the ruler of my country and I must choose my consort wisely, for the entire country of Madean depends upon it. I agree that it would be politically astute to link Frain and Madean by marriage, but right now, this werwinstans thing has all my wits scrambled, and I know I could never make as good a decision as I will when I return home. I have great affection for both of you, but I am not willing to commit my country or myself yet, until we see how things turn out with Korul and his invasion. Whatever happens in the future, I hope that the one of you that ascends to the throne will be willing to work with Madean at forging a reliable peace." Illera smiled at the two serious faces in front of her. "I know you will, for you will have the welfare of your people to care about and I don't think either of you has of the personality of your father."

Raven grinned and looked at his hands.

"Thank you, my Lady," he said sarcastically. "Does that mean that you are not rejecting us outright?"

Illera stretched her dainty hand across the table and settled it over his big one. "I'm not rejecting you in any fashion. You are my friend and whether we will ever be more than that remains for the future. I'm saying that I need to get home and take care of Korul before I make any decision regarding my future."

"Well, I am the oldest." Lark, face split into a wide grin.

Raven stared at her hand on his lying on the table. A strange chill worked its way from her hand down her spine, and she removed her hand, rubbing it down her skirt under the table.

"You're a fool, my Lady," grumbled Ashera. "Once the maidens of Carnuvon catch sight of these two, you won't stand a chance."

They all burst out laughing.

"I'll have to take my chances."

The door creaked open, and one of the sailors popped his head around the corner.

He spoke quickly with an edge of excitement in his voice. "The cap'n said to warn ye that we's fixin' to run b'fore a storm. An' a terrible one it looks like to be. Ye are all to go to yer quarters and batten down all yer gear. Don' know how long it'll be, but if the forecaster's right, should blow us all'a way to Carnuvon. No lamps, nor any kind'a fire, no cooking, no water, 'cept what blows over the rails. So hang on lubbers and brace yer bodies in yer bunks."

The sailor closed the door accompanied by a low moan from Ashera. Illera moved to her and put her arm around the larger woman. Rushing to tidy their own cabin, Lark and Raven hurried out. Illera scurried around making sure their few possessions were securely stowed. She returned and held Ashera in her arms, rubbing her back and giving her all the silent reassurance she could.

The rising and dipping of the ship increased. Water streamed over the porthole, blotting out their exterior view. The ship lurched from side to side and front to back, shaking its passengers mercilessly. The howl of the wind rose and rose until it penetrated into their cabin, vibrating their very bones. Ashera was sick. As Illera held the bucket for her, closing her mind to rising stench of vomit, her mind wandered back, reliving the interview just past. She wondered what she should have said to make them understand. The bucket jumped and sloshed its contents in an uncomfortable fashion. Rising, Illera slipped and staggered to the door, hoping to empty the puke over the rail topside. She managed to make it to the ladder unsoiled, but the ship was moving too much for her to climb to the deck. She could see fierce blue and purple lightning bolts striking downward from the sky. The Thunderer rode the clouds, drowning all sounds under his drums. A wild toss with a twist knocked her feet from under her. The barf bucket went one way and she another, rolling down the slanting deck to land with her feet against the Priestess's door. It opened, and Laughter helped her to her feet.

"You must stay in your cabin." She yelled to be heard over the voice of the storm.

"Ashera was sick, and I had to empty the bucket," Illera screamed back.

"Go to your room," commanded Rejoicing from her corner.

Laughter took her by the elbow and assisted her back down

the hallway to her own quarters. She pushed open the door and shoved Illera inside.

"Stay!"

Illera tried to make it to her bunk, but the floor tipped from under her, becoming a wall for a few seconds. She rolled to the table. The sounds of retching echoed through the gloom, and the sickening smell of bile rose around her in clouds. In the moment while the ship was almost level, Illera dashed for her bunk, diving for it and barking her shins painfully on the wooden frame. She braced herself on the headboard and footboard and gave herself to the storm and stink of their dancing cabin.

The tossing continued interminably; the whole world narrowed to the microcosm of the cabin. The walls were her horizon, the ceiling, her sky. Her boundaries narrowed, and her body was the enemy. The narrow world was trying to destroy her, shaking and bouncing her. She held on tight, concentrating on the thunder and pounding of the waves on the hull, trying to ignore Ashera's moans and sickness. Her mind revolved around the last weeks since her father sent her away. She felt young and uncertain. The priestesses seemed so certain of what she needed to do. Lark and Raven reached the same conclusions. Even Ashera supported their views. Who was she to swim against the current and defy the wishes of everyone she knew? However, it still did not seem right to go against her own mind and intuition. How could she choose between brothers? No matter whom she chose, someone would be rejected, and that could make them enemies. She would never want to be the cause of dividing them. Honestly, who else could she choose? She knew no other men of the right age, and she knew they were people of integrity. They had proven it time and again, but still, now was not the time to be making any decisions. She wondered: why did life have to be so baffling and so hard? The sea and wind concurred with her conclusion by heaving her halfway to the ceiling and dropping her back to the bunk.

After an eternity, the storm eased, the violent persecution of the waves had worn them out. The Waiting still battered from side to side and front to back, but without the ire of the preceding hours. Exhausted, Ashera and Illera fell asleep.

Illera dreamed. The sky was a lowering yellow, a color that should be cheery, but instead was menacing and evil. Wide plains rolled gently away in folds of gray, ashy and sere. She stooped to pick up some soil, but as far as she dug in the hard ground, only ash met her questing hand. She plucked a worm, limp and blue from the compacted dirt. It turned its face to the yellow sky and then to her. The worm wore the face of her father. Her heart lurched and sped within her chest.

"It is come, it is come!" The high piping voice issued from the worm, putting her in mind of Maggie.

"Maggie?"

"No, the doom blows from the north upon Madean."

"Who are you?" Illera cried.

The worm twisted on her palm and disintegrated into ash. Illera turned in a circle, but could not see the way to go. In all directions, the land looked the same, folded and gray. Not a single distinguishing feature was visible, no tree or dwelling or animal. There were no footprints to follow, no wind to scent direction from, just the small hole from which she had dug a worm. She tried to run, her feet heavy as though encased in mud. She looked down and saw huge and heavy boots on her feet, but they had no fastenings so that she could remove them. So she ran with them, tripping and falling down into the ash, which parted to let her through, and she fell and fell down an ash-coated tunnel.

With a start, she woke, drenched with perspiration. She stumbled from her bunk and slipped on the vomit coated floor. In disgust, she uttered an oath as she lurched towards the door. The ship was still rolling, but far less than before. Illera wandered into the hallway and up the stairs to the darkened deck. The sailors were busy, tending sail and minding the wheel. They ignored her.

A clean cold wind was propelling the ship forward at a wonderful rate of speed. She tottered to the bow and looked over. Below, riding the bow wave were a pair of seals, briefly lighted by one moon or the other as the wind, with heavy clouds, veiled and revealed the sky. The cold felt good after the funk in the cabin, and Illera wondered if she could sleep on the deck tonight instead of inside. The pounding of her heart quieted as the sweat dried from her skin. She shivered.

She jumped as a warm and heavy cloak settled around her shoulders, and strong arms encircled her.

"You shouldn't be on deck and not properly dressed, my Lady," Raven spoke from over her head.

Illera laughed. "You startled me. I didn't hear you come up behind me."

"Sorry. You looked lost in thought and then I saw you shivering."

"Thanks."

"Why aren't you below sleeping? Captain Rivard thinks we might make port tomorrow afternoon if this wind keeps up. You should be ready."

Illera paused; staring at the foam-flecked sea. "I...uh...I can't."

"Did the storm scare you?" The concern in his voice made her throat ache.

"No, I was sleeping, but..."

"What?"

She turned to face him. "Just silly stuff, like bad dreams."

He looked at her seriously. "Sometimes dreams are not silly. They tell us what is inside of us and sometimes that can tell us the way to go."

"I wish someone could tell me the way to go?" She turned back to the sea.

Raven burst into loud guffaws of laughter.

"What?" Illera drew herself to her full height and stiffened her spine, insulted by his hilarity.

"My dear Princess," he gasped between chuckles, "that is exactly what you told us was the problem this morning. I would think you have too many people telling you what to do?"

Illera chuckled, realizing the absurdity of her comment. "Sorry, you're right. Too many people are telling me what to do, but I can't see the right path to follow."

Raven smiled and leaned over the railing, watching the animals playing in the waves. "You just need to relax. You'll figure out what you need to do. Give yourself some time. We haven't had too much leisure for quiet reflection since we left Seven Spires."

The name of her home gave her a pang, and she moaned at its mention.

"So you're not angry that I didn't choose you this morning."

Raven smiled, his profile rueful. "No, not at all. I figured you would choose Lark anyway. Lark was born to be a leader; he is strong and always takes charge of everything. So, I just figured that it would be him you would pick, he is the logical choice. Hey, the longer the decision is put off, the longer I go without my dreams being crushed."

"Your dreams being crushed?"

Raven turned at the flapping of canvas, and with a brief wave, he hurried away to help the sailors draw in the line. Illera knew he wasn't going to answer, so clutching his cloak tightly about her shoulders and trying not to trip on its length she descended the stairs. Going to the galley, she implored a bucket of water and a mop from the cook. Cleaning the floor of their cabin was a dreadful chore in her inexperienced hands, so Ashera finally took pity on her and finished the job.

Illera went to the cabin of the female acolytes and asked if she could bathe. After the girls checked with the priestesses, Ashera and Illera were taken to the bow. The tubs were prepared, and Illera washed the stink of vomit from herself and her garments. Once she and her cabin were clean, she was finally able to sink into a restful slumber.

The morning dawned clear and cold with the Waiting still running before the wind. The gray sea was dotted with foam and flotsam from the storm. With Lark on one side and Raven on the other, Illera stood at the bow, watching for the first sight of the island of Carnuvon. She knew from her lessons that it pointed its narrow end in the direction of Madean, like an arrow shot from a bow and speeding toward the target. That was the way she had always thought of it.

The smudge on the horizon thickened. As the sun crept higher, rising in front of them, the line grew and developed a shape, sharp and angular against the cerulean sky and dark sea.

Ashera joined them to watch her home rise out of the sea to tower over the Waiting. The ship glided closer, and the land grew taller, rising far above the puny masts of the vessel.

"This somehow feels familiar." The giantess twirled about. "I must have some memory of this place buried inside."

Illera placed her hand over the other woman's.

"I'm sure you do. I don't remember much about my youngest years, but sometimes when the sun hits something just right, I know I've been there before and have seen exactly the same thing. You will probably find a lot of Carnuvon like that."

Ashera turned to her with an eager grin.

"Do you really think so? I've been different and a stranger for so long, I can't even imagine what it would be like to have some-place where I belong."

"I believe Illera's right," Raven told her. "Our earliest memories make us who we are. Myself, I grew up on the back of a horse, and there is nowhere I feel more at home, no matter where the horse goes."

Lark laughed and commented, "My brother, the gypsy."

Ashera sighed, a breath from the depths of her soul. "If only you were right. It would be worth everything I've suffered at Korul's hands to have a real home. I hope you are right."

Illera smiled up at her and put an arm around her waist. "Of course we're right. Have you ever known us to be wrong?"

They all laughed at Illera's remark. A pleased smile on his face, Captain Rivard joined them.

"I am pleased to see you are all happy to be home," he said.

"Yes," replied Ashera, "I feel I am going to be very happy here."

"Good." The sea Captain made a satisfied grunt. "I am going to be very happy myself."

The crew skittered about, reefing in sails and reducing the speed of the ship. A long tee shaped dock protruded from the steep cliff face like the tongue of a rude child. The Waiting swept smoothly alongside of the thick dark planks and one the sailors leapt agilely to the edge, trailing a length of rope. The companions watched as he snubbed the line around two of the bollards whipping it in and out in a figure eight. The Waiting drifted to a stop with a faint ripple through the deck, under their feet. The gangplank was lowered, and the Captain strode to the rail.

A tall, cadaverous-looking man stalked up the boards, bouncing a little with every step of his thin insect legs. He wore a heavy black uniform liberally decorated with gold braid and buttons that flapped around his body much the same as the sails had flapped on the masts. His long, narrow, hollow-cheeked face was grim with a thin line of mouth pulled back and down. There was a mighty frown between his narrow set hazel eyes as he peered around the ship, inspecting every visible rope, bolt, and board.

"Permission to come aboard," he asked in a high-pitched voice, incongruous in one so tall.

"Permission granted," returned the Captain.

"And you are?" the stranger continued as he stepped onto the deck.

"I am Captain Rivard of The Waiting."

A sharp intake of breath from the stranger surprised Illera.

"The Waiting? What do you do at Carnuvon Town's dock?"

Captain Rivard smiled, turning his face into a mass of wrinkles. "I bring you the lost."

The official started, "Surely, you don't mean…"

"I do indeed," the Captain said as he grinned away, "I bring the lost Princess of Carnuvon, Ashera, daughter of Uggarick and his first wife, Mae."

The Captain waved his arm for the four still standing at the bow to come forward. Ashera hung back until Illera grabbed one arm and Lark the other and pulled her to the Captain between them. The stranger's eyes fixed on Illera.

He demanded, "What sort of joke is this? Such a tiny child could not belong to Uggarick."

Lark laughed, "No, that is Illera, Princess of Madean. This," he said propelling Ashera forward with a hand behind her back, " is Ashera, daughter of Uggarick, so we have been told by the Darkliete."

"Darkliete," the man snapped as he looked Ashera over from head to toe, "You know the Darkliete do not have any influence in Carnuvon."

Captain Rivard bowed his head, "You know The Waiting is a Darkliete ship, so don't act surprised now. And the Darkliete are the ones that discovered your Princess."

"This will have to be verified by our own priests?" the stranger said as if uncertain.

"Nacherly," agreed the Captain, stiffening his spine. "Now are you goin' to take the Lady or do I sail away with her again."

The tall man bowed his head, "Very well then, come; I will take you to Uggarick."

He whipped around and bounced back down the gangplank. Ashera grasped Illera's hand and held it so tight that she soon had pins and needles coursing through her arm. She loosened the other woman's fingers but did not withdraw the hand. The

Captain, Lark, and Raven followed, while Maggie circled overhead.

They passed the dockworkers, swarming about different vessels tied to the docks, threading their way between bales and crates, dodging men while jogging to keep pace with the official. The yells and curses of the sailors and chandlers accompanied by the loud noises of the tools and thumps of crates made conversations impossible. The docks widened as they progressed inward, becoming busier and more crowded. The official had to stop more than once to allow them to catch up. His face grew angrier and angrier.

A shallow stone platform, of thirty or so feet, supported the docks. Rough storage caves had been chiseled out of the rock face, their mouths still bearing the marks of tools. To the right a switchback began, stitching up the sheer face of the cliff. The official headed for this and started up, his long legs making short work of the steep incline. Ashera and Illera were soon puffing behind him as the pace had quickened even more. Illera felt the strain in her thighs and calves as she boosted herself higher with every step, always a little nervous of the sheer drop over the edge to the dock or sea far below. Grunts of effort came from behind them as the men struggled to keep up.

When she thought she could not go another step, and her knees were about to collapse, the stranger stopped and turned to them with a tight smile.

"Stick close to me once we are in the city. We have a few...uh... unsavory characters there, and I wouldn't want to lose you until we have proven you are imposters."

Breathe heaving, Ashera looked at Illera, who shrugged. Ten feet of flat and level rock led them to imposing wooden doors heavily banded with iron. The official pounded on the surface. A small wooden window slid aside a foot above Illera's head. Two eyes examined them. Minutes later a small invisible door, set into the larger ones opened. The official ducked through it, followed by the others. Illera was the only one who did not have to stoop to enter. Illera noted that the walls of the town were six feet thick as they moved single file through a narrow stone lined and roofed corridor to another small door at the end. They sidled past a dozen guards all dressed in black uniforms with drawn weapons. Around the corner, the noise of the town hit them, a boisterous roar of hawkers selling their products and people conversing, all at the top of their lungs. Clusters of stone houses and market stalls lined the narrow cobbled streets. Cattle and sheep bawled, and chickens crowed from cages and ran loose in the streets. Scrawny dogs darted everywhere, chased by laughing, yelling children. Forges spat smoke and the reek of hot metal into the already thick and cloying air. Hands reached out on either side to pull the unwary traveler aside to the nearest vendor of vegetables, meat, livestock, jewelry, gold coins, fabric, tools, chests, woods, or clothing, new and used; more items than she had ever seen gathered in one place. Illera jammed herself tight to the official, walking on his heels and Ashera was tight to hers. The babble increased, making Illera nervous and jumpy, but still, the official forced his way through the churning multitude.

The shoving crowd thinned as they came to another set of tall gates, guarded by black-uniformed soldiers standing two deep in front of the entrance, blocking it completely. One of the men, with a tall black plume on his helmet, stopped the official, checking his face closely. From under his clothing, dangling from a long·cord on his neck, the official produced a signet. The plumed guard inspected it. A whispered conversation between the two men ensued in tones so low Illera could not pick up a single word. The guard continued glancing up at her and the others standing behind.

He barked an order, and the soldiers parted, making a human corridor to the heavy wooden door. The official proceeded, and Illera followed, trailing Ashera and the others. It was a short, claustrophobic passage, hemmed in by tall bodies before, behind and on either side. Feeling the beginnings of panic, she breathed deeply to quell her uneasiness. Around one side of the official's black shoulder, she could see a tall, wide copper-bound door. Two guards leaned their weight against the bars of copper stretching from the middle to a foot from the ground. Slowly, slowly with protesting groans, the heavy leaves parted. Illera and her companions trotted after the official as he strode through the doors. Grunts of effort echoed behind them as the guards struggled to close the massive doors.

They walked down a flagstone path winding through smooth green turf. Short, twisted trees dotted the lawn, every second one ringed by red or yellow flowers that nodded in the breeze. The mansion ahead soared into the sky with copper-topped minarets on round towers. A myriad of mullioned windows with arching tops faced them, punctuated by copper-bound doors at the ground level. It sprawled over much of the lawn; five stories high in the main area with its towers rising double that. Around the doors, servants hurried about their business, and six gardeners tended the wide beds of red and yellow blooms ringing the palace.

The official strode straight ahead moving without pause from the path to the wide flagstone paving separating the lawn from the flowerbed. He passed through the nearest door without a break in his stride, and they followed behind him like ducklings after their mother.

The main hallway was wide and magnificent, wooden paneled walls trimmed lavishly in gold. Dodging in and out among the many black liveried servants, they passed quickly to the great room. Here Illera stopped, astonished by the opulence, frozen until Ashera banged into the back of her. She scurried to follow the official, gazing around at the barbarous splendor. Cut crystal chandeliers filled with thousands of candles illuminated tables covered with gold worked into designs of animals and people. The chairs were glowing wood, upholstered with plush red velvet. Gigantic tapestries in glowing colors covered most of the walls, and the floor underfoot was polished marble. Twin thrones occupied the place of honor, gilded with gold and encrusted with red, blue and green gemstones the size of Illera's fist. The official halted just beyond the ruby colored carpet surrounding the thrones. Above the thrones, in a musician's galley, the players were providing soft music to the workers who scurried below.

A balding man, his head like a wrinkled peach approached the official, and another whispered conversation took place. With a quick glance at the travelers, the bald man hurried from the room. Before Illera had time to look around, a bevy of giants entered the hall.

The first man wore a crown, just slightly askew on his graying yellow curls. He was a bear of a man, thick and huge. A red face with small eyes and a large, thick-lipped mouth was supported on a neck that could have graced a bull without shame. He lumbered over to them and stared. His robes of royal purple proclaimed his status. The official went down on one knee. Captain Rivard followed, but Illera remained standing, staring at the giant. Behind him, she could see a woman almost as large. Her once reddish hair was graying, and her wide, flat face was deeply lined with wrinkles. Seven giant young men spread out behind the two older people, all bearing an uncanny resemblance to the king. Three young women hovered behind them, dwarfed by the massive size of the family.

"And who are you to look me so boldly in the face without bending the knee?" demanded the King.

Illera stepped around the kneeling official and trod upon the carpet to approach.

"I presume you are King Uggarick of Carnuvon?" she asked.

The room became still behind her, sounds of industry halted as if everyone and everything held its breath. The king's face grew redder as indecision hovered in his eyes.

"You cannot be my daughter. I would never have whelped such a puny offspring," he grumbled.

"No," she replied, holding out her hand, "I am Illera, daughter of King Ian of Madean. Until recently, your daughter was my guardian and maidservant."

A sharp intake of breath greeted her statement. Illera turned and gestured Ashera to come forward. Ashera tiptoed to her side.

"This is Ashera, your daughter," Illera introduced.

The king's burning gaze turned upon the giantess. Illera could see how she would fit into this family; there was no denying the resemblance. The king studied his daughter a long time.

"This one is possible. I can see that this could be her. Who claims reward if she is verified?"

Startled, Illera looked back as Captain Rivard jumped to his feet.

"I do," he exclaimed.

"Very well," continued the king, "see to the comfort of our visitors. The priests shall assemble this evening after the meal, and we shall determine if this Ashera is indeed my own blood."

The king spun on his heel and left through the door by which he entered. His family followed, turning to give the travelers long looks before departing. A small, black-clothed woman approached from behind and leaning forward so as not to step on the carpet; she tweaked Illera's sleeve. Illera turned and followed the woman, trailed by her companions. Mounting wide marble stairs, balustraded by gilded railings, they climbed to the third level and down a wide corridor as luxurious as the rest of the palace. At the first door, the servant opened it and gestured Illera inside. The door closed behind her and her companions separated from her. She gazed around the large open room. Two pale blue couches with gilded arms and legs occupied one corner. A solid gold circular table occupied the dark blue carpet between the couches. A massive canopied bed filled the opposite corner, gold accenting the blue patterned bedding. A wide door opened into a bathing room, tiled in blue and white with a deep tub, sunken into the floor, and golden fixtures gleaming in the bright candlelight. A wide mullioned window draped in dark blue looked down upon a circle of garden blooming far below. A blue and white window seat provided a comfortable resting-place for gazing from the window. Beside the window was a solid gold dressing table and chair with all the fripperies any woman could want. Illera moved restlessly from item to item around the room.

A timid tap came at the door. Illera opened it to see a young girl holding a length of midnight blue material over both arms. The child tiptoed into the room and draped the item over the nearest couch.

"My lady, Queen Dora, sent you this for to wear to the evening meal, Lady. I'm to stay to make sure it fits. If'n don't I'll take the measure and take it to the seamstress so you'n can be properly dressed."

Illera fingered the material. It was far finer than anything she had worn.

"Do I have time to bathe first?" she asked the girl.

"No, mam, if'n it needs fixin' we needs the time now."

Sighing, Illera took the dress to the bathing room and changed into it, holding it up in both hands. The girl gave a little giggle when she saw her, for the dress hung around her like a tent, bagging far down in the front and being a foot too big on the sides and bottom. The child got to work and had the dress pinned into a more dignified configuration in just a few minutes. Illera changed again and gave her the garment. She scurried out of the door.

Left to her own devices, Illera decided to bathe and prepare herself for the night to come. After a good wash and a short nap, she spent the time staring down from the window watching the servants trotting to and fro in the garden. As the sky began to darken, the same little girl knocked and entered Illera's room. She held out the dress.

Illera retreated to the bathing room. The dress fit perfectly, outlining her curves and emphasizing her proportions. It was cut lower at the front than Illera was used to, exposing her collarbones and revealing a lot of cleavage. Her riding boots did not go with the dress, but she had no other footwear, so she wore them. The girl was waiting by the dressing table when she emerged.

"Here, Lady. I'm to do your hair."

Obediently Illera allowed herself to be fussed over; her long copper locks were pinned into a high crown of curls on her head. The girl then produced a garish sapphire pendant and placed it about Illera's neck and matching earrings on her ears.

"There you go Lady, you are perfect," the child exclaimed.

Illera looked at herself in the polished silver of the mirror. She did indeed look different from her usual self, elegant and royal. She laughed a little at the image. The girl smiled.

"Come, I'll show you the way. The banquet should have begun by now."

Illera followed the child, retracing her steps of earlier, descending the great staircase. Every table in the great hall below was filled to capacity with people, and every face was turned to her as she made her way down the steps. A murmur ran through the crowd. Two men rose from the king's table and made their way to the foot of the stairs. With a start, she recognized Lark and Raven, washed, barbered and dressed in royal garments, waiting for her. The recognition almost made her lose her footing. She joined them, and they escorted her to the king's table. She sat at the Queen's left hand.

"I see my old dress was suitable after all," the Queen told her with a piercing gaze that examined her from head to foot.

"Thank you for your graciousness," replied Illera. "All my luggage remains at Korul's castle, and my attire has suffered dreadfully for it."

The Queen gave her a pleased smile. A loud "AH" rippled through the assembled throng and Illera turned. Ashera was poised at the top of the stairs, staring down at the great crowd. A flicker of uncertainty slipped across her face, immediately replaced with a wide smile. She had never looked so beautiful, in a blood-colored gown, liberally decorated with gemstones and golden threads. Her hair was piled high and glowed with more jewels. She descended like a true queen and Illera's heart sang with joy for her. King Uggarick himself moved to escort her to her place at his right hand. Illera sighed with pleasure. The Queen looked at her and smiled.

"You are not jealous of your friend?"

Illera shook her head, "No, why should I be?"

"If the priests prove she is Uggarick's daughter she will have untold wealth and luxury for the rest of her life."

"I hope she does. I really hope she does, after all, she's been through she deserves it."

"You don't want that for yourself."

Illera laughed out loud. "No, I only want to get back to Madean and live in peace with enough to eat. I require nothing more."

The Queen gave her an odd look and turned away to watch Uggarick with his daughter.

"Well, the resemblance is certainly there," the Queen murmured to herself.

"Yes," replied Illera, "but I thought Ashera's mother died in Madean."

"Yes, his first wife, Mae did. She was the mother of Roc, Gareth, Hobie, and Ashera. Roc is supposed to inherit the throne when Uggarick retires. Those boys are all married, and Roc even has a couple of boys of his own. But Ashera was always special to her father. He has seven sons, but only one daughter."

"Are the other boys yours?" Illera asked.

The Queen smiled expansively, "Yes. My sons are a little

younger. That's Dorian," she said pointing to a massive young man halfway down the table. "And that's Aelfred, Beorick, and Marstan. None of my sons are married."

She looked at Illera like she was a horse at the market. Illera squirmed in her seat, taking surreptitious looks at the sons of this Queen. All huge, all resembling their father to an uncanny degree, they made her nervous for a reason she could not define. They gave her long looks, turning away as if in deep discussion with their companions on either side, but when she glanced up she could see them all staring again.

The banquet was interminable. Fish, chicken and red meat, each with its own complement of vegetables and bread, followed soup served in bowls big enough to slop hogs. Finally, massive servings of pudding and cake were set before each of the guests. Illera was already full enough to be sick, although she had eaten less than half of her portions. She pushed the sticky concoction away.

"Is our banquet not to your liking?" inquired the Queen.

"Your pardon, Majesty but I have eaten more in this one sitting than in the past several weeks. I am sure I would not honor your lavish table by hurling the contents of my stomach to your clean and shining floors," retorted Illera.

The Queen stared at her, astonishment in the roundness of her eyes and the oh of her full lips. Her mouth split into a huge grin and she began to chuckle, then bellow with laughter. All the guests turned to stare, most laughing along with the Queen. Gasping for breath, she repeated Illera's comment to the King, who also broke into peals of laughter, followed by the whole room. Illera squirmed in her plush chair wishing herself a thousand miles away.

The entrance of four priests broke the uncomfortable tableau. They shuffled in, like cookies stamped from the same cutter, clad in identical frayed and grubby beige robes that ended in tattered fragments just below their knees. Each shaven head was of a height with the other three, and dark, mournful eyes drooped beneath shaggy brown brows. Narrow noses, concave and flaring at the nostrils perched above tight slashed mouths and receding double chins. Illera could not tell one from the other. Two boys, about twelve years old, scurried after the priests, lugging a heavy wooden chest between them.

As the servants cleared the dishes and remaining food, and pushed the tables and chairs back against the walls, the boys opened the chest and set out its contents. A thin woven circle of brown material was placed on the floor and a brazier set in the middle, filled with lumps of coal and set alight. A thin, round copper table was assembled and placed over the brazier. A small, shining copper bowl was placed in the center of the table. Incense was added to the coal, and a cloud of sweetish smoke wafted throughout the room. The four priests began to circle the table in a shuffling dance, raising one foot high in the air every fifth step. Their low chanting filled the great room as the odor had, and all the guests watched, mesmerized by the performance.

Illera's legs were feeling numb, from standing still so long, when the noise and motion suddenly stopped. Two of the priests fell to the cloth as if senseless. One of the others high stepped to the king and clasping his hand drew him onto the cloth in front of the table. The second then did the same with Ashera. One of the boys produced a stiletto and handed it to the priest holding the king. With a single sharp stab, he pierced the king's palm and let the blood drip into the copper bowl. The other boy handed the priest an opaque blue bottle. Dropping the king's hand, he removed the stopper and poured a few drops of clear liquid into the blood. It heated quickly and began to boil.

The other priest held Ashera's hand over the bowl and taking the knife pierced her palm. As the blood dripped into the bowl, a shaft of steam twined into the air, two columns braiding together then combining before dissipating high overhead. A loud 'ahhh' burst from the crowd at the sight. The unconscious priests on the floor began to speak in a language strange to Illera, babbling on in voices that rose higher and higher in pitch and power until they were shouting up into the air, each drowning out the words of the other man. As one they stopped. The silence felt oppressive after the sound, thick and malleable. One of the standing priests tossed a handful of something into the fire, and a thick smoke filled the room, obscuring the outlines of even the nearest persons.

It gradually dissipated, leaving only a single priest standing in the exact center of the brown circle. The table, bowl, brazier and other priests vanished in the cloud. The priest bowed low before the king and Ashera.

"My liege," he intoned in a deep and rumbling voice, "this woman is indeed your child who has been missing these many years. Twelve times now you have summoned the services of The Brotherhood, and eleven of those times has the result been negative, but today, the twelfth time, the results are different. Your blood and hers merged. This means they are the same; she is your own blood and your own flesh. Rejoice! The lost has been returned."

The room reverberated with loud cheers. Uggarick's face split into a grin that he could not repress as he turned and hugged Ashera to him, pushing her back to look at and hugging her again and again. When he finally released her and turned her to face the room full of people, he kept his arm firmly around her shoulders, tucking her under his armpit. Ashera looked stunned. The guests lined up to congratulate the king and his daughter.

When Illera's turn came, she hugged Ashera hard. "I'm so happy for you. You deserve to have found a home and a family who loves you."

"I'm scared, my Lady, I mean Illera. I can't do this; I wasn't raised to be like this. What am I going to do?" Ashera whispered as she hugged Illera back.

"You'll do fine. Your family will help you. It will be all right, just give it a chance."

Ashera watched her as she moved away, looking far more stunned than pleased by the situation. When the greetings were over, Uggarick led his daughter to the red carpet surrounding his throne and seated her on a plush chair on his left. Queen Dora seated herself on the right.

"Now," began the king as the crowd grouped in front of the throne, "I will be taking offers from sufficiently royal young men for the hand of my daughter in marriage. I will, of course, be expecting a large bride price for such a prize as my Ashera, so let the word go out."

Ashera turned pale, a look of horror spreading across her broad face.

"King Uggarick, I have unfinished business that I must attend to before you make such plans for me."

"Nonsense. You are finally home, and now you will work for the advantage of the Kingdom of Carnuvon."

Ashera looked about to panic. Illera stepped forward, her toes on the red carpet.

"King Uggarick, may I speak?"

The king frowned, and the pause was long as he regarded her, his eyes assessing what she would say. Finally, he nodded.

Illera drew a deep breath, "I am delighted that you have found your daughter after all these years and I am delighted that I had a small part in bringing her to you. Most, unfortunately, she has been through some difficult situations on her way back to you, so difficult and so insulting in fact, that the man who did this evil must answer for it, must pay with his life. I suggest to your majesty, that Ashera will not rest easy until this man has been repaid for his treatment of her."

Uggarick's face darkened, and his mouth turned down at the corners.

He rose to his feet and bellowed, "Who is this man who insulted my daughter?"

Illera looked at Ashera who rose herself and faced her father. She mouthed a quick, silent 'thank you' to Illera.

"Korul, King of Frain, has caused me great injury. As Princess Illera said, I cannot rest easy until I am assured of his death, to repay the treatment he gave to me. In fact, I demand that I be the one who removes his head from his body and brings it back to you father, on a pike."

Her grin was triumphant. "I have trained as a warrior. I was chosen as bodyguard, and companion to Princess Illera by her father. I will go, and I will fight with this spawn of demons, and I will return to you father and be obedient to your will. But first, I must eliminate this foul stench that hangs about me on account of the King of Frain."

"You have just returned to us; I cannot let you go again," Uggarick stated. "I shall also keep your friend, the Princess Illera. She shall wed one of my sons, and I shall allow her to choose which of the four who remain unmarried as she will. A well-bred Princess is a difficult thing to find in these days."

Without asking for permission, Illera spoke up, "I regret I must decline your offer, King Uggarick, but my own country of Madean needs me. King Korul will invade for the insult I did to him, and I must be at home to assist my Father in his defense of Madean."

The king was becoming angry, hands clenched into tight fists at his side and veins in his neck bulging under the strain.

"I am the king of Carnuvon. I have spoken, and I will not be contradicted by two willful females."

Illera felt a hand tug at her clothing. Turning her head, she saw Lark and Raven poised to fight their way out of the strong-hold. She held up a cautioning hand.

"My lord, I grant your right to control your kingdom, but if I have done you a kindness in helping to return your daughter, I pray you will also grant me a kindness."

He glared at her suspiciously. Illera could hear the tense whispers from the crowd behind her. Uggarick eased back onto his throne.

"Tell me your request before I say whether or not I will grant it?"

"Allow your own priest to determine whether or not I should remain here, and whether or not Ashera should be allowed her vengeance," Illera ventured, bowing her head.

Placing his chin in one hand, the king pondered.

"Very well, summon the priests," he commanded.

The four men reappeared by magic, the crowd parting to allow them through. The brown cloth was spread again, and again they danced in a circle and chanted, stopping suddenly. Each man withdrew from his robe a handful of bones. In unison, they tossed the bones into the middle of the cloth. Much muttering and pointing ensued. When they seemed to reach a consensus, they turned and approached the king, standing just beyond the edge of the red carpet.

As one, they bowed their heads and spoke, "My Lord, King, the bones have been tossed, and the omens read. They are dire indeed. The choice, of course, is always with you, O King."

"What did you learn?" Uggarick demanded, leaning forward from his throne.

One priest spoke, "If you choose to keep these woman in Carnuvon, a great evil will spread across the land. It will destroy Madean and Shul, then ooze across the Southern Sea to Carnuvon. For the first time in history, Carnuvon will be conquered, and its streets will run red with blood. Great indeed will be the slaughter and the plunder and the King of Frain will not stop until he has both Princesses in his power. You, yourself, O King, will be bound and have your eyes bored out after you witness the slaughter of your seven sons and the rape and slaughter of your wife. This is the omen we read."

Uggarick sat back on his throne, pale and unsettled at the words of the priest.

"If they return? What happens then?"

The priests conferred briefly, and a different one spoke, " The daughter of your body, O King, holds death in her hands for the evil spreading across the land. The Daughter of Madean must return and must rule her homeland, for only thus can the King of Frain be stopped. Light and dark must be her guide. The choice is yours."

Ashen-faced, the king, shook his head, "You leave me no choice, I must let them go to save my own kingdom."

"Yes father," interrupted Ashera stumbling over the word father, "you must let me go and finish off Korul. I give you my word; I will bring you his head on a pike."

Uggarick took a deep breath, "Very well, Princess Illera will return to her own country, accompanied by my daughter and some of my sons. When Ashera has taken her revenge, she will return to me. If Illera wishes to return as well, she will be welcomed in Carnuvon and into the royal family. All attacks on Madean are to cease immediately. We will attack Frain since their king insulted a royal daughter of Carnuvon. Plunder and loot every inch of coastline, make Korul pay for his lack of wisdom in choosing his enemies."

Uggarick rose and swept from the room followed by Dora and Ashera. Illera stepped back, shaking, to be supported by strong arms and wide grins.

CHAPTER 10

The column of air rising up the cliff face blew Illera's hair back from her face as she peered down the sheer drop to the ocean foaming against the rock below. She perched on the highest point of the outside wall, yearning towards Madean. She could feel her country's pull, tugging in a physical sensation in her chest and stomach. If she closed her eyes, she felt the magnetic attraction would draw her home through the air, but, she was solidly rooted to the stone. Maggie soared below, supported by the shaft of rising air, drifting along without moving a feather. She felt a vague envy, a mindless wish to soar over the sea on unmoving wings.

"Hey," a voice below called, breaking her reverie.

Looking down, she noticed Lark with his feet planted far apart and hands on his hips. He raised his hands and cupped them around his mouth.

"You should come down from there."

She looked out over the restless waves and sighed, reaching behind with one toe for the footholds to lower her body down the face of the wall. There had been precious little privacy in the last week. Everyone wanted her attendance at banquets, dances, small parties and walks around the town. The sons of Uggarick never left her alone for a minute and now, when she finally had an hour to collect her thoughts, here was another interruption. Inch by slow inch she stretched down the rocks until she joined him on the flagstones. The bright morning sun gilded his hair giving him a golden halo. Illera smiled up at him.

"Don't you realize you could fall to your death up there?" He raised one eyebrow his face stern.

Illera laughed. "After all, I have been through you are suddenly worried that I will fall off a perfectly secure wall that has stood for decades and plunge to my death in the ocean. I hardly think so. Besides, it is clean and beautiful up there, a good place to think."

Lark's smile was stunning. "And what was my Lady thinking of? Perhaps a suitable king for Madean?"

Illera groaned. "Not you too Lark. I've been accosted none stop for the last week by the four unmarried sons of Uggarick. They are courting me in case you wondered. Where have you and Raven been when I need protecting?"

Lark laughed. "Why taking notes of course. How else could we poor princes-by- default learn how to court a princess?"

Illera groaned again. "So why did you call me down and it better be something important?"

Lark sobered, a worried shadow in his eyes. "A ship from Madean has been sighted. It should have docked at the quay by now, and the officials have orders to bring any messengers straight to the king."

Illera tossed him a glance and began to trot towards the castle. She could hear the beat of Lark's feet in counterpoint to hers trailing behind. Servants toiled in the gardens as she jogged past, each looking up from his work to follow her with his eyes. She came through one of the side doors and slid around the corner and into a wide hallway. A pair of maids shook their heads at her hoyden behavior. Slowing to a swift walk, she moved straight to the Great Hall, interrupting a tension-filled tableau.

King Uggarick was poised to rise from his throne, a mighty frown on his broad face. A small brown man knelt before the red carpet his hands together in front of his breast in supplication. The courtiers and servants faced the pair, expressions of shock on their faces. Illera spied Raven standing in the back, his face drawn and grim.

"Ah, the princess Illera," called Uggarick as he caught sight of her, "she is the one who needs to hear your news."

The small brown man rose to his feet and faced her, entreaty alive on his brow. "Princess Illera? Is it really you? We had lost hope."

She moved forward, halting directly in front of him. "Why? What is the matter with Madean?"

Stammering, he replied, "Well, my Lady, the country is still there, I would not say fine and good, but she is holding her own, but the troubles, my Lady, the troubles."

Impatient Illera grabbed his shoulders and shook him.

"What troubles? Tell me, man!"

"Well, it's like this, see, the king of Frain, he is coming, is on Madean soil right now and the people, well, they are resisting, but he has hundreds and hundreds of men. We never seen the like of his army before and armed to the teeth; they's just brushing everything we can muster against them away and..."

"Get to the other part, about King Ian," growled Uggarick.

Illera shot a wild glance at the king, and her fingers dug into the brown man's arms until he winced.

"Yes, yes, of course, your majesty," he replied trying to bob a knee, but Illera held him too firmly. "Yes, the king, our king that is, King Ian, he is fighting against the King of Frain, and he was in this battle, at Ocean Perch it was, right by the border. Tough goin' it was, as all the knights from Frain had left, of course, they had to go, couldn't expect them to fight against their own..."

"The king," roared Uggarick, "tell her about her father!"

"He got hit. The king, good king Ian, he took an arrow in his shoulder. Right through the chain mail and all. The healers have been working on him day and night, but the green rot 's set in and like, well it don't look good."

Illera released the man, all her blood roaring in her ears, her muscles trembling. Strong hands behind her gripped hard around her shoulders and kept her from falling. She summoned strength and turned to King Uggarick.

"Sire, I beg you, give me leave to go. If you can offer support I would be most grateful and in your debt, but I pray you, speed me on my way."

"Make ready your ship. The Waiting is faster than any of mine, and it will sail you to your home. Ashera will go with you and any who wish to aid you in this war. I will prepare my ships and send men at less haste, but now, go to your father."

Illera turned and fled from the palace, running through the hallways to the front entrance and out into the gardens. Pairs of feet thudded behind her. Fear clutched her heart with an icy fist, sending shards of pain flowing through her blood. The castle doors stood open and guarded by troops who parted to allow her through. The townspeople took one look at her face and fell back from her path as she loped along the rock-paved streets. Raven sped past her to the outer gates, and they were waiting, opened as she dashed through. The switchback path was too steep to run down, but she hurried at her fastest walk, often stumbling and in danger of falling down the steep banks. With Raven in front and Lark behind, they threaded their way through the docks where sailors stood silent, watching their progress, the work frozen, paused for the rush of her passage. They thundered up the gang-plank of The Waiting, and Captain Rivard tipped his head to her.

Maggie sailed out of the sun to land in the rigging. Rejoicing and Laughter encircled her, one on either side and led her below. Others boarded behind her.

The lines were shaken out, and the Waiting eased from the dock, swinging her high prow to the open ocean. Facing the wind, they tacked forward, progress slow as the wind and current fought against them. Illera paced her cabin, the same one she had occupied before, while Rejoicing, Laughter, Lark, and Raven sat at the table and watched her.

Laughter sighed. "Enough, Princess. Rest. Your father will need you when you get there. You can't pace the cabin for the whole three days of crossing; the floor would be worn through."

"Three days?" wailed Illera. "I need to be there now, right now. I can't wait three days."

"Nevertheless," Rejoicing's voice was cool and logical. "It will take three days for The Waiting to make it to Ocean Perch. That's the closest port, and The Waiting is the fastest ship. If you went on one of Uggarick's barges, it would take you a week."

Illera buried her face in her hands. Unshed tears shone in her eyes when she raised her head.

"I should have demanded to leave as soon as Ashera was confirmed to be his daughter. I should have left that very night."

"Illera, I don't think you could have predicted what Korul would do..." Raven rose and lifted one hand.

Lark broke in. "No, we thought he would chase you until he caught you before he invaded Madean. That makes much more sense than just invading. What can he hope to accomplish?"

"What he always wanted to accomplish," Illera snarled, "to rule over my land and people."

Lark's head snapped back, and the others in the room stared at her. Illera let out a long moan and collapsed into a chair.

"Look at me," she cried, "I'm falling to pieces. How am I going to lead Madean against

Korul and help my father if I can't control myself?"

Raven placed an arm around her shoulders. "I'll help you Illera."

"And I," chorused Lark.

The door to the room swung open, and Ashera stood in the doorway dwarfed by her brothers Dorian and Aelfred.

"We'll help you too Illera." Ashera nodded her chin with a sharp motion. "Don't forget, I have the right to extract vengeance on Korul. You've stood by me; now I'll stand by you."

Illera rose and went to the other woman, putting her arm around her. She sobbed on her breast until the material was wet and clinging. Ashera led her to the bunk, and they sat down. The Waiting staggered west against the wind.

The cliffs narrowed on either side, looming tall and dark out of the very early morning mist. Illera shivered by the rail, Copper's reins clenched in one hand. The mare had been saddled for hours as The Waiting glided up Sea Reach bay. The landward rushing wind was, at last, pushing them toward their goal, but not fast enough for Illera. The last three days had been an agony of waiting. There was not enough work, nor food, nor bathing in all the world to keep her mind from her father and the plight of her people. Raven, Lark, and Ashera tried to occupy her, but it was in vain, for her brain held room for a single thing: her father. Dorian and Aelfred who thought to continue courting her, each competing to win her favor, strained her patience further. She had none to bestow right now, only grief, fear and a burning need to get home.

Sections of the town hovered above the fog in these predawn hours; the tallest steeple-roofed house of the gods and the square façade of the town hall. Individual houses clung to the steep hillside, blending into the background of mist with their silvered wooden walls and shake roofs. The mournful sound of the crying seabirds blended with the creak of sail and flap of canvas. The

Waiting slid in beside the docks, sails dropping with a muffled thud. They snubbed the ship tight and ran the gangplank down. Copper's feet were on the board before the dock end was secure. Skittering down the board, Illera pulled her up to a sleepy worker.

"Where is the king being kept?" she demanded, her voice imperious.

"Princess Illera?" The man goggled. "Thank all the gods ye have returned."

"The King," she demanded, "Where is the king?"

"Why, my Lady, they took him on to Seven Spires. They said he said he wanted to die at home where his memories were."

Without a thank you or a pause, Illera jammed her heels into the mare who broke into a wild career up the steep streets of Ocean Perch. She could hear the sound of hoof beats behind her, but Copper was born to run and run she would. None of the other horses would be able to keep her pace and Illera intended to force all the speed she could from her steed.

They clattered through the stone and dirt streets and out into the wilderness. The road ran straight here, straight until it intersected with the wide main road. Copper flew up and down the hills; soon dripping with sweat and bits of foam that flew back and spattered unheeded on Illera's cloak. She bent low over the mare's neck, her weight well forward and her knees urging the palfrey on with every stride. They ducked into the forest, and up the rocky hills and into the sunshine, then down again into the cool trees. When the mare's breathing became labored, Illera slowed her to a walk. A couple miles further, she lifted the horse into a gallop again. The sun was straight overhead when they reached the wide main road. She pulled Copper's head to the left and let her walk the next two miles. At a small creek running parallel to the road, she paused to allow the mare to drink when she was cooled. Pulling the horse's head around, she tackled the road again, urging the mare to greater and greater speed. The sun burned hot on their backs, making the mare sweat more. Illera ignored the sweat soaking her clothing and the foam that spattered her clothing. They dashed through small villages and past single family dwellings. The people ran to see her, but she cantered past without pause or greeting, hearing the sound of her name and cheers blowing to her on the wind. The day died around them in splendid colors of fuchsia and peach, fading into cobalt blue and black laced with stars. The mare needed a slower pace more often now, walking half the time and galloping the other half. First moon rose, bathing the road in light and making the footing surer. It was nearly set when second moon arose, and Illera thanked the powers that were watching over her that she would not have to contend with the tricky shifting shadows caused when both moons rode the night sky together. Her weary mind would have trouble comprehending what she saw. Copper plodded now, managing a slow canter from time to time, but lapsing into a heavy trot whenever Illera slackened the reins in the slightest. The mare's head was low, and she started to shiver when she walked for too long.

Feeling the pain in the mare's legs and her own bottom, Illera slid from the saddle. Her legs rebelled and refused to hold her. Thinking of her father, she forced strength into them, pulling Copper along behind. Second moon was sliding to its bed when Illera mounted again. In the pitch darkness, they wove their way towards Seven Spires, feet often leaving the road to stumble through the grass. Illera's sense of urgency was growing, dread rising up to smother her mind.

Pale pink fingers of dawn were streaking the sky when she caught sight of the tallest towers of the castle. Brutally she forced Copper into a gallop. The brave mare lifted her legs and ran, giving everything to her rider. They thundered up the approach to the drawbridge just as the sun lifted itself above the horizon. Illera pounded on the door that opened far too slowly for her. Scraping her knees and the mare's sides, she forced Copper through before the gates were opened fully. The horse staggered over the outer bailey to the inner gate, collapsing to her knees before the doors, her breaths coming with loud gulps and coughing. Copper collapsed. Tears streaming down her cheeks, Illera pounded until the gatekeeper opened to her. Tearing across the inner bailey, she dashed to the castle doors and threw them open. Weaving on unsteady legs, she raced up the stairs to her father's quarters and threw open the doors.

His breathing was audible from where she stood. The stench of rotting flesh smote her like a blow. Face pale and shrunken, he opened bright fever eyes and looked at her. The doctor standing beside his bed stared, mouth open. Maidservants scurried forward and led her to her father's side.

"Father, I'm here," she spoke softly. To the maids, she said, "Quick, go to my old room and bring me a bag with my herbs in it."

The women rushed to obey.

"Illera," Ian whispered, "Is it really you?"

She grasped his hand, cradling it to her face."Yes, father, it is really me."

King Ian waved his other hand feebly in the air.

"Have the scribe, the law keeper and Sir Garth come in here."

The doctor nodded and left.

"I'm here now father. I will make you well. Just hang on a little, and I'll soon have you back to your old self."

The withered, old white head shook from side to side.

"No, I'm sorry Illera. Not this time. I'm afraid you're just too late."

"Don't say that, I can't make it without you."

King Ian's fever cracked lips lifted at the corners. "Yes, you can. You always could, my precious, precious girl. Of all the good things in my life you were the best."

"No father, say I am the best."

"How I missed your sweet face."

"I missed you too, father, more than I can tell you."

A commotion at the door drew her attention. The maids were back with her herbs and the doctor with the scribe, law keeper, and Sir Garth. The scribe was a wizened brown man who had been a fixture in the castle so long his given name was lost. A stalking heron of a man, the law keeper, pranced to the bed with books and sheaves of paper tucked under the wing of one arm, held in place by thin insect fingers. Sir Garth was as always, dark, bearded and formidable. The scowl on his square dark face boded ill for any who crossed his will, while the powerful, heavily muscled hands and arms moved restlessly seeking an enemy to destroy. The doctor lifted the king higher on the bed.

"As you know, I appointed Sir Garth in charge of Madean when Illera was not here," the king began in a frail voice. "Now my daughter has returned, of course, the kingdom is to succeed to her and her chosen consort. Write that and publish it across the land."

Sir Garth's face darkened and with a mighty frown at Illera, he swept from the room.

"Beware Garth, daughter; he thought to gain where he had no blood right." Her father coughed.

"I'll see to it your majesty, now rest," the doctor told him.

"I'll rest for eternity when I'm done here, let me speak to my girl."

Sorting through her bag, Illera selected some blue mushrooms, now dried and shriveled. She tried to thrust them through her father's lips. The healing moss was dry and crumbly, but she gathered the bits with her hands and tried to insert them under the bandages to his wound. He slapped weakly at her hands.

"You must chew on these. I haven't got time to make tea, just chew on them," she begged.

He shook his head. "I'm tired Illera, too tired."

"Father you must try. I need you."

"Should the kingdom be lost, go to Faerie. They will always take you in, your mother's people."

"No!"

Raising both trembling hands, he clasped her face and looked long into her eyes.

"I'm sorry, my child. Sorry I have made such bad decisions for you. I pray you will forgive me."

Sobbing, Illera clasped his hands to her face. "There is nothing to forgive, nothing at all, Father please, don't leave me alone."

"I love you, my child. I love you as I loved your mother, more than my own heart," he whispered, his voice shaking with weariness.

As the first bright rays of sun lightened the window, a soft breath sighed from his lips, the light fading from his eyes. In horror, Illera released his hands, and they collapsed back to the bed. Shivers racked her body, and her teeth chattered as she backed away from the corpse of her father. She stared around. From the corner, the doctor was gazing at her with sympathy. The maidservants skittered to the bed, one closing the pale veined lids over the sightless eyes and the other lifting the sheet to cover his face.

A single sob forced its way past her lips and her eyes burned. She turned from the bed. On one knee, the scribe and the law keeper stared up at her. The doctor joined them.

"The king is dead. Long live Queen Illera!" the trio intoned.

The maidservants joined them.

"Long live Queen Illera!"

Shaking her head, she backed from the room into the hallway.

"No," she whispered, "No, it can't be. I won't have it."

The doctor strode to her and gave her a small shake.

"Then who will have it. Sir Garth? King Korul? It is your father's legacy to you. Would you let him down so?"

The pain of loss was a living thing inside of her breast, clawing and tearing her insides to shreds. Although her knees wobbled, she made her way to her old rooms, collapsing on the bed. The tears were dammed up inside, drowning her powers of thought and reason, waging their own war with the pain of her father's death. Maggie winged in through the open windows and perched on her lap making soft and sympathetic noises. Absently, Illera stroked the shining black and white feathers. Gradually a rising commotion in the courtyard grew upon her awareness. She moved to the window, but could make no sense of the noise. A timid tap on the door made her jump.

"Excuse me your majesty," Orille, the major domo said, "but the people wish to confirm for themselves that you are back and have taken your place as the rightful ruler of Madean."

His gimlet blue eyes regarded her with pity, and the light from the window bounced from his bald head as he bowed to indicate she should follow him. His slender hands, with long delicate fingers, pointed down the hallway, urging her without words. She looked at her dirty and travel-worn clothing, sweat-stained and spattered with lather. A queen should appear with dignity, but all her belongings were at Korul's castle, and the few remains left in her room would not create the impression of royalty. If the people could not accept her as she was, then so be it. She followed the butler.

Orille threw open the doors of the balcony. King Ian had used it to watch contests in the courtyard and to address the people when that was necessary. Illera had never stood on it before, and this time she wished she never had to. The babble of the crowd subsided as they beheld her approaching the railing. Squaring her shoulders, she marched to the front and looked down upon the gathered throngs. Never had she seen the courtyard so filled with bodies. The inner gates opened and more people continued to spill out onto the outer bailey. The grass was covered as far as she could see, right to the outer walls of the castle. The hush spread through the crowd like wind in grass and all faces turned up to her.

She tried to speak, but her voice cracked and would not come out of her mouth. A sigh rippled through the mob. She cleared her throat and tried again.

"My people," Her voice was weak and soft. She hardened her belly. "My people, to my great sorrow, my father, King Ian has died, murdered by the arrow of our invader from Frain, my personal enemy, Korul."

The wave of sorrow passed through the throng, and a few sobs reached up to her and tweaked her own waiting grief.

"I have a most difficult task ahead of me, to deliver Madean out of the hand of this madman and to avenge my father's death at his hands."

Sounds of fear lofted up to her from the crowd.

"We have allies in this fight. The King of Carnuvon will fight at our side as will the Sorwelk from the north. I have seen what life under Korul is like, the fashion of his people and servants. It is hard, hard and brutal and demeaning. You deserve far better than this and I can think of no better reason for me to lead you against him than the treatment he metes out to his own. Will you be with me?"

Silence, then a great roar shook the castle walls.

"Long live Queen Illera, Long live Queen Illera."

Most of the crowd was down on their knees offering their allegiance and loyalty to the new Queen. Illera bowed her head in acceptance, turned and left the balcony. Orille led her to new quarters, where a hot bath had been prepared. Illera tried to soak away the shivers as she battled the growing pain inside of her. Gowns were laid out for her inspection, but she did not care about what she was to wear. The serving girl selected a silver blue one and dressed her in that. She went to her father's library to meet with his officials.

The walls, windows, books, and furniture were all the same,

all screaming of normalcy on this most abnormal day. Illera felt things should have changed, the world should appear different, altered, but it just went on as if the best bit of it were still around and directing things. Seven people stood uncomfortably around the perimeter of the walls. Illera stalked to her father's desk and sat in his chair.

Orille assumed command of the meeting. "I don't know if you are acquainted with your father's right-hand people—you know Sir Garth, your father's head of the army, and Sir Trebut who is your father's quartermaster in charge of supplies." He indicated the lanky blonde man with piercing green eyes. "Of course we have the scribe. This is Sir North, a new man, just appointed by your father to be the royal armorer."

Sir North was a thick man, not that tall, but with arms and chest bulging with muscle. His face was flat and wide with dark, drooping eyes and a thick-lipped wide mouth. Beside him was a familiar face, the short, slender man she knew well, right down to the jagged scar across the bridge of his nose and one cheek. She had healed that wicked slash in better times.

"Jarot, the horse master, has a new assistant, Elisa who brought us many fine horses..."

Illera leapt from her seat with a cry. Lark and Raven's mother stepped from the shadows. Illera ran to her and embraced her, hugging her tight. The six men looked away and shuffled their feet. Orille coughed.

"I'm so happy to see you." Illera released the older woman. "How did you get here?"

"Female hysteria has no place in the ruling of a kingdom," Sir Garth muttered just audibly.

"Perhaps another time, your Majesty, I think the major domo wants to start the discussion." Elisa ducked her head.

Turning, Illera went back to her chair. She noted the contemptuous sneer on Sir Garth's face as she resumed her seat.

The scribe seated himself at a corner of the desk and the scratching of his pen filled the room.

She cleared her throat. "I think the first thing we should discuss is the funeral of my father..."

"I disagree," interrupted Garth, "we must discuss the troops and the protection of Madean."

Illera rose to her feet and pinned Garth with a gimlet stare.

"Would you have presumed to interrupt my Father in such a fashion?"

Startled, Sir Garth took a step backward. The scribe could not suppress a giggle, and even Orille was smiling at her imperious tone.

"Perhaps," Orille began in a conciliatory voice, "we should begin with the coronation of yourself, my Lady."

"No." Illera resumed her seat, "we will discuss the funeral arrangements for my father. We will lay him properly to rest before we have a coronation."

Sir North bowed low to Illera. "Your Majesty, I don't know how long Korul will hold his attack. We desperately need a plan of action."

"Then let us discuss the funeral so we can move on to that business."

The men of the convocation nodded.

"I want my father to lie in state with guard fore and aft the coffin for the full seven days. The coffin will be copper lined in blue. I want him prepared immediately, and all of Madean that chooses to pay homage to their former King is welcome to come into the castle in the front foyer and do so. Sir Trebut I want a table filled with food for the crowds as they depart."

Sir Trebut nodded his head, and Orille bowed low to the new Queen.

"It will be done, Queen Illera," Orille intoned.

"Very well, let's get to the war. What is the situation?"

Sir Garth spoke with a sneer in his voice. "King Korul is over the border with all the warriors of his kingdom, well trained and well armed. We have only farmers and a handful of knights, poorly trained and poorly armed. We are, fortunately; thanks to the mounts Elisa brought, very well mounted. It may be in the best interests of Madean to surrender."

"Never," Illera snapped. "We have men, we can make arms, and we have mounts. We need to mount a cavalry battle, a running one and to stretch his line of supply thin. Then, we sever that line. Sir North, how soon can you make enough arms for the men of Madean?"

"My Lady, with all due respect," snarled Garth, "you know nothing of military matters and have no qualifications to make such decisions."

"If I was given access to all the supplies and helpers I need," Sir North glared in Sir Garth's direction. "I could probably have enough swords and pikes in a fortnight. Shields take a little longer, and so does armor, morningstars, and javelins."

"I doubt Korul will give us that long, especially once he knows I am here. Weapons are to be given a priority status immediately. Take all the helpers you need and contact the miners. Who is in charge of metals Orille?"

"Meredan, your Majesty," the major domo replied.

"Send Meredan to Sir North, and they can work out the logistics of the matter. Sir Garth, you are to see to the training of the farmer's, merchants and their sons that are old enough to fight. I want all the able-bodied of Madean assembled..."

"Do you think I will take orders from a woman?" Sir Garth slammed his gauntlets against the desk.

Illera opened her mouth to reply when a loud commotion outside the closed doors disturbed them. When her keen ears picked up familiar voices, Illera commanded the doors be opened. A disheveled crew boiled into the room, Lark and Raven, worn and dirty, Dorian and Aelfred flushed and furious looking while Ashera managed to look cool, regal and utterly in control.

A cry of relief escaped Illera's lips, and she motioned them forward.

"What is this?" snarled Sir Garth. "How dare these strangers interrupt a council session?"

"Sit down Garth."

Sir Garth strode towards the travelers. "These men are with the enemy. They are Korul spies and squires..."

"They are my sons," interrupted Elisa.

"And they are my friends and Madean's allies in this fight. I said let them in," commanded Illera as Sir Garth blocked their passage.

With reluctant steps, the Madean knight moved aside, and the travel-worn entered the room.

"Orille, will you please arrange refreshments for our guests and have the maids prepare suitable quarters. These are Lark and Raven, illegitimate sons of King Korul of Frain and they will be taking rulership of his kingdom once we have eliminated him. Ashera is the lost daughter of King Uggarick of Carnuvon, and the reason he was raiding Madean these past twenty-five years. Now she has been returned to him, and he approves her accompanying us in the fight against Korul. Dorian and Aelfred are her half-brothers come to defend their sister against the hordes of Frain. And where are the Darkliete?"

Raven stepped forward. "They are following, with most of the crew of The Waiting, all fully armed, but we came on in haste. We thought you might need us."

Illera read the personal message in his blue eyes, a message of concern for her safety and the need to care for her well being. The grief within her chest eased the slightest amount.

"This is nonsense," Sir Garth blustered. "We can't include these strangers in our war council."

Illera stared at the big dark man until he stopped pacing and stood still. The silence stretched, broken by the scratching of the scribe's pen. Sir Garth faced her and stood still, fists planted on his hips.

Illera spoke softly. "Hear me and hear me well Sir Garth. Lark, Raven, and Ashera are not strangers to me. They have been the most faithful and trustworthy of companions, displaying honor and impeccable judgment at every crisis. To me, you are the stranger and should you question my instructions one more time; I will have you removed and replaced by one of my friends. Do I make myself clear?"

A sudden intake of breath from the residents of the room startled Sir Garth out of his glare.

"Oh, I hear you, your Majesty. Now you hear me. I have run this castle for your father for twenty years. There is no man in the kingdom of Madean more capable or qualified than I am to fight this war. You are a little girl, not even a woman yet and still; you presume to know more about fighting wars than I, a grown man and Knight with twenty years of experience. I will not be bullied by a child, and I will not be forced to fight in ways that will lose the kingdom. You are making a serious mistake if you alienate me."

Illera came from behind the desk and faced Sir Garth, craning her head back to stare into his eyes.

"You just counseled me to surrender to Frain. Are you not being rather inconsistent? Now you are the only one capable of saving Madean?"

"I am the only one capable of saving Madean. But for what? What do I get out of saving the country for you?"

"You get to do your duty, to serve Queen and country."

"If I do this, if I save the country, then you must marry me, and I will become king of Madean. As much as taking a child like you is beneath me, I will do so and thereby save Madean."

Illera turned her back and paced back to the desk where she sat down. She regarded Sir Garth through narrowed eyes. Beyond him, she could see Lark and Raven and the two princes regarding her with alarm. Illera smiled; a vicious feral grin. She waved one hand lightly in the air and leaned back in her chair.

"Was that a proposal?" she inquired the smile still on her face.

Sir Garth relaxed, a grin matching hers spreading across his darkly bearded face.

"I suppose it was, both a proposal and an ultimatum."

"Ah, how curious that my first proposal as queen should also be an ultimatum. 'a girl' likes a little romance, not a little force in her proposal. But being such a man of experience, I suppose you already knew that."

Sir Garth nodded, moving confidently forward to perch on the edge of her desk and stare down at her, triumph in the glint of his dark eyes.

"So you see, Lark, Raven, Dorian, and Aelfred, that is how you do not ask a Queen to marry you. Sir North, Sir Trebut, Orille, Jarot take Sir Garth and throw him into the dungeon. That is how I respond to threats and ultimatums. When you are ready to swear fealty to me and allegiance to Madean, we can have another discussion, Sir Garth." Illera slammed her small fist on the desk as the men grappled Sir Garth from the desk and out of the room.

The scribe, hunched over his ledger was smiling. Lark and Raven moved forward, looking at her silently. Dorian and Aelfred edged slightly towards the door as Ashera sprawled over the leather sofa facing the fireplace. A low chuckle escaped from her lips. Illera smiled as well.

"Now, I am in need of a man to head my army."

"Certainly," replied Raven

At the same time, his brother said, "I don't know, we should discuss this. After all, we are from Frain."

Looking at the desk and remembering how her father dealt with people, allowing them to reveal their hearts, she smiled again, a gentle pain-wracked curve of lips.

"Raven the job is yours if you want it. Lark, I'm sorry, but the position has been filled. Hasn't it?"

"Certainly, your Majesty. I am honored, and surprised that you asked me, but I will work for you to the best of my ability."

The other men returned from their unpleasant chore and Illera got down to serious discussion about the war and the tactics they might use.

Rising in the darkness, Illera paced the floor of her new quarters, bare feet padding soundlessly on the thick russet and blue carpets. Her body was exhausted, longing for the oblivion of slumber, but her brain would not be sated and let go of the day's events. Questions tumbled with ceaseless chatter through her mind: Was she insane to alienate Sir Garth? Would he have been the best ruler for Madean? Were Lark and Raven trustworthy? Would their meager experience be enough to save her land? What was she going to do with Uggarick's sons? Was the five days they had talked her into too long or too short a time for her father's lying in state? Would Korul attack before they could prepare? Illera rammed her fingers into her hair and pulled, willing all the nagging decisions to leave her alone. Her father was gone. It was enough to ponder the implications of that without polluting her mind with these necessary but unanswerable questions. She donned and tied a thick, red, velvet robe around her waist. The stairs were dark, the torches few and far between with menacing shadows reaching for her as she descended.

The bier was set in the foyer, in the mathematical center of the large space. Eight tall beeswax candles flickered, four at the head and four at the foot of the shimmering copper coffin. Her steps slowed as she approached, wanting to see, yet unwilling to believe in her heart what lay there. All day she had managed to avoid this, although they told her the village people were thronging by, leaving small offerings of woodland and garden flowers. The floor in front was littered with the wilted blooms. The women had been quick and efficient in preparing the body, and the cloying odor of cinnamon and cloves overlay the sweet corruption of wounds and death. The guard at the head of the casket shifted his position, his full armor catching the light and her attention.

"Is everything all right?"

Illera tried to smile and failed. "Yes, thank you. I just couldn't sleep, and I wanted to say my farewell without the entire country watching."

"Would you like us to leave?"

"No, he was a good king, and he deserves the honor you grant him by your presence."

The guard shifted back into the shadows, and Illera tiptoed to the coffin. The floor was cold on her bare feet, and she was shivering despite the warmth of the robe. She looked at the coffin material first. It was dark in the candlelight, dark, dark blue, shining where the light caught it. Obviously, they had given him the finest material from the storerooms. Her eyes traveled down the darkness to the pale face. His white hair was combed neatly, and the purple-veined lids were closed over his eyes. Except for the pale coloring of his face and its lack of movement, he could be asleep. She watched to see, if by some mistake he might take a breath or a nostril flutter with the indrawing of air. The lines of pain around his eyes reminded her of all he had been through in the last weeks since she was sent away. Some wicked sprite had graven sharp lines from his nose to the corners of his mouth and painted unhappy wrinkles on his forehead.

She took a breath and stood as close to him as she could. Unshed tears swelled in her throat, making breathing difficult. The smell and stillness of death rose about her threatening to suffocate her and take her to join him. For a moment, she thought that might be best, go with her father into death and let Garth have Madean. But the other love, the werwinstans rose unbidden at the thought. She loved this land, these people and all the creatures that lived in her demesnes. She could not abandon them and must struggle to do her best for they were hers and hers alone. A sob hiccuped in her throat. The clank of a knight walking across the floor disturbed her, and she looked up, grateful for the distraction.

Raven, dressed for battle, with his sword drawn, was walking towards her.

"My Lady, you should not be here alone in the night."

"And what of you?"

"I came to take my turn to stand honor guard for your father."

"Oh," was all she could squeak past a tight throat.

In two steps she went to him, collapsing against him as the storm of sobbing took her. Trembling so that she could barely stand, she clutched the interstices of his armor, her fingers grasping claws.

"I can stay another hour, take care of the Queen," the guard at the head told him as another knight relieved the guard at the foot of the casket.

Raven placed an arm about Illera and led her in stops and starts to the library. They sat down on the sofa, and she clung to him as she sobbed, using him as an anchor for her pain. The fire burned low, and Illera wept on, coughing and choking on the agony as she allowed it to flow from her. The embers fell to ash, and she was still, the odd tremor still racking her body.

"My lady, Illera, are you all right now?"

"No," she muttered back, her voice thick, "I'll never be all right again."

Raven held her tighter. "You will. You most definitely will. We'll all help you. Ashera and Lark and me. Even Dorian and Aelfred will help."

"You can't bring my father back."

"No, no we can't, but we can be your friends."

"Yeah." She sighed. "You are my friends, but I want my father."

Raven pushed her away and held her at arm's length.

"Illera, you can't have him anymore. You have your memories of him, and that has to be enough, because that is all you will ever have. You have to get over this sometime and now is a good time. You can decide to go on, or you can decide to wallow in grief. Your people need you. Your country needs you, and I need you."

"You don't understand." She wailed.

"You are right. I don't understand. I only understand Korul is coming and he wants Madean. Your people need you. You have a duty to them and to yourself, and I've never known you to shun your duty."

Illera looked at him strangely. His face was in shadow, only the far light of the torches glinting on his eyes and armor. His silhouette was dark on darker, an odd outline without features. She closed her eyes.

"I know you're right, but it hurts so much."

"I know it hurts. I can see it in your face, so darling Illera, grieve in private, or with me if you will, but be brave in public."

"I tried." She hiccuped as he drew her close to him again, the sobs returning.

"I saw," he replied, his voice rumbling directly to her from his chest, "You were magnificent this morning. I've never seen such royal authority on anyone. You truly are a Queen. And when you dismissed Sir Garth, I thought the others were going to swallow their tongues. All except the scribe, he enjoyed every bit of the incident."

"I did all right? It wasn't a mistake?"

He rubbed his hand in circles around her back. "No, you didn't make a mistake. If Sir Garth was allowed to rule Madean, I think it would shortly become another Frain. He didn't want to marry you because he loves you, he only wanted the throne."

"And what about you?"

Raven laughed, bouncing her head up and down.

"I think you are trying to trick me, but if you were to marry me, I wouldn't care if you were a penniless waif from the woods or the Queen of the entire world. I like you for being who you are."

Illera began to sob uncontrollably again, and Raven held her through the long dark night. Just before the dawn, she fell asleep. He carried her to her rooms and left her to sleep off her exhaustion while he stood guard over the departed king.

By midmorning, Illera was taking inventory in the armory with Sir North, Lark and Ashera. Their cache was indeed spare, but Sir North had seven smithies set up and working, day and night to build up the stores of swords and pikes at least.

From there they went out of the castle to the horse herds. Jarot and Elisa met them. Illera hugged the older woman.

"I regret I killed Copper getting back to my father. She was a fine and courageous mare."

Elisa smiled. "Relieve yourself of guilt on that account. When I heard you arrive, I went to the castle and got her. She was hard used, and her wind is be broken, but she can serve as broodmare for many years to come. See."

Elisa pointed to a fiery chestnut on the far side of the herd. Illera could make out the stockings and blaze down the face. A knot she had not known was inside her unraveled and smoothed out. A deep sigh from the center of her being forced its way through her lips. Elisa laughed.

"You are not the only one who can doctor animals."

"Your Majesty," interrupted Jarot, "as you can see, we have five times the number of horses that Korul does..."

"It was my understanding that these horses were Korul's." Illera cut him off.

"Yes, well yes, of course, they used to be, but…"

"How did they come to be here?"

Elisa laughed aloud. "Lark and Raven warned me that Korul was about to go on another rampage and that you had killed Torul."

"I didn't kill Torul, he fell, but go on."

"My husband, the boy's stepfather was sent to me with a note explaining the state of things and a suggestion that I take the herd and bring them to Madean in order to be safe. That is just what I did. Seth is here now, helping make weapons I think, although he is a blacksmith, not an armorer. Your father was most hospitable and offered me a place next to Jarot. I was happy to accept."

Illera grinned at the other woman. "As I am happy to accept your presence with my people."

"But when I become King of Frain, my mother and stepfather will return home with me." Lark placed a proprietary arm around Elisa's shoulders.

"That will be your mother's decision," Illera corrected him.

"Well, as you can see, your Majesty," Jarot said, trying to regain control of the situation, "we have a large number of well-trained war horses with which to fight."

"Can you train some of the farmers or their sons enough to be of use in the time we have?"

Bowing low Jarot replied, "I will do my best, your Majesty. I will do my best."

"I know Jarot. I know you always do your best, and I appreciate it very much, and so will all of Madean. I'll leave you to get organized while I meet with Sir Trebut."

Illera, Ashera, and Lark marched back to the castle, and to the stuffy supply rooms, Sir Trebut occupied. They spent several hours in close discussion with him about supplies, depots, caches and supply lines before the fussy knight was satisfied.

Orille prepared a banquet for the guests and knights. The Darkliete and sailors had arrived as well as a large contingent of Carnuvon, all excellently armed and ready to fight. Their troops had grown by one third, and the Darkliete promised warriors from Sorwelk would arrive within a few days. Although she wanted nothing more than to return to her room and wallow in grief, Illera made small talk and pleasantries to the guests and danced when required with the various hopeful suitors and dignitaries. She followed Raven's advice and poured her heart into the solidifying of Madean's friends, putting her personal desires aside.

The whirlwind of planning in the last few days had settled inside her head. It spun, around and around until Illera thought her stomach was going to turn. She had managed, and managed well these frightful days, always with her friends by her side, lending her their strength when her own was insufficient. The funeral cortege was waiting in the courtyard below her father sealed away forever and about to take his last trip, to the vault. She dressed in the flowing white mourning gown. The mourners with white ribbons on their arms waited; the honor guard mounted on black horses. Abbadon waited for her to mount and lead the way, Raven at his bridle, Lark, and Ashera following on foot, but her dizziness would not allow her to rise and descend the stairs to the waiting funeral.

The soft tap on her door brought her upright from the dressing table over which she was leaning. The two maids at her back whispered behind their hands, annoying her. The tap came again, and one of them scurried to open it after a quick glance at her mistress.

"My Lady," Orille stated, "the cortege is waiting for you. You must come, or you will shame your father."

She sighed. "I know Orille, but I'm sick. My head is so dizzy that I can't stand up let alone ride."

In three quick strides, Orille was across the room and lay a palm on her forehead.

"Highness, you have no fever. It is probably distress of heart. As Queen of Madean, you must control yourself. It is your duty."

Illera lay her head again on the desk. "I am getting heartily sick of hearing those words. I know my duty. I know I am Queen, but I am sick, truly sick."

Giggles from the girls behind made her raise her head and glare at them.

"What is so funny about being sick?"

Orille coughed. "It is the nature of your illness."

Illera looked at him one eyebrow raised in question.

"Well, you have been with the two squires from Frain and the two princes from Carnuvon a lot. Tongues will wag."

Illera felt her face grow hot as the meaning of his words dawned on her. Fury brought her to her feet, circles of bright red in either cheek. She took a step towards the now frightened maids.

"How dare the servants make my efforts to save Madean a matter of prurient gossip," she snarled.

"There," Orille said, smiling, "the sickness has past."

Illera spun to face him, realizing the dizziness had left her. It jolted her, making her realize that she must face the task ahead. Sighing, she obediently followed him out of the door, down the staircase, out the main door of the castle and through the throngs of mourners to the head of the line. Turning his great head, Abbadon whickered at her as Lark boosted her into the saddle. As Maggie glided down from the castle walls, the musicians positioned in front of the hearse began to play. The mournful, haunting notes of the flute silenced the low murmur of the crowd, and when the heavy drumbeat began in a slow cadence, Raven led Abbadon forward, one halting step at a time. Maggie perched on the stallion's poll and refused to be moved no matter how he tossed his head.

Everything had a surreal feeling, unlike the glamour of Faerie, but a clarity, a sharp-edged vision, and unnaturally keen hearing. She forced her spine straight and tall and held her chin high and face impassive. The long, slow march wound from the approach to the castle and through the nearest village to the edge of the quarry. Illera heard the murmurs of wonderment as the cortege passed by, the villagers standing in respectful stillness as their king went to his rest. The shuffling and whispers behind her were disturbing, but Illera stared straight ahead trying to shut out the others who were there to mourn with her. The pink marble of the crypt hove into view, nestled amid the carefully tended lawn and encircled by gnarled oak trees. The light reflected in painful fashion from the arches and columns polished to a mirror gloss. Raven led Abbadon to the left and halted. He lifted her down from the high saddle and gently squeezed her arm as he set her on her feet. She stood on shaking legs as the rest of the mourners formed a semi-circle beside and behind her.

Turning her head, she noticed what the whispering was about. Every dog, cat, pig, goat, sheep, donkey, horse, or bovine in the area had joined their cortege. A smile tugged at the edges of her mouth. From the surrounding trees crept rabbits, wolves, lynx, lions, deer, elk, as well as a myriad of birds that filled the trees and the surrounding lawn with their singing, far more cheerful than the flute. The people shifted nervously amid the press of creatures, tame and domestic. The casket was unloaded and placed in front of the wide double doors. Then the priests had their say, extolling the virtues of good King Ian and praising the excellencies of his reign. They committed his body to the memory of the gods. The Darkliete presented a service, and again Illera tuned her ears to the wind in the trees and the birds and rustlings of the wild things. When the ceremonies finished, the doors were unlocked and opened. Her father vanished into the darkness within. In her mind, she called a farewell to him.

She shook her head as the priests emerged and the doors closed with a loud crash. The sound of the tumblers turning as the vault was locked again, was one of the loudest noises she had ever heard. When Raven grasped her elbow, she realized she was shivering. She looked around. All the animals had surrounded her, with Raven, Lark, and Ashera in the middle with her. The rest of the human mourners had separated themselves and stood on the other side of the lawn. Illera went to her knees and thanked each creature as it passed by, bestowing her good wishes and blessing upon it. As she caressed each one, it vanished back to its normal place in the natural world. She turned to thank the humans just as a man riding a lathered horse burst into the clearing, waving his arms wildly over his head.

"Korul, Korul is advancing," the rider gasped as he tumbled from the horse. "He is on Madean soil and is razing the villages as he comes, raping the women and slaughtering the children. The men he binds and drags behind him. Please, Lady, help us."

Illera turned immediately to Abbadon. One of her friends, she knew not who, threw her to his back. She felt a body thump down behind her and turned her head to see Raven, his face grim urging her back to the castle. The war-horse needed little coaxing, lifting his mighty hooves into a gallop as they thundered back to Seven Spires.

The gates were closed and locked, and they lost precious minutes as the portcullis was raised and the gates opened. Abbadon raced to the next gate and through. Illera slid from his back and dashed to her room. Quickly donning the armor Sir North had made her, she sprinted back to the courtyard.

It was a madhouse of confusion. Men were running, and wagons were being loaded. Horses and women were screaming. Farrell, Kenna and Min, young people Orille had chosen for her, were packing a wagon loaded with tents, food and such items as the Major Domo deemed necessary for a Queen.

Elisa was at Illera's side, guiding her to the white war-horse she was to ride. He was a more slender build than Abbadon and Appolon, combining the look of speed with power. Gracefully, white feathers flowed up his legs, and his mane and tail were long and silken. The animal rolled a wild blue eye at her as she ran up to him. She stopped her rush and went quietly to his head, talking to him low and rubbing around his swiveling ears. The stallion lowered his head and smelled her. Rubbing his muzzle up and down her face, he accepted her.

"His name is Commitment," Elisa told her.

"Hello, Commitment." Illera sang to him. He snorted at her and pawed the ground with one hoof.

"Lady, hurry. The nearer Korul gets to Seven Spires the greater the danger," called Ashera from her tall gray mount.

"I'm coming."

Elisa gave her a leg up. She turned, checking that her saddle-bags of special supplies were in place. Out of the mass confusion of the yard, an army had taken shape. Knights were arrayed around and behind her as supply wagons completed their loading. Turning Commitment's head to the open gate, she put her heels to him. With a mighty snort, he charged out of the inner gate and then the outer gate, racing to meet the King of Frain.

The first mad dash to battle slowed; many miles must be covered before they met the opposing army. Light riders on fast horses raced ahead, bringing news of Korul's whereabouts so they might be able to choose the battleground. Information began filtering back: Korul had smashed all of the small villages visible from the main road. Korul made the captured men of Madean march ahead of his army to protect them from ambush and arrows. Korul had catapult and other war engines pulled by oxen because he was short of horses. Korul had almost a thousand men to fight against them, all armed and trained in warfare.

Korul was moving quickly and was already a third of the way to Seven Spires.

Illera called a halt just before dark.

Lark pushed Appolon close to Commitment as she was about to dismount.

"Your Highness, if we push on we can engage Korul before another day has passed. You are allowing him to kill and destroy more of Madean by this halt."

Raven cantered up to her other side.

"If we engage Korul tonight, after dark, we will be at a disadvantage. Let him tire his men and horses by pressing on through the night. We rest and come at him with all our power tomorrow. About five miles ahead, there is a wide grassy meadow beside the road. On either side are tall hills, perfect for hiding troops. Our horses will have room to maneuver, and our men will have a place to retreat to if necessary. Archers should be stationed on the hilltops to shoot down into Korul's men while sparing our own."

"But Illera, there are villages there. What about them?" Lark argued.

"They will take their chances with the rest of us," she spat, tired from the long day and the distress of her soul.

Reining Appolon around, he called back to her, "I hope you don't regret making such a mistake."

"It's all right your Highness; Lark is just full of nerves. I've heard other men talk about this before they go into battle." Raven turned Abbadon back towards her.

Illera smiled at him. "Thank you, my friend. The way Lark wants to organize things you'd think he was my troop leader instead of you."

Raven laughed aloud. "Lark has always been the leader ever since we were young. He just does what comes naturally, and he's good at it. I think it annoyed him that you picked me instead of him. I don't have as much experience at telling people what to do."

"I know." Illera slid down Commitment's side. "That's why I selected you. I don't want to argue about my orders every time I give one."

Raven followed her to the tent they had erected for her.

"And what are your orders, your Highness?"

Seating herself in a folding chair, Illera shook her head. The commotion of the camp had caused a return to the dizziness of the morning.

"I think you should station some men behind the one hill, good men, familiar with weapons and fighting. Some of the younger untrained men should be with them as well. Anyone who is good with the bow should be on the hilltops. They can shoot from there down into Korul's army and try to avoid our men, whom they are using as shields, as you said. When the lines are mixed, the archers can join the fighters below. I want the men behind the hill held in reserve and if it appears that Korul is pushing our men back, then bring them in behind Korul's army and sandwich him between two of our forces."

"Do you really think we have enough men to allow for that?"

"How can I say? I don't know, probably not, but I can't think of anything else to do. Ride in and strike and ride out again quickly. Try not to engage in hand to hand combat. His men are well trained, and ours aren't. Try to make it a running battle."

"I'll try your Highness; I'll try."

"Raven, I'm heartily sick of this Highness business. Can't you call me Illera still?"

Raven smiled and shook his head. "No, I can't. You are a queen, and I'm just the son of a wicked King and brother to the heir apparent. It wouldn't be good for morale. Good night, your Highness."

Sighing, Illera watched him go, wondering if he would be alive to argue with her tomorrow night. One of the attendants brought her a plate of food that she picked at until it had gone cold. She left it and went to her cot, determined to rest. Uneasy, her mind kept her tossing and turning, and calling out to the world until the early hours of the morning when she finally dozed off.

The quiet of the predawn hours was broken by the sounds of the camp being struck. Groggy and dizzy Illera was awakened by a sharp beak thrust into her tender parts.

"Aw Maggie," she mumbled, "I just got to sleep."

The attendant was there with warm washing water, and another brought her clothes and armor. Sighing Illera rose, preparing for the day she never wanted to see. She forced breakfast down her throat and strode from the tent to face her troops. One of the attendants helped her mount, and she turned Commitment to face her army, mounted and ready to fight.

She took a deep breath and called in her loudest voice, "You all know what you are fighting for. My prayer is that each and every one of you returns whole to your lands from this battle. But know, should the worst happen, that you are saving Madean for your children and your wives and for the future. You are keeping our country from the tyranny of Korul. I salute you all."

She wheeled her stallion around and set off at a slow canter to the sound of their cheering. Abbadon and Appolon surged forward to ride on either side of her, while Ashera and her two brothers followed behind. As they approached the twin hills, Illera reined Commitment to the left and up to the top of the hill. From there she could see far down the road. It was clear. No troops traveled down its dusty surface. She closed her eyes and called, bringing her talents to the battle.

The dust began to rise in the distance. Illera watched her troops split apart, a smaller portion disappearing behind the opposite hill and a group of riders behind her own. Archers rode up to the top, and some joined her on the crest of her hill. They dismounted and hid their horses behind the mound. Illera sat her horse and watched the procession wending its way down the road. Faint cries of pain and terror reached her ears from the men brutally thrust along at the front and leading sides of the column. She looked south. Raven had his men arrayed across the road, blocking any progress past the meadow.

The creak of leather and scent of dust and fear came to her, stretching her already tight nerves to the breaking point. Korul slowed his advance, shielding behind the captured men of Madean. His army ground to a halt between the hills and stretching far back along the road.

Illera began to hum, singing low in her throat as the armies paused at the cusp of battle, staring, assessing each other. A flashing beam of light sparked from Raven's standard and the bowmen drew their weapons. A flight of arrows rained down inside the protective ring to fall upon Korul's men. Screams of anger and a few of pain broke the tense, silent waiting. With a roar, Korul's men brutally pushed the Madean prisoners aside, trampling those who did not move fast enough. His knights sallied forth, javelins poised to strike Raven's army. The mounted Madeans swayed aside letting the Franians pass through their middle without engaging them and reforming behind them. Korul's army was split into two sections. Half of Raven's men faced the Mounted Franians and half the heavy weapons and footmen. The troops hiding behind the opposite hill crept behind the foreign troops and waited for the signal. Korul yelled, and his men drove into action, swinging swords, morningstars and all manner of weapons. The Madeans engaged in their clumsy way, trying to stop the force of the armed and experienced men.

Raven and his army were pushed back towards the waiting Franian soldiery. They fought fiercely, Lark and his brother accounting for half the downed enemy, but their troops were young and green, and they were no match for the seasoned fighters. Illera closed her eyes and began to sing. She felt her forces gathering. A gravelly voice joined itself to hers, and the wind began to rise, whipping sand and debris into the eyes of the Franians. From the north, a pair of dragons flew into view. One was very large and the other very small. They hovered over the cluster, heads wagging back and forth as if counting. A rain of fiery spit fell upon the catapults of Frain and among all their wagons. They burst into flame, scattering the soldiers guarding them. The oxen bawled and tried to bolt, but the dragons picked them off, carrying them away to nests to be consumed later. Three griffins flew in from the south, gliding on still wings through the wild whirling wind and wilder fighting. Illera watched carefully, and where the Franians appeared to be winning, she directed the great birds to attack. Stooping with extended claws, they lifted Franian knights from their horses, soaring high on straining wings then dropped them to plummet back to earth and seize another. The horses spooked and shied, bolting in uncontrollable fright. Snarling from the edges of the conflict told Illera that the lions and dire wolves were hard at work, selecting the Franians for their victims. The battle below had deteriorated into a vicious free for all. Thunder and lightning rippled through the morning; the sky grew dark as midnight. Sharp forks of lightning speared earthward, spitting Korul's men. The reek of burning human flesh rose up to her. Illera shook her head, knowing it was not of her doing, yet grateful for the assistance. Thick gloom enveloped the road between the hills.

The Madeans rode madly to and fro, slashing at the invaders. Small cyclones of wind obscured the battle, then revealed it again. The meadow was chaos. The hidden troops joined the other fighters, pinning Korul's men between them. The battle began to turn slowly in Madean's favor. Illera felt a tiny spark of hope kindle in her breast. The fighters mixed together now, and the dust and dark made it difficult to distinguish friend from foe. Raven's standard waved directly ahead, while Lark's plunged deep into the melee furthest north. Ashera was invisible in the murk, but it did seem as if they were winning.

A horse thundered up the path behind her. Illera turned, straining her eyes to see who was approaching. On the back of a large gray mount, his face drawn back in a rictus of rage, Korul loomed out of the dark. With two hands, he swung a double-bladed ax around his head. He screamed incomprehensible obscenities as he charged at her.

Belatedly, Illera put the spurs to Commitment, and he plunged down the hill in front of her, Korul only a stride behind. The white stallion stretched his neck and raced for the wild milling of the battle, with Korul gaining slowly. High overhead Maggie screamed as Illera tried to call one of the griffins. Their minds were full of bloodlust now and hard to control. She tried as the war-horse galloped over the rough ground, leaping over bodies and wounded, swerving around combatants. Korul pursued with a relentless focus. A miniature tornado of wind dashed between them, causing Korul's horse to shie. A piece of midnight lurched out of the surrounding darkness and confusion. His shoulder drove into the chest of Korul's mount, knocking it sideways and off stride. Turning, Illera saw the battle ax whistle over Raven's head as Abbadon leapt aside. Korul hurled the weapon, striking Raven on the shoulder, knocking him from Abbadon's back. Korul bounced from the gray's back and approached with his sword drawn. Another gray horse reared out of the mist and a sword sliced wickedly at Korul's neck. Illera saw the thin red line it left in its wake.

Korul spun around, his face showing surprise as Ashera dropped from her horse and confronted him. A cruel grin spread across his face. His weapon struck like a snake, aiming for her face. Her sword shrugged it aside and embedded itself in Korul's heart.

"Why prolong this. I just want you dead, dead, dead," Ashera spat at him as she stabbed again and again.

The King of Frain slumped to the ground, his face a rictus of horror.

She raised the sword high overhead and hacked through Korul's neck, severing his head from the body. Taking a pike, discarded on the ground, she impaled it and held it aloft, the horrified expression on Korul's face outermost.

With a grin she ran through the battle shouting, "Lay down your weapons, Korul is dead. Lay down your weapons, Korul is dead."

Illera hurried to Raven, slipping from her mount. Blood soaked his armor, dripping from a deep gash on his shoulder. She explored the wound with trembling fingers. It was clean but bleeding. She used her healing skills to staunch the flow of blood, then bound it in moss from her saddlebags.

The storm lessened, lightning ceased, and the clouds began to shred and blow away in the still violent winds. Illera stayed by Raven waiting for him to wake. Others of her people came to her, and she treated their injuries. Korul's men retreated to a position against one of the hills, pikes outthrust, waiting for a leader to take charge. When Illera had treated all of her own men, and Raven was still unconscious, she moved to the front of the Franian lines.

"Your king is dead," she told the frightened men. "He is dead and his bastard son, Lark, will be your new king."

Turning to her own people, she asked, "Where is Lark? Was he wounded in the battle?"

Sir North stepped forward. "No one knows, your majesty. Lark was with us through most of the battle, but vanished after Princess Ashera slew King Korul. He is not injured, nor is he slain. Just vanished."

"What do you mean just vanished? A knight can't just vanish in the course of a battle. He must be among the slain?"

"I'm so sorry, your Highness." Sir North indicated the battle-field. "But I have searched the wounded, and the dead and Sir Lark is not among them."

"Get me, Dorian."

Before she could catch her breath or further puzzle about Lark's absence, Dorian rushed up panting.

"Prince Dorian, I beg a favor."

A wide grin split his huge face. "Of course, Queen Illera. You know any assistance I can be to you would be a boon to me."

"Lark has vanished, and I must search. Would you act as my agent over the captured remains of Korul's army? I need them to be disarmed and treated for their wounds."

"I would treat them all to an icy hell," snarled Dorian, his handsome face twisting into a mask of hatred.

Illera snapped, "No! I wanted them treated with decency."

"After the crimes, they've committed?" Dorian hissed back.

"These men committed nothing but loyalty to their sovereign. They need proper treatment and food. I want friends here, not enemies."

"The Carnuvon always slaughter the wounded and captured of the enemy. That way you know your back is safe!" Dorian stamped about a circle.

Illera threw up her hands and strode away. Meeting Ashera waving her bloody pike through the air gave Illera an idea.

"Ashera, were there any unusual fighters in this battle, you know creatures that should not have been here?"

Ashera's smile grew smaller as she thought back over the past battle.

"Yes," she mused, "but maybe not. It might have been just a very big, ugly Franian, but I thought I might have seen a Shul skulking around the outsides of the battle lines. I might be wrong though."

Illera nodded her head. "No, I don't think you're wrong. It make perfect sense now. Ashera, would you take over the control of the army while Raven is indisposed. I need someone to watch over the Franians."

A smile of great beauty spread over Ashera's face, illuminating it with a great radiance.

"You want a woman to be in control of your army?"

"Of course? I had thought to ask your brother, but I think you are better qualified."

Ashera laughed out loud, drowning out the cries of the wounded and the loud voices of the victors.

Illera smiled with her. "You do know how I would wish the prisoners treated?"

Nodding, Ashera replied, "Cure what wounds as can be cured, make sure everyone is well fed and bedded down and take care of everybody."

The giantess rolled her eyes skyward as Illera laughed.

"Then be my vice-commander of the army until I return."

"Where are you going my Lady, I mean Illera?"

"I'm going to get Lark back."

CHAPTER 11

*I*llera paused once, at Raven's tent. In unconscious abandon, he lay still encased in his rent and bloody armor. Heavy shadows darkened his face, and she frowned at the sight of him lying there so helpless. Checking the wound, she knelt by his pallet; hands held flat above the bandages binding his shoulder. She closed her eyes and willed the flesh to heal, meshing her energy and life force with his. She poured her strength into him until she felt dizzy and just spared herself from toppling over with a hand on his belly. It came away sticky with drying blood.

Rising, she looked again at his face. It was pale, but the dark shadows had retreated. Unconsciously, she wiped her hand down one thigh, staining her armor with his blood. Sighing, she turned to go, pausing at the tent to look back once more.

"Heal well my friend. If circumstances were different I should stay and care for you, but Lark needs me, and I can't see you wanting me to abandon him. Heal well."

Maggie fluttered out of the descending twilight. Illera clutched her precious friend to her breast. With an indignant squawk, Maggie struggled loose and perched on her shoulder.

She stroked the bobbing head. Taking the bird on her hand, she turned towards Raven's tent.

"Maggie, stay with Raven. Take care of him for me."

The magpie shook her head and ruffled her feathers.

"Please Maggie," Illera pleaded. "I need to concentrate all my wits on finding Lark. If I don't, who knows what will happen in Madean? I need you to watch Raven for me. If, if something bad happens, you come and get me, and I will try to get back as quickly as possible. Okay?"

Grumbling, Maggie fluttered from her hand and landed at the entrance of the tent, walking with exaggerated steps into the darkness within. Illera turned and stumbled back to her tent. There was unease in her entrails at the thought of undertaking this journey bereft of all she had won, stripped of even her life-long avian companion.

One of her attendants bustled around outside her quarters, fussing with the fire and the evening meal. Commitment whinnied from the picket lines a few steps away.

The boy looked at her and blanched. "Your Highness! You are injured. I'll run to the physician immediately."

"Min, wait. This isn't my blood. I need you here. I want travel rations for my horse and myself for several days. I need them right now."

"Surely your Highness doesn't need to ride back to the castle in the middle of the night. In the morning the path will be clearer."

"I'm not going to the castle, Min. I have to find Sir Lark."

"I will run around the camp, Lady. I can go very fast, and I will find him for you."

Illera smiled at the boy, all long-boned, gangly adolescent eagerness. "Sir Lark has been taken by the Shul. It's there that I have to go, so just prepare the rations please."

She turned to the picket lines, refusing to take notice of the boy's appalled look. Saddling and bridling Commitment, she pulled him behind her to the tent. Min handed her tightly wrapped packages, which she stowed in her saddlebags.

"Highness, let me go with you," the boy begged.

Illera smiled at him. "You tempt me Min, but no, my own life is enough to risk on this foolish venture."

"Please, Highness. Give me a chance to prove myself."

Pausing, Illera consulted her inner compass. It was true her heart leapt when she heard she did not need to go alone, but what of the sense of failure that was dragging at her at the thought of this journey. The idea of Min lightened the despair and gave her the first slight glimmers of hope. She turned and looked at him, all angles, arms, and legs with nothing that quite fit together yet. His dark mop of curly hair and shining, hopeful dark eyes gleaming in the firelight accenting the parted lips full of the hope of glory and daring adventure.

"Very well Min. Get yourself a horse and supplies. And tell the other squires where we are going. Tell them to let Ashera know come morning, but not before. Understand? Not until the morning."

"Yes, yes your majesty, I understand," he called over his shoulder as he scrambled away to do her bidding.

The darkness inside of her vanished like the mist before the sun. She knew this would succeed, she knew it in her bones. Pulling Commitment around, she scrambled to his back.

Only muscles aching to the point at which she wanted to scream made her stop and allow Min to make camp. It would be only a few hours until dawn, and Commitment and Min's stocky bay were tired, glad to rest and graze. Illera lay on her back and stared at the night sky, the pinpricks of the stars glowed with unusual brightness in the absence of the moons. She was weary in every fiber of her body.

"Lady, why do the Shul want Sir Lark? I mean he never fought against them so's they'd want to kill him."

Without looking away from the arching heavens, she replied. "It's me they want Min, not Sir Lark. He's just the bait they are using to get me."

After a pause of a few minutes, he asked again, "Why do they want you Highness? Did you do something bad to them?"

Illera laughed. "No, Min, I did good things for them."

"Then why, Lady? What do they want with you?"

"It's not even really me they want. What Targ wants is gold. A friend of mine once told them, in order to save our lives mind you, that I was worth a large ransom of gold. So that's why they want me, to trade for gold."

Min pattered up and handed her a tin plate of steaming food. Illera's stomach rebelled at the thought, but she sat up and forced herself to eat. Across the fire, Min watched her as he bolted his own food.

"What do they want the gold for your Highness?"

Illera looked at him puzzled. "They just want the gold."

"But what good is it? You can't eat it, or wear it, or ride it. It just sits there, and you have to drag it around, and it's heavy. What good is the gold to the Shul?"

Illera set her plate on the ground and stared at the boy. His words echoed like one of the Thunderer's bolts in her mind. 'What good is it? What good is it? What good is it?' It was, as if, for one dizzy moment the world changed its configuration and settled into one more in harmony with reality; the eyes of a child seeing what the rest were too blind to notice. She grinned, her mouth stretching wide and her eyes lighting in sudden under-standing.

"Min, I think you just saved Madean, Frain and me. When we get back from this 'adventure,' you are going to be the personal squire of whichever man I choose to be King of Madean beside me. If he doesn't want you, then he doesn't get me either." Illera caroled a song to the stars, a shout of laughter.

"Your Majesty?"

She leapt to her feet and danced around the fire to the boy. Seizing his hand, she drew him to his feet and hugged him, a swift clasping of arms around his gangly frame. She moved back to her side of the fire and flipped the blanket over her shoulders.

"Go to sleep. We have a lot to do tomorrow."

"Yes, your Highness." Min huddled still against the ground, watching her, puzzled at her behavior.

Illera greeted the dawn with a lightened heart. Fully formed in her mind, the plan of action shaped itself while she slept, so that now she could approach the Shul full of confidence and goodwill. She called to the creatures she needed as she washed and groomed Commitment. After a quick bite of breakfast, she swung into the saddle, and they chased the shadows towards the mountains.

At midday, a pair of ewes and a splendid ram joined them on the trail, their shepherd boy puffing along behind them. Sweat trickled in runnels down the child's face, and he left a long smudge of dirt across his forehead and nose as he wiped it away with his tattered sleeve. Illera reined her stallion to a standstill and leaned down over the cantle.

"Greetings, boy. What is your name?"

The boy stared up at her with wide blue eyes, unspeaking. Min kneed his bay in to tower over the child almost knocking him down.

"Here now, answer the Lady. This is Queen Illera, ruler of Madean," he snapped, all bluster and authority.

"It's all right Min. Give the child some room." Illera noticed the child shrink away in fright. "I am Illera, Queen of Madean, and I need your help very much. If you will help me, it might just save our whole country."

She dismounted and tossed the reins to Min. Approaching

the boy she knelt before him.

"Won't you help me?"

"Y-y-yes y-y-your M-m-m-m-m-majesty," stammered the child. "M-m-my name is N-n-n-n-n-nar-r-r-in."

"Thank you, Narin. I know it is a big responsibility to take care of the sheep, for your parents?" At the boy's nod, she continued, "And I know you must do a very good job because you have chased them all the way here to me and that shows me you are a very good shepherd. But you see I called these sheep because I need them very much. I need them to save our country, so all our people can live in peace and have enough to eat and a good place to live. Do you understand?"

The boy nodded his head, his eyes wide.

"Now I know it is not fair to ask your parents to pay for the whole country, so I tell you what I'll do. I'm going to give you a piece of paper that your parents can take to the castle, Seven Spires, and one of my servants will give them some money to pay for the sheep. Is that okay?"

The boy nodded, his eyes wider than ever. Illera strode to her saddlebags and ripped a scrap of paper from one of the packages. With a small stick of graphite, she scribbled the note and gave it to the boy who tucked it into the pouch at his waist. She mounted the stallion, and they headed down the thread-thin path with the three sheep following. The child stood still on the trail, staring after them until they were out of sight.

They moved gradually into the rolling hills, gentle swellings of the ground at first, becoming higher as the day wore on. The row of hills heaved upward, growing ever steeper until they blended into the purple mountains ahead of them. A warning prickled down the back of her neck and unseen eyes bored into the back of her skull. Someone, somewhere behind, someone important was staring, was coming. She continued on, speeding the pace of the horses as the sheep fell behind. Their distressed baaing causing her to slow again.

The hills rose, giving a better view of the plains and road behind. She paused on every crest and glanced behind, searching for the eyes that followed. The horizon on all sides was empty of people of any sort, but the feeling persisted, strengthening as they approached the scrubby open forest. As they jogged through the aspen, birch and pine Illera listened to the bird's songs. These were normal, the larks and sparrows singing as usual from their leafy perches and fluttering past on urgent avian missions. The sights and sounds were all normal for this area, the insects and wind, small rustlings of rodents and the occasional crash of a larger animal fleeing from their path. Still, the sense of imminent confrontation with someone, some watcher from the rear pricked at her nerves and transmitted itself to Commitment, making him shy and duck from every shadow. The trees grew thicker as the land heaved upward. As twilight settled in, Illera told Min to make camp in a small clearing surrounded by birch and clean rock. He bustled around making a fire, fetching water and cooking, as Illera stared out into the darkening forest, trying to thrust her senses along with the wind, to discover who or what was picking at her nerves. The darkness kept its secrets, and she settled for the night, uneasy and unsatisfied; the morning's joy and confidence a fading memory.

The sharp crack of a snapping stick jerked Illera awake. A huge shadowy form moved between the fire and her bedroll. Illera leapt to her feet, tangling in the blankets and crashed to the ground. Huge callused feet shifted backward from her view. A low, gravelly chuckle rang in her ears. A hand lifted her to her feet as if she were thistledown and not flesh and blood. She struck and kicked at the huge form, screaming her defiance. He chuckled loudly.

"Princess Illera, I thought we were friends. So why are you trying to slaughter me?"

His chuckled became loud guffaws that woke Min on the other side of the fire.

"Frak?" Illera grew still.

"Who else?" he replied, "Who else would be guarding your way to the Shul? Why are you coming this way princess? You serve only to play into Targ's hand. I thought you would recognize a trap when you saw one."

He set her upon her feet, and she snapped the blankets around her shoulders to keep out the chill night air. A whippoorwill sang his lonely story from a nearby tree.

"I know it's a trap, but what can I do? I have to get Lark back."

"Is one squire so important that you would risk the Princess and future ruler of a country to get him back? I'm sure Targ means to kill you this time. He doesn't like to be made a fool of."

Illera sighed and trusted her instincts about Frak. "Lark is going to be King of Frain. He is Korul's son, and Korul is dead. Torul is dead as well, so Lark will be Frain's King. He's not just some squire; he's a king."

Frak sank to his haunches, staring at Illera, the horizontal pupils widened to large darkness in the center of his glowing eyes.

"I see, that does make things different. And you trust me with this information?"

Illera gave a short laugh. "I do, strangely enough, I do. You are a man of integrity and my friend. And without your help, I doubt if Korul would be dead or Lark King of Frain."

"Highness?" ventured Min from across the fire.

Illera gestured at him to remain seated and silent.

"Highness?" questioned Frak.

"Yes, my friend. I am now Queen of Madean. My father, all the gods, rest him, left me alone to care for his country."

A low whistle escaped from the ogre's lips as he shook his massive head.

"Don't let Targ know that. As a princess you are a valuable hostage, to be ransomed for gold then killed on the way home. An accident, I understand, has been well planned. But as a queen, why then you are nothing but the enemy and to eliminate you is to own Madean."

"But Frak, I must get Lark back. I must, and I have a plan, a way to make life better for all the Shul. Surely Targ will listen to reason."

Illera drew back at Frak's bellow of laughter.

"Targ listen to reason?" The ogre snorted. "Not until the moons go dark and hell becomes a green and inviting place."

Illera turned from him and paced around the fire, aware of his and Min's eyes following her every step. She shook her head.

"No, I have to go to Targ, persuade him to release Lark, and make a pact for peace with him."

Sadly, the large ogre shook his head. Rising to his full height, he stared down at her upturned face.

"Lady all you will accomplish is the destruction of the very things you seek to preserve."

Stubbornly she shook her head at him. "I must. I can feel it inside, and I know this is the right thing to do."

"Even if it costs your life?"

"Even if it costs my life."

"Very well then, Princess, I will guide you. I will tell Targ that I discovered you on the trail and am bringing you to him. That way at least you won't be killed on sight as an invader."

"Thank you, Frak. You're a good friend." Illera placed one small hand on his massive forearm.

The Shul shuffled his feet and looked away.

"Well, yes, best get some sleep now. The trail tomorrow will not be easy."

Illera nodded and rolled back into her blankets. Frak lumbered to the other side of the fire and flopped down beside Min who stared at him with distended eyes.

"Go to sleep, or I'll eat you," growled the ogre.

Min hastily pretended sleep that soon became a reality.

The dulcet shades of dawn were barely established when the

trio resumed the trail. The woods were dark, and grew darker as the day advanced, thick with spruce, cedar, and willow. Large canopies blocked the sun, leaving only startling lancets of brightness amid the gloom. The hooves of their horses and the sheep made little sound on the thick luteous moss. The narrow trace snaked between the massive boles of rough bark that snagged on mane, tail, and fleece. Frak led them forward at a steady pace, pausing only to allow the animals to drink from the small streams that seemed to nestle in the bottom of every dip in the landscape. The hills grew higher and the valleys shallower, and by nightfall, the woods were thinning, the trunks decreasing in size and further apart. The moss gave way to patches of rock or hard packed sand covered with a thick layer of reddish cast off needles.

Frak guided them to a clearing beside a jutting cliff face. It started to drizzle as they made their fire and the rain pounded down all night, effectively ending any hope of conversation.

They began the day, as damp and dark as the weather. The sky continued to weep, making the rocks slick. The horses slipped, again and again, forcing Illera to walk rather than trust the animal's balance on the steep switchbacks. The hungry bleating of the sheep caused her to divide the horse's grain and left the mounts unsatisfied. The world narrowed to rock walls, rain and Frak's back leading them ever upward; their ears filled with the patter of rain; the hungry complaint of horse and sheep.

At the higher elevations, the clouds shredded and fell away, blessing the travelers with a weak and watery sunshine. The wind prowled around the peaks and stole what heat they had in their bodies as it moaned and cried around them. Much of the journey was up and down now. They climbed a peak only to descend again and climb another. As the sun sank ahead of them, it robing the peaks in a glorious crimson and fuschia, Illera spied the Shul camp below.

As they inched down the switchback into the camp, a furor

exploded. Horns blew, and Ogres poured from buildings, some armed and some half armed. Illera smiled at the thought that they were so afraid of one small female and a half-grown boy that they must appear in full fighting gear. Thus, Frak led her into the camp. A young one appeared and took their horses the instant they dismounted. Commitment sent a whinny back to her, ringing in the cold air and drowning out for a moment the noise and conversation of the Shul.

The wind was strong, and the yellow feathers lining the doorway of Targ's hut beat a tattoo against the leather and stone as if attempting to fly again, far away from this place. They glowed in the dying rays of the sun. Frak roughly pushed her inside, and she stumbled, nearly going to her knees in front of Targ, but she caught herself and pulled herself erect in front of the Monarch of the Shul. Min, less disciplined, landed face down in front of the huge ogre. Frak strode in behind them, puffing out his chest and raising his crest high.

"What is the meaning of this Windsinger?" Targ's face bore a vicious snarl.

Frak puffed and strutted. "I caught this small female and partially grown male. I believe this is the one you have been looking for: the princess of Madean who is worth much gold. I wish to claim the reward of bringing her in."

Targ smiled, long yellowed fangs glittering in the dancing lamplight. His attention focused on Illera, peering at her with gimlet orange eyes.

"Are you the Madean Princess?"

"I am."

Turning to his attendants, he roared, "Give the Windsinger the reward. You are dismissed."

Frak bowed and left of the tent. Illera's heart clenched within her, tightening in a painful spasm as she questioned her abilities. What if she had judged Frak wrong and he betrayed her? Fear coiled poisonous in her gut. She raised her chin and stared boldly at Targ.

"I want my friend Lark," she demanded.

Targ laughed, and the attendants surrounding his throne laughed with him. "I will deal with you tomorrow, in front of the whole camp. Then you will learn what it means to try to make a fool of Targ."

He made a gesture with one hand, and Illera, with Min, was dragged from the tent and across the compound. They were thrust into a dark, tiny hut with barely room for the two of them. It was already occupied, and a scream of pain as they tripped over him alerted Illera and Min to his presence. Min pressed against the outside flap as Illera went to her knees and ran her hands over the crooked body. The body moaned and babbled deliriously.

Illera felt the face and whispered, "Lark?"

"M'Lady,"Lark's voice was thick and garbled. "Sh'd'n't be here. Gon' kill ya."

"Yes Lark, I know Targ wants to kill me. But I couldn't leave you in his clutches. What has he done to you."

"Beet'n." The reply was muffled.

Illera felt through the pouch at her waist. The mushrooms were easy to identify in the total darkness, both by feel and smell. She slipped one into Lark's mouth.

"Try to chew this. It will help you."

Beneath her palm, his jaws moved. She could feel the swelling on his lips, eyes and the side of his face. Crushing one of the leaves from her pouch to ascertain if it was the correct one, she sniffed. It had the right astringent odor. She placed it where his face seemed to be the worst and was rewarded by his sigh of relief. His arms felt intact, but when she got to his legs, one was bent underneath him at such an impossible angle she knew it had to be broken.

"Min," she called softly, "come here and lift Sir Lark so I can fix his leg."

Min shuffled forward, running into Lark and eliciting a bellow of pain. Illera guided Min's hands to Lark's hip and back. On her command, he lifted the older man as much as possible. Lark gave one sharp scream and passed out. Illera pulled the broken limb from beneath him and laid it out straight. Working by feel alone she aligned the ends of the bones, dripped the astringent sap from the leaves in the wound, packed the area with the healing moss and knitbone, binding it tightly with the thick leather of Min's jerkin and strips torn from her own petticoats. She placed her hands over the wound and willed her healing energy into damage, feeling bone and flesh knit together under her touch as the night crept away.

Fatigued and sleepless, she watched the crack around the door flap lighten. The howling wind eased, and the luffing of the leather stopped. The absence of the constant sound woke Lark. Raising himself to his elbows, he stared at Illera.

"I thought you were a fever dream," he muttered his voice hoarse and ragged.

Illera smiled at him. "Lucky for you I'm not. That was a bad break."

Lark looked down the length of his body.

"It itches like mad."

"That's because it's healing. You need another day or maybe two at least before it is better."

"Two days, Lady you are a miracle worker."

"Not yet," she whispered back at him, "not yet, but I hope to be by tonight, if all the gods and spirits of this world are willing, I will be by this night."

They heard the commotion long before it arrived at their prison. The screams and bellows awakened Min from his fetal position. He tried to stretch but had little success in the cramped quarters. The noise drew nearer, and the flap was whipped aside.

A dozen Shul, in full battle armor and armed with their spears blocked the entrance to the tent. Their faces were painted with yellow stripes and red circles, and full collars of red and yellow feathers circled their thick necks.

Growling, one reached in and hefted Lark over his shoulder. Another picked Illera up by her arms and carried her, feet dangling inches above the ground. A third elicited a yelp from Min as he dragged him by one shoulder. They paraded through the Shul camp as the males chanted, screamed and called names. Some of the males rushed from the openings of their huts to spit upon them or slap Lark and Min. Illera took note of the females and half-grown young pleading with the males and attempting to hold them back from these humiliating taunts.

The flames that burned without source heated the air around them. A huge construction of stone and timber soared to the height of the largest hut. Targ perched on top, barbarically arrayed in red and yellow enameled chainmail armor and liberally decorated with feathers. The crest on the top of his skull flamed a fluorescent red, engorged and swollen to twice its normal intimidating size. With lips pulled back in a rictus of fury and pleasure, he snarled down at the captives. The warriors holding the prisoners threw them at the foot of the throne structure.

Illera worried for a moment about Lark's injured leg as he struggled to stand. Then she got a good look at his face, which had been hidden by the darkness. One eye was swollen completely shut and his lips puffed on one side. A slash went from the corner of his mouth to the right temple. Despite her fumbling ministrations of last night, the flesh looked angry and infected. He balanced on his good leg and tried not to put any pressure on the bandaged leg.

Min remained crumbled at the foot of the structure, staring up at her with terrified eyes, unsure of whether to rise or remain where he was. She gestured for him to rise and take his position behind her, as a proper squire should. She herself rose from the mud at the foot of the throne with all the dignity of her heritage and the hope in her heart. She stared straight up at the towering menace of the ruler of the Shul.

Bowing low she rose. "Great Targ, I thank you for this audience with you in front of your people."

She gestured with her arms turning to encompass all the men, women and children of Shul pressed around them in a large circle. As she turned, she noticed a flicker of blue off to one side of the flame that soared up and up into the sky on her right. She completed the turn and faced Targ again. The murmurs of the women and men ran around the circle. Targ's glowing eyes were bugging out.

"How dare you as a prisoner and a woman have the face to speak to me first. You will be silent until I speak."

"Your majesty, how can I be silent when I come with an offer of peace between our two lands."

"Silence, I commanded silence."

One of the feather-adorned warriors stepped forward and bowed his face to the earth.

"Mighty one, let us listen to this insignificant creature's words that we may have some amusement in the long winter nights as we discuss the foolishness of its proposal."

Targ considered the words at some length, then nodded his ugly visage. "Very well, tell me your proposal of peace."

Illera stepped a pace forward. "Thank you mighty Targ. My father sent me with a gift for you, two ewes and a ram. These are excellent animals and will soon produce more of their kind."

"Targ cares not for sheep except to eat them," the monarch interrupted.

Illera nodded, staring into his furious eyes. "But the main problem with your people is that they are hungry. You obtain your needs by raiding and killing because your land is rocky and little grain grows here. The land cannot support cattle, but sheep or goats could do very well in these hills with the amount of grass and other fodder available. I could bring you a great deal of gold, but of what good is gold. It is heavy. You cannot eat it. You cannot wear it or ride it. But, with sheep and goats, you can feed and clothe your people. I am willing to give you herds and shepherds to train your young ones in their care, women to train your women to spin and weave. And with these animals, you can trade with the lowlands for grain or any other necessities you may need to make your lives better and…"

Targ's fist smashed down on the throne structure with such force that the very ground beneath their feet trembled and she wondered if it were going to topple to the ground.

"Shul have always lived by raiding. We are not farmers. We are warriors, and we live by fighting. Gold for your ransom, only gold for your ransom."

Illera took a deep breath. "But think, your Majesty, the women, and children would benefit so much…"

Targ smashed his fist down again.

"No! Gold, only gold!" he roared.

An ogress pushed forward to stand before the throne. She clasped Illera's hand in her own.

"Targ, you know me. I am your woman, the first woman in your harem. I carried your heir. Listen to this princess. What she says, all the women agree with. We need…"

"Silence. Since when do women of the Shul tell their men what to do? We are

Shul and we live by the sword. We have always lived by the sword and as long as I have the throne, we always will."

A small black form winged out of the clouds, landing on Illera's shoulder with a flurry of feathers and a loud squawk. Illera felt her heart clench. Raven, Raven, was worse, and she was stuck here and could not help him.

One of the men stepped forward as Targ's wife moved back into the pack. He was smaller than most and moved with a limp.

The crest on his head was small and withered, the same color as his face.

"The princess of Madean speaks sense. What use to us is gold? We need food and a steady supply to assure that we continue and that we can thrive..."

"Silence," screamed Targ as he smashed his fist on the throne again making it and everyone else jump.

"Do you challenge for the rulership of the Shul, Glup? It is your right." Targ's head turned to check the whole assembly of his people. "It is the right of any Shul to challenge. How about it? Do you think you can beat me in unarmed combat Glup?"

The burning eyes seared down at the unfortunate ogre. He shuffled his feet and shook his head, sliding back into the crowd and trying to lose himself.

Targ's head rose, and he peered over the crowd. "How about it? Does any creature challenge my leadership?"

Illera looked at Frak who was trying to efface himself to the side of the pile of stone and timber. The grounds were so silent she could hear only the hiss of the great fire.

"I challenge," a quiet voice spoke from the rear.

A vicious snarl twisted Targ's face into a mask of hatred. A corridor opened behind Illera, Lark, and Min, the ogres pushing aside into each other and crowding together in huddles of darkness. Turning they beheld the challenger. Darkness stood at the end. A dark-haired man in gleaming dark armor leading a giant dark horse. Illera's heart lifted then sank at the sight. Targ roared with anger.

"Do you, a puny human dare to challenge me in my own home?" he snarled, incredulous with anger.

"You offered the challenge to anyone Targ." Raven had a confident smile on his lips.

With three leaps, Targ was down from his throne, sword discarded next to the fire. A boy scampered to take Abbadon who kicked and snapped at him. The boy retreated. The Shul pushed back and formed a ring around the combatants, pulling Illera, Lark, and Min into their circle. Frak stepped forward.

"The rules, so you will know, puny human, are combat to the death, unarmed and without assistance by anyone. Should any interfere, they will be slaughtered without mercy, as well as the one they go to aid. Begin."

He stepped back into the circle of bodies, contriving to be next to Illera. She reached out and grasped his massive forearm with both of her hands. Maggie chirped from her shoulder and Lark placed one arm around her shoulders. His face was tight and white.

Raven discarded his sword, knife and the shield he carried on his back. Illera's viscera tightened. Raven was half the size and bulk of the massive ogre, probably not yet recovered from his wounds. Targ's crest was erect and pulsing with a heartbeat; its scarlet color eye hurting bright. Murmurs from the crowd came to her ears, groans and whimpers of fear from the women, mutters of disgust from some of the men and loud encouragements for their leader from others.

The fight started slowly, with circling and feints. Targ lunged, and Raven skipped nimbly aside. They circled again, around and around like a cat stalking a mouse. Raven moved closer, cautiously, slowly. Like a striking python of the jungles, Targ snapped towards him, pinning his arms to his sides and lifting him high off the ground, squeezing the air from his lungs, the life from his body. Raven ducked his head, and a shudder ran through his body. He slipped bonelessly to the ground and his knees, scrambling through Targ's widespread legs. Springing to his feet, he brought his arms under Targ's armpits and around the back of his massive neck, locking his hands together at the nape of the ogre's bulging crest. Targ roared and flung himself from side to side to loosen the grip of the man. Raven clung with stubborn strength, locking his legs around the King's midriff to keep from being unseated. Targ hurled himself onto his back, using his legs to grind Raven into the dirt. His face hard with concentration, Illera could see Raven compress the base of Targ's crest even more. The scarlet color became distinctly purplish with blue shadows in the hollows. Targ roared and howled, leaping to his feet with Raven still clamped to his back. The ogre jumped and twisted, flailing his arms wildly to throw the man from his back. He bucked and bent, rolled and twirled, but Raven clung like a hated bur. The entire comb of the crest was dark and blue. Targ's eyes were crazy with pain. The sweat poured from Raven's face with the effort of maintaining his position astride the giant.

"Quat," the Shul screamed, "take the sword and run him through."

One of the warriors in the feathered collar jumped and said, "Mighty one, the challenge?"

"Quiet you fool. This is a human, and no human can rule the Shul. The rules do not apply. Run this flea through." Targ bellowed.

The warrior strode forward hesitantly. Frak stepped forward as well.

The Windsinger called in a loud, clear voice; "The rules apply. Challenge was offered and accepted according to the traditions of our forefathers, and so all the rules apply."

"NOW!" screamed Targ, dancing and bending in the middle of the circle.

The warrior advanced. Another stepped in to stop him. Around her, Illera saw the Shul taking sides, some for allowing the fight to continue, others wanting to support their king and kill Raven. Arguments rose, drowning out the sounds of King and rider. Fearing an armed melee where all would be killed, Illera stepped to the side, moving quickly to the tower of flame. The small blue fire still hovered to one side. Holding her breath, she plunged her hand into the fire and felt it spread its euphoria and well being through her body. It covered her in its blue essence. She turned, glowing and glided into the middle of the circle where Quat was trying to stab Raven while Targ pranced and jerked around and Frak interposed his body between the two fighters and the armed warrior. Illera willed herself above the heads of the arguing crowds.

"Attend me!" she commanded in a ringing voice.

Flickering on the edges of her mind like so many bright fireflies, she could feel the minds of the Shul, fearful, amazed, dismayed, awed. All turned upward to gaze at her. Targ even stopped his wild fling to stare.

"This is over. Now. Raven, let Targ go."

Raven released his grip and slipped to the ground. Targ's crest deflated in seconds and lay flaccid and brown over his skull and obscuring one eye.

Illera lifted her hand and a dark cloud formed, narrowing down from the looming mountain.

"I control the flying mouse." She waved her hand, and the column of creatures changed course to circle around the outside of the camp. Cries of fear floated up to her.

"I offer you a better life, a better life for your wives and your children. I offer you acceptance and trade, medicine and industry. I offer you, the Shul, not Targ. Targ has lost his fight and his life by breaking your own rules. Kill him now."

The moment paused, hung in the balance of past and future. Illera called the bats just a little bit closer. One of the Shul leapt from the crowd and ran Targ through, piercing the heart. The leader of the ogres slumped to his knees and fell into the dust without a sound.

"Good. Frak Windsinger is now your new king."

"But the man won the challenge."

"Can a man understand the Shul? No, he cannot. But a wise king can lead his people to a good and productive life. Frak is a wise man."

Murmurs of assent drifted up. Illera willed herself closer to the ground, stopping when she was slightly above head height. All the faces focused on her.

"I will send animals, more sheep, and goats to you. So will the king of Frain. We will also send people to teach you, to help you to know the usefulness of the animals. We will send grains that will grow on these high mountains. You will never be hungry again. I will send healers to help your sick and injured. Together we can make our world a better place than it was for our parents and grandparents. We will give this as a gift for your children and grandchildren. Will you accept?"

A loud cheer shook the assembly and reverberated back from the mountains.

"Long live Princess Illera. Long live King Frak. Long live the Shul!" a thousand voices yelled.

Illera permitted herself to settle almost to the ground and gathering Lark and Raven with a look glided across the ground to Targ's former tent. Once inside she exchanged the light with Lark, telling Raven to be ready to care for them. They passed the light back and forth several times until it was too dim to see. The last thing she remembered was Raven lowering her to the smelly floor of the tent.

There was a wild uproar going on outside. Although her eyes were closed and her body flaccid, she could hear the cacophony of celebration, singing, fighting and general din on the other side of the thin leather walls. However, it was a closer sound that woke her; the furtive movements of someone close to her. She opened her eyes and stared cross-eyed into a pair of hot orange ones just inches from her face. Their owner reared back and thumped to the floor beside the low cot on which she was lying. Illera raised herself on one elbow and looked down at the ogre.

He laughed, a gravelly rumbling welling up from the bottom

of his chest.

"Why does it seem you always surprise me?" He chuckled, rising awkwardly to his feet and looming over her.

Illera swung her feet over the edge of the cot and gazed up at him, still a little dizzy.

"Frak?"

"What? Don't you recognize the changes you wrought?"

Frak's crest was larger, faint fingers of orange creeping from the edge of his skull to fan out through its increased mass.

"You look different," she commented.

Frak snorted. "Of course I look different. You proclaimed me King of the Shul. Will I, won't I the change has begun, and my body is determined to be King no matter what my mind says."

Illera shook her head. "I'm sorry Frak, I must be still in thrall to the Darkliete, but I don't understand you."

Frak paced back and forth his voice fading and increasing with his steps.

"Shul wear a sign of their position in the tribe, the crest. I am sure you noticed Targ's. It was the biggest and most flamboyant of all the living Shul. As a, a scholar, I guess you would call me I was exempt from the status games that others played. I worked with and for the King and my position was secure for everyone knows Windsingers never become Kings. But the rest of the rabble, bah, they are forever quarreling and arguing, jockeying for position with our ranks and as they go up or down in importance the crest swells or declines. Now here I am, a Windsinger and you proclaim me King. Half the camp is overjoyed, and the other half is ready to challenge."

Shaking her head, Illera replied, "I'm sorry. I should have discussed it with you, but at the time, it seemed the right thing to do. Besides what is so wrong with a King that actually has a brain instead of just muscle."

Frak laughed. "Nothing in theory, but whether the camp will support it or not remains to be seen."

Min dashed into the tent, elbows akimbo as he skidded into Frak.

With flying arms and legs he rushed outside calling, "She's awake my Lord."

With another about-face, he ducked inside again and moved to one side of the tent flap. Raven strode in, stalking in long-legged strides to her bedside.

"Are you all right your Highness? You haven't had much sleep, but I couldn't prevent the King of Shul from checking on you. It is his own tent now."

Frak grunted in the background as Illera laughed.

"I wouldn't expect you to try to keep Frak away from me. And thank you for coming to my rescue, although I don't think you should have jeopardized your health that way. You can barely be recovered from your injury."

Raven smiled, loosened the fine wool shirt he wore from about his throat and pulled it over his head. He knelt in front of Illera, scarred shoulder next to her. She reached out her fingers and traced the thick white line that ran from the top of one muscular shoulder and down across his chest to just above the sternum. It faded from a finger-wide welt to the size of a fine thread as it crossed his body.

She looked into his eyes and asked, "But how? Even my best herbs don't cure that fast."

Rising, he shrugged, slipping the shirt over his head and fastening it again.

"I only know that when I woke, it was healed but sore. By the time I found out where you had gone, the soreness was fading and by the time I arrived here it was as you see it now. I thought you could tell me what you did?"

Illera shook her head.

"Are you well?" demanded Frak. "Can you come with me?"

She rose and followed the King of the Shul outside into the uproar of the camp, trailing Raven and Min behind. The day was gloomy and dark with heavy, ominous clouds obscuring the sun and threatening to rain. Even the wind was still, as though oppressed by the dullness of the day. A sudden hush fell over the assembled ogres as they noticed her presence. One of the collared warriors lumbered forward and made a gesture as if the seize her arm. Raven blocked his grab with his own forearm.

"Treat the Princess with respect," growled Frak.

The warrior backed away bowing and gesturing for Illera to take the center of the circle. With low murmuring, the ring closed behind her. Lark pushed through the crowded bodies and into the center with them. An ogre whose crest was also beginning to swell and showed a pale yellow blush along the base stepped into the circle with them.

"It is not for a foreign creature to decide who will rule the Shul. I am Lort, and I slew Targ. The Kingship is mine!" he yelled in a deafening voice.

Comments both for and against ran around the ring of bodies.

Illera stamped her foot. "Wait!"

The crowds grew silent and unnumbered eyes fastened on her.

"This Lort claims kingship?"

"Yes, I shall be king for I slew Targ," Lort's voice was so loud she had to step back.

Illera turned to face him and raised her arm pointing her finger. "Then you deserve to die."

The ogre's jaw dropped open, and he took a step back from her. A loud murmur erupted from the watchers.

"You committed regicide at the order of a female, and a human woman at that. You interfered with the challenge when to do so means certain death, and yet you claim to be King. You are pathetic. A weak child of a creature with not even the strength of character to face challenges as it should be, hand to hand. You are a disgrace to your people."

Loud cries of agreement burst from the mob. Fists were shaken in his direction.

"But, but," the shaken ogre stammered, "you are the one who told me to do it."

"Yes, yes I did," agreed Illera, "and I also told you that Frak was to be your King. If you use me as an excuse for your deed, then how can you ignore my will for a successor."

Illera could see his crest deflating and the color fading. Lort turned to the crowd.

"The female is right. I withdraw my right to the throne."

He scuttled back into the crowd of villagers. Frak stepped forward. Before he could speak, Illera stepped beside him.

"You have never had a wise man to lead you before. I must tell all of you that I support Frak's rule one hundred percent. As long as Frak is your king and willing to deal peaceably with Madean, I will supply you with teachers and healers and trade. I will give you animals and grain to get started, and ogres will be welcomed as honored guests in my land at all times. The penalty for harming one of you will be the same as for harming another human."

Lark stepped between Frak and Illera.

In a ringing voice, he proclaimed, "And same shall be true of Frain. As long as Frak rules this people we will be friends and trading partners in peace."

Illera continued, "Should you decide on another ruler, then I shall take my sheep and my companions and go. Things will be as they were before. Remember you are making this decision for your children and the future."

Ogres turned to each other, and the babble of conversation grew. For long minutes they discussed and argued. As a body, they turned back to those in the middle. A dozen of the collared ogres stepped into the center with them, and one of them walked to stand just in front of Frak. Slowly, with massive dignity, the great creature lowered himself to one knee. Behind him, the other eleven followed suite.

In unison, they chorused, "We pledge allegiance to Frak Windsinger, King of the Shul. You are our liege and we your servants from now until your death or defeat in challenge."

Frak spread his hands out accepting their fealty. He began to sing, and the clouds parted, bathing him in a spear of brilliant golden light. Illera stepped back, bringing Lark, Raven, and Min with her until they melted into the cheering crowds.

The horses were fresh and eager to be away, skittering down the steep inclines at a pace far too brisk for Illera. Lark rode first, and she followed him with Raven and his new shadow bringing up the rear. Maggie scouted ahead, returning to scold often, as if she wanted them all to fly. The journey home was uneventful, long days of riding down, down and up, then down again. The stunted forest appeared, grew taller, thicker and denser and then dwindled again into open birch and aspen groves. Thinning trees signaled the end of the woodlands and the beginning of the hills and farms. They cut across the countryside so as to be nearer to Seven Spires.

On their last night, as they gathered around the fire, replete with a fine supper that Min had cooked, the conversation wandered again to the future.

"I want to increase the trade between Madean and Frain," Lark was saying.

Illera nodded her head in agreement while staring into the flames. He took a deep breath.

"Do you remember what the Darkliete said?"

Illera looked up, noticing the dance of flames in his eyes.

"The Darkliete said a lot of things."

"They said it would be best for the world if you married me. United, Frain and Madean could be such a force for good."

Illera smiled.

"Is that a proposal?"

Lark rose and approached her. He bent his knee before her and gazed into her face.

"I don't know if you realize what you mean to me, your strength and your goodness. You are queen of Madean and I king of Frain. This journey began to unite Madean and Frain, so would you complete the journey with me and become my wife and queen of Frain as well as Madean."

Illera felt the tears well up in her throat, and sharp prickles assailed her eyes. Breath grew short, and from the corner of her eye, she saw Raven hurry away into the dark, closely followed by his shadow. A promise sprang to her mind.

"Lark, would you be willing to take Min as your companion and train him to be a knight and your personal bodyguard?"

A frown clove the space between his eyes and Lark shook his head.

"I just proposed to you. You are supposed to answer yes or no, not ask irrelevant questions."

Illera smiled down at his upturned face.

"I love you, Lark; I really do, but like a brother. I hope I can always be your sister and a very good friend."

"Does that mean no?"

"It means no."

"Being king of Frain is good, but it's only second best compared to having you. Will you be choosing one of Ashera's brothers then?"

Illera smiled, a wild grin of pure delight and turned away from Lark and slipped from the firelight into the darkness.

"Where Maggie?"

The magpie fluttered ahead, visible only as a light patch in the dark. Illera followed, pausing as Maggie uttered an annoyed squawk. She almost ran into Min.

"Go back to camp."

He thrashed past her and vanished into the darkness. Maggie forged ahead. She could see Raven's silhouette, just barely visible leaning with his head against the lone tree gracing the side of the hill. Maggie landed on his shoulder and poked him in the ear.

"Go back Min, and take this pesky bird with you. Sometimes a man needs to be alone."

His voice was rough and uneven. Illera stepped beside him and laid a hand on his arm. Startled he jumped.

"I'm sorry, your Highness, I thought you were Min."

Maggie burbled and poked him the ear again.

"I need to ask you a question?" Illera's voice was strange in her ears.

"Certainly Lady," he replied, his voice more controlled and distant.

"Would you be willing to take Min as your squire and train him to be your companion and personal bodyguard?"

She could hear the smile in his voice as he answered. "Of course, your Highness. I love the kid like a little brother already. I would be honored to have him as a companion."

Illera's laughter was a merry tinkling on the wind. She spread her arms wide as if to embrace the sky.

"In that case, Raven, son of Korul, son of Rejoicing and son of Elisa, will you be my husband and King of Madean beside me?"

Stunned silence greeted her. In the starlight, she could see the flair of his nostrils and the sudden intensity of his eyes. Her wide-spread, empty arms filled as a hard, warm body rushed to her and squeezed her tight. He pushed her away and held her at arm's length. She could see a world of wonder reflected in his wide, dark eyes.

"Do you mean it? Do you really mean it? You want me?"

Illera smiled. "Ever since the day, we met in front of Abbadon's stall."

He crushed her in his arms.

CHAPTER 12

They arrived home the next evening as the sun eased behind the western mountains, gilding the seven tall towers with its last rays. Illera's heart throbbed with joy at the sight of home. As they rode slowly up the approach, a fanfare burst from the walls and the sound of a commotion disturbed the settling twilight. An approaching cavalcade of horses, knights, castle servants and village folks drowned the ringing echoes from the horses' hooves upon the drawbridge. Leading the charge, Ashera on the late King Ian's giant gray war-horse, screamed her welcome, waving her arms about in such a fashion that Illera wondered how she could keep her seat. Behind tumbled such a mishmash of bodies that the travelers could not distinguish faces or cries of welcome.

Ashera drove her horse next to Commitment, bent forward and lifted Illera from the saddle, squashing the air from her lungs.

"How did you do it? How did you do?" the giantess babbled. "We thought you dead. The priests were going to proclaim you dead the day after tomorrow and let Garth have the kingdom.

They let him go, and he's in your father's suites now. I'm so glad you're home. How did you do it?"

Illera struggled loose from the big woman's grip and thumped back down to her own saddle. The people were reaching up, touching her legs and hands, welcoming her back. At her back, she could hear Abbadon snorting at the nearness of so many people and Raven's soft words soothing him, encouraging him to be still. Illera rose in her stirrups and waved her hands over her head. Min seized a torch from someone and rode to her side using it to illuminate her face. A hush spread across the hordes of people crammed into the outer bailey.

"Thank you for the welcome!" cried Illera in her loudest voice.

A mighty cheer rose up from the assembled throngs.

"I come bringing good news, the best. Frain has its new king."

Lark rode forward into the small circle of the firelight and waved to the people.

"And I have still more good news. Targ, King of the Shul, is dead and Frak, the new king, will work with us for peace and trade between our two people."

The people cheered long and loud, many throwing caps or bonnets into the air at her announcement.

In the pause, she added, "And perhaps the best news of all, Madean will have a new king as well as a new Queen."

She gestured, and Raven thrust Abbadon forward as Lark eased aside.

"Welcome, Sir Raven, my betrothed and soon to be your King."

A hushed pause preceded the wildest screams and cheering yet. The crowd boiled with adulation, and the throngs pushed closer, each individual determined to touch the Queen and her chosen. Night drew velvet curtains around them as they pressed towards the castle, one slow step after another. Ashera tried to break the trail, and with Lark to one side and Raven the other, they reached the inner gates. Here the people finally stepped aside to let them pass into the relative quiet of the inner bailey and the keep. Only the castle servants followed them now, laughing and cheering still.

Dismounting in front of the stables, Illera's weary legs wobbled. Raven was there in an instant, supporting her with a hand under her elbow. The stableboys led the horses away with wide grins and whispering behind their hands. As they made their way to the doors of the castle, the servants melted before them. The doors were locked and bolted.

Illera pounded on the doors and demanded that they be opened. Only icy silence met their ears. Then she snorted and turned to face Ashera and the men.

"Does Garth think that he can keep me from my home by locking the front door?" she asked.

Ashera looked at the ground. "I'm sorry Illera. I tried to stop the priests, but they insisted that King Ian wanted Garth to be King, if you couldn't be found. I told them to wait for you, that you would be back, but they said the omens insisted that you had been eaten by the Shul. I have to go back to my own land, so what could I do? I brought all the people to meet you so Garth couldn't have you killed and then say you didn't return."

Illera placed her hand on her friend's heavy shoulders.

"It's fine, Ashera, just fine. You did exactly right. I hadn't known, and if you didn't act exactly as you did, we would have ridden into a trap and all been killed. This, this is nothing. Gather some of the knights who are still loyal to me and meet me in the stable."

Ashera nodded and trotted off into the night. Raven chuckled as he followed her to the stable. Bare minutes later, Ashera was back with fifteen well-armed fighting men in full armor. Illera nodded and slipped aside the panel that gave her access to the hidden passages of the castle. In single file, they followed her into the bowels of the building, gliding silently between the walls. Illera moved from peephole to peephole looking for Garth.

At the spy hole in her father's rooms, she saw him preening in front of the dressing mirror King Ian had always disdained. She pressed one ear to the wall and listened hard. His voice was just audible to her sharp ears.

"Yes," the pretender was saying to himself, "I do believe I am the best King Madean has ever known. How perspicacious of you to notice, have a knighthood."

Illera's lips drew back in a snarl of anger, and she tripped the latch and slid the panel aside. Raven, Lark, Min, Ashera and the fifteen knights poured into the room. She followed slowly, noting Garth's hand poised in mid-grab for his sword hanging on the back of the chair.

"I hardly think that anyone will tell you that you are the best king Madean ever had, especially when you are not her King and never will be," Illera snarled.

Garth's face flushed red to the roots of his carefully coifed hair. He hurled himself forward, hit the ground with his shoulders and rolled to his feet beside the door to the hallway. As the knights lunged at him in a group, he whipped the door aside and vanished, Ashera and the fighting men in pursuit. Raven paused and looked at Illera.

"Go back into the walls. Garth doesn't know them, and you do. You'll be safe there."

"No, I won't hide like a rat between the walls of my own home." She shook herself indignantly.

Raven smiled and took two steps to her, grasping both shoulders in his big hands.

"Illera, if he kills you, he wins. And you thought that it was quite okay to be a rat while you were princess. No?"

Illera thought, then nodded, turning back to the wall and sliding the panel closed again. She watched as Raven ran from the room following the others. She moved from place to place, checking each room, searching in her own way for Garth. The knights split up and searched the castle room by room, starting at the top. Illera moved to the dungeons on her invisible pathways. In Garth's old cell, she found her retainers chained to the walls. She slipped from her hiding place and strode to the jailer's bench at the foot of the steep stairs.

"Release Orille and the rest of my people at once," she commanded the rat-like keeper.

A slow and greedy smile spread across the man's narrow face, and his long red nose twitched. His hand glided downward towards the sword he wore strapped to his skinny hips. Illera was faster, whipping her long dagger and pricking the base of his throat with it. The jailer dropped his weapon to the stone floor with a loud clang. Pointing, Illera directed him to the cell where her people were chained. He hesitated before the bars. She probed with the razor sharp blade and sped his fumbling hands. A thick trickle of blood seeped down his neck and under the collar of his greasy shirt.

Illera prodded him over to Orille, and grunted in the direction of the iron cuffs holding the old man's hands tight to the walls. The jailer began to back away. Illera twisted the blade, and the man skittered back to Orille's side, inserting the key and opening the cuffs. Orille slumped to the dirty floor and crawled towards the door.

She lowered the blade just enough to shove the jailer's wrists into the cuffs and close them again. Sheathing the knife, she took the keys from his belt and tried the keys one by one until she had all her people loose. With a hand to her lips, so they would be quiet, she led them into the dark, hidden passages. In starts and stops, she directed her weakened people to the big kitchen of the castle. After checking that the place was deserted, even the gigantic hearth fires were cold, she slipped the catch, and they toppled into the huge, flagstoned room.

Illera busied herself giving them food and water with her own hands. Elisa grabbed her hands and brought them to her lips, but Illera forestalled her with a shake of her head.

"You mustn't."

Elisa stared at her, a puzzled frown between her brows.

"You will be my mother-in-law, so it wouldn't be appropriate."

There was no mistaking the joy in Elisa's face. Despite the deprivations she had suffered, she was full of joy and hope.

"So you will marry Lark after all?"

Illera shook her head. "Raven."

Elisa's eyebrows rose to her hairline.

"But isn't Lark to be king of Frain. Don't tell me something happened to him; I thought when you returned, well..."

Illera interrupted, "No, Lark is fine and is acclaimed King of Frain, but Raven, well Raven is for me, and I am for Madean."

The understanding flowed into Elisa's face. She threw her arms around Illera and hugged her tight.

"Welcome daughter, may you never have to leave your home again."

Startled, Illera hugged her back, her heart thumping at the older woman's words. When the servants settled, Illera disappeared behind the walls to see how the hunt for Garth was coming. The knights were on the main floor now, still searching from room to room, apparently without success. The night was wearing away, and still, the sounds of turmoil rang through the castle.

Weary to the depths of her bones, she made her way to her old rooms to begin the search once more from the top. Moving confidently in the dark, she ran into an obstacle in the corridor. Rough hands grabbed her and held her tight. Her knife was taken. A flint struck, and a light flared, all but blinding her in the sudden glow. With an animal snarl of pleasure, the arm crushed her, squeezing harder.

"So, my great lady, you still prowl the walls at night. You are not the only one who can sneak behind the backs of others. And with you out of the way, I can become King of Madean and my first job will be to hunt down your boyfriends and have them killed."

Illera struggled, kicking and clawing, until Garth struck her a blow across the face that made her head reel and her balance go. He heaved her over one shoulder and moved downward, awkward on the stairs. He paused and looked out a peephole, uttering a low chuckled and a barely breathed word, "Fools."

Hanging head downwards, Illera spied the faint gleam of a catch. Shifting her weight just slightly she reached down and tripped the spring. With a sudden lurch, she threw Garth off balance as she palmed the panel open. He reeled out onto the musician's gallery, Illera still clasped over his shoulder.

In a flurry of feathers and a sharp, high scream Maggie arrowed out of the shadows, aiming for Garth. Her sharp beak stabbed straight into his left eye. With a shriek of pain, he threw Illera from his shoulder. Cartwheeling through the air, she added her screams to his. Her flailing hands grasped the hard, slick edges of the gilded railing.

The knights rattled into the room, drawn by the screams.

"By all the gods, Illera hang on!" yelled Raven from many feet below her.

A wild clatter of feet galloped up the stairs. Garth succeeded in prying the furious magpie from his face and lurched for the hidden passage, locking the catch just as the first of the knights reached the top of the stairs.

Illera looked down. Raven still circled below orbited by Min, and she wondered how long she could keep her fingers locked on the shiny surface. Already she could feel slight movements despite the pressure of her grip, almost as if the rail were turning under her hands. She held still and stiff. A hand reached from above, one of the knights trying to reach her to pull her back up. His weight against the rail shifted it just enough that it cast her loose and she fell, plummetting to the hard flagstone floor below.

She closed her eyes, and the impact came. It was not the bone-crushing splat she expected but rather, a hard jarring. Breath exploded past her face. Quickly she rolled to her knees and stood wobbling with the nearness of her escape. Raven lay before her, writhing and gasping to inflate his lungs. Dropping to her knees, she checked him, but other than having the air knocked out of his lungs he was intact. Winning the struggle to breathe he sat up and grinned. Illera hurled herself into his arms again. Crying with relief, she sobbed against his hard chest until the world was right side up again. She looked up at him, eyes wide and wet, watching his smile as he bent his head and kissed her.

Eternity in a moment she thought when they parted, and as she left him to instruct the knights where to search for Garth, she carried the feeling and taste of his lips with her. The night revolved to dawn in its slow way and the report filtered back to them from a shepherd youth taking the sheep to graze, of a man in fancy clothes with one eye streaming blood suddenly appearing from beneath a bridge. The strange figure ran off into the forest.

With a sigh, Illera tramped down all the hidden passages of the castle, placing locks on them so that Garth could not reenter the castle through the back doors. Only the feeling of Raven's mouth on hers sustained her during the weary hours of tramping and climbing through the dark and dusty corridors. With the castle secured, she summoned the priests who had released Garth and exiled them from Madean. The day was wearing away when she finished and giving in to her exhaustion she fell into her bed and a deep dreamless sleep.

The castle, indeed the country, was in turmoil of joy and anticipation when she awoke. A flurry of preparations; sewing, cooking, arranging the wedding bower and coronation platform was in full swing. Artisans from all over Madean arrived at Seven Spires, hawking their wears and offering their services. Orille was in his glory arranging for the double ceremony, and Illera was content to sit back and allow him to take charge. She was measured and poked, asked questions, then ignored, chivvied about and told to rest. Raven and Lark were separated from her, involved in their own whirlwind of preparation, only having contact with her at mealtimes. Ashera spoke to her briefly, a few minutes a day before she hustled off to other tasks. Two weeks flew by without a single pause for breath. Frak arrived with an entourage of Shul and was welcomed into the castle, although Illera noticed a certain unease on both sides, human, and ogre. King Uggarick, Queen Dora and the rest of their sons arrived to join in the festivities. Rejoicing and Laughter, and all of the Darkliete and ship's crew moved through the chaos with brilliant smiles and suggestions.

Frak sang them a magnificent day of sun and warm, gentle breezes. The trees dressed in their finest colors, brushed with yellow, gold, crimson and scarlet. The fields lay reaped, fawn and fallow, while copses of night dark green punctuated the garish splendor of the land. Illera was up early and whisked off to the pavilion erected especially for her beside the Royal River. A wide path of white stone ran straight and true to the soaring white arches of the wedding bower. Peeking from one drape of the pavilion on that side, she could see the path on the other side of the bower, as white and unbending as her own leading straight to where Raven would be being prepared for their nuptials.

The servant girls fussed around her, doing her hair and organizing her garments. Ashera and Laughter in one corner were likewise fussed over, they being the women who would stand with her on the outer ring of the bower. Queen Dora had offered to conduct her to the bower, a job that should have been her mother's. Thinking on her mother, Illera stared out at the river, wishing she had had a chance to know the woman that gave her birth and missing what all the others seem to take for granted.

A small mist rose from the water, for the air was cool in the early morning. As Illera watched, the mist began to thicken. A servant girl tugged at her sleeve, but Illera brushed her off and stepped from the tent towards the water. The mist continued to thicken and began to swirl. It revolved to the near bank and parted. Two beautiful women stepped from the fog, alike as two peas in a pod.

Illera recognized the porcelain face with the wide-set violet eyes and delicately pointed chin. Their hair was the color of moonlight on snow, long and flowing and accenting the beauty of the long-lashed eyes. One of the women had delicate upswept ears and the other plain, round human ones. Both wore silken capes of a pale azure color. Heart thumping, Illera stepped to meet them.

"Illera, my beloved," called the woman with the pointed, elven ears.

"Mother?"

The woman rushed forward and enfolded Illera in a tight embrace. Hot tears ran down her face and stained Illera's red dressing gown a darker hue. Illera pushed her away and stared into her face.

"You are my mother?"

"Of course my dear, I am your mother. I could return to you but three times in your life and I chose your wedding day as the first."

"Why?"

"What do you mean why?"

"Why did you leave me? Why did you stay away? Why didn't you give me some help when I needed you? Why? Just why?" Illera cried.

Lera sat down on a folding chair, beside a table littered with cosmetics.

"Dear, dear child, you know the power of the werwinstans. I stayed as long as I could. I dearly loved your father, you know.

Now you have experienced love; I was hoping you would understand."

Illera sank down on the tent floor at her mother's feet. "Then why have me at all? I know you can control such things, so why have me if you were just going to leave?"

Lera closed her eyes and leaned her head back as if watching some inner scene that would give her the words. A sigh escaped her shapely lips.

"I'm so sorry for any pain I might have caused you, but please understand I would do anything to please your father. And Ian, oh my Ian, he wanted a child more than anything else in the universe, even more than me. I told him I couldn't stay, and I asked him what gift he would have before I left. He asked for you. How could I deny him that when he was the beating of my heart?" Lera placed a hand on each side of Illera's face. "So, you were born out of my great love for Ian and his love for me and hope for you."

A single tear squeezed from Illera's eye and tracked down her face, making a runnel in the careful makeup of the servant girls.

"I miss him so much," Illera whispered.

"As I have missed him every moment of every day since I left to return to Faerie. But I, too, took a gift from him when I left. This is your sister Cantrell. She was raised in faerie and has never been to human worlds before."

Lera indicated the other woman who had accompanied her and looked like a twin. Illera rose and approached her sister. The young woman swallowed nervously. Illera held out her arms.

"Welcome. I always wanted a sister or a brother, and I'm sorry we didn't get to grow up together, but you are most welcome now."

Lera sprang from her chair. She embraced the two of them.

"I'm so glad that you feel that way Illera. You see, Cantrell would like to stay with you, in Madean."

Illera turned to face her mother, who walked away and began to pace nervously, wringing her hands together.

"You see, my dear, we can't control what our children inherit from their parents. It's true; the elven can control the conception but not the quality of that conception. So here you are, half-elf with more of the gifts and the same werwinstans as a full-blooded elf, yet raised human in a human world." She gave a small laugh. "If you had come to faerie with me you would have been accepted without question, because of your gifts which are in you in stronger measure than most elves, myself included. But Cantrell, I'm afraid that as much as I loved your father, I did her no service in bringing her to faerie. She has no gifts, no werwinstans, no elven traits at all. She is as human as her father."

"But, Lera, Mother, she doesn't know anything about Madean." Illera eyes widened, her face pale.

"But she can't stay in faerie. She is a reminder of the world we left behind and all its evils. The ruling counsel asked her to leave. That is why I brought her to you; I knew you would make room for her in Madean. She is, after all, your full-blooded sister."

The servant girl ventured a timid tug on Illera's dressing gown.

"Your Majesty, we must be about the dressing, or you will miss the appointed hour."

Illera turned away, allowing the maids to repair her makeup and hair and dress her. Her wedding gown was white, inset with sky blue panels on the sides, with delicate blue butterflies embroidered around the hem and up the outsides of the long sleeves. The neckline swooped in a graceful curve from shoulder to shoulder. A sapphire butterfly necklace clasped her throat, and a circlet of sapphire butterflies and blossoms graced her brow. Lost in thought, Illera did not notice the ministrations of the maids. This new wrinkle in her life occupied her until Queen Dora bustled into the tent to escort her down the path. Ashera and Laughter left to take their places on the outer ring of the marriage bower. Illera heard the tuning of the musical instruments as the players readied themselves. Birds twittered in the trees round about the bower and small rustlings in the grass and bushes indicated that her nonhuman animal friends had arrived.

Illera decided and turned to Cantrell with a smile.

"You are welcome sister, to make a home with me for as long as you need to."

With that statement, she forgave her mother of any duplicity in attending her wedding.

"Queen Dora, I thank you for volunteering to escort me to the wedding bower, but would you be insulted if I asked my Mother and Sister to do so instead?"

Dora smiled and bowed to those ladies. "Surely, it is the privilege of the mother and sister to do so. I only offered when it seemed you had no one."

"And I thank you for that." She seized the older woman's hands and lifted them to her lips. "You have been a faithful and true friend, and I will be eternally grateful."

The opening chords of the wedding music penetrated the flaps of the tent. Heart thumping, Illera held out her hands, shoulder high. Lera grasped one and Cantrell the other. As the servant girls held the flap open, they stepped from the tent. The path stretched wide and white ahead of them. Illera looked down the trail to the white wicker bower rising gracefully against the bright background of trees. All the vegetation was loaded with birds, singing fit to burst. Small animals, deer, and elk peered from the underbrush. On the open side of the bower, row on row of people stood, watching, all eyes fixed on her. Whispers ran through the crowds at the sight of Lera and Cantrell.

They moved a step forward. Looking ahead, Illera saw Ashera and Laughter waiting for her just inside the circle of the bower. Lark and Min stood opposite them on the other side, and past them Raven, hands stretched out like hers, escorted by Elisa and Rejoicing. She noticed the wide and silly grin he seemed unable to take off his face for this solemn occasion. Her own face answered that grin, and everything else ceased to exist for her. She moved on dream clouds towards him, single step after single step. At the edge of the bower, her hands floated down, and she stepped between Laughter and Ashera, seeing them only as the gateway to the white circle in the center of the space. Without will, her hands rose and grasped Raven's outstretched ones

"When had he suddenly become so handsome?" She wondered in silence.

The music sighed away, and the bird chorus shrilled once and fell still. Illera stared into Raven's eyes, lost in their darkly blue magic.

The young priest stepped from the audience, dressed in brilliant yellow with the book of ceremonies in his hand. He stood behind them and faced the crowd. The words he spoke were inaudible to Illera as she gazed at Raven, nothing else existed for her in this moment but him. Orille whispered her name from behind a post, and she laughed, still looking at her beloved.

"Raven, son of Rejoicing and Korul, deceased King of Frain, son of adoption by Elisa of the horse herds, I give myself to you in body, mind, and soul. I choose you to be my companion through life, the father of my children, the support during my trials and the compass of my thoughts. I choose you to rule my country of Madean beside me as equal. I pledge my love to you and only you, from now until death separates us. Will you accept?"

"I accept with gladness. Illera, daughter of Lera of the elven and Ian, deceased King of Madean, I give myself to you in body, mind, and soul. I choose you to be my companion through life, the mother of my children, the support during my trials and the compass of my thoughts. I pledge my love to you, my protection, and my willing heart from now until death separates us. Will you accept?"

"I accept."

Raven's head bent, and his lips captured hers as the trees and rivers rang with the cheers of the crowd. When they reluctantly parted, a path opened for them between the hordes of visitors. They moved regally between the columns to the end of the audience. Waiting there were Abbadon and Commitment gloriously caparisoned in gold, white and sky blue. Min and Ashera carried banners of blue with the white griffin rampant on them, leading the way to the stage of coronation. Overhead birds wheeled and dipped in joy.

Because the crowds were so large, Orille erected a grand platform outside the walls of Seven Spires. Benches framed the space before the platform in a semicircle, with ornate chairs in the front row for the royal guests. Illera and Raven rode to the platform where he dismounted onto it and lifted her from her horse to stand beside him.

Two new priests, looking young and nervous waited. Illera could see their golden robes trembling as the knees shook beneath them. She gave them a flashing smile which seemed to make them more nervous than before. Strongmen heaved two gilded thrones to the platform. The crowd cascaded into the benches behind them. As the priest began their singsong rituals, Illera reached out and clasped Raven's strong hand. He gave it a gentle squeeze. Birds wheeled overhead in flocks and Maggie smugly detached herself and perched on the back of the nearest throne. The forest creatures slipped back into their homes, and even the birds gave up as the ceremony went on and on. Illera concentrated on the warmth of the hand in hers and the feel of their flesh together. With an abruptness that startled everyone, judging by the numbers of the audience that jerked upright, one of the priests left the stage, returning with two heavy circles of jewel-encrusted gold.

At his signal, Illera knelt and felt the literal weight of Queenship for the first time. The priest muttered over her head, and as she arose, a giant white griffin plunged from the sky and hovered behind the platform. Many of the crowds fell to the ground, fearful of the huge predator. Illera smiled and walked towards it. She sang a thanks to it for its support and appearance at this special time. Throwing its head back it warbled a high and wild cry, then it flapped into the sky, disappearing into the sun. An awed whisper ran through the people.

Raven knelt before the priest and received his crown. Moving to join her in front of the thrones, they sat down together. The rest was an ordeal of endurance. Every person present passed before the couple, the Madeans offering fealty, the foreigners friendship. The crown weighed heavier and heavier as the hours passed and their cheeks grew fatigued with smiling.

When the last person had passed, and the torches lighted to show the way, for the night had fallen, the feasting and dancing began. Illera and Raven consigned their crowns to the keeping of Orille and ate and danced with the rest of the giddy crowd.

Looking for her mother, to introduce her to Raven, she found only Cantrell.

"Where's our mother?" Illera asked, towing Raven behind her.

"She left. She told you she could only stay for the day. You see, over there the rules are kind of crazy, so unless she was going to stay forever, she had to leave before sundown. Told me to tell you she'd be back when your first son is born."

"But I never got to know her, to visit with her," mourned Illera.

Cantrell shrugged her shoulders as Lark materialized out of the darkness. He was grinning from ear to ear.

"So, now Illera, who is this lovely young thing and why have you been hiding her from me?"

Raven snorted with laughter.

"This is my sister, Cantrell. My mother has already left, but Cantrell is going to be staying with Raven and I."

"Not for long judging by Lark's smile," Raven whispered into her ear.

Throughout the night, Illera noticed that Cantrell was shadowed by Lark, as well as by Ashera's unmarried brothers. The girl enjoyed the attention, flirting and dancing with an abandon Illera could never attain. She knew Raven was right and Cantrell would not be with them very long.

The long day and night finally drew to a close. As they retired to the king's and queen's chambers for the first time, Illera's heart thumped, and she felt fear picking at her nerves. Raven took her in his arm, and she placed an ear on his bare chest, over his thumping heart.

He whispered down into her hair, "Don't worry, it's going to be all right. Everything's going to be all right."

Illera knew within herself, with the certainty of her inner feelings that never let her down, that he was right. She moved her head and lost herself in the sweetness of his kiss.

EPILOGUE

The commotion in the camp woke Illera. She turned on her side to greet Raven for the morning, but he was gone, only a lingering trace of his scent still on the pillow. Leaping from the bed, Illera hurried into the outer chamber of the tent seeking the services of her maid. Today they would welcome home her first and second born sons from their year-long visit to Rejoicing in Sorwelk. With a pang, she also remembered that Raveena and Alora, just sixteen and fifteen respectively would be leaving on the ship that brought her sons home.

"Regain my sons and lose my daughters," mused Illera as the maid hurried into the tent and prepared her for the short trip through the town to the ship.

Owl and Jay, the younger boys, interrupted her toilet. At ages ten and nine they were a handful, and she didn't recall Ian or Eagle being as rambunctious.

"Mom are you ready yet?" asked Jay with his usual irrepressible grin.

"Not quite yet, my darling. Do you know where your father is?"

Jay laughed. "It was supposed to be a surprise, but I can't wait to tell you."

"Tell me what?"

"Daddy is letting me ride Blackness," Jay babbled on, nodding his wise dark head.

"No!" breathed Illera, pretending to be horrified. "You are much too small to ride such a big war-horse."

Unable to contain himself Jay bounced up and down crying, "Yes, yes, yes Daddy said I could ride him to the quay to surprise Ian and Eagle. I can't wait. Won't you hurry?"

Illera smiled and tousled his black hair as she turned to the older boy. "And what about you? Do you have a shocking revelation for your mother?"

The golden head dipped, and Owl peered up at her with his shy, hesitant smile.

"Well," he drawled, "Daddy did say I could ride Night if I wanted to."

Illera clapped a hand theatrically to her forehead and collapsed into a folding chair.

"No, no not my two precious little boys, forced to ride on giant, fierce war-horses. I can't abide it."

Jay giggled and launched himself into her lap. She tickled him mercilessly, reaching out and snagging Owl into the play. They all ended in a heap on the floor, rolling and tussling.

Raven pulled the curtain aside and strode into the tent.

"Ah, a fine picture I see here," he exclaimed in a mock rough voice. "Here I am letting my youngest sons begin their training as Knights of the realm and what do I find? A free for all on the floor of my own tent. I never..."

With those words, Raven launched himself into the pile and tickled the boys until they were screaming for mercy. Laughing, he caught his wife and planted a kiss on her lips. The boys made gagging noises and ran from the tent. Raven stood and pulled Illera to her feet.

"Are you ready my dear?"

Illera permitted the servant girl to tidy her hair and then, arm in arm with her beloved, they left the tent. The royal encampment set on the crown of a hill, looked down into the town of Ocean Perch. The tall peaked roofs of the town lay below like patchwork quilt. The long finger of the sea was just visible as a narrow thread of gray framed by the jutting cliffs.

The town and its people looked fat and prosperous, as indeed it should. Did not all of Madean prosper in the twenty-five years since she and Raven had ascended the throne? The alliance with the Shul had proven more beneficial than just an end to raiding their food stores. King Frak's young wind singers found employment in every community, thereby ensuring the ideal weather for their type of crops. The Shul also prospered, their population increasing to the point where King Frak felt safe sending scouts to the west to open new lands.

Illera sighed with pleasure as Raven slipped his hands around her waist and kissed the top of her head.

"Where are you off to in your mind my love?"

"I was thinking how far Madean has come these last few years. Our lives have been wonderful."

He released her and turned away muttering, "Except now our girls are going off into the unknown."

Laughing, Illera moved to him, circling him with her arms and laying her head on his back. "You didn't mind when my boys left."

"No, but Ian was twenty-two at the time, and Raveena is only sixteen; Alora a year younger. I don't think they are old enough."

She could feel the tenseness of his muscles.

"But doesn't it make sense for them to go now? Lark's and Cantrell's Sparrow is going, and she's twenty. She'll take good care of them."

He turned to her with a frown between his brows. "Maybe it

makes sense, but I don't like it. It sounded okay at first, but, now, I wish I had said no."

"Raveena wouldn't like that. She has her heart set on going." Illera laughed. "You know how much success you have in forbidding Raveena to do anything."

Raven gave her a wry smile and took her arm.

"We'd best be going, or the ship will be docked. Ian and Eagle will think we've forgotten them."

Illera nodded and followed him to the middle of the encampment. The boys were already mounted on the tall black horses, excitement shining from their eyes. Alora also waited on horseback, her pale head the color of her palomino's mane and tail. Her long blue cloak blew back from her shoulders in the strong breeze of the hilltop. Porters started out, carrying the luggage to the docks. Raveena's gray palfrey danced impatiently, as Raven and Illera mounted.

"Where is that girl?" Illera shifted in her saddle, anxious to be off.

Raveena emerged from the tent she had shared with Alora, wrapping the thick blue cloak more tightly. Of all their children, Raveena was the only one with Raven's midnight blue eyes. The rest carried the violet elf eyes of their mother, but Raveena resembled her father, tall, slim, dark, a strong face with prominent bones and those piercing blue eyes that dominated her face. The instant she entered a room, she automatically becomes the focus of everyone's attention. As now, all eyes watched as she glided to her horse and into the saddle. She was away without a word, the rest of the party trailing behind her.

The ship was just completing its last tack to the dock as the entourage arrived. Raven lifted Illera down from her horse and escorted his wife and oldest daughter to the pier. Alora and her little brothers trailed behind. Respectful crowds babbled and murmured at their backs, wanting in their small way to watch this homecoming and home leaving.

Eagle hung from the prow as the ship slipped up beside the bollards, throwing lines to the waiting dockmen. Tearing her eyes from her second born, Illera spied Ian, standing with regal dignity beside the rail, his eyes boring into her own. She felt hungry for the sight of him; a year like eternity when a loved one is gone. She feasted on her boys, eyes darting rapidly back and forth between them. How she wanted to scold Eagle for hanging from the front of the ship that way, exposing himself to danger. But the wind was ruffling his curling light brown hair and bringing bright spots of color to his cheeks. He was grinning, the same convivial smile that charmed her on his father's face.

Ian, of course, looked solemn, wrapped as ever in his massive dignity. It seemed odd to see a face so much like Raven's in such a serious mien. Illera smiled and waved to him. He replied with a gracious nod of the head.

The ship snugged to the dock and Eagle bounded down the gangplank. Seizing his mother, hugged her until she was almost suffocated. Then he moved to his father and repeated the exercise. Illera moved to greet the waiting Ian. He bowed to her, reddening slightly when she hugged him in front of the watching townfolks.

"How are you? I've missed you so much. I'm so glad you're home."

"Thank you, mother. It was an experience I shall treasure forever. Grandmother is an amazing person."

He turned to indicate Rejoicing, just descending the gangplank. Illera held out her hands and Rejoicing clasped her in a tight embrace.

Porters loaded the girl's luggage, and the dock was crowded with bodies. Rejoicing pulled Illera and Ian to a less busy section.

"So, are my granddaughters all ready to go?" she asked with a wide smile. "The boys were an enormous pleasure, but now, I am ready for girls."

Illera smiled as Raven hurried over, throwing his arms around his mother and lifting her off her feet. Rejoicing laughed until he set her down.

"How have you been Mother?"

"Busy, busy, busy. And we are in a rush right now. The captain wants to catch the tide to return to Sorwelk, so he wants to leave right now. Are the girls ready?"

Illera noted Raven's stricken face.

"I think their baggage is being loaded now," Illera answered for him.

Raven frowned and turned away. "But Sparrow isn't here. You can't go without her."

Ian pointed, and there, coming through the crowds was Sparrow, a thin, fragile girl with light brown hair and pale, almost colorless eyes. Her face was pale, the wide-set eyes terrified and the delicately pointed chin quivering. Lark helped her down from her stolid mount and wrapped the thick red cloak more firmly around her shoulders. Porters streamed from behind them, carrying crates and chests to the waiting ship. Lark steered Sparrow over to the four of them.

"Lark," cried Raven thoroughly thumping him on the back.

"Raven," Lark exclaimed returning the thumping.

Lark placed a brief kiss on Illera's and Rejoicing's foreheads. He bowed his head to Ian.

"I don't know if this is a very good idea, Rejoicing. Sparrow has changed her mind about wanting to see Sorwelk."

"Nonsense Lark," the priestess dark replied, "It will make for an excellent education for her. She is your heir after all, and she will need a knowledge of other lands."

Lark's face furrowed into a mighty frown. "You don't understand, Sparrow, she isn't like your other girls."

Ian laughed, a tightly controlled explosion of breath. "Uncle Lark, don't worry. They take excellent care of you in Sorwelk. It's absolutely fascinating."

Rejoicing edged away. "Do get the girls now. It's time we were boarded."

"But we never got to visit." Raven strode after her.

Rejoicing took his hands. "Next time. I promise. For now, Ian and Eagle can tell you all about my doings during the last year."

Eagle teased his younger brothers, straightening up as they approached. He became quiet and turned to his sisters, giving each one a warm hug and stepping away. Illera reached Alora first. She felt the tears forming in her eyes but forced them away. This was a happy occasion; her girls were going out to learn of the world. Alora smiled at her and Illera kissed her goodbye. Alora moved to her oldest brother and father, and Illera stood looking up at Raveena. The girl stooped down, hugging Illera with unexpected strength.

"Do be good Raveena. Remember your father and I are counting on the both of you to be true representatives of Madean."

Raveena grinned and moved to her father. As Illera turned to watch, she could see how hard it was for him to let her go. Rejoicing tugged at one hand and pulled her from her father's embrace. They ascended the gangplank and turned. Sparrow crept up behind them.

The plank was pulled up, and the sails zipped to the top of the mast, catching the breeze. The ship wallowed a few minutes then turned, becoming graceful as the sails filled with wind. Illera waved and waved to the three figures standing at the rail. Raveena, Alora, and Sparrow waved back until the ship was too far away to make out individual people. Illera turned to Raven, understanding his stricken face and taking him by the hand. She willed comfort down that bond of flesh.

"Let's go to the encampment. Ian and Eagle can tell us all about Sorwelk."

They turned from their daughters and started home.

MESSAGE TO THE READER

To all my readers: I hoped you found pleasure in the adventures of Illera and her band of companions. I can and do write for myself, but it feels so much nicer to know that you are reading along with me. Thank you for your time, and I hope you will continue to read with me. Daughter of Darkliete is in the process of being written, so if you have enjoyed this adventure, I most sincerely hope you will join us in the next one. The world is out of balance without you dear readers to read my words, and I appreciate every single one of you.

ABOUT THE AUTHOR

Gail Gernat lives in Northern Ontario, in the country with her beloved husband, Norman, a crazy dog and two aging tom cats. While being involved in many projects, this award-winning author enjoys being very close to nature. Gail is also living with lymphoma and these factors inform much of her writing.

f

LERA'S SORROW - (Darkliete Book 1)

Lera and her cousin have completed their long childhood and their training as healers. Sent to their grandparents back in Madean, they must negotiate the strange new world, attain their werwinstans. Fate intervenes in the shape of handsome young Ian, very human and very poisonous to the elven. Trying out her independence for the first time in her life, what will Lera decide? Where will she discover her loyalty to lay, with love or with duty?

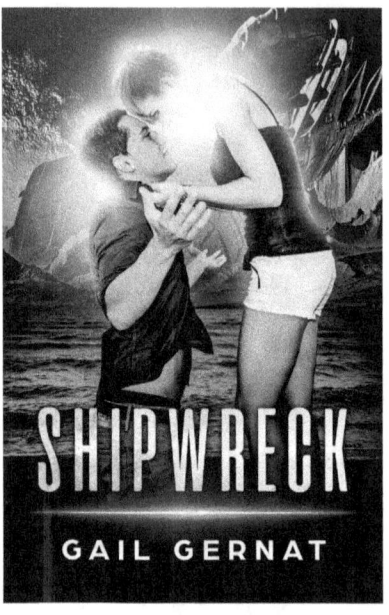

Fiery-haired Bridgit has a temper as hot as her hair, so when the colony transport gets into trouble in deep space she must work with the only other person awake; the man she most despises. Despite their best efforts, the ship crashes on an unknown planet. Bridgit is forced into impossible situations in order to survive and protect the remaining colonists.